PROMISES OF THE HEART

ALSO BY NAN ROSSITER

PROMISES
OF THE
HEART

a novel

NAN ROSSITER

HARPER

NEW YORK · LONDON · TORONTO · SYDNEY

HARPER

PROMISES OF THE HEART. Copyright © 2020 by Nan Rossiter. All rights reserved. Printed in the United States of America. No part of this book may be used or reproduced in any manner whatsoever without written permission except in the case of brief quotations embodied in critical articles and reviews. For information, address HarperCollins Publishers, 195 Broadway, New York, NY 10007.

HarperCollins books may be purchased for educational, business, or sales promotional use. For information, please email the Special Markets Department at SPsales@harpercollins.com.

P.S.™ is a trademark of HarperCollins Publishers.

FIRST EDITION

Designed by Jamie Lynn Kerner

Library of Congress Cataloging-in-Publication Data has been applied for.

ISBN 978-0-06-291773-7 (pbk.)
ISBN 978-0-06-297213-2 (Library edition)

20 21 22 23 24   LSC   10 9 8 7 6 5 4 3

For my sister-in-law (and in-heart), Terry,
who is one of the kindest people I know,
and who blessed our family by saying yes to my brother . . .
and for my brother, Gary, who didn't give up until she did!

For where your treasure is, there will your heart be also.

MATTHEW 6:21 (KJV)

PART 1

1

MACEY SAMUELSON STOOD ON THE WRAPAROUND PORCH OF THE OLD
Victorian home she and her husband, Ben, had been restoring for
the past nine years. She gazed at the long silky garlands of Spanish moss hanging from the oak trees in the yard and crossed her
arms stoically. She had been through this before, and she would
get through it again, but her heart was still a big ache—a phrase
her little sister, Maeve, had used when they were kids to describe
the way her chest felt when Grandy died, and now a term they both
used when they felt the unbearable sorrow of loss.

Placing a hand on her abdomen, Macey dreaded what was to
come and, despite her resolve to not cry, felt tears welling up in her
eyes. She looked at the still-illuminated screen on her phone. It
read, BEN, and then, CALL ENDED. They'd been through this before,
and as soon as he had heard the quiver in her voice, he'd said, "I'll
be right there."

It had been raining for days, the result of lingering bands of
a tropical storm that had stalled off the Georgia coast, making the
Savannah skies look just like she felt—weary, somber, and hopeless. In high school, Macey had been voted class optimist, but now,

after her fifth miscarriage, she felt anything but. Each time she got pregnant, her heart swelled with hope. Maybe she'd carry to full term this time, instead of barely two months. Maybe she and Ben would bring home a sweet, healthy baby—a baby for whom a nursery was already painted and furnished. They'd even picked out names: Harper for a girl, and Emmett, after her grandfather, for a boy. But now Macey's heart was so broken she couldn't even think about trying again, and at thirty-six, she felt like time was running out.

Feeling the familiar dull pain, she curled up on the porch swing and pulled a pillow against her abdomen. How long would it take for her body to realize the baby had died? Dr. Baxter had asked her if she wanted to schedule a D and C, but she'd declined. It wasn't that she didn't believe her doctor when she'd confirmed that morning that there was no heartbeat. It was just that . . . well, what if she was wrong? What if the baby just had a really quiet heartbeat? Or was tucked into a position that made the heartbeat hard to hear? She knew, of course, deep down, that the chances were nearly impossible, but she had to be absolutely sure. She could hear Grandy's voice telling her gently that things that are impossible with men are possible with God, and she wanted to hold on to that one last thread of hope and let her body make the final call. It was the only way she'd be sure.

"Oh, Grandy," she whispered. "Why does this keep happening? Don't you have some strings you could pull?" As if on cue, the wind chime she and her grandfather had made from flattened silver spoons tinkled above her head. She looked up, smiled wistfully, and pictured her grandmother bending God's ear just as intently as she had bent Grandpa's.

"That's too much, Emmett," Grandy had often scolded, eyeing her husband's piled-high bowl of ice cream they'd made with the peaches they'd picked that afternoon. "It's not good for your cholesterol."

"Oh, Millie," he replied, winking at his two little granddaughters. "We have fresh peaches only once a year. I'm sure a little extra ice cream won't kill me."

"There's enough in that bowl for *all* of us!" Grandy admonished, but her childhood sweetheart just grinned at her impishly as he licked his spoon.

Macey and Maeve couldn't have loved their grandparents more. Some of their most precious childhood memories were of long summer days at their farm, helping with all the chores, so when Grandy died in her sleep one snowy winter night, leaving their bereaved grandfather to fend for himself, they all felt the loss keenly. And even now, almost thirty years later, that big ache had never lifted.

Macey wished she could talk to her grandmother now—she would know just what to say. Grandy would pull Macey into a long hug and gently whisper it was all part of God's plan . . . that she'd understand someday. But the words sounded hollow when Macey said them to herself. She would *never* understand this. She and Ben just wanted to have a family. They wanted to fill their big Victorian home with the sound of giggles and the pitter-patter of little feet. They wanted to look at each other over mugs of steaming coffee, piles of wrapping paper, and a passel of happy, toddling little people on Christmas morning.

"Is having a family too much to ask?" she whispered.

Macey heard Ben's pickup in their driveway and wiped her

eyes. She sat up, bracing herself for the all-too-familiar sorrow in his eyes. She knew they would get through this, but how much more could they bear? The only affection they seemed able to muster these days was holding hands, and when they did stir the embers and make love, it was bittersweet. *It isn't supposed to be this way*, she thought—*young married couples are supposed to look forward to making love. They're supposed to steal romantic moments when their kids aren't around, or laughingly try to be quiet when they are. They aren't supposed to be worried about what might happen. Loving each other isn't supposed to be so shadowed with fear.*

Macey looked out at the line of ancient willows planted along the river and watched their long slender leaves swirling like gold confetti up into the stormy sky. She'd always loved willow trees—when she and Maeve were little, they'd sat out on their grandparents' front porch and watched the willows dancing in their yard. "No matter how fiercely the wind blows," Grandy explained, "they just bend and sway, and their deep roots are so wide and strong, they rarely fall. They may lose a few branches," she added, "but if you leave them on the ground, they'll take root and become a new tree."

Macey watched the weeping willows now and pictured their roots winding deep into the earth, seeking moisture and life, while high above, their long wispy branches danced with the storm.

"Oh, Grandy," she whispered, "help me be more like a willow."

2

AT THE VERY MOMENT BEN SAMUELSON PARKED HIS OLD CHEVY PICKUP next to the house, the skies opened. Through the rainy windshield, he looked up at the dark sky and tried to decide if the cloudburst would pass or if he should make a run for it. He knew Macey was waiting, but he needed a minute to pull himself together. He'd left the job site so quickly, only waving to his crew as he pulled out, that he'd hardly had time to think about what had happened. Now, as he gazed at the house, he couldn't help but recall the hopes and dreams they'd had when they bought it.

They'd been on their way home from North Beach when Macey had noticed a new real estate sign posted at the end of the long driveway. "Wow! Mrs. Latham's house is for sale. My mom used to run errands for her." The abandoned Victorian was set so far back from the road they could hardly see it, and what little they could see was veiled by long curtains of Spanish moss hanging from the line of majestic live oaks flanking either side of the driveway.

"I know that old place, and I'm sure it needs a ton of work," Ben said, slowing down. "Besides," he teased, "I've heard it's haunted."

"It is not," Macey said, rolling her eyes.

"Indeed it *is*," Ben insisted in his slow drawl. "A Southern belle died waiting for her soldier husband to return from the War of Northern Aggression and still paces its halls."

"*The War of Northern Aggression?*" Macey asked, raising her eyebrows.

"Yes. I think you Yankees call it the Civil War, though I don't know what was 'civil' about it, with Northerners behaving so unkindly toward the South."

"Oh, really? Is that how Southerners view it?"

"Mm-hmm, some," he said. "Not me, though," he added with a grin. "I have nothing against Northerners."

"That's good, because you married one. And I still don't believe it's haunted."

"It is . . . *and* I'm pretty sure this property was part of an old Native American burial ground."

"Oh my goodness! You can't just build a house on top of a cemetery."

"Early colonists did whatever they pleased. And you know as well as I do that Savannah is known to be haunted . . . especially the cemetery," he added, referring to Bonaventure Cemetery, Savannah's famous, historic resting place for loved ones who'd gone on to their final reward.

Macey rolled her eyes. "C'mon, let's go look."

Ben sighed and turned reluctantly into the driveway, and as they drove slowly up to the grand old house, Macey caught her breath.

"It's beautiful," she whispered, and for a brief second, Ben saw it through her eyes, as it might have looked in its glory days, all intricate woodwork, tall windows, and decorative molding. A moment later, he came to his senses and saw what was really there—peeling paint, broken windows, and rotting wood.

"Like I expected," Ben said, surveying the porch. "It needs a ton of work. Look at those steps."

"Why are you always so negative?" Macey asked, climbing out. "Can't you see its potential?"

"Um, no," Ben answered flatly.

"C'mon," Macey said, motioning for him to follow.

"No, thanks," Ben replied, waving.

He watched Macey walk around the house and then closed his eyes. *I have more than enough work to do without buying a money pit,* he thought, recalling the funny scene from the movie with the same name of a claw-foot tub falling through the floor and Tom Hanks—the new owner—laughing maniacally. He smiled to himself. *Yeah, not a chance.*

"C'mon, Ben!" a voice outside the truck called. He opened his eyes and saw Macey standing with her hands on her hips. "Let's just look."

He shook his head. There was no way he was getting pulled out of his truck *or* into this conversation.

Macey raised her eyebrows, and Ben groaned. Why couldn't they just go home, like they planned, shower off the sand from the beach, have a nice cold beer, and make dinner?

He climbed reluctantly out of his truck and followed her up the walkway, and then, to prove his point, kicked the front step, causing a big chunk of wood to break off and clatter to the ground. "See?" he said.

"I'd be careful if I were you," Macey warned with a slow smile. "You might be the one who has to fix that."

Ben chuckled. "I don't think so," he said, but deep down, he was already worried where this conversation was going. He knew all too well that once an idea lodged itself in Macey's stubborn head, it was hard—if not impossible—to dislodge it. As his best friend, Henry, always teased, "What Macey wants, Macey gets."

Ben looked at that step now—he *had* been the one to fix it— along with everything else that needed fixing. In fact, in the nine years since that day, they'd spent nearly every spare penny and every free minute working on it, and it still wasn't finished.

Having the old house to work on, though, had turned out to be a blessing because every time Macey had lost a baby, they'd dealt with their grief by throwing themselves into the house. The end-less scraping, painting, and restoring had been cathartic. Even Macey, who'd been a newbie at restoration when they started, had meticulously sanded and painted every baluster of the elegant winding staircase in the front hall after she lost their second baby.

As the rain let up, Ben gazed at the single candle flickering in the window and remembered the first night they'd stayed in the house. It still wasn't finished, but Macey had wanted to stay there because it was Christmas Eve. On that night, they'd sat in front of the fireplace, and he'd pulled a small gift bag from behind the iron firewood ring.

"What's this?" Macey had asked in surprise. "I thought we said no gifts this year."

"Just a little something," he'd replied with a slow smile, "for our first night."

She'd reached into the bag and pulled out a window taper wrapped in tissue paper.

"Just one?" She'd looked puzzled. "We have thirty windows."

He'd nodded. "Just one. During the war . . . you know, the War of Northern Aggression," he added with a wink, "families put a single candle in the window to guide a loved one—usually a soldier—home." He'd nodded to the candle in her hands. "It's not a Christmas decoration. It's a guiding light for the husband of the Southern belle who waited for her husband to return . . . and it's a guiding light for our family—the family we're going to have someday."

Macey had smiled. "Thank you," she'd whispered. "It's perfect." She'd walked over, set it on the front window stool, and it had flickered to life. Then she'd snuggled next to him. "How 'bout a little *friendly* Northern aggression?" she'd teased, leaning into him.

"Mmm . . . I'd love some," he'd murmured, "especially since your dad thinks it's time for some grandkids."

Macey chuckled. "Do you think he could've been any more direct at dinner tonight?"

"No. I think asking: 'When are we gonna have some grandkids around here?' is about as straight-arrow as it gets."

"Sorry about that. He's always been one to speak his mind."

"That's okay . . . now I know where his daughter gets it," he teased.

"Hey!" Macey said, laughing.

"Hey, what?" he asked softly, pulling her next to him and kissing her softly on the neck and then slowly making his way down her body.

The first time they'd made love in the big old house had been by the light of the flickering fireplace and that candle. One month later Macey had discovered she was pregnant. Two weeks after that, she had her first miscarriage.

BEN CLIMBED OUT OF HIS TRUCK, PULLED HIS JACKET OVER HIS HEAD, trotted up the steps, and pushed open the door. Macey was leaning against the doorway into the kitchen, fighting back tears.

"Oh, Mace," he said, pulling her close and gently brushing them. "I'm so sorry."

"I'm sorry, too," she said softly, shaking her head.

Ben wrapped his arms around her again and gazed at the candle in the window. Ever since that first Christmas Eve, it had glowed all night . . . and sometimes, when it rained, it flickered all day, too.

3

TWENTY-TWO YEARS EARLIER

"WHO'S *THAT*?" FOURTEEN-YEAR-OLD BEN SAMUELSON ASKED, NODDING to a tall, slender girl with long strawberry-blond hair in line ahead of them.

"*That*," Henry Sanders said dramatically, "is Macey Lindstrom." Henry was Ben's best friend—a friendship that had begun in kindergarten when Henry's last name serendipitously placed him in line behind Ben.

"Did she just move here?" Ben asked, reaching for a lunch tray and putting an overflowing fried clam roll on it.

Henry nodded, eyeing the menu options and taking a clam roll, too. "She's from Maine—Cape Beth or something. Today's her first day." Henry scanned the bowls of canned fruit cocktail for one with a cherry. "She has a sister in sixth grade . . . May something."

"How do you know so much?" Ben asked, distractedly reaching for a fruit cup.

Henry reached for a carton of chocolate milk. "Were you asleep this morning? She's in our algebra class."

"I'm *not* in your algebra class," Ben reminded as he grabbed a milk, too.

"Oh, right," Henry said, handing his lunch money to Mrs. Lyons.

As Henry stood waiting for Ben to dig his money out of his pocket, he saw the new girl step back in line, and even though he tried to get Ben's attention, it was too late. His friend turned at the very moment she passed behind him, and the scene that followed was just as cliché and mortifying as any teen rom-com. Hard plastic dishes clattered across the floor as Ben lost control of his entire lunch tray, causing everyone in the cafeteria to look up and begin clapping and cheering.

"Oh, Ben!" Mrs. Lyons said in an exasperated voice.

"I'm s-sorry," Ben stammered, his cheeks aflame.

Henry and the girl both knelt to help him pick up the clams and chunks of fruit that had scattered and splattered all over the linoleum floor.

"Thanks," Ben mumbled, feeling humiliated.

"No problem, kiddo," she said, smiling as she tucked her long hair behind her ears.

"Okay, kids," Mrs. Lyons said. "Thank you for trying to clean up. Mr. Fielding is on his way with a mop . . . and, Ben, you better get yourself another tray or you won't have time to eat."

Ben stood up, and the girl handed him the one thing that hadn't spilled—his milk. "Thanks," he said, realizing, now, that she towered over him.

"I'm Macey," she said, extending her hand with a grin.

Ben looked up and was immediately captivated by her sparkling green eyes and her sun-tanned face sprinkled with cinnamon freckles. He looked down at her outstretched hand and, barely mustering the presence of mind to not lift it to his lips and kiss it, replied, "It's nice to meet you. Welcome to our humble school."

Macey's smile immediately stole Ben's heart, and he stood dumbfounded, gazing into her eyes until another girl called her name and she turned away. "Coming, Steff." She turned back to Ben. "See ya 'round, kiddo."

He nodded, awestruck, and seemingly nailed to the floor, watched as she walked away.

"*Kiddo*?" Henry teased, elbowing him. "*Welcome to our humble school*?"

"I know," Ben said, shaking his head. "I didn't even tell her my name."

"That's okay," Henry said. "I think she knows it."

But in the months that followed, Macey never let Ben forget their encounter, and if she knew his name, she never used it. "Hey, kiddo," she'd tease whenever she walked by with her friends, "it's clam-roll day—try to keep 'em on your tray this time."

Ben would feel his cheeks get hot, but deep down, he didn't mind. In fact, he loved it. It meant she knew who he was—she *remembered* him.

Ben and Macey's friendship didn't truly blossom until the following year, though, when they found themselves in the same honors French and geometry classes.

"I don't know why I'm even in this class," Macey said gloomily as she plopped her books down on the desk next to him. "I barely passed algebra."

Ben looked up in surprise. "Geometry's different," he offered. "It's about shapes . . . *and* it's easy."

"Easy for you, maybe," she said, rummaging through her

backpack for a pencil. "My brain isn't equipped for equations that include letters . . . or for calculating the hypotemus of a triangle. I honestly don't know when I'll ever use algebra *or* geometry anyway."

"You'll use them someday if you ever have to remodel a house," Ben said with a grin, "and it's hypote*nuse* not hypote*mus*."

"There you go," she said, laughing. "My hypotenuse has already crossed paths with a hippopotamus *and* we can only hope my kids will be smarter than me." She continued to unzip the pockets of her backpack. Finally, she gave up. "Ben, would you happen to have an extra pencil?"

"I would," Ben answered, astounded to discover she knew his name. "Here," he said, thrusting his only pencil, new and freshly sharpened, in her direction and pulling a pen out of his corduroy pants pocket.

She looked up. "Now you won't have one."

"I don't think I need one. We're just going over stuff from last year."

"Are you sure?"

He nodded—he would've given her his kidney if she asked.

When the bell rang, she tried to give it back to him, but Ben shook his head. "Keep it."

"Thanks," she said, smiling. "Where're you headed next?"

"French," he said, gathering his things and sliding them into his backpack.

"With Mrs. Pease?"

"Yes," he said, looking up in surprise. "You, too?"

She laughed and nodded. "I heard she wears her hair in a bun most of the time, but when there's going to be a quiz, she wears it down."

"I heard that, too."

"I saw her this morning, and her hair is down. How can we be having a quiz on the first day?"

Ben shrugged as he held the door open. "I don't know, but it can't be too hard."

"Well, it will be just my luck to start off the year with an F."

"That won't happen," Ben said, laughing. "Believe it or not, teachers are *not* out to get us on the first day."

"Ha!" Macey said. "I had social studies before this, and we already have three chapters to read about primitive man."

Ben smiled. "Mr. Hughes?"

Macey nodded.

"I heard he's really hard."

"Great," Macey said, shouldering her backpack. "So are you going to help me survive geometry? Because I'm already confused."

"Sure," Ben said, smiling.

In the years that followed, Ben helped Macey survive more than geometry. He got her through Advanced Math and Calculus, as well as all four years of French, making sure she knew, early in the day, if Mrs. Pease had her hair down. He also helped her with her jump shot when she made the basketball team, her pitch when she played softball, and his was the reliable shoulder she cried on every time another boy broke her heart. All the while, he fell more deeply in love with her.

4

NINE-YEAR-OLD HARPER WHEATON FINGERED THE FRAYED HEART stitched on the chest of the tattered bear in her arms. She fiddled with its ear—the fur of which was completely rubbed off—and strained to hear the phone conversation in the next room. Even though she was practically holding her breath, she couldn't make out the hushed whisper. It didn't matter, though. She knew what was being said, and, finally, she shouted, "I don't want to stay in this stupid place anyway!"

The door to the next room clicked closed, further muffling the voice, and angry tears slipped down Harper's cheeks. With a clenched fist, she brushed them away and then pulled the bear tightly against her chest. She hated not having control over things that happened in her life.

She stared at the raindrops trickling down the smudged window and noticed a man walking a dog. The dog had long, silky hair—just like Tom and Mary's dog. The sudden flash of memory made her sad. The big golden had loved to curl up on the end of her bed when she lived with them. He'd nuzzle his head into her lap and gaze at her lovingly with those sweet brown eyes. Someday, she was going to have a dog just like Sundance, and when she did, she would never make him walk in the rain and get wet! She continued to watch the man holding a small umbrella over both their heads, and then she rolled her eyes. *He needs to get a bigger umbrella or raincoats for both of them! People are so stupid sometimes*, she thought, propping the musty, flat pillow against the wall and leaning against it.

The tiny room was cleaner than most she'd been in, and she had it all to herself, which had never happened before in her whole life. She loved it, even if it did look like a jail cell. There were no pictures, and the furniture was old and chipped. The narrow bed creaked when she moved, and it smelled like mildew. The only other piece of furniture was a heavy wooden bureau, which was missing three knobs and had *C.T. was here* carved into its side. Harper stared at the initials. *C.T.* had to be Connor Taylor, she decided, another kid who was staying at the same foster home *and* who was Harper's current nemesis. She could still hear his stupid singsong voice: "Harper's a baby! She carries a bear with scabies!"

Everyone on the playground had laughed, and Harper had felt her cheeks turn bright red as hot tears filled her eyes. She'd clenched her fists. There was no way she was going to let them see her cry. "I'm gonna kill you, you little shit," she'd seethed, lunging at him and hurling her fist squarely into his smug face, and then landing a second blow to his soft stomach.

"Who's the baby now?" she'd sneered as he doubled over in pain.

Afterward, she'd stumbled back, rubbing her chest. She'd closed her eyes, trying to catch her breath, but when she'd turned to sit down, she'd bumped right into Mrs. Lewis. "I don't feel so good," she'd mumbled, the rosy flames of embarrassment draining from her face.

"I'd be sick, too, if I behaved like you," Mrs. Lewis had said unsympathetically.

Harper rubbed her chest again now—the pain was gone, but why did it keep happening?

There was a knock on the door. "Harper?" Mrs. Lewis's stern voice called.

Harper rolled to her side and pretended she was asleep, but Mrs. Lewis continued.

"Mrs. Grant is on her way over to pick you up," she said, opening the door. "I'm sorry, this isn't going to work out. Please get your things together."

Harper didn't move. Fresh tears slid down her cheeks and plopped onto the musty pillow. "Why doesn't Mrs. Grant pick up stupid Connor instead?" she muttered after Mrs. Lewis closed the door.

Harper had been only three years old when one of her mother's misguided friends knocked on their apartment door because her mom wasn't answering the phone.

Harper had opened the door, wearing only a T-shirt and underwear. "Mommy won't wake up," she explained matter-of-factly.

"Shit," the stringy-haired woman had muttered, glancing around the filthy apartment as she stepped over beer cans and spilled Cheerios. She'd followed Harper down the hall, and when she saw the splayed-out position of the body on the bed, she'd covered her nose, stepped closer, and stared. "*Holy* shit!"

Harper had lost track of how many foster homes she'd been in since then. Most had other foster kids, and she'd learned that, although some adults opened their homes out of the goodness of their hearts, others did it for the money they got from the state—or, at least that's what she'd overheard some other kids say. Harper fully believed she'd landed in more homes of the latter than of those who truly cared, and that was probably why she couldn't get along—no one gave a crap about her *or* how she felt—they just wanted the money for taking her in. In all the years she'd been shuffled from one foster home to another, she'd only truly felt welcomed by Tom and Mary . . . and, of course, Sundance.

Within the fostering community, Tom and Mary Larson had been famous for their warmhearted kindness. Their gentleness could turn any child around—no matter how wayward. The child just had to be lucky enough to be placed there. Unfortunately, Tom and Mary had only fostered, they didn't adopt, and right after Harper was placed in their home, Mary had been diagnosed with cancer. After much deliberation, Tom and Mary had decided they needed to take a break from fostering while Mary recovered from surgery and chemo. Not long after that, Harper overheard Cora Grant, her case worker, telling someone at DFCS that Mary had died and that Tom wouldn't be fostering any more kids, at least for now.

Harper sat up, wiped her eyes, and touched Bear's heart, remembering how Mary had carefully cut it out of some pink felt she'd had in her closet and then sewn it over the hole in Bear's chest. She'd handed Bear back to Harper and, smiling, pulled her into a hug. "Love you, sweetheart," she'd whispered. It was the only time anyone had ever told her they loved her, and she'd stood there blinking, trying to discern the warm feeling in her chest.

She looked out the window and saw the old man walking back up the street with the dog—both of whom were thoroughly soaked now. The dog stopped to shake, and the man tried to shield himself from the shower, but his umbrella wasn't big enough. "Get a freakin' bigger umbrella!" she yelled through the smudged glass. The man didn't hear her, but the dog looked up and gazed right at her.

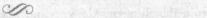

5

MACEY WAS USED TO SEEING BLOOD. WHEN SHE'D FINALLY RETURNED home from her post-undergraduate escapades in Europe, she'd buckled down, decided what she wanted to do with her life, and gone back to school to become a physician's assistant. In the ten years she'd worked at Savannah Pediatrics, she'd become a pro at drawing blood, giving shots, weighing, measuring, consoling, and making little people laugh. Given what she dealt with on a daily basis, blood was no big deal. Except when it was her own.

"I can't come in today, Marilyn," she said into the speaker of her cell phone—which was lying face up on the bathroom counter. "I—I think I just lost the baby."

"Oh, hon, I'm so sorry." Marilyn's voice echoed through the bathroom. "You take all the time you need. We'll be fine. Call if you need anything."

Macey nodded tearfully, and because she was so preoccupied with what was happening, tapped END CALL without realizing her coworker couldn't actually see her nodding. It didn't matter. Marilyn—and everyone else in the office—knew and understood; they'd watched her go through it before. Macey turned on the shower, pulled the old shirt she wore to bed every night over her head, and stood under the streaming water, letting it cascade over her weary body. When she looked down, she saw even more diluted red swirling toward the drain.

She ran her hand lightly over her flat belly. What was wrong with her? Why couldn't her body carry a baby? She leaned against the shower wall, letting her tears mix with the water streaming down her cheeks.

Macey didn't know how long she stood there, but when she finally pulled on Ben's frayed waffle Henley shirt and her old Bowdoin College sweatpants, she felt physically and emotionally spent. She slid into her slippers and shuffled to the kitchen to make a cup of ginger tea, and while she waited for it to steep, glanced at her phone and realized she'd missed five calls. She tapped the speaker to listen to the messages. The first call was from her mom, of course—Ruth Lindstrom always knew when something was up with one of her girls; the next three were from Marcy and Heather and Melissa, friends at work who'd called to express their sympathy; and the last was from her sister. Maeve worked at Willow Pond Senior Care, and Macey was convinced that her little sister was the only human on earth who—like Tom Sawyer painting Aunt Polly's fence—could make working in a nursing home sound like fun. Maeve loved recounting stories about the residents and their antics. "I'm off to the Sundowners' Club," she often said as she left for work with a smile that was truly genuine. She didn't dread going to work, as did so many people who worked in this setting. She enjoyed being around "the old folks," as she called them, and she loved helping them navigate their senior years—a time that is all too often a lonely stage of life. Maeve was a blessing at Willow Pond and a breath of fresh air to all who knew her.

"You're not going to believe this, Mace," Maeve's cheerful

voice said in her message, "Mr. Olivetti told me that he and his twin brother were in an orphanage for two years before they were adopted by a couple who couldn't have children. He said the couple made all the difference in their lives . . . and there's much more to their story—which I can tell you over lunch or coffee. By the way, when *are* we going to lunch or coffee? We are way overdue! Anyway, I think you and Ben should reconsider. Love ya! Call me!"

The message ended, and Macey dunked her tea bag several more times before squeezing a sliver of lemon into her mug. Maeve knew the baby had died—which was probably why she was hot on the topic of adoption (again)—but her little sister didn't know that the actual sorrowful evidence had shown up in the bathroom that morning, so her timing couldn't be worse. Macey shook her head. Maeve could be relentless sometimes. It was for good reason their mom called her Miss Persistence. But it didn't matter how tenacious Maeve was on *this*—there was no way she was going to adopt. For one thing, Macey had never even considered adopting, so she couldn't *re*consider it. Not to mention that, deep down, she didn't know if she could ever love an adopted child as much as she would love one who had come from making love with Ben, and that wouldn't be fair to the child.

Macey cupped her hands around her mug and sank into Grandy's old armchair. Whenever she sat in it, she felt like her grandmother's loving arms were around her—something she needed more than anything right now. She'd almost called Ben before she'd stepped into the shower, but because the loss was still so real and raw, she'd decided to wait until she could pull herself together. Besides, she knew he was overwhelmed at work and she didn't want him to feel like he had to rush home just to put his arms around her. No matter how loving a hug, it wouldn't bring their baby back. They'd both known this was coming, and now, she just needed to give her body—and her heart—time to heal.

She took a sip of her tea, savoring the lemony-ginger combination. She'd recently read an article trumpeting the health benefits of ginger and lemon, and at this point she'd drink just about anything if it would make her feel better. *Too bad my extra-healthy body can't carry a baby*, she thought miserably, as she cradled the mug in her hands and noticed the sun peeking through the clouds.

She stood up and looked out the window. Golden sunlight streamed through the Spanish moss, and she recalled the time Ben had pulled her behind a misty veil of moss to kiss her. She'd looked up at the shimmery curtain around them, and he'd explained that Spanish moss isn't a moss at all. It's not even Spanish, he'd added softly. It just floats in the breeze and attaches to trees, living solely on the moisture and nutrients in the air. Now, as she gazed at the drops of rain sparkling like thousands of tiny diamonds on gossamer veils, she put her mug on the table and studied the diamond on her hand, recalling the day Ben had given it to her. They'd been the only ones walking on Tybee Beach Pier on that absolutely frigid—even by New England standards— Christmas Eve afternoon. The sun was sinking below the horizon, and the Savannah sky was on fire, making the beach and ocean glow in an ethereal light.

"Mace," Ben had said, pulling her to a stop.

She'd turned and realized his hands were trembling.

"I told you to wear gloves," she'd teased with a grin as the wind whipped all around them, blowing her hair in every direction. She'd reached up and tried to tuck it behind her ears, but it was hopeless, and Ben had smiled, gently placed his hands on the sides of her head to hold it in place, and searched her eyes.

"What's the matter?" she'd asked, frowning, suddenly worried.

"Nothing," he'd said. "It's just . . . Mace, I hope you know how much you mean to me." He'd lightly traced a finger over the speckled map of freckles on her cheeks. "I want you to know that I can't imagine my life without you in it. Even though we were just friends when you went away to college . . . and then to Paris, I felt lost without you. I felt like I'd lost my *best* friend, and I don't ever want to feel that way again." He'd paused and smiled. "I also want you to know that I already talked to your dad . . . and your mom, of course, because she refused to be left out"—he'd grinned—"and they . . . well . . . they approved." Then he'd let go of her hair so he could reach into the pocket of his jacket.

Suddenly, Macey realized what was happening and felt her heart start to pound.

What came next, she would never forget: Ben had knelt on the wooden pier, mustered a brave smile, and said, "Mace, I've loved you since the moment I saw you in the eighth-grade lunch line . . . and I will always love you." He'd opened the small black box and held it out, revealing a gorgeous pear-shaped diamond. "Macey Lindstrom, will you marry me?"

"Oh, Ben," she'd said, tears filling her eyes. "Yes, yes, of course I'll marry you!"

Ben had stood up and held her face in his hands again and kissed her for a very long time.

They'd both been shivering when they finally got back to his truck. "This is so perfect," she'd said, admiring her new ring. "Now we can tell everyone at my parents' tonight."

Ben had looked over and smiled—it was all part of the plan.

Macey slowly turned the ring on her finger now, wondering, as she did every time she lost a baby, if Ben had any regrets. They'd talked so often about having kids. "A whole basketball team," he'd joked, smiling. But in the years that followed, she hadn't been able to give him a single point guard, and she'd often wondered if he'd have been happier if he'd married someone else—someone who didn't cause him so much heartache.

She slumped back into the chair, closed her eyes, pulled the soft afghan Grandy had made around her shoulders, and drifted off, temporarily leaving her struggles and her sadness behind.

6

BEN REACHED UP TO FIT THE NEW FRONT DOOR ON THE HINGES OF THE entrance to the stately Federal-style home he and his crew had been working on for the last year. The restoration had been challenging because the owners were constantly making changes to work that had already been completed, and now, Mr. Jackson, a prominent attorney in town, had informed him that he and his wife hoped to move in before the holidays. Ben had advised his crew that they would need to put in some overtime, and even though they had three months, when he thought of the old oak flooring that still needed to be sanded and refinished; the Sheetrock that still needed to be taped, plastered, sanded, primed, and painted; the kitchen overhaul—cabinets, granite countertops, and new retro appliances that still had to be installed; and the tile floors in the bathrooms that still needed to be laid, he felt overwhelmed.

He finished hanging the door, gathered up his tools, and locked the house. Climbing into the cab of his truck, he looked at his phone and realized how late it was. He quickly pulled out of the driveway and turned toward home, but as he drove along the

Savannah River, he slowed down. The luminous pink-and-coral sky reminded him of the day he'd finally found the courage to ask Macey to marry him, and the memory made him smile. It seemed so long ago . . . and to think it almost hadn't happened.

All through middle school, Ben had been the shortest boy in class. His mom even had him tested because he was so much shorter than Henry, but when the results came back, they said he was a perfectly healthy late bloomer. This revelation, though comforting to his mom, was little consolation to a five-foot-two boy in love with a five-foot-eight girl. Being small hadn't helped his aspirations on the cross-country team, either—as it turned out, having short legs was a handicap.

In his junior year, though, Ben had a growth spurt and grew six inches! It was a boon to his self-esteem, but the miles of running he'd been logging also triggered Osgood-Schlatter disease, a common condition among growing teens—especially boys—where the tendons attached to the knees become stretched, inflamed, and tender, making it painful to run.

Undeterred, Ben soldiered on, and by his senior year, the condition eased and he became one of the team's top runners. He was tall, lanky, and handsome, and although Macey couldn't help but notice the change in his stature, she didn't let on . . . and she still called him *kiddo*.

In the summers, Ben worked for his dad's construction company, and although his high school guidance counselor tried to get him to consider college, Ben loved Tybee Island and couldn't imagine living anywhere else. He also loved working with his hands while figuring in his head. "Measure twice, cut once," his dad always said, and although the long days left him exhausted, they also left him fulfilled. He found satisfaction in doing a job well and completing it with precision and meticulous care.

Macey, on the other hand, had a heart for wanderlust. She applied to several colleges and ended up venturing off to Bowdoin, where her grandfather still lived. In the summers, she stayed in Maine, keeping him company, helping him on his farm, and exploring the rugged coastline with her college friends; and since her parents always returned to Maine to visit her dad's dad—and only surviving grandparent—during the holidays, Macey never came home.

Ben had been lost without her, and although they exchanged letters—her letters always closing with the words: *Leave a light on for me, kiddo! xo Macey*—he missed riding bikes and going to the beach with her. He missed talking late into the night and hanging out. But most of all, he missed her wild, free spirit, so different from his own. For four long years, Ben wondered if Macey was ever going to come home. He counted the days until she would graduate and then learned her parents had given her a trip to Europe as a present. He shook his head in dismay—he needed to, once and for all, let Macey Lindstrom go—he'd already wasted too much time waiting. And since this had still been his mind-set that fall when their high school classmates decided to have an impromptu reunion at Doc's the night before Thanksgiving, it had been fairly easy for Henry to convince him to invite someone.

"Like a date?" Ben asked skeptically as they'd run along the river.

"Yeah. I'm bringing Lindsey," Henry panted, referring to his new girlfriend. "We could double. It'd be fun."

"And who, exactly, do you have in mind?"

Henry pulled to a stop and leaned on his knees, trying to catch his breath. "Hayley," he puffed.

Ben stood next to him and frowned. He'd always thought Henry's little sister was cute, but she was still *Henry's little sister.* "Nah," he said.

"Why not?" Henry pressed. "She just got home from Tulane and . . ."

"Wait . . . Hayley's in college?" Ben looked dumbfounded. He still thought of her as a high school kid.

"She is," Henry said with a laugh, "*and* she's old enough to drink!"

"No way! Little Hayley is twenty-one?"

"I know, hard to believe, right? You forget . . . she's only two years younger than us, and she knows just about everyone in our class. She would love to go."

"She can go . . . but she doesn't have to be my date," Ben said, shaking his head. "Sheesh, I can't remember the last time I saw Hayley. It must be at least three years. Does she still wear those bright red Chuck Taylor Converse high-tops?"

Henry laughed, remembering his sister's signature footwear when she was younger. "No, she traded those in for high *heels* a few years ago, and her hair is longer."

"Wow, I can't picture her with long hair. She always wore it short." He remembered hearing how Hayley had stepped up and filled Macey's shoes on the basketball court after they'd graduated and eventually became one of Maeve's best friends. "Does she play at Tulane?"

"Nah," Henry said, starting to trot along again. "She was good, but she wasn't D-One material. She's focusing on her studies . . . or so she says." He laughed. "Honestly, Ben, you wouldn't know her, and she's always thought the world of you."

Henry was right. When Ben knocked on the Sanders' front door that night and Hayley opened it, he *didn't* recognize her. Gone was the cute athletic look she'd always sported in high school. Gone were the red high-tops and the Nike sweatshirt. And gone was the short—almost boyish—haircut. Now, dressed in a casual outfit that included black suede boots, tight jeans, and a burgundy curve-hugging V-neck sweater, along with a stylish silky haircut that fell at her shoulders, she had the sophisticated look of a young college undergrad. "H-hey, Hayley," he stammered shyly.

"Hi, Ben!" she gushed, wrapping her arms around his neck, and Ben, who—because he'd been waiting since middle school for Macey to come to her senses—didn't have much experience with girls, felt awkward and uncomfortable. He gently pried himself from Hayley's embrace, and then saw Henry and Lindsey standing there. *Thank goodness!*

When they got to Doc's, Henry pointed to an empty table, and Hayley and Lindsey hurried to grab it while Ben and Henry headed to the bar to order drinks. On the way, they stopped to shake the hands and slap the shoulders of several old classmates, but it was the familiar voice Ben heard as he reached for his wallet that made his heart stop. Without turning, he felt a lump forming in his throat because—after waiting for so many years—he suddenly wished he had come alone.

"Well, well, look who's here," he heard Henry murmur under his breath.

Ben slowly turned and saw Macey making her way through the throng of their classmates.

"Hey, kiddo! Look at you!" she'd teased, standing on her toes to kiss his cheek and realizing he now towered over her.

Ben blushed and felt his heart resume beating, but now at a ferocious rate. "Hey . . . look at *you*! I . . . I didn't know you were going to be here."

Macey grinned. "I know. I wanted to surprise you."

7

"I DON'T KNOW WHAT'S WRONG WITH YOU, GIRL! WHY DO YOU INSIST ON making trouble everywhere you go?" Cora asked.

"Connor started it."

"Well, how come I'm picking up *you* instead of him?"

Harper stared out the window and didn't answer.

"I think you like spending time with me."

"Maybe."

"Well, child, I cannot adopt you."

"Why not?"

"Because I have three kids of my own, I don't make enough, and you're white."

"I don't think that's politically correct."

"What's not?"

"You can't adopt me because I'm white."

Cora Grant chuckled. "I'm sure it's not." She looked over. "So Mrs. Lewis said you didn't feel good. You all right now?"

Harper shrugged. "I guess."

"One thing's sure—you don't eat enough," Cora said, reaching into her purse. She pulled out a candy bar. "Want this?"

Harper looked down at the Snickers bar. "You trying to kill me, Cora? I'm allergic to nuts, remember?"

"Oh, that's right—I forgot. I'm sorry. Too many damn kids to remember who's allergic to what."

"I *am* hungry, though," Harper added, spying a McDonald's ahead.

Cora chuckled. "Does that mean you want the golden arches?"

"Only if you do."

Cora shook her head. "I could use a nice big-ass coffee," she mused.

"Me, too."

"You don't drink coffee."

"Yes, I do."

"Lordy, girl, you are ten years old. . . ."

"Nine," Harper corrected.

"Nine . . . ten—don't matter, you should *not* be drinking coffee."

"*It's my source of comfort*," Harper said, repeating the words she'd often heard Cora say.

Cora looked over and chuckled. "We need to find you a home. You're way too smart for your own good."

"So find me one."

Cora turned into McDonald's and as she pulled up to the drive-through, she rummaged in her purse. "What do you want?"

"Chicken McNuggets, fries, and a big-ass coffee."

"You're *not* having coffee."

"Coke, then."

Cora shook her head. "That's probably worse."

"Probably, because it's like drinking straight sugar."

Cora edged up to the speaker to place their order: "A six-piece

McNugget, value fry, value Coke, and a large coffee—light and sweet."

"Barbecue sauce," Harper whispered.

Cora nodded. "And barbecue sauce."

"You're gonna hafta stop and pee if you drink all that coffee," Harper teased after they'd picked up their order.

"Probably," Cora said, chuckling again as she reached for a fry.

"I thought you gave up fries," Harper said, eyeing her.

"That was the other day. Today, I'm hungry."

"Well, have some more, then," Harper said, holding out the bag.

Cora looked over and took a handful. "You only live once!" she said with a sigh.

Twenty minutes later, they pulled into the DFCS parking lot and Harper sighed. "Home sweet home."

"Girl, if you didn't have such an attitude, you'd *have* a home sweet home."

"Yeah, yeah, that's what you keep telling me, but if people weren't such a-holes, I wouldn't have such an attitude."

"There you go again," Cora said, scooping up her purse, paperwork, and coffee. "You can't go 'round calling people a-holes."

"I'll just call them by their full name, then—because, unfortunately, the world is full of 'em."

Cora sighed. "Please grab your garbage. I have to hurry inside."

"I told you you'd have to pee," Harper called, laughing as Cora waddled across the parking lot. Harper stuffed her wrappings into the McDonald's bag and threw a fry she found on the floor out into the parking lot. Almost immediately, a seagull swooped down and snagged it while three other gulls cried out indignantly. Harper looked up and thought of the seagulls in her two favorite movies,

Finding Nemo and *Finding Dory*. "Mine! Mine! Mine!" she mimicked in her best seagull voice, and then she noticed the sunset. The rain had stopped, and the bright orange sun, slipping below the horizon, was turning the lingering clouds purple and pink and coral. She stared at it and then crumpled the bag in her hand and slammed the car door. She looked back at the ever-watchful gulls. "Mine! Mine! Mine!" she teased again.

8

It was still dark when Ben got up the next morning. He dressed quietly and headed down the stairs to make coffee. When it finished brewing, he filled his thermos, but left enough in the pot for Macey to have a cup. An hour later when she found it, she smiled. Ben knew she wouldn't make a full pot just for herself, and his kind gesture provided just enough caffeine to get her day started. She warmed it up in the microwave and then headed back upstairs to shower.

Ben was usually off on Saturdays, but the Jackson house was taking up all his time, and she missed him. After she showered, she stood in front of her bureau in her underwear and pulled out her favorite T-shirt. The heather-gray V-neck had a picture of Tybee Island's famous lighthouse on the left chest and, on the back, "From Rabun Gap to Tybee Light"—referencing the diverse geography of Georgia—from a steep mountain pass in the state's northernmost tip to the historic island lighthouse. Even though it was a tourist shirt, it had fit her perfectly—soft and not too tight. The instant she saw it in Tybee Tees she'd had to have it, but lately she'd been wearing it so much it had started to look a little tattered. Maybe she'd see one today if she could convince Maeve to go into some of the souvenir shops.

She sat on the bed, pulled on her jeans, now too loose—she hadn't had much of an appetite since her doctor's visit—and slid her phone into her pocket. She hurried downstairs, slung an oversize canvas bag over her shoulder, slipped into her flip-flops, grabbed her keys, and glanced in the mirror. Her eyes were still puffy, but at least she'd stopped crying.

Twenty minutes later, Macey turned into the historic section of downtown Savannah, skirted Ellis Square—one of the twenty-four squares originally laid out by James Oglethorpe, founder of the colony of Georgia and designer of the city of Savannah—pulled onto Barnard Street, and got lucky with a spot right in front of Goose Feathers Cafe, her sister's favorite breakfast spot. She looked over and saw Maeve standing out front and waved.

"Sorry I'm late," Macey called.

"No worries. . . . I just got here," Maeve said, giving her a hug. She stepped back and searched her eyes. "How're you doing?"

"Okay," Macey said, mustering a brave smile.

"Yeah?"

Macey nodded. "Want to go in?" she said, blinking back tears.

"Mmm, I'm starving," Maeve said, "and I *desperately* need some coffee," she added with a grin.

As they turned to the door, an older gentleman came out and held it open for them. "You two must be twins," he commented with a smile.

"Sisters but not twins. Believe it or not, there're two years between us," Macey said.

Macey and Maeve were used to being mistaken for twins—

they'd been cut from the same cloth, and it hadn't helped that when they were younger their mom had dressed them in identical outfits. By the time they were in high school, though, their true colors had started to shine through. Macey was taller and wilder while Maeve was petite and quiet. She was also a better ball handler, and when she made the varsity basketball team as a freshman, the Lindstrom sisters—Maeve at point and Macey at center—became an indomitable force dreaded by opposing teams.

"What're you having?" Macey asked, looking up at the menu. "Let me guess," she teased, knowing her sister's favorite dish. "The Bird's Nest."

"How'd you know?" Maeve said, laughing. The Bird's Nest—grits with homemade salsa, two poached eggs, a pinch of cilantro, and a ring of shredded cheddar—was the signature dish at Goose Feathers, *and* Maeve's favorite.

They stepped up to the counter, and Maeve ordered while her sister tried to make up her mind. Macey shook her head indecisively. "I'll just have a coffee and . . . a chocolate croissant," she finally said with a smile, pushing her little sister's wallet away.

They took their coffee outside and sat at one of the tables to wait for their food.

"Have you talked to Mom?" Maeve asked.

Macey nodded. "I stopped by yesterday. She and Dad were working in the garden. They're pruning everything back already." She smiled. "Dad just stands behind her with his pruning shears and rolls his eyes."

Maeve chuckled. "She's just like you—hardheaded and demanding."

Macey laughed—she knew her sister was right. Their mom was

the most determined woman they knew. She was also the reason her daughters had such competitive spirits.

Ruth O'Leary had married Hal Lindstrom right out of college. She'd been twenty-two years old, and Handsome Hal—as she always called him—a shy farmer's son, had been twenty-five. Through the years, Hal always said it was Ruth's auburn hair and green Irish eyes that stole his heart, but Macey and Maeve both knew just by the way she looked at him that their mom was equally smitten.

Macey nodded. "So, how's Gage?" she asked, raising her eyebrows and smiling. The newest guy on Ben's crew, Gage Tennyson, had been dating Maeve for almost a year.

"He's fine," Maeve replied with a half smile.

"Just fine? Have you been doing anything fun?"

"Not really—Ben works him too hard. He comes over, has one beer, and falls asleep on my couch." She stirred a little of her grits into her eggs and scooped it up with her spoon. "When are they going to finish this job anyway?"

"Hopefully by Thanksgiving," Macey said, sipping her coffee.

"I'll be thankful for that," Maeve said. She eyed her sister's croissant. "You need to eat," she said nodding to her plate. "You're too skinny."

"I am eating," Macey said, cutting off a corner of the chocolate-oozing pastry with her fork. "I don't have much appetite."

Maeve nodded thoughtfully. "Hey, did you get my message about Mr. Olivetti?" she asked, trying to sound casual.

"I did," Macey said. "But I'm not adopting."

"I didn't say anything about adopting."

"Yes, you did."

"Oh, I guess I did," Maeve said with a sigh, regretting how this conversation—which she'd hoped would be upbeat and low-pressure—had started. "Well, Mr. Olivetti and his brother were wards of the state during the Depression because their parents had too many kids and couldn't afford to keep them all."

"I *wish* that was my problem," Macey said.

Maeve frowned. "Anyway, they were in an orphanage for two years before they were adopted by a young couple who couldn't have kids. And that couple raised them to be wonderful, successful men. Their adoptive father was a woodworker, and he taught them the trade—that's how they came to have their own furniture company. They also went on to have families of their own, making their adoptive parents grandparents. They ended up with eight grandkids between the two of them! What a legacy!"

Macey nodded. "Things were different back then, Maeve. We have state kids as patients, and some of them are sweet and cute, but some have real problems. Even Cora—you know, the lead case worker at DFCS—says things are different these days. There's too much risk involved in adopting—too many kids are born to drug-addicted mothers, or have developmental issues . . . or their parents turn up years later and want them back, and then you have a huge custody battle on your hands. You just never know what you're gonna get . . . and you could end up being very unhappy."

"*Or* you could end up being very happy," Maeve pressed.

"I know, Maeve, but we've been over this. I'm not interested in adopting, and you know it. Mom has been suggesting it, too, now, so I think you two must be in cahoots."

Maeve shook her head innocently. "I haven't said a word, but it does seem like a good option—there are so many kids who need homes. Have you even talked to Ben?" she asked, not willing to give up so easily.

Macey shook her head. "Maeve, stop. I'm pretty sure Ben feels the same way, and besides, he's so busy he can't think of anything but that house."

Maeve looked stung. "I'm sorry," she said, and when her sister didn't reply, she glanced down at their plates and realized, except for her first bite, Macey hadn't eaten any more. "You need to eat, Mace."

Macey sighed and sipped her coffee. "I'm not hungry." She pushed the plate toward her. "Want it?"

"Just a taste," Macey said. She cut off part of the croissant, transferred it to her plate, and took a bite. "Oh my goodness—this is amazing."

Macey laughed and slid the rest of it onto her sister's plate. "Just take the whole thing—I'm not going to eat it."

"Are you sure?"

Macey nodded.

"So, what do you want to do today?"

Macey pulled a list out of her pocket. "I need to run to Home Depot and see what they have for mums and pumpkins, and I'd like to stop at a couple of souvenir shops and see if I can find another shirt like this," she said, gesturing to her shirt.

"You need a new Tybee Island T-shirt?" Maeve asked, raising her eyebrows.

"I *do*," Macey said. "I *like* this shirt."

Maeve laughed. "Whatever it takes to make you happy."

"I'm afraid it's gonna take a lot more than that."

BEN PULLED INTO THE DRIVEWAY OF THE JACKSON HOUSE AND SAW HIS crew already hard at work. He didn't like asking them to work on Saturdays. Except for Gage, they all had kids with weekend activities, but no one seemed to mind. They all had bills to pay.

"Hey, Gage," Ben said, climbing out of his truck with his thermos and a brown paper sack.

Gage Tennyson looked up from measuring a piece of oak flooring. "Hey, Ben."

"How's it going?"

"Pretty well. You?"

"Okay," Ben said with a half smile.

"Maeve told me about the baby. I'm really sorry, man."

Ben nodded. "Thanks."

"I hear the girls are going out to breakfast."

"Yeah. I hope Maeve can cheer Macey up—I'm beginning to wonder if she'll ever smile again."

"If anyone can, it's Maeve."

Ben nodded and turned to go inside, but then looked back over his shoulder. "Where's your pal?"

Gage looked up from measuring. "Gus? Oh, he's around here somewhere. Probably down by the river."

Just then, a lanky yellow Lab came tearing around the house with a heavyset man chasing him.

"What's he got now, Jim?" Gage called.

"My bagel!" Jim hollered.

"Do you really want it back after he's had it in his mouth?" Ben called, chuckling.

"No, I don't want it back! I want him to stop taking my food!" Jim shouted, gasping for air and slowing down. Gus looked back, realized the fun was over, and wagged his tail as he wolfed down the bagel.

"I'll pay you for it," Gage offered, suppressing a smile.

"*That* is not the point," Jim said, his hands on his hips, still breathing heavily. Gus wiggled over to him, but Jim shook his head. "Don't you come over here, mister," he scolded.

"Aw, he loves you," Ben teased, "and he obviously thinks you need to eat less bagels and exercise more."

"Yeah, well that's the third time this week he's taken something."

"And he's wondering why you aren't getting the message."

Gus tried to nuzzle Jim's hand, but he pulled it away. "Nope, we are *not* friends," he said, "Go bother someone else."

"Jim's mad at you, Gus," Gage said. "You've snatched one too many bagels."

Gus wandered over to Gage with his tail hanging low and laid down with his head between his paws.

"Look, Jim," Ben said, shaking his head. "You've made him sad."

"He *should* be sad," he said, scowling and trying to sound angry. He eyed him. "I *always* save you a bite, Gus . . . so you don't need to steal."

The very tip of Gus's tail wagged, but his eyes were still forlorn, and Jim shook his head. Finally, he walked over, knelt down, and stroked Gus's big head. Gus thumped his tail and licked Jim's hand and then rolled onto his back for a belly rub. "I'll forgive you this time," Jim relented, "but next time, we're through."

"I hope you're listening, Gus," Ben teased. "Jim says, next time you're through, and *this* time, he means it."

Gus thumped his tail and Jim chuckled. "I honestly don't know how anyone can stay mad at you."

Gus thumped his tail again, and Jim stood up and turned his attention to Ben. "It's about time *you* got here," he teased. "Are ya gonna finally do some work?"

"Yup," Ben said, holding up the paper bag in his hand. "Right after we have these bagels."

10

"I don't know why nobody's answering their phone," Cora said, eyeing the list of numbers on the paper in front of her. She looked up at Harper. "Probably 'cause it's Saturday and word's out you been displaced . . . *again*."

Harper shrugged. "I guess I'll just have to stay with you."

Cora sighed. "I am *not* supposed to take you home. My house is not a foster home."

"Well, it should be—it's the best one I know of . . . and trust me, I've seen 'em all."

"That's the understatement of the century," Cora said, shaking her head.

"Rudy and Frank and Joe'll be glad to see me," Harper added. She'd secretly been praying no one would answer their phone.

"Let's just go," she said, standing up, hoping Cora wouldn't try to call anyone else. "It's getting late and I just wanna go to bed."

"Go to bed?! Ha!" Cora snorted. "If I bring you to my house, you an' Rudy'll be up half the night!"

"No, we won't," Harper countered, trying to suppress a smile.

Cora looked at the clock and watched the second hand click slowly around its face, marking time. It was already seven thirty and her kids hadn't even had supper yet. "You are going to be the death of me, child," she said with a sigh.

She picked up the phone again, and Harper's face fell. Still, Harper crossed her fingers and squeezed her eyes shut, praying, and then heard Cora say hello—which meant someone had answered. Her heart sank as she pulled Bear against her chest.

"I'd like to order a large pepperoni pizza . . . mm-hmm . . . for pickup . . . yes, thank you."

Harper's face lit up with a grin. "I *love* pepperoni!"

"You just ate," Cora said, standing and pulling her threadbare coat off the back of her chair.

"I'm still hungry."

"I thought you were tired."

"I'm tired *and* hungry."

"Well, let's go," Cora said, stuffing a pile of papers into her oversize, cluttered bag.

Twenty minutes later, they pulled into the driveway of the one-level apartment complex where balls and bikes of every shape and size were strewn across the grass. Cora started to pull into her spot and almost ran over a bike that was lying on the ground.

"Damn it, Rudy," she muttered. "That child is always leavin' her bike where she shouldn't. I should take it away."

"I'll move it," Harper volunteered, handing the pizza—which had been keeping her legs warm—to Cora and getting out. She steered Rudy's bike—a bike she'd ridden many times—over to the side of the building and leaned it against the brick wall. Then she walked back to the car and took the pizza from Cora's outstretched hands.

The outside lights blinked on and the door opened. "Mama!" eight-year-old Joe cried.

"Pizza!" fourteen-year-old Frank said, smiling.

Then, nine-year-old Rudy appeared. "Harper!" she shouted, running out in her stocking feet to give her best friend a hug.

"Hi, Rudy," Harper said, smiling shyly.

"What'd you do now?" Rudy teased, putting her hands on her hips.

"It wasn't my fault . . . ," Harper said defensively.

"Ha!" Cora interjected, lifting the gallon of milk off the back seat. "That boy didn't hit himself."

"No, but he *did* make fun of me in front of everyone."

"Okay, that's enough. It's water under the bridge," Cora said, glad to be home and ready to put the long day behind her. "Who's hungry?"

Four hands shot into the air as a chorus of voices cried, "Meee!"

Cora handed a gallon of milk to Frank and ushered everyone— including McMuffin, the family's gray tiger cat—inside, where Harper immediately knelt down to stroke the cat's silky fur. Harper had always wanted a pet. She had adored Tom and Mary's dog, and whenever she stayed at Cora's, she loved playing with McMuffin.

"How come that pile of laundry is still on that chair?" Cora asked, eyeing Frank.

"Because I've been doing homework," Frank said, putting the milk on the counter.

"You have not," Rudy tattled. "It's Saturday and all you been doin' is watchin' videos on your laptop."

Frank gave his little sister a dirty look. "*You* know how to fold clothes, too."

"It's *your* job this week," Rudy said, climbing up on a chair to get a stack of white-and-blue Pyrex plates out of the cabinet.

"It's also my job to make sure you and Joe are safe while Mama's at work," Frank said matter-of-factly. "Laundry's a girl's job."

"Laundry is *not* a girl's job," Cora scolded as she slid four slices of pizza onto plates. "Pour the milk please."

Frank set out five glasses. "You want some, Mama?"

"No, thanks," Cora said. "I'll just have water."

Frank poured the milk and ran the tap until it was cold and filled the last glass with water. Then he set all the glasses on the table and brought the folding chair from the computer desk in for Harper.

"Thanks," Harper said, sitting down and taking a big bite out of her pizza.

She felt a bony elbow bump into her ribs and looked over at Rudy. "What?" she asked, frowning.

"You're supposed to wait till everyone is served . . . *and* we say grace," Rudy whispered.

Harper felt her cheeks flame. "Oh, I forgot," she whispered back, putting her pizza slice down. Cora's house was the only one besides Tom and Mary's where people said a prayer before they ate. It was also the only place where everyone politely waited for everyone else to be seated and served, too.

"Ay-men," everyone—including Harper—whispered reverently when Cora finished giving thanks and asking for continued guidance in their lives.

Cora smiled and finally relaxed long enough to look around at her beloved brood. She took a sip of her water and then a small bite of her pizza. With Harper there, she'd have only one slice so all the kids could eat their fill. She knew Frank could easily eat half the pie himself!

After the dishes were washed, dried, and put away, and everyone's teeth brushed, Cora pulled an old squeaky cot out of the closet and set it up next to Rudy's bed. Then she found the sheets and blanket on a shelf and set them on the mattress. "I'm going to be folding the laundry, and I don't want to hear you two talking half the night."

"We won't," Rudy promised.

Harper stretched the bottom sheet over the flimsy mattress. "I wish I could live here," she said softly.

"I wish you could, too," Rudy agreed, shaking open the top sheet. "Then we could take the bus together and do our homework together and everythin'. It would be so great." She looked up from fluffing the pillow. "Why don't you ask my mom?"

"I did," Harper said, tucking in the blanket. "She said it wouldn't work—she doesn't make enough money, and there isn't enough room, and this isn't a foster home . . . and I'm not black."

"She said all that?" Rudy asked in surprise. "I don't think that last part matters."

"Matters to her," Harper said, flopping onto the cot, and smiling when McMuffin hopped up next to her.

Rudy frowned. "Maybe she's worried you won't get along . . . or kids will make fun of you."

"Maybe," Harper said, stroking McMuffin's fur, "but it wouldn't be any different."

"I thought people who took in foster kids got paid."

"They do, but I guess it's not enough."

Rudy nodded. "So, what do you want to do tomorrow?"

"I don't know . . . ride bikes? Go to the playground?"

"Okay," Rudy said. "How about Monopoly or Clue?"

"Okay."

"Rudy?"

"Yeah?"

"Wouldn't it be great if we were sisters?"

"It would be," Rudy said, pulling up her covers. "But we'll always be best friends."

"Cross your heart?"

Rudy smiled. "Cross my heart," she said, crossing her finger in front of her chest. She reached over to turn off her lamp. "At least we have this weekend."

"Yeah," Harper murmured sleepily, still petting McMuffin while pulling Bear against the twinge in her chest. "It'd be great if it lasted forever."

"It would be," Rudy agreed, and then she heard Harper breathing softly and knew she'd fallen asleep. It would be so great if she had a sister. She was tired of only having brothers.

11

"WHAT DO YOU THINK OF THIS ONE?" MACEY CALLED, HOLDING UP A large chrysanthemum covered with burgundy buds and blossoms.

From the other side of the display, Maeve gave her sister a thumbs-up, and Macey set it in her cart. She looked around, spied another one about the same size with copper blossoms, set it in the seat, and pushed her cart over to where Maeve was looking at gourds. "They have some really weird ones this year," she said, pointing to an orange-and-dark-green gourd that looked like it had a smaller one growing out of its top.

"Look at this one," Maeve said, holding up a creamy pumpkin with bumpy warts all over it.

"Whatever happened to plain old pumpkins?" Macey asked. "I need a bunch for jack-o'-lanterns."

"I think they're over there," Maeve said, motioning to the other end of the storefront.

Macey looked in the direction her sister was pointing. "They must have some kind of special event going on today."

"The Boy Scouts are probably selling popcorn," Maeve said, setting a snow-white mum in the seat of her cart. "They're every-where this time of year."

"I think it's something else," Macey said. "There's a tent and a hot-dog truck and a van. . . ."

"Maybe it's a fall festival," Maeve said, preoccupied with her decorating ideas. "Stores are always trying to draw people in with special events on the weekends."

Macey nodded. "Maybe."

Maeve finally looked over, too. "The only way to find out," she said, pushing her cart in the direction of the tent, "is to go see."

Macey lingered over the gourds, picked out a couple more unusual ones, and then followed.

"It's the animal shelter," Maeve said as Macey caught up. "They're having an adoption day. I remember hearing about it on the radio."

Macey nodded and started to walk toward the store. The last thing she needed right now was a pet, but as she rounded the fenced-in area, she noticed a beautiful golden retriever lying in the sun with a festive bandanna with autumn leaves on it around his neck. "Is he yours?" she asked the volunteer sitting next to him.

The lady looked down. "Keeper?" she said, and the big dog immediately lifted his head. "Oh, no. He *is* getting to be our mascot, though—he's been with us ever since his owner died two years ago."

"He's beautiful," Macey said. "How come no one adopts him?"

As she said this, the handsome retriever pulled himself up and hopped over, swishing his tail, and Macey, realizing he had only three legs, bit her lip. She reached out her hand, and he licked it and then nudged his head into her hand.

Maeve came up beside her. "Oh, no, what happened?" she asked.

"He had cancer," the volunteer explained, kneeling down and putting her arm around Keeper's broad shoulders. He turned and licked her cheek. "The only way to save him was to amputate. That's why no one adopts him—they think he'll be too much trouble or get cancer again."

"What are the chances he *would* get cancer again?" Maeve asked.

"Same as a human's. Some will, some won't. It happened before he came to us . . . before his owner passed."

"That's so sad," Macey said, stroking his soft fur and looking into his sweet brown eyes. "I can't believe no one wants you."

Finally, she stepped back. "Thank you," she said, nodding. "I hope you find a home for him."

She started to walk away, with Maeve reluctantly following her. "You *hope* she finds a home for him?" she asked. "Boy, you're more hard-hearted than I thought. Why don't *you* give him a home?"

Macey turned and gave her sister a look that spoke volumes. "First, you want me to adopt a child, and now you want me to adopt a dog. Maeve, you need to stop. I can't give him a home."

"Why not?"

"Because of our steps—he wouldn't be able to get into the house."

"You're married to a woodworker. He could build a ramp."

"Ha! Ben definitely doesn't have time to build a ramp right now. And he would never go for getting a dog."

"You don't know that. You haven't even asked him."

"If you feel so bad for the dog, why don't *you* adopt him?"

"Because I live in an apartment and I work all day. Besides, Gage already has a dog."

"That's a lame excuse. I work all day, too, and if you adopt him, Gus would have a friend."

"It's just . . . he seemed so sweet, Mace. I think he'd be good for you. We always had a dog when we were growing up, and you know how good they are at consoling—they're the best kind of friend you can have. I bet he'd help take your mind off things."

"I don't need a dog to take my mind off *things*," Macey said, starting to sound annoyed as she loaded several large pumpkins into her cart.

"I just mean he might take your mind off yourself. . . ." But as soon as she said it, Maeve knew it was the wrong thing to say. "I'm sorry. It was just a thought."

"Well, thanks for thinking of me," Macey said, her voice edged with sarcasm. She walked over to the checkout counter and plopped her mums and gourds on the belt. "I also have ten pumpkins," she told the cashier. She was definitely annoyed now—she didn't need to feel guilty for not adopting a handicapped dog on top of everything else.

Macey felt like storming off, but she wasn't fond of drama, so she waited for Maeve to finish checking out. They walked outside in silence and saw Keeper lying in the same sunny spot.

"It's really sad no one wants him," Macey said. "He has such beautiful, sad eyes—he looks like Tucker."

"He does," Maeve agreed, recalling their parents' last dog. "And I think you should think about it—wouldn't you want a sweetheart like Tucker?"

"Oh, you!" Macey said, throwing up her arms. "You never give up!"

"I know," Maeve said, laughing as she loaded her purchases

into the trunk. "Thanks for breakfast. I'm sorry we didn't find a shirt."

"It's okay," Macey said, giving her a hug. "Some things aren't meant to be."

Maeve nodded, knowing her sister's words rang true for more than a shirt. She looked over at the pet-adoption event. "Think about it," Maeve pressed, grinning.

"Okay, Miss Persistence!" Macey said. "I'll think about it."

As Maeve pulled away, she waved, and then Macey walked over to her car and put her mums and gourds in the trunk. She closed the door and when she returned her cart, the big golden picked up his head and swished his tail.

"Don't you start, too," she whispered, feeling his sweet, solemn eyes tug at her heartstrings.

12

"Mmm . . . what smells so good?" Ben asked when he came into the kitchen.

"Supper," Macey said, taking a sip of her wine.

"And *what* is supper?" He lifted the top off the slow cooker to release a savory steam.

"Chicken soup—my own recipe."

"Well, it smells amazing," he said, pulling her into his arms. "I knew I married you for a reason—you're beautiful; you have a sweet, sexy *Northern* accent . . . *and* you can cook!" He kissed her neck. "Mmm . . . and you smell good, too."

"Thanks," Macey murmured, loving his arms around her.

He softly kissed her lips. "Missed you."

"Missed you, too."

"How was breakfast?"

"Good."

"Just good?" he said, breaking off a piece of French bread and dipping it into the olive oil she'd drizzled on a plate.

"Yeah, just good. I mean it was great to see Maeve, but I wasn't very hungry, and when we went shopping, I couldn't find a shirt

I've been looking for, and then we went to get mums and there was a pet-adoption event in the parking lot and we saw this beautiful golden retriever who's been in the shelter for two years and Maeve kept . . ."

Ben frowned. "How come no one adopts him?"

"He only has three legs."

"What happened to him?"

"Cancer. They had to amputate one of his front legs."

"Oh," Ben said quietly. "Does he have trouble getting around?"

"Not really—I mean he hopped over to say hello, but I don't know how he manages stairs."

"How did he end up in the shelter?"

"His owner died."

"Wow, that's really sad."

Macey nodded. "Maeve thinks *we* should adopt him. I told her there was no way, but you know how persistent she can be, and she just kept pressing it, and now I can't stop thinking about him. He must really miss his owner, and he must wonder what in the world happened that he has to live in a kennel."

Ben nodded sympathetically. "I'm sure he does, but you're right—we can't take on the responsibility of a dog, especially one that's handicapped. "

"I know," Macey agreed, "but I keep picturing him lying on the cold kennel floor all by himself."

"I'm sure he has something soft to lie on—a bed or a blanket."

"I doubt it," Macey said skeptically.

Ben slipped two ice packs from his cooler into the freezer, closed it, and opened the fridge for a beer. He flipped the cap into the garbage and took a sip. "What time is supper?"

"Now," Macey said, drizzling homemade dressing onto their salads. "You can serve your soup, if you want," she added, motioning to the bowls next to the slow cooker.

Ben scooped a generous ladleful of soup into a waiting bowl and grated some pepper on top. "Want me to serve yours?"

"No, thanks," Macey said, slicing the crusty baguette. "I'm not very hungry."

"You need to eat, Mace. To heal," Ben said softly.

"I know," Macey said, putting a couple slices of bread on Ben's salad plate. Then she ladled a small amount of soup into a bowl, sat down across from him, and took another sip of her wine.

"You also need to eat because you shouldn't drink on an empty stomach."

"I *am* eating," she added, motioning to the steaming bowl of soup in front of her.

He eyed her. "I want to see it empty."

"Yes, sir," she said, dipping in her spoon and gently blowing on it. "How's the house coming?"

"Slowly," he said, breaking off a piece of bread and dipping it in his soup. "Gus stole a piece of Jim's bagel again this morning," he said chuckling. "He's so funny—he waits until Jim's not paying attention and then he races off with whatever Jim was snacking on."

Macey smiled, picturing the scene, and then her face grew serious. "You know, if Gage brings his dog to work, why couldn't you?"

"Well, for starters, I don't *have* a dog. . . ."

"But if you did?"

"You know I love dogs, Mace. We always had one when I was growing up, but my mom was home all day. We both work all day, and from what you say, if he only has three legs, I'm sure getting around must be a challenge. He certainly doesn't need Gus chasing him—which I'm sure he would do if I brought him to work with me."

"He might be fine with it."

"He might be, but what if he isn't? Then what? Do we take him back?"

"I don't know," she said. "We would figure something out."

Ben could tell the wheels in Macey's head were spinning—which always meant trouble. He also knew her emotions were raw from losing the baby, but was getting a dog the solution? Would a dog—especially one with a handicap—ease their grief or only add to it?

"I don't know, either, Mace. It's a pretty big risk, and if we have to give him back, it will just cause more heartache."

"I guess you're right," Macey said with a resigned sigh. She pushed her barely touched soup away and pulled her glass closer.

"But if you never take a chance," she added wearily, "how do you know?"

"I don't think it's a chance we should take right now," Ben said softly. He mopped the bottom of his bowl with the last of his bread and realized she had barely touched her soup. "Are you going to finish?"

"No. I'll have it tomorrow."

Ben frowned. "I'll get the dishes. Why don't you go relax?"

Macey nodded, refilled her glass, and took it out on the porch while Ben put the remaining soup in a Tupperware and filled the sink with hot, sudsy water. As he washed the dishes, he looked at the long shadows stretching across the lawn and heard Macey's question echoing in his head. The Macey he'd known and loved all his life had always been eager to take chances. She'd ventured off to college, and then all across Europe—Paris, Munich,

London, Geneva—and when she'd finally come home, she'd taken a chance on him. After they'd married, she'd pressed him to buy a big Victorian house that needed a ton of work. Nothing daunted her. Nothing stopped her from moving forward. She was always eager to learn, to explore, and to love with all her heart. The five miscarriages, one right after another, had taken the wind out of her sails, though, and they'd broken her heart. Those losses had changed her. She wasn't the free spirit who always threw caution to the wind anymore. And just now, when she half-heartedly asked the question, *If you never take a chance, how do you know?* it sounded as if she was trying to remember something she'd once believed but had, somehow, lost.

Ben dried his hands and went out on the porch to sit next to her. She smiled. "I can't believe it's the end of September. Where did the summer go?"

Ben looked at the fading light. "I don't know where it went. I don't know where the years have gone. We just keep getting older, and the older we get, the faster time flies."

"Before you know it, we'll be members of the Sundowners' Club."

Ben smiled. "We will." He hesitated, turning the words he wanted to say over in his mind. He wanted to tell her he was willing to go see the dog, but he knew, if he did, there'd be no turning back, and as much as he wanted Macey to feel better—to be the feisty passionate woman he loved—he wasn't convinced that adopting a dog was the answer.

13

"Mo-om! Come quick!" Rudy cried. "Harper doesn't feel good!"

"I'm coming!" Cora called back, throwing off her covers and almost knocking over her bedside lamp as she tried to find her glasses. She pulled her robe around her, hurried down the hall, and found Harper curled up in a tight ball, moaning.

She knelt next to her. "Baby, what's the matter?"

"I don't know," Harper whimpered. "My whole chest hurts."

"Can you straighten out and lay on your back?"

"Noo," she moaned. "It hurts too much."

Cora's heart pounded. "Rudy, get the phone!"

Rudy hurried down the hall and came back with the phone, and Cora dialed 911. "Hello? Yes, I need an ambulance—I have a little girl with chest pains. . . . Yes, she's ten years old. . . ."

"Nine," mumbled Harper.

"What? Yes . . . no, nine."

"I can't breathe," Harper cried. "Please help. . . ."

"She's having trouble breathing!" Cora cried. "Oh, Lord, send someone right now!" She gave them her address, looked up, and saw her boys standing in the doorway, their faces drawn and frightened.

"Mama, what's wrong with Harper?" Joe asked softly.

"She doesn't feel good, baby."

She turned to Frank. "Go wait outside and show them where we are."

Frank hurried outside. He could already hear the siren whining in the distance.

"It's all right, baby," Cora soothed, rubbing Harper's back. "They're almost here."

Frank waved to the ambulance driver and he stopped behind Cora's car. Two EMTs hopped out, and while one hurried inside, the second one unloaded a stretcher. It was raining, and the red and white lights splashed eerily across the brick buildings, shining on the curious faces peering around curtains and people stepping out into the rain to watch the commotion. Moments later, the EMTs bumped the stretcher out to the ambulance with Cora hurrying along beside. Harper reached out her hand, her eyes wild with fear.

"Cora!" she cried, but her voice, muffled by an oxygen mask, was barely audible.

"I'm comin', baby. I'm comin'," Cora said, squeezing her hand. She let go as the stretcher was lifted into the back of the ambulance.

Just then, Janelle Williams, Cora's next-door neighbor, came up beside her and put her arm around her. "Cora, who's that?" she asked in her lilting Jamaican accent. "Is she a friend of Rudy's?"

"She *is* Rudy's friend, but she's also a foster child who shouldn't be staying with us. Lord, I am going to lose my job."

"Mama, is Harper goin' to be okay?" Rudy asked, coming out into the rain.

"Go back inside, Rudy," Cora said sternly. "Harper's going to be fine. They're taking her to the hospital, and they're going to find out why she doesn't feel good."

"You want me to stay with the kids?" Janelle asked.

"Would you, Janelle? Just till the morning? Then Frank can take over."

Janelle nodded. "You go. We'll be fine."

"I have to change," Cora said, looking down at her nightgown and robe. "C'mon inside."

Cora's mind raced as she tried to think of everything she needed. She quickly changed and then they all watched, wide-eyed, as she hurried about, grabbing her bag and keys and phone.

"Here, take this, too, Mama," Rudy said, thrusting Harper's teddy bear into her arms.

"Be careful, Mama," Frank said in a worried voice.

"I will—don't you worry. Be good and go back to bed."

They nodded.

"Thanks, Janelle," Cora said, turning to her friend and giving her a hug. "I owe you one."

"You owe me nothin', girl," Janelle said. "Now, go."

"I'm goin'. I'll call you in the morning." She looked at the clock. "The *real* morning."

They watched her pull away, and Janelle closed the door. "I know you three are wide awake," she said with a gentle smile, "but I bet if you lie down, you'll fall back asleep."

Reluctantly, Frank and Joe shuffled to their room and closed the door, while Rudy lingered, looking out the window. Finally, she wandered down the hall, too. Every light in her room was on, illuminating the hurriedly thrown-off sheets and blankets. She gazed at the cot where her friend had been just minutes before, and sat down—it was still warm. She folded her hands to pray, but then dissolved into tears and buried her face in her hands.

Janelle heard her crying, peered into the room, and sat down next to her, making the cot groan. "It's okay, baby," she whispered, putting her arm around her. "Everything's goin' to be okay."

"Why does everything have to be so hard for Harper?" she sobbed. "Nothin' ever goes right."

"I don't know, baby," Janelle said softly. "All we can do is pray."

"I been prayin', but it doesn't help."

"Would it be okay if I prayed, too?"

Rudy nodded, and Janelle held her hand and whispered a prayer for healing and for things to go better for her friend Harper.

"Thanks, Janelle," Rudy said, wrapping her arms around her wide middle.

Rudy curled up on the cot, and Janelle pulled the blanket up around her shoulders.

"Things will be better in the morning, Rudy. You'll see." She gently wiped away Rudy's tears and kissed her forehead. A moment later, Rudy was sound asleep.

14

MACEY LAY AWAKE FOR A LONG TIME. SHE COULDN'T SEEM TO SHUT OFF her worried thoughts—they ran together, making her mind spin, and when she finally did doze off, she had an unsettling dream about a three-legged dog struggling to swim, its sweet brown eyes full of fear. Later, deep in the night, she was awakened by the haunting sound of a siren, and she whispered a prayer—as she always did—for whomever needed help. She lay still, trying to fall asleep again, and heard light rain hitting the windows. *Will it ever stop?* she thought, rolling to her side. She could hear Grandy's voice whispering, "'He will come to us like rain.'"

"What does that mean, Grandy?" she'd asked when she was little.

"It's from the book of Hosea, Macey dear. It means the Lord is always near when we need him—you just have to draw on your faith."

Macey listened to the rain now and tried to do just that, but her faith felt nonexistent. "Where are you, Lord?" she whispered, trying to think of a time when she'd felt God's presence, or truly at peace. Her mind drifted to the day she'd come home from Europe and heard that everyone from her class was meeting at Doc's. No one had known she was home, so she'd been excited at the prospect of surprising Ben. She had missed him. They'd written back and forth often, and she'd looked forward to seeing his familiar neat handwriting on the envelopes leaning inside her mailbox. His letters were warm and funny, and he often talked about running. Every day, it seemed, he'd get home from work, lace up his shoes, and "put in an easy ten or twelve miles"—like it was nothing!—and then, added with a smiley face, that it got him through missing her.

Was he teasing, she had wondered, or did he really miss her? She couldn't be sure, but every time she'd gone out with a guy in college, she'd found herself comparing her poor unsuspecting date to Ben—*Was he as fit? As caring? As funny?* Most of the guys, she'd decided, didn't measure up.

And then, when she'd traveled across Europe with her friends from Bowdoin, she hadn't been interested in going out with any of the guys they met. Not even tall, blond, blue-eyed Per who they met one night at the Lamb & Flag. The handsome Scandinavian was pub-crawling with his equally handsome brother, Olaf, and their friend Nils, and the young men had paid for several rounds before trying to convince the three American girls to accompany them to the Star Tavern—the next watering hole on their itinerary. Bridget and Jen had been all in, but Macey—who was usually the first to say yes to more adventure—had hesitated.

"Per likes you," Bridget had whispered, trying to convince her.

"That's what worries me," she'd replied, laughing.

"Just one," Jen pressed. "It'll be fun! Then, we'll go home. Promise."

But just one had turned into *one too many*, and things had

gotten out of hand. Regrettably out of hand. When Macey had opened her eyes the next morning and blinked at the light filtering into the room, the first person she'd thought of was Ben. She'd clenched her jaw in dismay and remorse, and rubbed her aching head. What would Ben think if he could see her now? And why, for heaven's sake, did it matter? It's not like they were dating, or had any kind of commitment whatsoever. Heck, they hadn't even *seen* each other in four years . . . so why then did she suddenly feel so . . . guilty? *Damn him*, she thought, tears stinging her eyes. All he does is work hard, be cheerful and honest, eat the lunch he gets up early to make for himself, go running, come home tired, and find time to sit at his desk and write her sweet, funny letters. *That's the whole problem, right there*, she thought, *he is too good!*

After that night, all Macey had wanted was to go home. She'd had enough of traveling, sightseeing, and partying, and she'd begun to wonder if something—or someone—was playing a role in guiding her. Because it certainly seemed as if subtly, without any one occurrence she could pinpoint, she was falling in love with her old friend. The idea was crazy, she knew, because back when they were spending all their time together in high school, she'd seen the tender look in Ben's eyes, and she'd ignored it. After all, it was just Ben, her best friend, the boy she always called *kiddo*. But, somehow, the old adage *absence makes the heart go fonder* was proving true, and the gentle unspoken patience of Ben's heart was . . . well, it was driving her crazy!

Needless to say, when Ben Samuelson walked through the door at Doc's, her heart had skipped a beat. And as she made her way toward him, she'd realized he wasn't the skinny kid she'd said good-bye to four years earlier. He was six-foot, tan, and handsome, and his chiseled chin was accentuated by a scruffy beard. And although his shoulders and chest were broad and muscular from working construction with his dad, his faded Levi's still hung casually from his slender runner's hips.

"Hey, kiddo! Look at you!" she'd said with a smile as she stood on her tiptoes and kissed his cheek. The look on his face had been priceless.

"Hey . . . look at *you*! I . . . I didn't know you were going to be here."

Macey grinned. "I know. I wanted to surprise you."

Just then, Henry had peered around Ben, and Macey had looked over in surprise. "Oh no! Double trouble!" she'd said with a laugh, taking in the adult version of Ben's best friend. Henry, too, had changed. He was still handsome, but his chestnut-brown hair was receding, and he was heavier than she remembered, as if maybe he'd been to too many frat parties.

"Hey, Mace," Henry said, giving her a warm hug. "Care to join us?" He nodded to the table in the corner where Lindsey and Hayley were sitting.

Macey looked over at the table. "Oh my goodness! Is that Hayley?"

"It is," Henry confirmed.

"She came along because she knows so many people in our class," Ben added quickly, which prompted Henry to raise an eyebrow.

"Are you sure there's room?"

"We'll make room," Ben asked, reaching for his wallet. "What would you like to drink?"

Macey eyed the pitchers in Henry's hands. "I'll just get a glass and have whatever you're having . . . if you don't mind."

"We don't mind," Ben assured her.

They made their way through the crowd to their table, saying hello to several more classmates before Ben grabbed an extra chair and pulled it over.

As soon as Hayley saw Macey, she stood up. "Hi, Mace!" The two friends hugged. "Is Maeve here, too?"

"No, she's home with a sore throat—but she sends her love to everyone!"

Henry set the pitchers on the table and introduced Lindsey to Macey, and the two girls, discovering they had New England roots in common, immediately hit it off.

"How did you two meet?" Macey asked, looking from Lindsey to Henry.

"At college," Henry answered as he filled their glasses.

Macey knew Henry had gone to the University of North Carolina at Charlotte, but she wasn't sure what he had majored in. She gave him a puzzled look. "Remind me what your major was, Hen."

"Business . . . and Lindsey majored in education," he added. "In fact, she just started teaching kindergarten at an elementary school in Charlotte."

"Nice!" Macey said. She turned to Lindsey. "Do you like it?"

"Love it! The kids are so sweet."

"And . . . what are you doing with your fabulous business degree?" she teased, eyeing Henry.

Henry chuckled and took a sip of his beer. "Figuring things out . . . and bartending, but I'm definitely staying in Charlotte." He smiled at Lindsey, and then looked around the table. "One of us has to break away from this old town."

"Well, I'm done breaking away," Macey announced. "I'm moving back to Tybee."

They all looked surprised, and she smiled. "I've been accepted to a pediatric PA program in Savannah, and since my parents are getting older, I want to be nearby."

"Your parents aren't that old," Ben said, although he was happy to hear this news.

"They're not, but they will be, and it would be better if I settled nearby. I've missed them . . . and Maeve. Besides, Tybee is the most beautiful place on earth . . . *with* the best people," she added with a smile, "so why would I want to be anywhere else?"

"That's what I've always thought, too," Ben said with a grin.

The conversation turned to Hayley, and she talked about the nightlife in New Orleans and invited them all down for Mardi Gras. "We have plenty of room," she added, smiling at Ben even though it was obvious to everyone that the embers slowly burning in his heart for Macey had been fanned to a flame.

He should've stayed with Hayley, Macey thought sadly as she lay in bed now. *She has three kids!* She pushed off her covers, slipped out of bed, and shuffled downstairs to make a cup of tea. She looked at the clock—it was 5:00 A.M. There were five hours to kill until church. She sighed, and as she waited for the water to heat, she pictured the big golden retriever curled up on a cold cement floor. The image made her feel worse. "Poor guy," she said softly. "Life isn't fair."

She heard a sound, turned around, and saw the boy she'd missed so much when she was in Europe leaning against the doorframe in his boxers, and she realized some greater force *must* have played a role in weaving their lives back together. Now, if she could only find the faith to believe there was more joy and wonder in store for them. "I'm sorry if I woke you," she said, smiling sadly.

"I was awake."

She nodded.

"Mace," he said softly, "if you want to go see about adopting that dog, I'll go with you."

"Yeah?" she said, half smiling.

"Yeah," he said, putting his arms around her. "What did you say his name was?"

"Keeper."

He smiled. "I guess you can't go wrong with a name like that."

She leaned into him and smiled. "No, you can't."

15

Over an hour had passed since Cora found a seat in the crowded emergency room. She was surrounded by people who were either waiting to be seen, or were waiting—as she was—for news. Every ten minutes or so, the ER doors would glide open, and along with the wind, leaves, and rain, another stretcher would be whisked in. "Must be a full moon," a nurse behind the desk said.

Moments later, a slender Asian woman appeared in the doorway and looked down at her iPad. "Cora Grant?" she said, glancing around the crowded room. Cora waved her hand, and clutching her bag, hurried over.

"How's Harper?" she asked anxiously.

Seeing Cora, the woman frowned. "I'm guessing you're not her kin."

Cora shook her head. "No, Harper has no kin we know of. She's in the custody of the state. I'm her case worker. How is she doing?"

The woman nodded. "I'm Dr. Chu. Why don't we go back to one of the consultation rooms?"

Cora followed her through the doors, and Dr. Chu guided her to a small private room and they sat across from each other.

"Harper is stable," she said with a smile, "and she's feeling much better, but we need to run more tests. Do you know where we can get copies of her medical records?"

Cora took a deep breath and shook her head. "DFCS usually uses Dr. Hack at Savannah Pediatrics, but not all the kids go there, so I'm not positive and I don't even know how complete Harper's records are. She didn't come to us until she was three—her mother died of a drug overdose, and we've never been able to find her father."

"All kids get sick from time to time. Do you happen to remember a time when she didn't feel well?"

Cora shook her head. "I keep track of so many kids, it's hard to keep 'em all straight."

"It would help tremendously if you could remember."

Cora rubbed her forehead, thinking. "I know she's had strep a few times—it's very common with all the kids comin' and goin' . . . oh! and she's also allergic to nuts—just so you know . . . but I think, one time, she might've had strep and not had the usual symptoms—just had a headache."

"Did she have a fever?"

"She may've, but I don't know that we have a record of that. She's been in and out of so many homes the last couple years—she's kind of a tough cookie, you know." Cora shook her head, trying to remember. "I'm sorry, but I'm really not sure."

Dr. Chu nodded as she tapped notes into her iPad. "Thank you, that's more helpful than you know." She looked up. "Harper's chest pains seem to be caused by a weakened heart, but we won't have more details until we have all her test results back."

Cora frowned. "A weakened heart? What in the world would've caused that?"

"Well, she may have been born with it—congenital heart

defects are more common in children than most people realize, and if she didn't have regular checkups as a baby, it may never have been diagnosed. There are other possibilities, too, though. You said her mom died of a drug overdose? She may very well have been a user when she was pregnant with Harper—and that could've played a role. Also, a fever that goes untreated can damage the heart—it's hard to say without her records. We will run more tests and reach out to the doctor's office to see if they have any records, but until we have all of the information, we really won't have a complete picture."

Cora nodded. "Can I see her? I have her teddy bear," she said, holding up the tattered bear. "I promised I'd come."

Dr. Chu smiled. "Of course, but just for a few minutes. We're also going to be keeping her overnight. In fact, we might keep her longer, depending on what we find and how she feels."

They stood up and walked to Harper's room.

"Hey, Harper," Dr. Chu said cheerfully as they walked in, "I brought someone to see you."

Seeing Cora, Harper mustered a weak smile. "Are you feeling better?" the doctor asked as she checked the most recent readings on her monitor.

Harper shrugged. "I guess."

Dr. Chu nodded. "I'll let you two chat, and then we're going to take you upstairs for more tests."

Harper nodded, and as the doctor stepped out, Cora pulled a chair up next to the bed. "How're you *really* feeling?"

"A little better," Harper said.

"Rudy made sure I brought Bear with me," she said, tucking the bear next to her.

"Thanks," Harper said, lightly fingering the pink heart. She looked up and her lip trembled. "What's wrong with me, Cora?"

"Nothin', baby," Cora whispered, her voice choked with emotion.

"I heard the doctor say there's something wrong with my heart."

Cora swallowed and reached for Harper's hand. "Don't worry, baby. They're goin' to do some more tests and find out what's going on, and then they're gonna fix you up like new. Don't you worry one bit."

Tears spilled down Harper's cheeks. "Am I going to die?"

"No, baby, you are *not* going to die," she said, squeezing her hand. "You are much too stubborn for that!"

Harper half smiled, and Cora gently brushed her tears away.

"That's better. . . . Now, promise me you won't worry."

Harper nodded.

"Everything's goin' to be okay," Cora said, sweeping Harper's copper bangs out of her eyes, and Harper pressed her lips together and nodded.

Just then, a young technician peered around the door. "Harper Wheaton?" he asked. Harper looked up and nodded, and he stepped into the room. "I'm Bryan and I'm going to be taking you for a couple more tests. . . . But don't worry, they're easy . . . not like math or anything." He helped her into a wheelchair. "Ready, my friend?"

Harper nodded and then looked worriedly at Cora. "Will you be here when I get back?"

"I have to go home and check on Rudy and the boys, but I'll come back as soon as I can."

"Okay," Harper said, and as Bryan clicked off the brakes on the chair, Cora leaned down and gave her a hug. "Don't worry, baby," she whispered.

"I won't."

"Promise?"

"Cross my heart," Harper said, pulling Bear against her chest.

16

"I'm sure Keeper is not meant to spend the rest of his days in a shelter," Macey said as they climbed into Ben's truck. "He's already been through so much. Can you imagine? Losing an owner who loved him enough to pay for an expensive surgery? There must still be something good in store for him . . . and maybe it *is* us. Maybe *we* are the plan."

Ben looked over. He loved seeing her smile and sounding like her old self, but he still wasn't sure this was the answer. He took a deep breath and let it out slowly. "Where was the adoption event?" he asked, turning the key.

"Home Depot."

"Do we have time to grab some breakfast sandwiches first?" he asked, realizing as he backed down the driveway that he'd only gulped down a cup of coffee.

Macey shook her head. "I'm not very hungry, and I think we should go right there before someone else takes him."

"I think, if *we* are the plan, he can wait till after breakfast—I mean he's already waited two years. Another hour wouldn't hurt."

Macey shook her head again. "Let's just go."

Ben sighed. One thing hadn't changed—once his girl got an idea lodged in her head, nothing would shake it loose.

Macey gazed out the window as they drove, lost in her own thoughts, but when Ben pulled into the Home Depot parking lot, she perked up and pointed to the tent. He drove over slowly and parked nearby while Macey tried to see if the big golden was still there. "There he is," she said, pointing again. Keeper was asleep in the same sunny spot, and as they approached, he opened his eyes and swished his tail. The volunteer looked up, too, and immediately recognized Macey. "I thought you might be back," she said, smiling.

"You did?"

She nodded. "I had a feeling."

Macey smiled. "Can we come in?"

"Of course."

When they stepped inside, Keeper pulled himself up and hopped over, wagging his tail. "I think he likes you," the volunteer said, laughing.

Macey cradled the big golden's noble head in her hands and looked into his sweet brown eyes. "Do you?" she whispered, and he wagged his tail harder and pushed his head into her chest. She turned to Ben. "Isn't he beautiful?"

Ben nodded, watching the dog balance his massive chest on one leg.

"You *are* beautiful," Macey whispered, kissing his copper forehead and then turning back to Ben. "What do you think?"

He reached out to stroke Keeper's wispy fur. "Hey, fella," he said softly as the dog licked his hand. "He *is* beautiful, Mace . . . and he's sweet . . . but I'm still not sure."

"Why'd you say you'd come see him then?" Macey asked, frowning.

"I don't know . . . I'm just not sure. I want you to be happy, but I'm just not convinced this is the answer. I mean, we both work all day and—"

"Ben," Macey interrupted, her voice insistent, "if we had a baby, we'd have to figure something out. At least a dog can be left alone."

Ben took a deep breath and let it out slowly.

"It's inhumane to make him spend his days in a shelter," she added softly.

"Lots of dogs spend their lives in shelters, Mace. I know it's sad, but it's reality."

"I'm so tired of reality, and I think we can make a difference by doing this. It's not like we have any other responsibilities," she added.

Ben was quiet. He could hear the sad, almost bitter edge to her voice. Finally, he relented. "Well, I'm sure we can't just walk out of here with him," he said. "There must be some paperwork involved and, hopefully, a waiting period. It will give us a little more time to think."

Macey nodded. It wasn't the resounding yes she was hoping for, but it wasn't no, either. Deep down, she wasn't sure, either, but at least she was willing to take a chance. She walked over to where the volunteers were sitting. "Hi—uh . . . are there any forms involved in adopting?"

"Yes, we have an application, and we do a background check," one of the volunteers said, handing Macey a clipboard and pen. "It takes about a week."

Macey carefully filled out the form and handed it back to her. "I hope he doesn't get adopted by someone else before we're approved."

"No worries—if someone is interested, we put the pet on hold until the family has time to be approved." She looked over at Ben, who was scratching Keeper's long belly, and then smiled at Macey. "I think it's meant to be. We're going to miss him—he's such a sweetheart."

17

As Rudy walked over to her bike, still leaning where Harper had left it, she heard Frank calling her name, but she ignored him. She was tired of her brother telling her what to do—*and* what *not* to do. She was also tired of her mom working so much. Here it was, Sunday, their favorite day of the week, and they weren't even going to church because her mom had gone back to the hospital. She'd begged her to let her go, too, but she'd said no, adding she didn't know if she would be allowed to visit since they weren't related.

"How are they gonna know we're not related?" Rudy asked with her hands on her hips.

"Because you're chocolate and she's vanilla."

"So? Jesse Davis is black and her sister is white."

"That's because her mom married a white man who already had a daughter."

"Well, that could be the same for me and Harper."

"But it's not," Cora said, "and if I drive all the way over there and you can't go in, what do I do?"

"I'll walk home."

Cora rolled her eyes. "Rudy, I'm sorry this happened. I'm sorry we can't go to church, and I'm sorry you can't visit Harper. I'll try to get home as soon as I can."

Rudy sighed. "Whatever," she said sarcastically, plopping on the front step as McMuffin swished against her legs.

Cora kissed the top of her head. "Please do what Frank says."

"Yeah, right," Rudy mumbled.

After she left, Rudy climbed on the seat of her bike and rolled across the parking lot . . . right in front of old Mr. Glover, who was pulling in. He beeped his horn, and she looked up in surprise.

"Sorry, sorry," she said, seeing his annoyed face.

"Rudy!" Frank called from the front door. "You're not supposed to be out there."

"I'm fine!" Rudy shouted back, pedaling her bike along the parked cars to the sandy playground at the end of their unit. She climbed off her bike, dropped it on the ground, wandered over to the swing set, and plopped onto one of the swings.

"Stupid Mr. Glover needs to watch where he's going," she mumbled. "They should take his license away. He's gotta be ninety years old and his car has a million dents in it from all the things he's hit." The black rubber swing was warm, and she just sat there, dragging the toes of her shoes in the sand. Slowly, she began to push off, and then she kicked her legs straight out as she went forward, throwing her weight into it. She looked up at the cloudless blue sky and then glanced at the swing next to her—she could almost hear Harper's voice. "Higher, Rudy! Higher! Let's see if we can go all the way around!" She swung higher and higher until the legs of the swing set started to bump off the ground. She smiled, thinking of her friend, and then suddenly remembered she was in the hospital, and stopped pumping. Oh, how she wished Harper really was her sister—it would be so perfect! Frank was so bossy, and Joe was such a baby. If Harper lived with them, things would be so much better.

"Rudy!" Frank shouted, standing next to her bike. "Let's go!"

She shook her head, and he stormed toward her. "Rudy, I can't watch you here, and Joe at home, and I'm damn tired of you not listening."

"Well, I'm damn tired of you telling me what to do!" Rudy said, angry tears filling her eyes. "Leave me alone."

"No," Frank said. "Get home." He stood in front of her with his arms crossed, blocking the swing. "Trust me, girl, no one's more tired of this than I am."

Rudy stalked to her bike, picked it up roughly, and marched defiantly back through the middle of the parking lot.

"I'm telling Mom," he shouted after her.

"Fine! Tell Mom!" she shouted back. "I don't care!" She threw her bike on the small patch of grass next to the front step and stomped into the apartment, slamming the door behind her.

Frank followed her inside. "Listen, Rudy, if you think this is fun for me, you're wrong. I get stuck here every day, after school, watching you two when I could be playing basketball. Mom doesn't seem to understand that I could get a scholarship if I could play sports instead of babysitting."

"Then go play basketball," Rudy shouted back. "I'm not a baby, and I don't need you *babysitting* me. I can take care of myself."

"Yeah, right," Frank muttered, sinking onto the couch and staring at the video game Joe was playing on their TV.

"I'm not staying in this house all day—it's too nice outside," Rudy said defiantly, her hands on her hips. She kicked the side of the TV. "And you're not playing stupid video games all day, Joseph Raymond Grant."

Joe barely glanced up, and Frank didn't say anything—he just stared blindly at the TV, his anger raging inside him. He didn't blame his mother, or Rudy, for the situation they were in—he blamed his father, who'd moved out a year ago because he'd "met someone new." As far as Frank was concerned, his father could rot in hell. After he'd left, they'd had to move to this tiny apartment because they didn't have enough money, and now he had to share a room with Joe—who was six years younger. Not to mention, he had to take care of them all the time. He didn't mind helping out, but he had a life and friends, too—friends he never saw anymore.

"I don't get to see my friend, either," Rudy said sullenly, as if she could read his mind. She plopped into a chair. "Because mine's in the hospital." McMuffin jumped up on her lap and she gently stroked her fur.

"I'm sorry Harper's in the hospital, Rudy, but it's not my fault, so you don't need to act up."

Rudy played with the cat's tail and didn't say anything, and Frank looked over. "We'll go for a bike ride later, okay?" he said softly. "After Mom gets home."

Rudy nodded and sank farther into the chair with McMuffin purring loudly on her lap.

18

HARPER GAZED AT THE BLUE SKY OUTSIDE THE HOSPITAL WINDOW AND prayed Cora would find her. She'd been moved to the children's hospital that morning, and as the nurse had filled out her paperwork, Harper had repeatedly told the nurse she needed to find Cora Grant, her case worker, and tell her where she was. The nurse had nodded and assured her she would, but Harper didn't believe her. She didn't believe anyone anymore. Now, she rolled onto her side as hot tears trickled down her cheeks. She'd pretended to be sleeping after all the tests, and she'd overheard one of the doctors say her heart couldn't handle much stress, and although she'd promised Cora she wouldn't worry, she couldn't help it. She wanted to know what that meant.

She rubbed her chest. The pain was gone, but there was still a funny ghostlike sensation where it had been. She brushed back her tears. She wanted to go to Cora's—the only place that felt like home—and play with Rudy, like they'd planned. She tried to remember all the homes she'd been in over the years, and she realized Cora was right—she hadn't been able to get along in any of them. After Tom and Mary's, she'd been moved to a home that already had three foster kids, and that had been a disaster. Bob and Deloris had been so short-tempered, she hadn't stood a chance. Bob had watched her every move, leering at her with dark, creepy eyes. One time, he'd come into the kitchen when she was reaching for a cookie and he'd backhanded her so hard she'd landed on the other side of the room. It wasn't until Cora stopped by and saw all her bruises that she and the other kids had been taken from the home.

Nine more years, she thought. She just had to survive nine more years, and then she could be on her own. No one would ever again be able to tell her what to do, or where she had to live. She'd buy her own house and have her own job and get a dog like Sundance or a cat like McMuffin. She was certain she could take care of herself. She could do it now if she didn't have this stupid pain in her chest. Maybe after she got out of the hospital she could find Tom and ask him to let her stay with him. She'd promise not to be any trouble; she'd learn to cook, and do laundry, walk Sundance, and help out in any way she could. After all, he had to be lonely without Mary, and if she lived there, he wouldn't be lonely anymore. Suddenly, she wondered why she hadn't thought of that before. And if Tom couldn't take her, she'd run away. She was sure she could make it on her own.

There was a knock on the door, and a moment later, a different nurse came in pushing a cart with a laptop on it. "Hi, Harper, my name's Jill," she said, smiling.

Harper watched Jill erase the name on the white board at the end of her bed and write *Jill*. "If you need anything, just ask."

Harper nodded.

"How're you feeling?"

Harper shrugged and watched Jill check the tube in her arm. "What's that for?" she asked.

"It's an IV," Jill explained. "It's to make sure you stay hydrated, and it's also giving you a little medicine to help you feel better." She tapped some notes into her laptop as she spoke.

"Did anybody find Cora Grant?" Harper asked.

"Not yet," Jill said, "but I'm sure she'll come as soon as she can."

"She doesn't know where I am," Harper said.

Jill smiled. "Well, I bet she'll keep asking till she finds you."

"Maybe," Harper said. "Or maybe she'll just leave me here since I cause so much trouble."

"I doubt that," Jill said, laughing. "How much trouble can you be?"

"Oh, I can be a lot of trouble," Harper said with a sigh.

Jill looked up but showed no sign of hearing what Harper had just said. "Have you had breakfast?"

"I'm not hungry."

"Well, you have to eat to feel better," Jill said, smiling. "I'll make sure they bring your breakfast soon."

Harper watched Jill roll the cart out the door and then looked down at the IV in her arm and wondered if it would hurt or bleed if she pulled it out. She knew her clothes were in the plastic bag on the chair. All she had to do was pull out the IV, untangle herself from all the wires attached to the stickers on her chest, and get dressed. No one would even miss her.

She sat up, ran her finger lightly over the needle. She had just started to peel back the tape when there was a knock on the door, and she quickly pushed the tape down and looked up.

Cora was peering around the doorway with a large McDonald's coffee cup in her hand. "Hey, baby," she said softly.

Harper's face brightened. "Hi, Cora! Did you bring me a big-ass coffee?"

Cora laughed. "Lord, no!"

19

"OH MY GOODNESS, JOSH, YOU GREW AN INCH AND A HALF!" MACEY exclaimed. "Gimme five!" She held out her hand and, beaming proudly because he'd accomplished something so amazing, four-year-old Josh Lang slapped her hand. "*And* you gained five pounds—you're growing like a weed, little man!"

Josh grinned. "That's because I eat so much."

"Well, you keep eating like that and you'll be as big as Matty Ice."

"You think so?" Josh asked, awestruck at the prospect of being as big as the Atlanta Falcons' star quarterback.

"Maybe bigger. Especially if you eat all your veggies," she said with a wink to his mom as she showed them to an exam room.

Josh turned and looked at his mom, his mouth open in surprise—*How does she know I don't like veggies?*

His mom raised her eyebrows and nodded, as if to say, *See, I told you.*

"So, Josh," Macey continued as she put her blood pressure cuff on his arm. "Are you really four now?"

Josh nodded.

"Did you start preschool?" she asked as she squeezed the bulb.

He nodded again as she paused to listen.

"Do you like it?" she asked, gently pulling the Velcro cuff off his arm and taking the stethoscope out of her ears.

He nodded again. "This is my second year!"

"Oh, wow!" Macey said with a smile as she tapped on her computer. "Who's your teacher?"

"Ms. O'Connor."

"Is she nice?"

Josh nodded enthusiastically. "She's *really* nice."

Macey laughed. "I guess you like her then."

He nodded again.

"Let's see . . . ," Macey said, trying to think of the other questions she asked the younger patients to gauge how they were doing socially and developmentally. "Do you have a best friend at school?"

He nodded. "Luke."

Macey looked up to see what he was wearing—light blue shorts and a John Deere T-shirt. "Did you pick out that groovy outfit?"

Josh looked down and nodded. "My mom wanted me to wear a different shirt." He looked at his mom and grinned as he said this. "But this is my favorite."

"Favorite shirts are the best, aren't they? They just make you feel comfortable."

Josh nodded.

"Do you like John Deere tractors?"

Josh nodded. "My dad has an M he's fixing up—sometimes he lets me drive it."

"An M?" Macey asked, looking puzzled.

"That's the model," Josh said matter-of-factly, his face solemn. "Early John Deere tractors have letters. Newer ones mostly have numbers."

"I didn't know that. You taught me something new today, Josh," she said, tousling his hair. "*You* are doing great, my friend."

Josh nodded, and Macey smiled at his mom. "Dr. Hack will be right in." She closed the door, changed the notification color outside the door to show Dr. Hack his patient was ready, and walked back to the staff room to finish some paperwork. She nuked her coffee (for the third time that afternoon) and sat down at her desk. It had been a long day—a long week—and she was exhausted.

"Hey, Mace," Melissa called, peering around the doorway. "I have one more for you."

Macey looked up and gave her coworker a weary smile. "Of course, Meliss—anything for you," she teased affectionately.

Melissa smiled and set a thin file on the table. "Sorry. These are the only records we have. She was rushed to the ER with chest pains early Sunday morning, and they ended up keeping her several days. She doesn't seem to have a regular doctor, so they don't have any other records—not even immunizations."

"How has she been able to go to school?" Macey asked, frowning.

Melissa shrugged. "I don't know—she's a ward of the state. The hospital thinks her heart condition might've been caused by rheumatic fever."

"Sheesh," Macey said, shaking her head. "How in the world, in this day and age, does something like that happen?"

Melissa shook her head. "I don't know. Somehow, these kids just fall through the cracks."

"Is Cora bringing her in?" Macey asked, her face brightening.

Melissa smiled. "I think so."

"That woman is amazing. I don't know how she does it—juggling all those state kids and raising three of her own. Her Rudy is a pip!"

"She is," Melissa agreed, laughing, "and you're right—they definitely don't pay Cora enough. She would adopt all those kids if she could."

Macey laughed and nodded in agreement. "She would. She'd restart the orphanage program and be the house mom. Probably do a darn good job of it, too." She closed the file. "What time are they coming?"

Melissa glanced at the clock and realized it was quarter to five. "Any minute—let me go see if they're here."

Macey nodded, opened the file, pulled her reading glasses down from their perch on top of her head, and tried to discern the doctor's scribble.

Harper Wheaton, age 9, admitted with severe angina and rapid pulse.

Guardian and contact: Cora Grant, DFCS

Insurance: State of Georgia

Echocardiogram and Cardiac MRI results to follow . . .

Melissa popped her head back in the doorway. "Mace, they're here."

"Okay," Macey said. "I'll be right there." She quickly scanned the page and then closed the file and took it with her. She pushed open the waiting room door and looked around. "Harper?"

A little freckle-faced girl with copper-red hair stood up tentatively, and then reached for Cora's hand.

PART 2

20

BEN TIGHTENED THE LACES OF HIS RUNNING SHOES AND STRETCHED THE arch of his foot on the curb. He hadn't run in more than two weeks because of a mild ache in his arch that he hoped wouldn't flare up today. He heard the familiar squeak of a screen door, looked up, and saw Henry crossing the porch of his parents' house, wearing an old cross-country singlet.

"Where'd you get that?" Ben asked, shaking Henry's hand and eyeing the faded relic from their high school days.

Henry looked down. "I've had it."

"Swiped it?"

"No," Henry said, feigning innocence as he trotted toward the beach. "I might have another one if you want it."

"Yeah, I'll take it—it doesn't seem fair that you have two," Ben said, falling into step beside him. "Besides, that one looks a little tight," he teased.

Henry patted his belly. "That's what craft beer does for you. Anyway, I'll have to look around for the other one—it might be at home in Charlotte."

Ben's face grew serious. "How's your mom?" Henry's dad had

died of a heart attack four months earlier. The two friends hadn't seen each other since the funeral, and because things had been so hectic that day, they hadn't really had time to talk then, either. So when Henry texted Ben to let him know he was going to be home, visiting his mom, Ben had jumped at the chance to get together.

"She's okay. She misses him. I still can't believe he's gone. Every time I come home, I expect to see him out washing the car or cutting the grass, but he isn't . . . and then I remember. I'm sure it's much harder for her, surrounded by all the memories."

"He wasn't even that old . . . and he seemed to be in such good health."

"I know, and ever since it happened, I've heard more stories about people dying within a year of retiring. My dad retired exactly a year ago this week."

Ben shook his head. "I guess we better avoid retiring."

Henry nodded. "They had so many things they were looking forward to—like a cruise next month. It's all paid for, and now she has no interest in going. Hayley even offered to go with her, but she turned her down."

"I bet they would give her a refund if she explained the circumstances."

"They probably would, but she doesn't even want to ask. Maybe I'll look into it for her." He shook his head. "I wish I could get down here more often. I know she's lonely, but the job and family keep me so busy."

They turned onto Meddin Drive—the quiet road that led past Tybee Light. "How *is* the job?" Ben asked, ignoring the pain already flaring up in his arch.

"Busy," Henry said, smiling. "Who knew craft beer would be

so huge! We got into it at just the right time, and being near the NASCAR track and museum has been a boon for business. We named it Bump n' Run Brewery, and our catch phrase is *Celebrate the Checkers or Forget the Wreckers!* In fact, we're doing so well we're looking into opening a second location in Daytona."

"That's awesome," Ben said. "My parents are down that way now."

"That's right! I forgot your parents retired to Florida."

Ben nodded. "Well, it sounds great, man. I'm so happy for you. Your business degree *and* your first love have paid off."

"My first love?" Henry asked, looking puzzled.

"Beer!" Ben teased.

"Ha!" Henry laughed. "True that! The only trouble is the brewery takes me away from the family . . . and I swear those two kids conspire to drive Lindsey crazy."

Ben chuckled. "How old are they now?"

"Ryan's six and Chloe's four. I don't know where the time goes."

"I know what you mean."

"How 'bout you guys? Are you still trying?"

"Yes . . . and no. I mean, we *did* try again, but we lost the baby. Mace was crushed and I, well, at this point, I'm just numb. I feel like I'm always expecting bad news."

"I'm really sorry."

Ben nodded. "Thanks. I don't know how much more heart-break we can take. It's changed Macey—the spark is gone from her eyes. She's always been a take-the-bull-by-the-horns kind of girl, as you well know, but now she's just going through the motions."

"Have you thought about adopting?"

"Not really. I mean, I know there are a lot of kids who need homes, but I don't know if we're cut out for that. And now Mace's got it in her head that she wants to adopt a dog."

"Well, that might take her mind off things . . . plus, you'd have a running partner."

"Yeah, no. The dog she has her heart set on only has three legs."

"Seriously? Wow! What happened?"

"He had cancer and they had to amputate."

"What happened to his owner?"

"Macey said he—or she—died, and the dog's been in a shelter for two years."

Henry raised his eyebrows. "Sounds like he's not well and getting older, and if that's the case, he might end up just adding to your heartache."

"That's what I said, but you know Mace . . ."

Henry laughed. "Yeah, you're going to end up being parents to a three-legged dog."

"Probably," Ben agreed.

When they reached the lighthouse, Ben stopped to stretch his arch and Henry took advantage of the break to catch his breath. He looked around, recalling how much he and Ben had loved history when they were younger. As boys, they'd explored every corner of Tybee Island, riding their bikes from Fort Pulaski at the mouth of the Savannah River all the way to the Tybee Island Light Station. They'd raced each other up the steps to take in the amazing view, and they'd listened raptly to the park ranger tell harrowing tales of life as a keeper of the oldest lighthouse in Georgia. They'd heard Mr. Danton's spiel so many times, they'd known it by heart.

As they stood there now, Henry wondered if he could still recite the whole thing. Smiling, he swept his arm dramatically across the landscape and solemnly began, "Tybee Island is a strip of land seventeen miles off the coast of Savannah. Native Americans— most notably, the Euchee—were the first to inhabit the area, fishing and navigating the pristine waterways in dugout canoes. The Euchee also gave the island its name: *tybee*, the Euchee word for 'salt.'

"In 1520, Spanish explorers arrived and claimed the island as their own. They changed the name to Los Bajos, and many years later, English settlers arrived and started to carve a colony out of the vast coastal wilderness. They named it Georgia—in honor of King George, and they named its first settlement city, Savannah." As he said this, he bowed with a flourish, out of respect for the king, in a perfect imitation of Mr. Danton.

Ben laughed. "But let's not forget that for a long time Tybee Island was Georgia's best-kept secret. It was only as the years passed that word of the island's beauty spread, and it became a vacation destination. Now during peak months, shops, beaches, and restaurants are overrun with visitors." He paused and smiled, and just like the old park ranger, when he regaled tourists with his slow Southern drawl, he finished with a wink: "But usually, by late September, Northerners have headed back where they belong, and life gets back to normal—it becomes quiet and peaceful, just the way we like it."

"Nice," Henry said, nodding his approval. Then, he looked up at the lighthouse. "Race you to the top. . . ."

Ben shook his head. "It's nine bucks, and I don't have my wallet."

"What? It used to be free!"

"Nothing's free anymore," Ben said, trotting off.

"That's for sure," Henry agreed, jogging after him.

THE SUN WAS SETTING WHEN THEY GOT BACK. "THANKS FOR THE RUN . . . *and* the beer," Ben said, gesturing to the six pack of Intimidator Black Lager Henry had retrieved from the fridge in the garage.

"You're welcome. I hope you like it. And when you come to the brewery, just hold up three fingers for Dale Earnhardt's number"— Henry showed him the gesture—"And they'll know what you're asking for."

"Cute," Ben said with a chuckle. "You headed back to Charlotte tonight?"

"I am, but I'm having supper with my mom first. Ryan has soccer in the morning, and the brewery will be busy all weekend."

Ben nodded. "Let me know when you'll be in town again."

"I will," Henry said, shaking Ben's hand. "I'd hug ya, but you're all sweaty."

Ben rolled his eyes. "Don't forget my singlet next time."

"I won't. Good luck with the new dog. What's his name?"

"Keeper."

Henry nodded. "Meant to be."

"Maybe."

"Love ya, man," Henry said, smiling. "That's one thing I've learned . . ." he added, gesturing to the house. "Say how you feel, because you might not get the chance."

Ben nodded. "Love you, too, bro. Tell Lindz and your mom I said hello."

"You can come in and say hi yourself."

"Nah, I better head home."

"Okay," Henry said, waving.

Ben watched his friend climb the steps of the house that had been a second home to him when he was growing up. He felt he should go in and say hello to Mrs. Sanders, but he knew she would ask about Macey, and he would have to go through it all again, so he turned in the direction of the old Victorian, picking up his pace until he saw the single candle flickering in the window.

21

MACEY SMILED AS SHE WATCHED THE LITTLE GIRL WITH COPPER HAIR and cinnamon freckles reach for Cora's hand. *She looks like I did when I was little*, she thought.

"I'm a-comin', honey, I'm a-comin'," Cora said, propping her glasses on top of her head and gathering her things.

"Hello, ladies," Macey said, holding the door. "How've you been, Cora?"

Cora squeezed Macey's hand as she walked by. "I'm doing okay, but my friend Harper, here, had a pretty big scare th'other day."

"So I heard," Macey said, her face shadowing over with concern. "How're you feeling today, Harper?"

"Okay," the little girl answered with a shrug. "My chest doesn't hurt."

"That's good," Macey said, squeezing her shoulder and feeling Harper pull slightly away—it was just enough for Macey to realize her touch wasn't welcome.

"Let's see how much you weigh," Macey said, stopping at a scale in the hallway. Harper stepped on and watched Macey slide the weights back and forth. "Sixty pounds . . . *and*"—she slid the measuring rule down on top of her head—"fifty-two inches."

"Four-foot-four," Harper whispered, calculating in her head.

"That's right," Macey said with a smile. "Are you a basketball player?"

"No. Rudy and I play H-O-R-S-E sometimes, but that's it."

"I bet you're a good shot."

Harper shrugged, and Cora laughed. "She's a better shot than my Frank!"

"No, I'm not," Harper countered, rolling her eyes. "Frank's really good."

Cora sighed, shaking her head, and Macey laughed. "If you're good at sports, it's better to be modest—that way the other team is caught off guard."

Harper crossed her arms, rolled her eyes again, and didn't reply. Macey chuckled to herself—Harper reminded her a little *too* much of herself. She continued down the hall to an open exam room and motioned for her to hop on the table. "So, Harper, when was the last time your chest hurt?"

Harper shrugged and looking questioningly at Cora.

"Only you know, baby."

"In the hospital, I guess."

Macey looked at Harper's file again. "It says here you were released this morning. Does that mean it hurt this morning? Or yesterday? Or a few days ago?"

"A few days ago."

Macey nodded as she typed the results of Harper's temperature, pulse, and blood pressure into her laptop. "And how long have you been having these pains?" She looked up and noticed Harper's eyes for the first time—they were the same beautiful color as Ben's, except she had specks of gold flecking the blue around her pupils.

Harper shrugged. "I dunno. Since I was seven? It's been worse lately."

"Can you show me where it hurts?"

"Right in the middle," Harper said, pointing to her sternum.

Macey nodded and looked at Cora. "Heather said there are no medical records, other than this file?"

Cora sighed. "We know Harper was born in Atlanta, but I don't know if they have anything up there."

"When's your birthday, Harper?"

"March first."

Macey tapped this last bit of information into her laptop and looked up. "All right. Dr. Hack will be right in. Always good to see you, Cora, and it was really nice meeting you, Harper."

She closed the door behind her, and then closed her eyes, trying to shut out the image of the little girl with the potentially serious heart condition sitting bravely on the exam table. With some patients, she'd learned, it was better to not get emotionally involved. She had enough going on.

She walked back to the staff room, took a sip of her coffee—now cold again—and sat down to finish her paperwork for the day. Just as she was gathering her things, Dr. Hack came in, looking dismayed.

"How'd it go?" she asked.

He shook his head. "I can't believe the state doesn't have *any* medical records—how was she even able to go to school?" He rubbed his eyes. "Melissa is making an appointment at Savannah Children's Heart, and I told Cora that Harper needs to take it easy until she goes. I also told Cora to call nine-one-one immediately if the pains comes back."

Macey shook her head but didn't say anything, and Dr. Hack looked over the file again. "I think she may've had undiagnosed strep at some point and ended up with rheumatic fever—without her medical records we'll never know, but that seems the most likely cause."

Macey nodded, her heart suddenly aching for the little girl. "I wish there was more I could do to help. Please let me know if you need me."

Dr. Hack looked up from the file. "We always need you, Mace," he teased, "but you can head home." He smiled. "Have a good weekend."

"You, too," she said, hoisting her bag onto her shoulder. She said good night to Melissa and went out into the cool autumn air. As she walked across the parking lot, she noticed Harper swinging Cora's hand as they walked toward their car.

"Lord, please take care of that little girl," she whispered. "If anyone needs you, she does."

Fifteen minutes later, Macey pulled into her driveway and saw all the lights on. She frowned, trying to remember what Ben had said he was doing that night. He'd mentioned Henry, but she'd been so preoccupied that morning, she'd only half listened.

"Hey," she said, coming into the kitchen. "I didn't expect you home. What smells so good?"

Ben turned, his hair still wet from showering. "Supper—isn't that what *you* always say?" He smiled, too, as she leaned up to kiss him.

"And *you* smell good, too."

"Thanks," he said, taking a sip of his beer.

"What are you making?" she asked, lifting the lid of the pan and releasing a cloud of steam.

"Sausage and peppers."

"Do we have rolls?" she asked, reaching for his beer.

"We do," he said, watching her take a sip.

"I thought you were doing something with Henry tonight."

"I did—we went running, and he gave me that beer."

"Oh, right! I couldn't remember what you said."

"You couldn't remember . . . or you weren't listening?" he teased gently.

"Probably both," she said, smiling sheepishly. "You know how I am before I have my coffee."

"I do," he agreed.

She took another sip. "This is pretty good." She studied the label and eyed him questioningly. "Intimidator?"

"It's Bump n' Run's signature beer, named for Dale Earnhardt."

Macey raised her eyebrows. "Bump and run?"

"Yeah, Henry's brewery is in the heart of NASCAR country, so everything about it has a racing theme," Ben said, taking a sip of the beer and pulling her toward him.

"Oh, by the way . . . the shelter called this morning . . . ," Macey said as he kissed her neck. "And you'll never guess what . . ."

"What?"

"Keeper's all ours! We've been approved!"

"Great," he said with a hint of sarcasm.

"And we can pick him up tomorrow at ten . . ."

"Mmm," he said again, kissing her eyelids.

"But I'm supposed to get my hair cut . . ."

"And I'm supposed to work . . ."

"Can you work a little later?"

Ben pulled back and searched her eyes. "See what I mean,

Mace? He's already causing conflicts—just picking him up is a problem. Not to mention, we aren't ready to pick him up—we don't have a collar, a leash, a crate. We don't even have dog food!"

Macey frowned. "It's not a conflict. I'll cancel my appointment if you have to work. And we *do* have those things. Except a crate. But I don't think he needs to be in a crate—he's not a puppy, so I got him a bed, and it's supposed to come tomorrow."

Ben pulled away completely. "You mail-ordered a dog bed? From where?"

"Bean."

"I should've known."

"They make the best beds . . . *and* it was on sale."

"Yeah? How much?"

"I used the gift card you gave me for my birthday."

Ben sighed and took a long swig of his beer. "I think a crate would be better. What do we do if he gets into stuff?"

"He's not gonna *get into stuff*," Macey said, frowning. "Ben, you said you were on board with this."

"I was on board with putting in an application, but I'm still not as sure as you that this is meant to be. Mace, a dog is going to tie us down. There will be no more picking up and going away whenever we want. We'll always have to think of him and find someone to dog-sit. Not to mention, he's going to be inside all day when we're at work, which won't be much fun for him, and you can't guarantee he won't get into stuff."

"We *never* go away, so that's not going to be a problem, and he's definitely not spending all day in a crate. If you're so worried, we'll get a gate and he can stay in the kitchen." Macey leaned her back against the counter. "I can't believe you're making such a big deal out of this. Lots of people have dogs! And if we had a baby, we'd be even more tied down. We'd figure things out."

"We would take a baby with us if we went somewhere."

"Not to work."

Ben rolled his eyes. "What we'd figured out, Mace, is you'd be a stay-at-home mom."

The words *stay-at-home mom*—and the fact that she may never be one—struck a sensitive chord. Macey's eyes glistened.

"I told them we wanted him, and I'm not backing out," she said with quiet conviction.

"Oh, Mace," Ben said, reaching for her hand. "Please don't cry. I'm just trying to be realistic."

She pulled her hand away. "That's the trouble, Ben," she said. "You're *too* realistic. *Too* cautious. You never want to take a chance on anything. You're not spontaneous or compulsive. Everything always has to be all figured out. In advance."

"That's not true. I take chances—I took a chance on this house!"

She laughed. "Yeah, under duress."

Ben worked hard to suppress a smile and shook his head. "Not true."

"So true!"

"I took a chance on you."

"Yeah, well"—Macey looked away—"maybe you shouldn't have."

"Yeah, I should've," he said softly, reaching for her hand again and pulling her against him. "I'm sorry I'm such a stick in the mud sometimes."

Macey rested her cheek on his chest and swallowed. "And I'm sorry I'm such a pain in the ass."

Ben smiled and kissed the top of her head. "It's okay." Ben leaned back and searched her eyes. "If you weren't such a pain in the ass, my life would be really boring. I'd probably still be single . . . and I'd most likely live in a small, finished, simple house with no mortgage, minimal bills, and a healthy retirement portfolio. Instead, I have a whopper of a mortgage, a maxed-out home-equity loan, a car loan, someone else's student loans, a house that needs endless work, and a retirement account I can never afford to add to." He paused, smiling. "But I also have someone beautiful and loving to spend my retirement *with* . . . even if it's in a tent."

"Hey now," Macey said, mustering a smile. "It's not that bad—my school loans are almost paid off, and we will *never* live in a tent."

"We might."

Macey rolled her eyes.

"Do that again."

"What?"

"Roll your eyes."

She shook her head. "How long before supper?"

"I think it should simmer a bit. Want a drink?"

"Sure," she said.

"Beer? Wine?"

"I'd take one of Henry's Intimidators if you're sharing? Pairs best with this menu."

Ben opened a black bottle for her and pulled her closer, slowly unbuttoning the top of her shirt.

"So, what do you think about Keeper?" Macey pressed, trying to keep him on topic.

"I'm *not* thinking about Keeper," he murmured, kissing the curve of her neck.

Macey leaned into him. "If you said yes, I wouldn't be thinking about him, either," she teased, unbuttoning his shirt and tracing her fingertips along the smooth skin of his chest.

"You know, if I didn't know better, I'd think you were trying to bribe me."

"I would never do that," she whispered innocently as she pressed against him.

Ben took a deep breath and let it out slowly. Then he leaned back and searched her eyes. "I know you have your heart set on getting him, Mace, so how can I say no?"

"I don't want you to just *not* say no . . . I want you to want him, too."

"Do you want me to be honest?"

"Yes."

"Well, I'm not convinced that getting a dog with three legs is the best idea, but time will tell, won't it?"

Macey pulled away and pressed her lips together in a sad smile. "I guess." She put her beer on the counter and looked out the window. "I've had a long day and I'm going to get my pj's on."

Ben watched her go and took another long sip of his beer. "So much for what *I* had in mind," he muttered, lifting the lid and giving the sausage and peppers a stir.

22

Harper opened her eyes and blinked at the bright sunlight streaming through the window. She was so glad Cora had been able to get special permission for her to stay with them. She looked around the room and rubbed her chest, but the pain was gone. She pushed back her blanket and sat up, making the cot squeak. "Rudy, you awake?" she asked softly.

An unintelligible mumble came from the bed next to her.

"It's morning."

"Mm-hmm."

"I smell bacon."

"Mom's making pancakes," Rudy murmured sleepily.

Harper's eyes brightened. She couldn't remember the last time she'd had pancakes. "Is it okay if I go see?"

"Mm-hmm."

Harper tiptoed down the hall and saw Cora standing at the stove. She was humming something, but as soon as Harper peered around the doorway, she stopped. "How you feelin', baby?"

Harper's eyes grew wide. "How'd you know I was here?"

Cora smiled but didn't turn around. "Because I have eyes in the back of my head."

"You do not," Harper said, inspecting the back of Cora's curly salt-and-pepper head, just to be sure. "What are you making?"

"Blueberry pancakes."

"Can I help?"

"Sure." Cora took a sip of her coffee and turned the bacon, which was sizzling and popping in an old cast-iron pan. She looked down at Harper's tangled red hair. "You have some serious bed head goin' on, girl."

"I know," Harper said, peering at the bacon. "Mrs. Lewis said it's a rat's nest, and it hurt when she brushed it. She said I need a damn haircut."

Cora sighed. "Maybe we can fit one in. And you don't need to repeat everything Mrs. Lewis says exactly the way she says it."

"Oh, that's nothing! She says a lot worse than that."

"Well, it's not very ladylike, and if you want to be a lady, you won't copy her."

Harper grinned. "Yes, ma'am."

"You're such a fresh kid," Cora said, chuckling.

"I know."

Harper watched Cora scoop flour into a measuring cup. "What can I do?"

"You can start by rinsing the blueberries," Cora said, pointing to a container on the counter, "and then you can help make the batter."

"Okay." Harper turned on the cold water and held the container under it, popping several plump blueberries into her mouth at the same time. "Mmm, these are good!"

Cora looked over. "Don't eat 'em all or we'll be having plain pancakes."

Harper popped one more in her mouth and then turned off the water and set the container on a paper towel. She watched Cora pour milk into the flour mixture.

"Do you know how to crack an egg?"

Harper shrugged. "I guess."

Core looked at her and frowned. "You're ten years old an' you never broke an egg?"

"Nine."

"Nine, ten"—Cora sighed as she reached for an egg—"High time you learn, regardless." She cracked the egg on the edge of the bowl, pulled the edges apart, and released the egg with a dusty plop onto the flour. Then she nodded to the other egg. "You try." Harper reached for the egg and tapped it gently on the edge of the bowl. "A little harder," Cora instructed, and Harper tapped the egg harder, but because she was holding it too tightly, it broke in her hands. "That's okay," Cora said, pushing Harper's hands over the bowl. "Jus' let it go."

Harper dropped the whole egg, shell and all, into the bowl and then held her dripping hands over it. "Sorry," she said softly, feeling stupid.

"It's okay, baby," Cora said, reaching into the bowl to pick out the pieces of shell. "It takes a little practice. You'll get the hang of it. Wash your hands good, though."

Harper started to rinse her hands, but when Cora looked over and realized she was only using cold water, she turned on the hot. "You have to use hot water *and* soap."

"Why?" Harper asked, frowning.

"Salmonella."

"What's sam-o-nella?"

"It's bacteria that can make you sick."

"Oh," Harper said, frowning again. "Can you die from it?"

"Probably not, but it'll give you the runs and make you real sick, so anytime you handle eggs or raw meat, you have to wash with hot sudsy water."

Harper squeezed more soap onto her palms and washed her hands again—she had enough to worry about without worrying about getting the runs from sam-o-nella, too.

"Can I help?" Rudy asked, coming into the kitchen.

"Sure," Cora said, handing her the spatula.

Rudy pulled a chair up to the counter, and without needing any direction, started to stir the flour, eggs, and milk. "How come there's eggshell in here?"

"Because we wanted crunchy pancakes," Cora said, winking at Harper—who grinned and winked back.

A moment later, Harper was on the chair next to Rudy, both eating just as many blueberries as Harper was dropping into the bowl. "It's ready, Mama," Rudy announced.

Cora peered into the bowl to check the consistency. "Okay," she said, nodding. And as Rudy ladled generous scoops of batter onto the hot griddle, Harper hopped down to set the table.

"I just love it here," she announced, bending down to stroke McMuffin's soft fur. Then she poured orange juice into the glasses Cora had set out and hopped back on the chair with Rudy.

"How they comin', Rudy?" she asked, draping her arm over her friend's shoulder.

"They's a-comin'," Rudy said, laughing and putting her arm around Harper's shoulder, too.

Cora took a sip of her coffee and watched them. Just a week

earlier, Harper had been in the emergency room. Now she was hopping around, helping make pancakes.

"Don't be fooled," Dr. Hack had warned. "Things can change in a heartbeat."

Cora sighed—she'd had to do some serious wrangling to get permission for Harper to stay with her, even temporarily. In the end, the only reason her boss had given in was because Harper's medical issues were so serious . . . and the fact that other foster homes weren't available. No one wanted Harper. She had literally nowhere else to go. Still, Cora wished she could do more for her. Every once in a while a child came through the system who found a special place in her heart, and that fresh little redhead was definitely one of them. As tough as she was on the outside, Cora knew it was all a front—a defense mechanism to protect her from getting hurt again—and she was really a softy on the inside. She'd thought seriously about adopting her—she'd even prayed about it, but she just didn't get the sense that it was the right answer. The good Lord must have someone else in mind, and she wished he would show his hand.

23

"I'm coming!" Macey called, pulling her fleece over her head and reaching for her keys and the new cobalt-blue collar and leash she'd picked up at the feed store during her lunch break the day before. She hurried outside and saw Ben standing in the driveway, looking at his phone. When he heard her on the porch, he looked up and smiled.

"At least you're smiling," she said, her heart feeling lighter. She'd been so worried about getting Keeper without Ben's full support that she'd hardly slept, but this morning she'd heard him call Gage and the other guys and tell them they had the day off, and now he was waiting patiently for her, his tan face accentuated by sun-streaked hair, reminding her of the boy with whom she'd fallen in love. To this day, when she paused to really *see* Ben and not take his presence for granted, he still made her heart skip. And now, as he stood there in the morning sunlight, his faded jeans hanging loosely on his hips, and his blue button-down oxford neatly tucked in under his canvas Carhartt work jacket—he was obviously trying to look like a responsible pet owner—she wished she'd let him have his way last night, instead of being the spouse who played her *I've had a long day* card a little too often.

"Of course I'm smiling! I'm married to the prettiest girl in the world."

"I think you must mean the most headstrong."

"Well, that too," Ben teased, putting his arm around her. "I'm also smiling because Gage and Maeve think it's funny we're getting a dog when Maeve said you were adamant about *not* getting one. She says you're an old softy."

"Hey, it's a girl's prerogative to change her mind."

"It is indeed," Ben teased. "Anyway, they want to come by and meet him, and Gage said he'd help me build a ramp if we need one."

"But Maeve already met him! In fact, this is all her fault."

"Well, she must want to meet him again."

Macey rolled her eyes, even though she was glad they were coming over.

Fifteen minutes later, they pulled into the parking lot of Noah's Ark Animal Shelter. "You're positive about this?" Ben asked, looking over.

"I am," Macey confirmed. "I have this feeling we're supposed to give him a home. He belongs with us."

"Okay," Ben said with a resigned sigh, but when they opened their doors and heard a chorus of barking, he added, "I hope he's not a barker."

They walked inside, and the receptionist, who was on the phone, smiled. She gestured that she'd be right with them, and Macey nodded and stood next to Ben. The room smelled like wet fur and pet food, and although there was a full dustpan and broom in the corner, wispy hair floated everywhere in the morning sunlight. Macey looked around and noticed a gray tiger cat curled up in one of the chairs, sunning itself. She smiled and turned to Ben. "I wonder what his name is."

"Whatever it is, we're not getting him," he whispered.

The receptionist hung up the phone. "How can I help?"

Macey cleared her throat. "We're here to pick up Keeper."

The receptionist smiled. "Oh! I heard our Keeper was getting a fur-ever home! He is such a sweetheart. We're going to miss him."

Macey nodded, not knowing what to say.

"Hang on," she said, getting up. "I'll let them know you're here." She disappeared down the hall. A moment later she was back. "Okay, I need you to sign some papers and . . ." She looked up. "You know there's an adoption fee, right?"

Macey frowned. "No. How much is it?"

"Well, it's really a suggested donation—it covers expenses. It's a hundred dollars."

"Oh," Macey said. "They didn't tell us. I'll have to get my . . ."

"Here," Ben said, stopping her and pulling out his wallet. "Use this." He slipped a neatly folded hundred-dollar bill from behind his driver's license.

"No, not your lucky hundred," Macey said, putting up her hand. "I'll just go to the car."

Ben shook his head and looked her in the eye. "What better way to spend it?"

She half smiled. "Okay, but I'm paying you back."

"Mm-hmm," Ben said, handing the bill to the receptionist.

"Great," she said. "Now, I just need a signature here . . . and here," she said, marking the form. Macey looked it over, and with a slightly shaking hand, signed her name. As she did, the gray tiger cat got up, stretched, and strolled along the counter. "Hey, there, Big Mac," the receptionist said, stroking his soft fur.

"He looks like a Mac," Macey said, smiling. "How long has he been here?"

The receptionist frowned, trying to remember. "He's been here a while, but I'm fairly new." She looked over the forms and reached for a bag on her desk. "These are Keeper's things—his favorite toys and a vest he used to wear—they said he was a therapy dog. Anyway, he's all ready. You can follow me back." She motioned for them to follow her, and as they walked down the hall, she looked over her shoulder. "He just had a bath, so he smells really good." She held the door open at the end of the hall and then led them past a long line of kennels filled with dogs of all shapes and sizes who were barking excitedly, hoping it was their big day. Macey pressed her lips together, feeling sad—there were so many dogs in need of homes, she wished she could take them all. The receptionist stopped in front of the second-to-last kennel.

"Here he is," she announced. "Hey, Keep! Guess what? Your mom and dad are here to take you home!"

The big golden was lying quietly on an old blanket, wearing a new bandanna with pumpkins on it, but as soon as the receptionist started to unlatch his gate, he sat up, his eyes bright and his tail swishing tentatively. She opened the gate and stepped back. "You can go in," she said, smiling.

Macey's heart pounded. "Hey, ole pie," she said softly, kneeling in front of him. "Do you want to come home with us?"

Keeper stood up, his tail wagging, and nuzzled his head into her chest. "I guess that's a yes," she murmured, her eyes filling with tears and her heart swelling with a boundless love for a dog she hardly knew but who needed a home. *A forever home.*

24

"WANT TO RIDE BIKES?" HARPER ASKED, DRAGGING THE TIPS OF HER sneakers in the sand under the swing. She and Rudy had already played hopscotch, which, as usual, Rudy had won.

"Sure," Rudy said, hopping off. "You can ride my bike. I'll ride Joe's—all he does is play stupid video games anyway."

Harper dropped off her swing and tripped after her. "I can ride Joe's. You don't have to."

"I don't mind," Rudy said, moving several lawn chairs and tugging a rolled-up hose from under the makeshift storage area her mom had made—using a length of perforated green aluminum for a roof—between the low brick buildings.

Harper watched Rudy struggling to free her brother's bike and realized it was caught on a rake. "Let me help."

"No," Rudy said, tugging harder. "You're supposed to take it easy, remember?"

"I'm fine," Harper insisted, reaching down to pull the rake's tines out of the wheel's spokes.

"Hold on," she instructed, slipping her hand between the spokes.

Rudy waited as Harper untangled the long metal tines.

"Okay," Harper said, holding the rake to one side.

Rudy pulled back on the bike. "Thanks!" she exclaimed breathlessly.

Harper grinned. "That's what friends are for."

Rudy hopped on her brother's bike and rolled toward the parking lot. "Want to ride to the big playground?"

"Sure." Harper climbed onto Rudy's bike, knowing she meant the playground down the street. "Shouldn't we tell your mom?"

"She's not back from the store."

"Should we tell Frank?" Harper asked, pushing down on her pedal.

"He'll just say no," Rudy said, bumping off the curb. "Besides, we'll be right back."

Harper shrugged and bumped off the curb, too.

They rode through the parking lot and saw a man helping his daughter get into her car seat. "Hi, Mr. Jefferson," Rudy called, waving.

The man looked up and waved back. "Hi, Rudy!"

Harper pulled alongside her. "Do you ever hear from your dad?"

"No," Rudy said, shaking her head. "My mom said he moved to California."

"That stinks."

"He doesn't care about us, so it doesn't matter," Rudy said indifferently as she pedaled slowly down the street. "Do you remember your mom?"

Harper reached up to brush her hair out of her eyes. "Not really. I have a picture of her in my backpack, though."

"How come you never showed me?"

Harper shrugged and turned onto the street behind Rudy. "It's wrinkled, so it's hard to tell what she really looked like. She was pretty, though—she had long brown hair."

"You're such a good artist, you should draw her while you can still make out the picture. Then you won't forget what she looked like."

"I don't have anything to draw with."

"I do! I got a sketch pad and pencils for Christmas, but I can't draw worth a hill o' beans. You can use them. In fact, you can have 'em."

"Okay," Harper said thoughtfully. "Thanks!"

"I wonder," Rudy mused. "If your mom had brown hair . . . maybe your dad had red hair?"

"Maybe. I wish I knew who he was," she added wistfully.

"Does he know about you?"

"I don't know. I asked your mom, but she said they have no record of him."

"I bet if he knew about you, he'd come and get you."

"Maybe," Harper said doubtfully. They rode slowly past a man blowing leaves into the street and shielded themselves from the swirl of scarlet and gold projectiles. "What an idiot," Harper muttered. "Doesn't he know the leaves are just gonna blow back into his yard? He needs to bag 'em!" She turned around to look back and saw a car careening around the corner. "Rudy, look out!" she shouted, but Rudy had swerved out into the street to avoid the storm of leaves. "Rudy, look out!" she shouted again.

Rudy turned to see what she was shouting about and, at the very last second, saw the car barreling toward them. Her eyes grew wide in alarm as she instinctively veered away but hit the curb and fell

in the opposite direction—right in the path of the car! Harper pedaled harder and skidded to a stop right in front of Rudy and started
waving her arms frantically. At the very last second, the driver—a
kid wearing a crooked baseball hat—laid on his horn and swerved
away, shouting profanities through the open passenger window.

"Watch where you're going!" Rudy yelled back, her heart
pounding.

The boy gave her the finger, and tears sprang to Rudy's eyes.

"Jerk!" she called after him.

"You okay?" Harper asked, hopping off her bike to help her up.

"Yeah," Rudy said, gripping her handlebars to keep her hands
from shaking.

"What an a-hole," Harper seethed. "He didn't even slow down."

"He should be arrested and thrown in jail."

"Yeah—they should throw away the key!"

"Yeah," Rudy agreed. She looked up and smiled weakly at
Harper. "Thanks for saving me."

"I didn't do anything."

"Yes, you did—he would've hit *you* before he hit me."

"No, he wouldn't've."

Rudy looked back up the street. "Do you still want to go to the
playground?"

"Not really. You?"

"Not really," Rudy said, picking up her bike.

"I feel a little tired anyway." They started walking back, rolling their bikes through the swirl of blowing leaves, and when
Harper slowed down to catch her breath, she realized the man still
didn't see them.

"That leaf blower is so freakin' loud, you can't hear cars, never
mind see them through all these leaves," Harper said.

Rudy nodded.

Harper looked over. "You really okay?"

"Yeah." She hesitated, wondering if she should ask her friend such a question. "Harp, are you . . . are you scared of dying?"

Harper kicked through the leaves. "I was scared when I was in the hospital, but your mom came in and said I wasn't going to die, and she made me promise not to worry." She paused and looked over. "Are you?"

Rudy's eyes glistened and she nodded. "Especially at night. Some nights, it's all I can think about, and then I'm afraid to fall asleep because I'm afraid I won't wake up. I know we go to heaven, but I just can't imagine being without my mom—that's what scares me most. I'd miss her so much . . . and I know she'd miss me."

Harper nodded but didn't say anything. The only people on earth who would miss her if she died were Rudy and Cora, and maybe Frank and Joe. No one else on the whole earth even knew she was alive, so they certainly wouldn't notice if she died. "I don't think either of us are gonna die, Rudy. Your mom says I'm too stubborn, and I'm sure she'd say the same thing about you," Harper teased reassuringly.

Rudy laughed. "You *are* pretty stubborn."

They turned into the driveway of the apartments, and Harper looked over at the end unit. The curtains were drawn tight, and the yard was empty and overgrown. "Does anyone live there?"

"Mr. Peterson used to live there. He was really nice. His cat was McMuffin's brother. We got them from Janelle when her cat had kittens, and after he learned we named ours McMuffin, he named his Big Mac."

"No way!" Harper said, laughing.

"Way! And he had a dog with . . ."

Just then, Cora pulled into the parking lot and stopped next to them. "Where are you two comin' from?"

"Nowhere," Rudy answered. "We been here."

"Where are your bike helmets? You know you're not supposed to ride without helmets."

"Do we look like we're riding?" Rudy asked.

"Don't be fresh with me, Rudy, or you really *won't* be riding."

"I told you my helmet's too small, and I don't know where Joe's is."

"You did *not* tell me your helmet is too small."

"I did so!"

Cora shook her head and rolled forward. "Come an' help me with the groceries," she called.

"We're comin'," Rudy said, pushing her bike forward.

"So, what happened to Mr. Peterson?"

"He died," Rudy said matter-of-factly, "and now his place just sits empty."

"How come no one buys it?"

Rudy shrugged. "I don't know. His family owns it. Mom was going to offer to take Big Mac, but his family took his pets to a shelter."

Harper nodded, glancing back at the abandoned apartment. "You want to play Clue?" she asked, changing the subject.

"Sure," Rudy agreed, nodding.

"At least we know we won't die by candlestick, knife, revolver, lead pipe, or rope," Harper said, laughing.

"Ha! You never know," Rudy replied.

Harper kicked through a pile of leaves and imagined the gruesome wounds the weapons from Clue would inflict. "Yeah, I guess you're right."

25

"Welcome to the world of nose-smudged windows," Ben said, looking in the back seat of Macey's Outback. "Which is why he'll always ride in your car."

Macey looked in her rearview mirror and saw Keeper pressing his nose against the glass. "Do you want the window open, buddy?" she asked, pushing the button on her door panel. She smiled as she watched him put his head out the window. "I can't believe he was a therapy dog. I mean I *can* believe it—the way he nuzzles his head into your chest." She laughed. "What could be more therapeutic than that?"

"I nuzzle my head into your chest—is that therapeutic, too?"

"Well, it's not quite the same," Macey said, rolling her eyes and reaching an arm back to rub Keeper's head.

Ben looked in back again. "Well, Keep, I can already tell who's going to be getting the most attention."

"Oh, you've had your time in the sun," she teased, laughing. "Isn't that right, buddy?" She looked back again. Keeper's barrel chest was pressed against the door, his nose quivering, taking in all the wonderful scents as his jowls flapped in the wind.

"Never mind window smudges," she said, laughing, "there's going to be slobber all down the side."

"Which is why, I repeat, he's always riding in your car."

"You'll take him places."

"I doubt it," Ben said, shaking his head. "This is all you."

"We'll see," Macey mused, turning into the driveway.

"Besides, he probably won't be able to get into the truck."

Macey opened the back door. "Hold on, Keep," she said, reaching for his leash. "Okay." He hopped out, swishing his tail, and towed Macey toward the grass.

"He probably doesn't need to be on that leash," Ben called. "Where's he going to go?"

"They said to keep him on it until he's familiar with his surroundings," Macey called back.

Ben leaned against his truck and watched Keeper pulling Macey toward the nearest tree. The big golden lifted his leg, expertly balancing on two legs. "Hey! There's no peeing there!" he called, but before Macey could reply, he'd pulled into a squat, too.

"You're cleaning that up!" he added.

Macey looked back. "Get me a shovel."

"Oh, no! No, no, no. You're not using *my* good shovel to pick up dog poop."

Keeper finished his business, saw Ben watching, and hopped back to him. "Don't try to be friends after you made a mess in my yard," he teasingly scolded, but Keeper just wiggled around him, tangling his leash between his legs, and Ben laughed. "What the heck are you doing?"

"He's winning you over," Macey teased, leaning up to kiss him. "Thank you," she added.

"You're welcome," he said softly, pulling her against him.

Just as they started to kiss, they heard tires on gravel, looked up, and saw Gage's truck pulling in. Before they'd even parked, Maeve was hopping out and Keeper was wiggling over to her.

"Oh my goodness!" she exclaimed as he nuzzled her hands. "You're even sweeter than I remember, and I love your new bandanna." She held his head in her hands. "You look so handsome." Her kind words made his hind end wiggle even more.

"I think he's happy to be out of the shelter," Macey said, laughing.

"I bet he is," Gage agreed, kneeling down to say hello, too. "Hey, there, big fella, you glad to be home?"

Just then, an impatient bark came from the back of Gage's truck, and everyone—including Keeper—looked up and saw Gus with his paws on the edge of the bed, contemplating jumping.

"Hold on, mister," Gage said in his soft Southern drawl as he walked around to the back of the truck. "You can say hello, but you have to take it easy. Keeper's getting used to his new home." He looked him in the eyes. "If I let you out, you promise not to be crazy?"

Gus wagged his tail and licked Gage's cheek in agreement, but as soon as Gage let the tailgate down, Gus leaped through the air like a trapeze artist, landing ten feet out, and then made a beeline for Keeper. Both dogs pranced up to each other, sniffing all quarters until a joyful approval was reached and their tails wagged like flags in the wind. Gus jumped back, front legs flat on the ground with his hind end up in the air, an invitation to play, but Keeper just stood at attention, his nose quivering. Suddenly, Gus jumped up and started racing around, running circles around everyone, including Keeper, who just wagged his tail and watched until Gus came to a screeching halt right beside him. He gently sniffed Keeper's chest where his leg had been amputated, licked his cheek, trotted off, and looked back to see if he was coming.

"Let him go," Gage said, and Macey unhooked the leash. Keeper hopped after Gus, happily sniffing and peeing everywhere he did. Then he came back and laid on the sunny grass at their feet.

"You're such a good boy," Macey said, kneeling next to him. A moment later, Gus nosed back over to them and laid down beside him.

"It doesn't get any better than this, does it?" Ben said, putting his arm around Macey. "I think our boy has found a friend."

"*Our* boy?" Macey teased. "And here I thought he was all mine . . ."

"Nope, he's definitely *our* boy," Ben said, and Macey laughed.

"So, Ben," Gage said, looking at the front porch. "Do you think he needs a ramp?"

"I don't know," Ben answered. "We haven't found out if he can make it up the steps. At the shelter, they said he can get up a couple of steps without any trouble, and if that's the case, he could just use the back steps."

They walked toward the house with the dogs leading the way. "The house looks great," Gage said, nodding approvingly.

"Thanks," Ben replied. "Lots of things left to do, but we're getting there."

"That's when things start to fall apart," Gage teased.

"Don't even say it," Ben said. He looked up on the porch and noticed a box had been left next to the front door. "Looks like your dog bed is here."

Macey looked up. "Oh, good! Just in time!"

"Where'd you get it? L.L.Bean?" Gage asked.

"How'd you know?" Macey asked.

"Because that's where Gus's bed came from, too."

Ben chuckled. "These Northern girls think they know everythin'. Personally, I don't see why a dog even needs a bed, never mind a mail-order one all the way from Maine, but then again, what do we Southern boys know?" he teased, elbowing Gage.

"Yeah," Gage agreed, laughing.

"Y'all know how to dig yourselves a deep hole," Maeve teased. "*That* you know very well!"

"Sounds like a threat, don't it, Ben?" Gage asked, his eyes twinkling mischievously.

"Indeed," Ben agreed.

Macey rolled her eyes. "You two are like peas in a pod."

"Ain't that the pot callin' the kettle black?" Ben said, eyeing Gage again.

"Well, if you boys want lunch, you need to decide about a ramp."

"Well, see if he'll go up first," Ben said, nodding toward the steps.

Macey climbed the front steps of the old Victorian and looked back. "C'mon, Keep," she called. Keeper started to follow, and even set his one front paw on the bottom step, but then changed his mind, sat down, and gazed at her, as if she were asking him to do the impossible.

"You can do it," Maeve encouraged, kneeling down next to him. "Call Gus," she suggested, looking up at her sister.

"C'mon, Gus," Macey said, and the hapless Lab bounded up the steps and almost knocked Macey over.

"Go ahead, Keep—just like Gus," Maeve said softly. Keeper stood up again, tentatively placed his paw on the step, but then barked, backed away, and sat down. "I guess not," Maeve said glumly.

"Let's see if he can make it up the back steps," Macey said. She picked up the box and walked around the wraparound porch to the back door, with Gus at her heels while Maeve and Keeper followed in the yard. "How 'bout here, buddy?"

Keeper eyed the three steps, and then, with a happy bark, easily hopped up. "Good boy!" Macey said, giving him a hug. "I knew you could do it!" Gus bounced around as if he were spring-loaded, and then the two dogs ran the length of the porch and back.

"Looks like we get to have lunch without doing any work," Gage said, smiling.

Ben laughed. "Oh, I'm sure Macey can find something for us to do. I never get off that easy."

Macey ignored him. "C'mon, Keep," she called, holding the door open. "C'mon in and check out your new home!"

26

HARPER STUDIED HER REFLECTION IN THE MIRROR AND THEN REACHED around the edge of the hairdresser's cape to wipe away a bead of water that was trickling down her cheek. "I think I'd like it cut really short."

"How short?" Janelle asked, dabbing her cheek with a towel.

Harper looked at one of the pictures on the wall. "Like that," she said, pointing to a picture of a girl with a pixie cut.

"That's pretty short, hon," Janelle said, frowning, but seeing the disappointment on Harper's face, added, "but I bet it'd look real cute on you."

Harper turned her head, trying to imagine how she'd look with short hair. "What do you think, Cora?"

"I think you should get your hair cut any way you like, baby, but you need to decide soon because we have a doctor's appointment in . . ." She trailed off as she glanced at her watch. "One hour."

"Just like that then," Harper confirmed, nodding toward the picture again.

As Janelle combed out her long hair, Lana, the stylist cutting an older woman's hair in the next chair, looked over. "Your hair is such a beautiful color, you should consider donating it."

Harper frowned. "Donating it?"

"Mm-hmm . . ."

Janelle nodded. "That's a good idea!" Then she looked at Cora. "Cora, this is Lana. She just moved into our complex, and she has a little girl, Kari, who's the same age as Rudy, and a little boy, Kayden, who's the same age as Joe."

Cora smiled. "It's nice to meet you, Lana. Maybe we can get our kids together sometime."

"That would be nice," Lana said. "They need someone to play with so I can get them outside *and* outta my hair!" She turned back to Harper. "Anyway, child, there are quite a few organizations like Locks of Love that make hair pieces for kids who've lost their hair."

"Why have they lost their hair?"

"Mostly because of medical reasons."

Harper considered for a brief second. "What do you think, Cora?"

"I think it's up to you, baby."

"I'll do it!" Harper said, a smile lighting her face.

"This child's going to donate her beautiful hair to Locks of Love!" Janelle announced, and all the other stylists and patrons stopped their chattering and cheered.

Harper smiled shyly and felt her cheeks get warm as Janelle reached for her hair dryer. She gently brushed out Harper's silky hair. "You definitely do not have a rat's nest, child—I don't know *what* that lady was talking about. You have the most beautiful hair I've ever seen—and I've seen a lot of hair! It just needs a little TLC."

"What's TLC?"

"Tender loving care," Janelle said, gently braiding Harper's hair and putting a hair band around it.

"Last chance, now. You sure?" she asked, reaching for her scissors. "Because once I start, there's no turning 'round, and it'll take a year to grow back."

"I'm sure," Harper said, squeezing her eyes shut and feeling the gentle tug on her head as Janelle started to cut. A few seconds later, she held the ponytail up for everyone to see. "Look at this beautiful ponytail some little redhead's going to get!"

"That is one gorgeous ponytail," Lana said, smiling and winking at Harper.

Everyone cheered again, and Harper opened her eyes and tried to picture a little kid wearing a wig made from her hair. The idea made her feel oddly warm inside, and she smiled. "Maybe I'll grow it so I can donate again."

Cora smiled to herself. This poor little girl—who has nothing and no one—is still willing to give what she can. She might be a scrappy, foul-mouthed tomboy on the outside, but inside, she has a good heart.

Janelle adjusted her glasses and got to work, snipping, trimming, eyeing, and snipping some more, and all the time, humming. "Where were all those pictures taken?" Harper asked, looking at the photos tucked into the frame of her mirror.

"Tha's my home," Janelle said, and then she started to softly sing the lyrics to the song she'd been humming—"Jamaican Farewell."

Harper listened to the words and smiled. "You're a good singer."

"Thank you."

"Do you ever go to Jamaica?"

"Not as often as I'd like. See that picture there?" She pointed to a photograph of two young men wearing shorts and flip-flops with their arms draped over each other's shoulders.

Harper nodded.

"Those are my babies. Ma boys!"

"How come they're in Jamaica and you're here?" Harper asked.

"Oh, it's just the way things worked out," Janelle said with a sigh as she dried and brushed Harper's hair. She paused. "So what do you think?" She turned the chair so Harper could see her reflection.

"Wow," Harper said softly. "I look totally different." She turned her head and reached up to touch her hair. "I love it! Thank you!"

"You're welcome, child. I'm glad you *love* it."

"Cora and Miss Lana, what do you think?"

Cora smiled and nodded. "It looks real nice."

"It looks real cute!" Lana said, giving her a thumbs-up.

"Thanks! Wait till Rudy sees me," Harper mused, turning her head again.

"She probably won't recognize you," Cora said with a chuckle.

Janelle smiled, lightly fluffing her handiwork and unsnapping the cape. "Now we can see your ears, so you'll have to get your ears pierced and pick out some cute earrings."

"Ooh! Can I?" Harper asked hopefully, looking at Cora.

"One thing at a time," Cora said, reaching into her bag.

Janelle looked up, saw her friend pulling out her wallet, and shook her head. "Oh, no . . . There's no charge for donations to Locks of Love," she said.

"Are you sure?" Cora asked, frowning.

"I am *positive*," Janelle replied, folding the cape and laying it on the chair. "Now, scoot or you'll be late for your doctor's appointment."

"Well, please take a tip," Cora insisted, trying to press a bill into her hand.

"No, no," Janelle said, pulling her hand away and reaching for her broom. "I'll see you later."

Cora sighed. "I'll get you back."

"You can try," Janelle said, chuckling.

"Don't even," Lana said, laughing.

Twenty minutes later, Cora and Harper were sitting in the waiting room of the Children's Heart Center and Cora was bent over a clipboard, filling out paperwork.

"How'd you get today off?" Harper asked, leaning back in her chair and touching her head—which felt lighter.

"I told 'em they are just going to have to manage without me," Cora answered as she checked boxes. "I don't know half the answers to these questions," she said with a sigh. "When's your birthday again, baby?"

"March first," Harper said, fiddling with a loose thread on her chair. She looked around the busy waiting room. "Look, Cora, they have one of those coffeemakers—just like Janelle has in her salon."

"Mm-hmm," Cora murmured distractedly.

"Do you want me to fix you a cup?" Harper asked hopefully.

Cora, absorbed in her task and searching through her bag for Harper's insurance information, didn't hear the question.

"Can I make a cup?" Harper repeated, sitting on the edge of her seat, but Cora still didn't answer, so she stood up. "I'm just gonna make one," she said softly, hoping Cora wouldn't say no. She walked across the room to the coffee machine and then glanced back to see if she'd noticed, but Cora was still engrossed in her paperwork, so Harper turned to the display rack and looked at the flavors. Finally, she reached for a pod, dropped it into the coffeemaker, and clicked it closed. She positioned a paper coffee cup under the dispenser, and pushed BREW, and the coffeemaker spritzed to life, spilling out a stream of dark coffee. Harper tore open three sugar packets, dumped them in, and then added a generous amount of cream. She gingerly took a sip, hoping it wasn't too hot, licked her lips approvingly, and walked over to look at the fish tank. She lightly tapped the glass near an orange-and-white clown fish.

"Hey, Nemo," she said softly. Just then a blue-and-yellow surgeonfish emerged from behind a treasure chest. "Dory!" she squeaked, almost spilling the coffee.

Cora looked up, saw the cup in Harper's hand, and frowned. "What are you drinking?"

Harper looked down as if she didn't know what Cora was talking about. "This?" she asked innocently. "I told you I was making it. I made it for you—just the way you like it—light and sweet."

Cora eyed her suspiciously, and Harper handed it to her.

"Here," she said. "See if it's all right."

Cora took a sip and smiled. "Mmm . . . it's perfect. Thank you."

Harper sat down next to her and nodded. "It's called Donut Shop."

The door to the waiting room opened, and a physician's assistant holding an iPad surveyed the waiting room. Finally, her eyes settled on Harper. "Harper Wheaton?"

Harper nodded, wishing her heart would stop racing, and reached for Cora's hand.

27

MACEY FELT A WARM BODY STIRRING NEXT TO HER AND OPENED HER EYES. The kitchen was dark except for the soft light coming from the night-light next to the coffeepot. She looked at the clock and groaned—it was after midnight! Why hadn't Ben woken her? She sat up and stroked Keeper's silky fur. "Night, ole pie," she murmured sleepily, kissing his head. "It's time for me to find my own bed." Keeper opened one eye, yawned, and snuggled his head deeper into the side of the soft fleece.

Macey left the night-light on and trudged upstairs. It had been another long day at work—the rhinovirus *and* a nasty stomach bug were both working their way through the local elementary schools, and some poor kids had been lucky enough to catch both. She closed the bathroom door, turned on the light, and looked at her reflection. After falling asleep on Keeper's bed, her mascara was smudged, her eyes were puffy, and her hair—yikes! She'd canceled her haircut and now she really needed to reschedule. She brushed her teeth, threw her clothes in the hamper, and pulled on her pj's—Ben's old waffle Henley and a pair of boxers. She rubbed a copious amount of cream into her hands—which were dry from all the hand sanitizer she'd used at work—switched off the light, and tried to find her way in the dark, but when she reached the bed, she swung her foot forward and smacked her toe. "Ouch!" she cried. "Son of a bitch!" she added for good measure, falling onto the bed and tearfully rubbing the offended toe.

Ben sat up groggily. "What'd you do? Are you okay?"

"I stubbed my toe," she cried, "and no, I'm not! I think I broke it."

"You probably just bruised it," Ben consoled, rubbing her back.

"How come you didn't wake me when you came up?"

"Because you looked so comfortable, and Keeper looked so content. Besides, I'm beginning to think you like him more than me."

Macey frowned, still rubbing her toe. "You sound jealous."

"I *am* a little jealous," he admitted sheepishly. "There's another handsome blond male living in our house, and ever since he moved in, he's been getting all the attention."

"Poor you," Macey said as she gingerly slipped her still-throbbing toe under the covers. "I'm just trying to help him adjust. I want to make sure he knows he's loved."

"I'm sure he knows. Last night, he got grilled hamburger mixed in with his kibble, and tonight, he got roasted chicken." Ben propped his head up on his elbow. "How 'bout making sure the other male in your life knows he's loved?"

"I don't think he deserves it after he left me downstairs."

"I just thought you two looked cozy," he said, intertwining his fingers with hers.

Macey sighed, relenting a little as the pain in her toe subsided. "You'll be taking your life in your hands—I took the vital signs of at least thirty vomiting, sneezing children today."

"That's a chance I'm willing to take," Ben said, sliding his hand along the elastic waistband of her boxers. "Hmm, didn't you get the memo?"

"What memo?"

"It's no-boxer night."

Macey reached over to see if he had his boxers on, but nope, as usual, he was buck naked. "No, I didn't get the memo."

"Well, we'll just have to fix that," he said, sliding his hand inside her boxers and pushing them down as he softly kissed her.

"I'm sorry you've been feeling neglected," she whispered into his kiss. "Thank you for letting us get Keeper. He's such a sweetheart, and I know he's much happier now . . . and he's been so good. Did you notice he hasn't gotten into anything? And he's been fine by himself when we're at . . ."

"Shhh," Ben whispered, kissing her again. "It's *our* time."

In the darkness, Macey smiled, and even though her mind continued to race on, she didn't say any more. *Our time*, she thought. *Is this what our time is going to be like? Just Ben and me and Keeper? No little kids for Keep to love, either? No little fingers and cheeks for him to lick peanut butter off?* She realized her heartache could indeed be compounded by a dog. Now, she would not only feel sad for them, she'd also feel sad for Keeper, because he'd never get to know what it was like to have little people chasing him around and falling asleep on top of him.

"Hey," Ben said softly, bringing her back to the present.

"I'm sorry. My mind just keeps going along on its own."

"We don't have to do this. . . ."

"No, no—I want to," she said, rolling onto her side to face him.

"After all," he said softly, "you're the one who keeps talking about being in the moment."

"I am," she admitted sheepishly.

"What did you call it . . . momentness?"

"Mindfulness," she answered, smiling.

"Ah, mindfulness." He pulled her against him, and she felt how aroused he was. "See if you can wrap your mind around this," he whispered.

"I can wrap more than my mind around it," she teased, slipping her leg over his.

"Maybe we can lose this sexy shirt, too," he said, sliding his hands along the curves of her body and pushing it over her head. He traced his fingers lightly along her thighs, lingering here and there until she felt a tingling rush between her legs.

She breathed in the clean scent of soap mixed with the familiar scent of his body. "Mmm, you smell good," she murmured, reaching for him and teasing him, too, until, finally, unable to hold on, she moved her hands to his hips and tried to ease him on top of her.

"What's your hurry?" he whispered, hovering above her.

"I'm in no hurry," she said, smiling.

He brushed his long, hard body against hers, and she tried to pull him closer, but he just ran his lips along the nape of her neck. "Should I stop?" he whispered in her ear. "Because I can. . . ."

"No, you can't," she said, laughing.

"Yes, I can," he said, grinning.

"You better take it while you can get it, mister," she said, pulling him against her.

Ben smiled, covering her body with his, and moving slowly up and down, pressed against her, penetrating more deeply with every upward motion. "You feel so good," he whispered.

"So do you," Macey murmured, lifting her hips and pulling

him deeper. Finally, she heard him breathe faster and felt him surging inside until she, too, caught her breath. They lay still, their bodies intertwined, their hearts pounding.

"When we were younger, I had no idea you would be so good at this."

"I know—so much untapped potential just waiting to be appreciated!"

"Foolish me for taking so long," she teased, wrapping her arms around his waist. "I certainly appreciate it now."

He kissed her softly. "Oh, Mace," he said, his voice turning solemn. "I love you so much."

"I love you, too," she whispered, breathing in the lovely scent of him. She thought she could never get enough.

Ben's soft, steady breathing told Macey he'd fallen asleep. She sighed, wishing she could fall asleep so easily. Their whole marriage, Ben had always been first to fall asleep. He could even fall *back* asleep after being woken up. She, on the other hand, had one precious opportunity for a good night's sleep. If she fell asleep on the couch—or on the dog bed, as she had tonight—it was nearly impossible for her to fall *back* asleep. And she could tell tonight would be no different. Tired as she was, her mind was already picking up where it had left off.

She closed her eyes and tried to keep her nightly worries at bay by recalling the very first time Ben had kissed her—the first time she'd tapped into all that potential of his! It hadn't been long after she'd come home from Europe. Ever the gentleman, he'd taken Hayley home after their impromptu class reunion, thanked her for adding to their fun, and kissed her on the cheek—or so he said, and she had no reason to not believe him. The next day, he and Henry had run in the Tybee Island Turkey Trot, and the girls had all come along to cheer them on. After the race, they'd parted ways, and Ben and Macey had walked along the beach.

"Want to come over for dessert later?" she'd asked.

Ben had raised his eyebrows. "Is your mom making her famous apple pie?"

"She is," Macey said, laughing. "She said to be sure to ask you because she knows how much you love it. She's also making pumpkin."

Ben didn't need to hear more. "I'll be there," he said, smiling, and then he'd stopped walking and reached for her hand. "Mace, I can't tell you how good it is to see you. It's hard to explain, but when you weren't here, well . . ."

"I know what you mean," she'd said, studying him. "I missed you too, Ben."

He'd searched her eyes, leaned down, and softly kissed her lips . . . and when they'd pulled apart, he could hardly contain his smile. "I've wanted to do that for a very long time."

Later that night, after the pies were put away and Macey's parents had bid them good night, and followed Maeve—whose sore throat had blossomed into a cold—up to bed, Macey and Ben had sat on the couch and talked into the night. Finally, Ben had looked at his watch, realized how late it was, and pulled on his jacket, but when they got to the front door, Macey had leaned against it and pulled him against her. "I've wanted to do this for a long time," she'd said softly.

"Be careful," he'd warned with a grin, "or you'll get more than you bargained for . . . and your parents will hear . . ."

"You wouldn't," she'd said, laughing as he kissed her.

"I might," he teased, pressing against her. "I want you so much, Mace," he'd whispered.

Now Macey eased to her side, replaying the lovemaking they'd just shared, and suddenly her mind began to play the educational film they'd all watched in their eighth-grade health class. The image of a cartoon sperm swimming up a fallopian tube in search of an egg was as clear in her mind as if she'd seen it yesterday. "It's a long way," the narrator warned as the sperm swam along like salmon swimming upstream to spawn. "Only a few hardy travelers will reach their destination." She remembered the one happy sperm, smiling triumphantly as he approached an eager-looking egg. Then, she pictured Ben's sperm, looking fiercely determined, swimming up her fallopian tube at that very moment.

"Go, baby, go!" she whispered. "You can do it! Get that egg!" Then she realized what she was asking for, and tears filled her eyes. She squeezed them back and as she tried to quiet her mind, she heard a loud clump in the kitchen. She continued to listen for more sounds, but she didn't hear anything, so she felt around for her sweatpants and shirt, stopped at the bathroom—praying she wouldn't lose too many precious, determined swimmers—and went downstairs.

Keeper was lying on the floor next to his bed, but when he heard her, he looked up and thumped his tail. "How come you're not *on* your bed?" she asked softly, sitting next to him. "C'mere," she coaxed, patting the bed, and he pulled himself up, hopped over, and pushed his bowed head into her chest. "I wish you could come upstairs," she said softly, kissing the top of his head. He swished his tail, and she knew he wished it, too. "Maybe we'll have to move our bedroom downstairs . . . or maybe we'll have to put in an elevator! How fun would that be? Riding up and down in an elevator?" Keeper licked her cheek and curled up next to her, and Macey lay back and put her arm around him. Within minutes, they were both sound asleep.

28

"Look at you!" Rudy exclaimed as Harper climbed out of the car.

Harper reached up and touched her hair self-consciously as her freckled cheeks turned pink. "Do you really like it?"

Rudy nodded. "It looks nice."

"Thanks," Harper said, half smiling. "Janelle said I should get my ears pierced, too."

"You should!"

"Your mom would have to take me."

Cora reached into the back seat for her pocketbook and the grocery bags. "As I said, one thing at a time. Rudy, please come take these."

"I can take something," Harper offered.

"No. Remember, Harper? The doctor says *you* have to take it easy."

"I'm not made of glass, you know," Harper replied glumly.

"Mm-hmm," Cora said, handing the bags to Rudy. "Where are your brothers?"

"Inside."

She reached for the dark red chrysanthemum Harper had picked out for Janelle. "Here, you can take this, though." Harper took the mum from her and cradled it in her arms while Cora reached in back for the milk. She closed the door. "You kids are goin' through milk like it's goin' out of style."

"I won't drink any more," Harper volunteered hopefully. "I'll just have water and I'll eat less, too."

"That's not the answer, baby," Cora said softly, eyeing her.

Harper looked away. She would never understand why it couldn't be the answer.

"Do you wanna see if Janelle's home right now?" she asked, nodding in the direction of her neighbor's apartment.

"Sure," Harper said. Cora watched her walk over and knock on the door, but there was no answer. "She's not home," Harper called.

"C'mon then," Cora called. "You can try again later." She walked toward the front door, where McMuffin was meowing impatiently. "Did anyone feed this poor cat?" she asked as Harper knelt down to pet her.

Rudy shrugged. "I don't know—it's Frank's job."

Cora opened the door and the gray tiger scooted in, right past Joe, who was immersed in a video game, and barely looked up. "Have you done your homework, mister?"

"Don't have any."

"Ha! I find that hard to believe! You have five more minutes on that game, and then, off."

"But I need a half hour to finish this level," Joe protested.

"That's unfortunate, because you only have five minutes."

Joe frowned but knew better than to argue.

"Where's Frank?" she asked. Joe shrugged—he wouldn't tell her even if he *did* know.

"Frank, did you feed Muffin?" Cora called. There was no

answer, so she plopped the bags and milk jug on the table and headed down the hall. She knocked on his door, but there was still no answer, so she pushed it open. "Frank!" she shouted, and Frank looked up, startled, from his old laptop, pulled an earbud out of his ear, and quickly tapped his browser to a different page.

"What are you watching?" Cora asked, eyeing him.

"Nothin'."

She frowned. "You better not be somewhere you shouldn't be."

"I'm not, Mama," Frank said, sounding annoyed.

"Did you feed the cat?"

"No, I thought Rudy did."

"Have you done your homework?"

"I'm working on it—I'm almost done. Now that you're home, can I go shoot some hoops?"

"When you've finished your homework."

Frank groaned. "It'll be dark by then."

"Well, if you weren't wasting your time on some foolish website, you'd be done and you'd be going right now."

"I'm not wasting time, and I can finish later."

"Finish *now*," Cora said firmly.

Frank slammed his desk drawer. "I swear, Mama. I never get to go anywhere."

"Don't you raise your voice with me, young man, or you *won't* go anywhere."

Frank clenched his jaw. "You know, if I didn't have to babysit all the time, I could make the team and I could get a scholarship."

"I'm sorry, Frank, but if I have to pay a babysitter, I won't be able to pay the rent and we'll be living on the street."

"Why can't they go to an after-school program?"

Cora stepped into his room and closed the door. "Maybe that's something we can look into," she said in a low voice, "but, at the moment, I have my hands full. Harper is not well, and I don't know what I'm going to do with her. I'm sorry all this is happening right now, and I'm sorry that this is falling on you. But it is not my fault."

Frank shook his head and looked away. "Well, it sucks."

"I would appreciate it if you wouldn't use that kind of language."

"*Sucks* is not a bad word."

"Would you like me to use it?"

Frank just rolled his eyes. "Whatever."

"Get your homework done and you can go."

"It'll be too late."

Cora looked at her son leaning back in his chair. His lanky arms were attached to big strong hands with long angular fingers, and his legs stretched all the way under his desk—he had to be almost six feet. *Good Lord! When had he gotten so tall? And he was probably right. If he had the opportunity, he might very well be able to get an athletic scholarship.*

"When are tryouts?" Cora asked softly.

"Right after Thanksgiving," Frank said, perking up.

Cora opened the door. "I will try to figure something out. But I'm not making any promises."

Frank nodded. "I'm sorry for what I said."

"I'm sorry, too."

"It's okay."

"Leave your door open," Cora called back as she headed for the kitchen. She passed through the living room and realized Joe was still playing his video game. "Off!" she commanded. "You've had *more* than five minutes!"

"Five more?" Joe pleaded.

"No. Get off now, or you won't go on again this week."

Joe turned off the game and slumped dejectedly on the couch. Maybe Frank was on to something, she thought. If Joe and Rudy were in an after-school program, Joe wouldn't be spending all afternoon playing video games and Rudy wouldn't be venturing off on her bike without a helmet. She *would* have to look into it . . . just as soon as she found a foster home for Harper.

29

THE BELLS TINKLED CHEERFULLY WHEN MACEY PUSHED OPEN THE DOOR of Janelle's salon, now quiet after the long day. "Hey, Janelle," she called. "I'm sorry I'm late."

Janelle looked up from her newspaper. "It's quite all right, child. I needed a break anyway."

"Tell me about it," Macey said, shaking her head. "I think every kid in Savannah has the stomach bug or a cold . . . or both!"

"Well, I hope you left those germs at the office," Janelle said, eyeing her over the stylish scarlet reading glasses perched on the end of her bronze nose.

"Oh, don't worry! I took a bath in hand sanitizer before I left."

"Good. Well, c'mon over." she said, closing the newspaper and reaching into the cabinet for a clean towel. Macey hung up her jacket and sat down, and Janelle swirled a cape around her, tucked the towel under its collar, and snapped it closed.

"How've you been?" Macey asked as Janelle reclined the chair.

"Busy! I don't think I've ever been so busy."

"That's good," Macey said. "Word must be spreading about how great you are."

"Maybe," Janelle said as she lathered up Macey's hair. "'Cause I certainly haven't taken out any ads." She quickly lathered up Macey's hair, massaged it in, rinsed out the suds with warm water, poured conditioner into her palms, and smoothed it onto Macey's head. "Mmm, I just love this new conditioner—it smells so good!"

"It smells like coconut," Macey murmured, closing her eyes and feeling like she could fall asleep in the chair.

"You need to pamper yourself more often," Janelle teased, laughing as she gently toweled Macey's hair and brushed it out.

"I do," Macey agreed, smiling.

"So what are we doing today?"

"Oh, the usual, I guess. Maybe a little shorter so I can make it through Thanksgiving."

Janelle nodded as she reached for her scissors, and Macey looked over at the next station.

"Locks of Love?" Macey asked, gesturing to the long copper braid laid out neatly on a towel on the counter.

"Yes," Janelle said, nodding.

"A sweet little girl came in here today to get her hair cut and she donated it," Janelle said. "In fact, her hair's almost the exact same color as yours—it's just a hint brighter."

Macey smiled, and then frowned. "What was her name?"

"Harper."

"Harper Wheaton?"

"I don't know her last name. My friend Cora brought her in."

"I didn't know you knew Cora."

"Oh, yes. Cora and I go way back—she's my neighbor."

"Wow! I had no idea."

"Mm-hmm. How do you know Cora?"

"She brings the state kids in for checkups sometimes. She is the nicest person."

"She is," Janelle agreed, smiling.

"She just brought Harper into Dr. Hack's office on Friday."

"Well, then, you must already know that poor child had another appointment today. They were going there from here."

Macey nodded, wondering how much Janelle knew about Harper—she also knew that, no matter how curious she was, privacy laws would prevent her from saying anything further, so she changed the subject. "I should donate *my* hair."

"You should," Janelle said, combing it out. "You have beautiful hair and the people who make hair pieces could combine your hair with Harper's—no one would ever know the difference!" Janelle paused, wondering how much Macey knew about Harper. "You want to take the plunge today?"

Macey pressed her lips together, considering. "No, not today, Janelle—I'll need to think about it a little."

Janelle nodded. "I understand. I would, too, if I had such long beautiful hair. That little girl, though, she didn't give it a second thought. She must be very brave—and have a very big heart. When I asked her if she wanted to donate, she didn't even blink. Here she is, a little girl who has no family and not a thing to her name, and she's willing to give somethin' she *does* have to a child who needs it."

Macey bit her lip, wishing she had the same courage. She pictured Harper sitting in this very chair, getting her hair cut, and she remembered how tough she'd acted in the office.

"I don't know what Cora's gonna do with her," Janelle mused out loud. "She's having a heck of a time placing her in foster care. I guess she can be a bit of a challenge, and with heart problems, too! Poor thing!"

Macey nodded, still feeling as if she shouldn't talk about Harper's foster status or health problems.

"Cora called me when she got home from the doctor, and I know she was trying not to let it show, but she is beside herself. She doesn't even want to send Harper to school because she's afraid something's gonna happen to her. She loves that little girl, but there's no way she can adopt her. She has her hands full with her own kids." Janelle smiled sadly. "I told her to jus' keep the faith— the good Lord has somethin' in mind. He has a plan. We may not see it yet, but he does."

Macey nodded again, trying to picture the turmoil in Cora's house. The poor woman. She tried to imagine doing right by three kids as a single parent while holding down an overwhelming and thankless job and coping with the heartache of all those poor foster kids. It was hard enough for Macey to not get emotionally involved with the kids who came into the office, so she could only imagine how hard it was to know each child's complete history— the hardship, abuse, loss, and heartache they'd endured—and not become emotionally attached.

"So, how're you doin', hon?" Janelle asked as she snipped and trimmed, interrupting Macey's runaway train of thought. "Any news on the baby front?"

"No *good* news, Janelle. I miscarried again a couple weeks ago," Macey answered.

"Oh, baby, I'm so sorry," Janelle said, squeezing her shoulder. "I know how much you were hoping this time would be different. Isn't there anything the doctor can do to help you keep it?"

"We've tried everything, and I'm just about ready to give up. . . ."

Janelle nodded knowingly. "Life's hard. I know. I love my babies. They's grown now, but I loves 'em and they're far away. I ne'er get to see 'em." She shook her head. "You just need to keep the faith, baby. That's always been my mantra—keep the faith. It's never failed me."

"You remind me of my grandmother, Janelle. She had unwavering faith, too."

Janelle smiled, clicked on the hair dryer, and gently brushed out Macey's hair until it shone. "There you go," she said, unsnapping the cape and lifting it off her.

"Thank you," Macey said. "I really needed that."

Janelle pulled her into a hug. "Maybe, next time, you'll donate those lovely locks."

"Maybe," Macey said, laughing, "if I can get up the courage."

30

"Why're you still up, child?" Cora whispered softly, peering into Rudy's room.

Harper looked up from Rudy's desk, where the light from a small lamp softly illuminated the drawing pad Rudy had given her. "I couldn't sleep," she whispered back.

"Whatcha working on?" Cora asked, walking over, and Harper sat back so Cora could see her drawing.

"Who is that, baby?"

"My mom," Harper said, pointing to the tattered photo next to the pad.

"I remember that picture," Cora said, half smiling. "It used to be in your file."

"You gave it to me."

Cora nodded thoughtfully. She picked up the picture, and a smile slowly crossed her face. "She was pretty—your mom," she mused. "You look just like her."

"You think so?"

Cora nodded.

"Except for my hair. Rudy thinks my red hair came from my dad."

Cora nodded. "It might've . . . it might very well have." She looked at the drawing. "I didn't know you were such a good artist—that drawing looks just like the photograph."

"Thanks," Harper replied softly, adding a little shading under her mom's chin.

"Well, you have school in the morning, so you better get to bed—it's very late."

Harper nodded, switched off the light, and wrapped her arms around Cora. "I love living with you and Rudy."

"And we love having you here, baby," Cora said softly, resting her chin on Harper's head, hugging her and wishing she could do more. She kissed her on the top of her head. "Don't you worry, child, we'll find you a good home—one where you are just as happy as you are here." Cora lightly brushed the bangs off Harper's forehead. "Now go to sleep—tomorrow's your first day at Rudy's school."

Harper nodded and pulled up her covers, but she didn't smile. Even though she was going to school with Rudy—something she'd always wanted—they'd found out they weren't in the same class. They weren't even going to be in the same lunch period. So what was the point? Once again, she'd be on her own, and she couldn't help but wonder why the people in charge couldn't try a little harder to make things a little easier for her. It seemed like all the adults she'd ever encountered in her life—except for Cora—went out of their way to make her life as hard as possible. She stared into the darkness, wishing she could just go to work with Cora. At least there she'd know Cora was looking out for her . . . and maybe they could even get McDonald's for lunch.

CORA TURNED OUT THE LIGHT, WALKED BACK DOWN THE HALL, AND SANK into her chair. She did love having Harper there, and she knew

Rudy did, too—the two of them were as close as sisters—but Harper needed so much more than she could give her. Heaven forbid, if she ever needed round the clock care—which seemed more and more likely—she didn't know how she would ever manage. She felt tears stinging her eyes and brushed them away. "Oh Lord," she whispered, "please help me find that little girl a good home."

THE NEXT MORNING CAME ALL TOO SOON, AND, AS USUAL, THE GRANT household was in total chaos as Rudy, Joe, Frank, and now Harper scrambled to have breakfast, brush their teeth, and gather their schoolwork. Usually, there were two buses to catch in the morning, but Frank had already caught his to the high school, and since Cora was driving the other three so she could help Harper get settled, she'd waved off the second bus.

"I can help Harper, Mama," Rudy insisted. "I *know* where everything is."

"I know you do, baby, but I'm sure there will be more paperwork to fill out," Cora replied, "and besides, I need to stop at the nurse's office." She picked up her big canvas bag. "You kids got everything? Joe, you have the homework you said you didn't have?"

"Yes, Mama," Joe answered, stuffing his lunch into his backpack.

"Harper, have you got your lunch?"

Harper nodded, wishing again that her heart would stop racing.

"Baby, you look pale—you feel okay?"

"Yes. I just want to get this over with . . . are you sure I can't go to work with you?"

"I already told you, baby, I have a lot to do today."

"I promise, I won't be any trouble."

Cora looked up. "No," she said firmly. "It will be better if you're in school—you keep missing days and you're gonna get left back."

Harper rolled her eyes.

"But you must remember, if you don't feel good, you have to head right to the nurse's office—I'm gonna show you where it is."

Harper took a deep breath and let it out slowly. "Okay, I will."

"Let's go, then."

Cora pulled out and turned toward the school. Harper pointed as they passed the house where the man had been blowing leaves, and Rudy shook her head—the yard was covered again.

"What an idiot," Harper whispered, and Rudy nodded in agreement.

They pulled into the school parking lot, and Rudy and Joe suddenly realized that the buses had already come and gone.

"C'mon, Mama, we're late!" Joe called as they hopped out.

"I'm a-comin'," Cora called, reaching for her bag. "You two go ahead. We'll see you later."

"Okay," Rudy called, hurrying after her brother. Then she stopped in her tracks. "Good luck, Harper! I'm in Ms. Jones's room if you need anything."

Harper nodded. "Thanks, Rudy."

Rudy headed off and then turned around again. "We catch bus number five after school!"

"Okay," Harper called back, tucking away this important bit of information, but still hoping she'd see Rudy before the end of the day.

"Let's go, baby," Cora said, locking the car.

Harper started to reach for Cora's hand but then stopped, stuffed her hands in her pockets, and clenched her jaw.

"You okay?" Cora asked, eyeing her.

Harper nodded. "Fine."

"I know what 'fine' means, you know," Cora said gently.

"Well, I am," Harper said stonily.

"I know it's difficult to keep changing schools, Harper, especially since this one is probably going to be temporary, too, but I don't know what else to do. You *have* to go to school, and I *have* to go to work."

"I know, I know," Harper said. "It's no big deal, Cora, but there's no point in making friends when I'll probably just move again."

Cora swallowed. There were no easy solutions for this child, and the worst part was, she knew it.

"C'mon," Harper said, pulling open the door. "I'll be *fine*."

31

MACEY REACHED INTO THE BACK SEAT FOR THE GROCERIES SHE'D PICKED
up on the way home and noticed a plastic bag sticking out from
under the driver's seat. She pulled it out, frowning, and then remembered it was Keeper's things from the animal shelter. She
walked around back and peered in the window as she tiptoed up
the steps. No matter how quiet she tried to be, Keeper was always
sitting right by the door cocking his head. "There is no sneaking
up on you, is there, mister?" she said, laughing, and he began to
swish his tail.

Macey opened the door. "Hey, there, ole pie." She knelt down in
front of him and he pushed his great head into her chest. "It's always
so nice to come home to you," she whispered, kissing his bowed head
and then lifting his chin. "I love you . . . you know that?" She looked
into his chocolate-brown eyes and he wiggled all around, giving
her wet kisses. "Thank you so much!" she said, laughing.

"Do you need to get busy?" she asked, holding the door. He
hopped down the steps, hurried into the yard, took care of business, and came right back. "And now I bet you're looking for your
supper." She picked up his food bowl, scooped a cup of kibble into
it, added a little water, and walked over to put it down next to his

water bowl on the new mat she'd bought. Without being asked, Keeper plopped down on his haunches and gazed longingly at his bowl.

"Okay!" she said, and he hopped over and wolfed it down. "I don't know where you learned to be so polite," she teased, "you must've had a good owner, which reminds me . . ." She opened the plastic bag and looked inside. Soon Keeper, who'd already finished eating, came over and started wagging his tail as she pulled out an old tennis ball and a stuffed animal that looked like a hedgehog. She gave the hedgehog to him, and he immediately started to squeak it. "Oh, boy! Your dad's going to love that!" she said.

"His dad's going to love what?" Ben asked, coming through the door.

"A squeaky toy," Macey said as Keeper hopped over and playfully pushed the stuffed animal into Ben's crotch.

"Hey, watch that!" Ben said, reaching down to tousle his ears.

He leaned over to give Macey a kiss. "It's so nice to see you smile . . . *and* hear you laugh."

"It feels good to laugh," she said. "It's nice to come home to someone who is so happy to see me."

"Hey! I'm happy to see you."

"I know, but I usually get home before you, and this time of year, the house is dark."

He pulled her into his arms. "Well, as soon as the Jackson house is finished, I'll be home earlier."

She smiled. "But you still won't wag your tail."

"I can wag my tail, if that's what makes you happy," Ben teased, swiveling his hips.

"Just kiss me, you fool," Macey said.

Ben kissed her softly and murmured, "Nice haircut, by the way."

"Thanks," Macey said.

Suddenly, her stomach growled and Ben pulled away. "Hungry?" he teased.

"Famished."

"Well, that's a good sign. What are we having?" he asked as he emptied his lunch cooler and put his ice pack in the freezer.

"*We*," she said as she pulled groceries out of bags, "are having spaghetti and salad." She set a box of angel hair, a pound of ground sirloin, a can of tomato paste, an onion, and a jar of sauce on the counter.

"With meat sauce?" he asked hopefully, sliding an ice cube across the floor and watching Keeper block it with his foot and chomp it down.

"With meat sauce," she confirmed, reaching into the utensil drawer for a corkscrew and handing it to him. "Right after you pour some wine for the chef."

Ben opened a bottle of wine, poured a generous glass, and set it on the counter. "Want help?"

"No, thanks. I got it."

"Okay," he said, reaching into the fridge for a beer. "I'm going to shower then."

She nodded as he opened his beer and headed up the stairs. Then she looked down at Keeper, who was stretched out contentedly in her work area. "That's all right—don't mind me, I'll work around you." She stepped carefully over him to get her frying pan, set it on the burner, turned the flame to low, drizzled in a tablespoon of olive oil, and while it heated, diced the onion. She scraped the chopped onion into the pan, sipping her wine as it sizzled, and let her thoughts drift back over the day. She thought about all the sick kids she'd seen that day . . . and then she remembered how Janelle had talked about Harper donating to Locks of Love.

A few minutes later, Ben came back downstairs—his hair still wet from showering—and started to throw together the salad. "We're gonna need more croutons," he said, dumping the last of the bag onto the washed Romaine and popping two in his mouth.

Macey groaned. "It never fails," she said with a sigh, jotting a note on the sticky pad she kept in the drawer. "As soon as I get home from the store, I have to start a new list."

Ben chuckled. "Tell me about it. The same thing happens when I go to Home Depot."

Macey broke the spaghetti in half, dropped it into the pot, stirred it, and refilled her glass. "How do you think I'd look with short hair?"

Ben looked up from grating fresh Parmesan. He'd learned from experience—although he'd been a painfully slow learner—to proceed with caution when Macey posed odd questions out of the blue. "Hmm," he said, considering his answer.

She looked up. "That good, huh?"

"No, no," he said, "I'm just trying to picture you with short hair." He paused. "I think it would look good . . . I mean you'd look beautiful no matter what," he added, feeling as if he'd come up with the perfect answer. "Why?"

"Because I was thinking of donating my hair to Locks of Love."

He frowned. "Locks of Love?"

She nodded, tucking her hair behind her ears. "They make hair pieces for kids who have lost their hair due to medical issues, like cancer."

Ben drizzled dressing onto the salad. "I think you should do it," he confirmed.

Macey smiled. "I think I will," she said, taking a sip of her wine.

32

"I saw the whole thing, Mama, and it wasn't Harper's fault!" Rudy said indignantly. "Latisha pushed Harper, and then all her stupid friends told Ms. Jones that Harper started it."

"Yeah!" Joe piped. "I saw it, too."

"Well, how come you didn't say somethin'?" Cora asked.

"We tried!" Rudy cried out, "but they wouldn't listen!"

Harper sat next to the window and felt the cool breeze drying her tearstained cheeks. She fiddled with the broken zipper on her backpack, slipped the tattered photograph she kept in the pocket out, and tried to hold the two ragged edges together.

"Did *they* do that?" Rudy asked, looking horrified.

Harper nodded as fresh tears spilled down her cheeks.

"Do what?" Cora asked, trying to see into the back seat.

"They tore Harper's picture!"

"Of her mama?"

"Yes!" Rudy confirmed angrily.

Cora shook her head. "I don't know how you do it, child. This week was going so well! Did you say something to make them so mean?"

"No."

"You sure?"

"Mm-hmm," Harper said, nodding.

Cora eyed her in her rearview mirror, but Harper looked out the window and wouldn't make eye contact. Cora didn't say anything more, and they drove home in silence—each lost in their own thoughts.

Cora parked in her spot and waited for Rudy and Joe to get out. "Harper, could you wait a minute?"

Harper looked at Rudy and rolled her eyes and then climbed out and leaned sullenly against the car. "Rudy, you can go inside," Cora said, gathering her things.

"Why can't I stay?" she asked, frowning.

"Because I want to talk to Harper. Now, scoot!"

Rudy let out an exaggerated sigh, kicked the tire, and trudged toward the door.

Cora closed her door and studied Harper. "Look at me, child," she said softly.

Harper looked up and Cora could see the frustration and sorrow in her eyes—too much for a nine-year-old child. "Now. What *really* happened?"

"I already told you. Latisha came up and pushed me into the fence, so I pushed her back."

"How'd your picture get ripped?"

"It fell out of my backpack because the zipper's broken and she picked it up and ripped it."

"So, you hit her?"

"Yeah, I hit her—she's a freakin' idiot."

"Did you say something to make her push you?"

"No," Harper said, rolling her eyes and looking away.

Cora sighed. "Baby, you do *not* have a lot of options here, which is why you need to try extra hard to get along with people. What are we goin' to do now?"

"Take me to work with you."

"I *cannot* take you to work with me. You are supposed to be in school, learning—and *that* is never going to happen if you keep getting yourself suspended."

Harper shrugged. "I don't wanna go to that stupid school anyway," she mumbled.

"I thought you did. I thought you wanted to go to school with Rudy."

"I did, but why couldn't they put us in the same class? Why does everyone have to make everything so hard?"

"Oh, baby, people are not trying to make things hard for you."

"Sure seems like it," she mumbled. "First, my mom dies . . . and my dad doesn't even know I exist . . . and then I get put in all these stupid foster homes . . . and now I have a weak heart."

"Harper, I know it seems like things aren't going well. You have reason to be upset," Cora said, "but you need to start thinking about the good things in your life."

"Yeah? Like *what*?" Harper said, crossing her arms defiantly.

"Like having Rudy for a friend. Like riding bikes together or helping make pancakes. Like knowing I'm doing the best I can to find you a home . . ."

Harper rolled her eyes. "Yeah, like that's goin' real good."

"Honestly, Harper, you don't make it any better by having a chip on your shoulder—like it's you against the whole world."

"It *is* me against the whole world," Harper said defiantly, fresh tears springing to her eyes.

"Oh, baby," Cora said, pulling her into a hug. "It is *not* you against the world. *I* love you . . . and so do Rudy and Frank and Joe." She held Harper at arm's length and searched her tear-streaked face. "We love you so much."

Harper blinked back her tears and sighed heavily, feeling a wave of nausea wash over her, even as the weight of the world rested on her thin shoulders.

"Let's go inside," Cora said gently. "At least we have the weekend to figure things out."

Cora followed Harper inside and found Joe already planted in front of the TV playing a video game. "Frank?" she called, glancing down the hall, but there was no answer. "Rudy, go see if Frank has those confounded earbuds plugging his ears."

Rudy pushed open the door to her brothers' room and looked around. "He's not here," she announced, shuffling back to the kitchen and pulling open the fridge door.

Cora glanced up at the clock. "Where can that boy be?" she murmured to herself, frowning as she put on the kettle. "He doesn't know I had to pick you up, so he should've been here to get you off the bus."

"Mama, Frank doesn't need to be here. Harper and I can be here alone and take care of Joe. All he does is play video games anyway."

Cora snorted. "You are nine years old—you *cannot* come home to an empty house.

"Lots of kids go home to an empty house," Rudy protested. "I heard the teachers talking about it. They called 'em latchkey kids."

"Well, you are not a latchkey kid," Cora said, pouring the now-steaming water over her teabag. While it steeped, she reached into her bag for her phone and texted her son. Then she stared at the screen, waiting for the reassuring little dots to appear, telling her he was alive and capable of writing back, but no dots appeared and finally, the screen went dark. She bit her lip and dunked her teabag. "Where is that boy?"

"Mama, can we go to the playground?" Rudy asked.

Cora looked up distractedly and then glanced out the window. "It's getting dark. I think you should stay in. Besides, don't you have homework?"

"Mama, it's Friday."

Cora sighed. "Half an hour, and Harper, no running!"

Rudy pulled Harper out the door before Cora could change her mind and she went back to staring out the window, her mind running wild with thoughts of her oldest son in every worrisome scenario a mother's mind could imagine. She turned on her phone and stared at the unanswered text, willing him to reply, but there was still nothing.

"Oh, Frank, where are you?"

33

"You're such an overachiever," Ben teased as Keeper dislodged three soggy tennis balls from his mouth and nosed them in the direction of Ben's feet. He bounced back a few steps, tail wagging, and as soon as Ben reached for them, he tore off, completely uninhibited by his handicap.

"He's too funny," Macey said, sitting on the porch steps, cradling a cup of tea. She and Ben had learned early on that their new charge had an unabashed penchant for tennis balls. He was never without one, and he wasn't content with *just* one. He would press as many as he could, one by one, into his mouth. His record was five. "Can you imagine how sad he must've been when he was cooped up in a kennel with no tennis balls?"

"I'm sure they played with him," Ben said, tossing the balls again.

"I doubt it."

"I bet they did."

"Why do you always say the opposite of me?"

"Because it's fun," Ben teased, grinning. "By the way, is that what you're wearing?"

Macey looked down at her sweatpants and fleece. "Is there something wrong with it?"

"No. You go right ahead."

She smiled. "I'm actually gonna take a quick shower."

"Well, you better hurry up—it's getting late."

"Are you showering, too?"

"Not if you take too long."

Macey stood up reluctantly. It was a beautiful October afternoon, and she was enjoying the golden sunshine and bright blue sky, and watching them play. "I'll be quick."

Ben threw the tennis balls a few more times and then called, "That's it, buddy. Let's head in and get a treat."

Hearing the word *treat*, Keeper rounded up his tennis balls and hopped up the steps. "Good pup," Ben said, tousling his ears.

He gave him the promised treat and then grabbed a cold beer from the fridge and headed up the stairs.

"Mace, have you seen my blue shirt?"

"Which one?" she called from the shower. "You have at least five."

"My oxford."

"I think it's still in the wash," she called, rinsing the suds from her hair.

Ben stepped into the bathroom. "I thought you did laundry."

"I did, but I forgot to throw the last load in the dryer."

Ben peered around the shower curtain. "Hmm . . . I bet you wouldn't've forgotten if there was something of yours in there."

Macey rolled her eyes and then saw the beer in his hand. "Hey, are you sharing?"

"That depends . . . are you?"

She rolled her eyes again, but when she reached for it, he pulled it back. "Oh, no . . . if you're not sharing, I'm not sharing."

"There's no time for sharing."

"Have it your way," he said with a shrug.

"Just a sip."

He handed the bottle to her and watched as she took a sip, but when she seductively licked the lip of the bottle, he raised his eyebrows.

"Don't be a tease," he warned, "or you'll get more than you bargained for."

As if daring him, she playfully took another sip, and Ben shook his head.

"Your mom is going to be mad when we're late."

She laughed and started to hand it back to him, but he was pulling his shirt over his head. She raised her eyebrows. "Oh, no! We do not have time, mister. We're going to be late, and you know how unhappy that makes her."

"Your mom would never be unhappy with me. She loves me," Ben said, dropping his jeans and boxers to the floor in one fell swoop.

"We *really* don't have time for this," she said.

"I know," he said, gently brushing drops of water away from her face and softly kissing her. "But it's your fault."

"It's not my fault."

"It is, and I'll have to tell your mom it was all because her daughter was misbehaving."

"And how was that?" she murmured, pressing against him.

He chuckled. "Just like that," he said, kissing her again. "Mmm, you taste good."

"I'm sure I taste like beer," she murmured, melting into his kiss.

"Mm-hmm . . . my favorite flavor." He slid his hands down the curve of her hips and she leaned against the shower wall and watched his lowered head kissing her breasts, his blond hair and eyelashes sparkling with beads of water. Then she closed her eyes, and as the warm water cascaded over their shoulders, she felt him slowly easing himself deep inside her.

"Want me to stop?" he teased softly. "Because I can."

"No, you can't," she murmured, kissing him. And just like that, he stopped his slow rhythmic movement, and she opened her eyes and laughed.

"You better hurry up or you're going to be out of luck," she teased, starting to move, but he held her hips firmly in place and slowly shook his head before ever so slowly starting to move again, lifting her off the tub floor as she wrapped her legs around his thighs and closed her eyes.

When he finally set her down, she was smiling. "Well, now we *really* need to get going!"

"I know," he teased, reaching for his shampoo. "You've made us very late!"

She shook her head as she climbed out, dripping with water, quickly dried off, and threw on her clothes.

TWENTY MINUTES LATER, THEY WERE PARKING BEHIND GAGE'S TRUCK IN front of the New England farmhouse-style home Macey's parents had built when the downturn in the economy in the early nineties had forced them to move from Maine to Georgia. "You can take the boy out of New England," Hal had said, "but you can't take New

England out of the boy!" In fact, he had been so reluctant to uproot his family and leave his parents that he'd even considered taking over their farm. But then a job offer from Gulfstream Aerospace had come in that was so lucrative, it would've been foolish to turn it down.

"Well, well, look who's finally here," Ruth Lindstrom teased affectionately as they came into the kitchen. She kissed the top of Keeper's head. "Hello, there, sweetie pie, I'm so glad you came, too," she whispered into his fur, making his whole hind end wiggle. Then she gave her daughter and son-in-law hugs.

"It's Macey's fault," Ben said, his eyes twinkling mischievously.

"It's *your* fault," Macey countered, setting the dessert she'd made on the counter.

"You're here," Ruth said. "That's all that matters . . . and your apple crisp looks like a picture!"

"Thanks, Mom," Macey said. "It's your recipe. Hopefully I did it right this time."

Ruth smiled. "I don't know how you could do it wrong—it's so easy."

"You can do it wrong by using baking soda instead of baking powder—which makes the crisp lumpy."

"And there's nothing worse than lumpy crisp," Ben teased, grinning.

Ruth laughed. "I'm sure it wasn't that bad."

Keeper hurried into the living room, happily greeted Gage and Maeve, and then rested his head on Hal Lindstrom's lap.

"Hey there, big fella," Hal said jovially, stroking Keeper's soft brow—he was an old softy when it came to dogs, especially golden retrievers, and Keeper seemed to know it. "I can't believe how much you remind me of Tucker," he said wistfully, still missing the golden they'd had to put down several months earlier. "That old pup never left my side."

He kissed the top of Keeper's head, and then pulled himself out of his recliner. "Hey, there, Mr. Samuelson," he said, shaking his son-in-law's hand. Then he turned to Macey and gave her a hug. "Hullo, sweetie."

He watched his girls and their significant others greet each other and then called out, "The gang's all here, dear!"

"I know!" Ruth called back. "Come fix your plates."

"Where's Gus?" Macey asked, eyeing Gage as they followed Keeper—whose favorite word besides *ball* and *treat* was *dinner*—into the kitchen.

"He's not quite ready for polite social settings."

"Well, he won't learn if you don't bring him," Hal said.

"You're right," Gage agreed. "Maybe next time."

"I'm sorry to serve buffet-style," Ruth said apologetically when they came in, "but I think it's easier than passing because, by the time everyone has everything, it's cold."

"That's because you make too much food," Hal said, surveying all the dishes. "There's enough here to feed an army!" He eyed his daughters. "You girls better plan on taking some home or *I'll* be eating it for a month!"

"We will, Dad," they assured him, knowing he wasn't fond of having leftovers more than once.

Macey turned to her mom. "Dad's right, Mom. Look at all this food! Lasagna and salad would've been enough, but you made a turkey, stuffing, potatoes, and green beans—it's two meals."

Ruth waved her off. "Oh, it's nothing—I was just thinking about the holidays, and turkeys were on sale!"

"That's the thrifty Irish heritage in her blood. Dates back to the potato famine," Hal teased.

Ruth shook her head and handed them plates. "Get it while it's hot," she commanded.

"Besides," she added, smiling, "I'm sure these two strapping boys will be able to put a dent in it."

Ben and Gage both nodded, anxious to dig in, but hanging back politely for the girls to go first. While Hal waited, too, he freshened up his gin and tonic, and then offered the same or beers to the boys. "You girls having white?" he asked, holding a bottle of chilled chardonnay over the glasses on the counter.

"Yes, please," Macey said, putting a little extra salad on her plate.

Maeve nodded. "Thanks, Dad," she said.

"Hurry up and fill your plate, dear," his wife scolded, handing him the plate he'd put down to fix drinks. "Everyone's food is going to get cold."

"Man does not live by bread alone," he said, refilling her glass with merlot and putting his arm around her. "Nor does woman," he added with a grin, kissing the top of her silver head.

Ruth poked him in the side. "Oh, you!" she said, sounding exasperated, but the girls knew she loved their dad's teasing.

Hal filled his plate, and when he came into the dining room, Ben and Gage were standing behind their chairs, waiting for their hostess to come in and sit down. He smiled, pleased by their awareness of the same social etiquette he'd been taught as a boy.

"Thank you, gentlemen," Ruth said, finally coming in and sitting down. She eyed her husband. "Dear, would you say grace?"

Hal reached for their hands, bowed his head, and reverently offered the blessing he'd been saying since his girls were little. Then he looked up, and with a smile, remarked, "You know what would really help with all this food?"

Ruth raised her eyebrows, wondering what profound thought her husband was going to share—she never knew what he might say. "What?" she asked worriedly.

"Grandkids!" he said, smiling. "Wouldn't it be great to have a few ankle biters running around here to liven things up?" He looked around the table, feeling proud of his idea.

"One of these days, Dad," Macey said, her face revealing the sadness with which she was constantly struggling. "In the meantime, we brought Keeper, and I'm sure he'd be happy to help with leftovers."

Ruth sighed, aware of the pain her husband's comment had caused. "We're in no hurry for grandkids, Macey, dear. Dad and I know you and Ben have a lot going on."

"Maybe you should consider adopting," Hal offered unwittingly. "There are so many kids in the world who need . . ." But when he saw the daggers in his wife's eyes—a look he'd seen many times before—he clamped his mouth shut.

Macey shook her head. "Dad, please. Not now." She turned to Ben for support, but he was focusing on his plate and avoiding eye contact. "We're not interested in adopting, right, Ben?" she asked, elbowing him—which made it impossible for him to not engage.

He looked up. "Yeah, I don't think we're ready for that." He squeezed Macey's hand, confident that he'd said the right thing.

Ruth sighed, and, in spite of the look she'd just given her husband, turned to Maeve for her own support. "Maeve, don't you think they should consider it?"

"I do," Maeve said, "but it's up to them. Adoption is a big commitment."

"Thank you," Macey said, feeling vindicated.

"It *is* a big commitment," Ruth agreed, "but there *are* so many children who need good homes, and you and Ben would make such wonderful parents." She took a sip of her wine. "You know Cora Grant? From church? She works so hard trying to find homes for . . ."

"I know Cora, Mom, and I know she works hard—I know all this . . ." She looked at Ben, hoping he would chime in again—after all, he had known her parents since they were kids. He had spent so much time in their house, he'd practically been a third child. And he was her husband. Didn't he have something more he could add in their defense? But when his glistening eyes met hers, she realized he wasn't saying anything because his emotions were getting the best of him.

"Can we please just talk about something else?" Macey asked.

"Of course, dear," Ruth said.

"I shouldn't have brought it up," Hal said apologetically. "I meant it to be funny, but after everything you two have been through, it was thoughtless. As much as we joke about it, your mom is right—we are in no hurry to have grandkids. When the time is right, it'll happen . . . or not—I'm sure God knows what's best, and regardless, we have this wonderful granddog." He looked down at Keeper lying at his feet. "And that's more than enough."

He smiled, took a sip of his drink, and with his blue eyes sparkling mischievously, turned to Maeve and Gage. "Guess this means we'll just have to talk about the wedding. . . ."

"Dad!" Maeve said, looking horrified.

"I'm just kidding!" he said, chuckling and squeezing his wife's hand. "What would these kids do without us to embarrass them? How did we end up with such serious children?"

Ruth rolled her eyes, and in an effort to change the subject, asked, "Will we see you all in church Sunday?"

Macey nodded, but Maeve shook her head. "I have to work."

34

"Where in heaven's name have you been?" Cora asked when Frank finally came through the door. She was relieved he was home, but she was so angry she didn't know whether to hug or ground him on the spot.

"I'm sorry, Mama. My friend James said he saw you picking up Rudy and Joe, so I figured you didn't need me, and then he asked if I wanted to shoot some hoops. I was in such a hurry to go with him, I left my phone in my locker, and when I went back to get it, the school was locked."

"It's ten o'clock, Frank. Surely you haven't been playing basketball all this time."

"Is it that late?" he asked sheepishly. "I didn't know what time it was because I didn't have my phone, and then we went to Mickey D's and hung out."

"And no one there had a phone you could borrow to call your mother who was worried sick about you, or find out the time? We waited and waited for you to have dinner." As she said this, she held up a plate that was covered with aluminum foil.

"I'm sorry, Mama. I lost track of time, and I didn't want to ask anyone to borrow their phone."

"Why not?"

He shrugged. "Because I felt stupid."

"I don't know what there is to feel stupid about," Cora said.

"Because I *stupidly* left it in my locker."

"That's ridiculous," Cora said angrily, "and you shouldn't care what they think. You have to be responsible!"

"But I do care, Mama. They want me to try out for the team, and I don't want to do anything dumb to change that."

"Well, not calling your mother to tell her where you are is dumb, and those boys—if they're decent young men—would know it."

"Why'd you pick up Rudy and Joe anyway?" Frank asked, trying to change the subject.

"Harper got herself suspended."

"What'd she do now?" he asked, thankful he wasn't the focus of the conversation anymore.

"She got into a tussle with another girl."

Frank shook his head. "When's she ever gonna learn?"

"Probably the same time you do," Cora said, eyeing him so he knew he wasn't off the hook.

Frank nodded. "Well, I'm tired so I'm going to bed. Good night."

"Good night," Cora replied curtly, still standing stubbornly on her convictions.

"I love you," Frank said.

"If you loved me, you wouldn't make me worry."

"Mama, I said I'm sorry. I don't know what else to say."

Cora softened. "You can promise me you won't let it happen again."

"I promise," Frank said solemnly.

"And you can give your poor ole mother a hug."

Frank smiled, and towering over her stout five-foot-two frame, gave her a long hug.

She looked up at him with tears in her eyes. "I don't know what I'd do if something happened to you, Frank."

"Nothing's gonna happen to me, Mama," he said. "You worry too much. You tell us and everyone you meet to have faith, but you worry more than anyone."

"I know," Cora said, shaking her head. "But I'm glad you're listening."

"Of course I'm listening. I'd be a fool not to."

Cora smiled. "When did you say tryouts are?"

"After Thanksgiving."

"Okay. I still can't promise anything, but I will try to find out about that after-school program soon."

"Okay."

"I still don't know what I'm gonna do with Harper."

"You know, Mama, that elementary school is a tough place. Maybe, instead of looking for a family in the foster system, you should look for someone who wants kids but can't have them."

"It's not just that, Frank," she said, lowering her voice. "Finding a home for Harper will be more challenging now that she's on that transplant list."

Frank lowered his voice, too. "Does she know she needs a new heart?"

"She does. The doctor told her all about it . . . but I'm not sure she realizes how serious that is. The doctor assured her it wasn't immediately urgent, and she seemed okay with it. He didn't want to upset her, but how do you even give news like that to a child? It's like walking a tightrope."

Frank nodded. "You know, Mama, maybe you should have Harper put on the prayer list at church. People are always lifting up . . ."

Cora's face lit up. "Oh my! That is a good idea!" she said. "From the mouths of babes . . . thank you, Frank!"

"No problem, Mama," he said, smiling and giving her a hug. "Night."

"Night, Frank. Love you."

"Love you, too, Mama."

35

"WHERE DO YOU WANT TO SIT?" BEN WHISPERED, SURVEYING THE crowded sanctuary.

"Are my parents here?" Macey asked, shaking the raindrops off the hood of her raincoat.

"I'm sure they are—your mom is never late."

"Unlike us," Macey said as the congregation stood to sing the second hymn.

Ben looked for Hal and Ruth in their usual pew. "They're here," he confirmed, "and there's room near them."

They made their way down the side aisle, and when Ruth saw them standing at the end of her pew, she nudged her husband to move over, and then handed her open hymnal to her daughter. They edged in and Macey glanced around the sanctuary to see if Maeve and Gage had made it to church, but she then remembered her sister said she had to work. She saw Cora, though, and her choice of pew made Macey smile—it was just like Cora to position her children in the front row where they would have to stay alert. She looked at Frank, towering over his mother, with Rudy and Joe between them, and then Macey noticed a little red-haired boy standing next to Rudy, and wondered what wayward child Cora had with her now.

As Macey fell into the rhythm of the service, her mind wandered. She gazed out the window, recalling the unwavering faith of her grandmother and her commitment to the work of her church. Back in the day, Grandy would've been in charge of all the upcoming events the minister had just brought to the congregation's attention—the Christmas fair; the pies the youth group was making to help pay for their mission trip; and she would have even picked up a paintbrush and started painting the church herself, if that was what was needed! That's how Grandy had lived. No matter how much she had going on, she had always been the first to volunteer, and the legacy of her can-do spirit sometimes made her granddaughter feel like a slacker. Just then, Macey's thoughts were interrupted by the mention of a familiar name, and she looked up to see the minister adjusting the mic.

"Our dear Cora may be short in stature," he said, "but her heart is a mile wide!"

At this, the congregation chuckled, knowing it was true.

"Thank you, Reverend," Cora said, smiling. "I know this is unusual, and I will keep it short because I don't want to take up your time, but I'd like to make a very special prayer request today." She paused and looked over at Harper. "Visiting our church today is my friend Harper Wheaton."

Macey realized with a jolt that the child with Cora wasn't a boy at all. It was the little girl who had just donated her hair to Locks of Love!

Cora smiled. "Child, why don't you stand up so everyone can see you?"

But when she said this, Harper's eyes grew wide with horror and she sank further into the pew—a response that made everyone chuckle again.

"No?" Cora asked, eyeing her. "That's okay.

"Anyway, I'm here to ask for your prayers for my friend Harper because she has recently been placed on the heart-transplant list . . . and not only does Harper need a new heart, she also needs a new home." She paused again, looking around. "Harper's situation is unusual and complicated, but I know that if we all keep Harper in our prayers, they will be answered in ways beyond our expectations." She smiled. "Thank you."

As Cora made her way back to her seat, the minister smiled at Harper, who was now so low in her seat, she was barely visible. "We will *indeed* keep Harper in our prayers," he said, "for *both* a new heart *and* a new home." Then he looked up. "Now, if you will all stand and join me in singing our closing hymn, 'Here I Am, Lord.'"

Macey opened her hymnal, glanced at the title, and took a deep breath. The hymn was one of her favorites—they had sung it at both of her grandparents' funerals, and she knew, as soon as the familiar chords drifted from the piano, tears would well up in her eyes. Ben knew it, too, and put his arm around her and kissed the top of her head, but when he looked down and saw her solemn eyes searching his, he realized the flame of something much more complicated was stirring in her heart.

After church, Ben followed Macey down to coffee hour, and from across the room, he watched as she talked to Cora—but when she said hello to Rudy and Harper, Rudy gave her a warm hug, but Harper hardly looked at her. And then she and Rudy hurried off to see what snacks were on the kids' table.

36

Over the next week, Macey couldn't get Harper off her mind. She usually tried to not get caught up in the problems of patients, but the plight of this little girl was tugging on her heartstrings . . . hard. And even though Ben knew something was brewing—he could tell by the look in her eyes—when she finally opened up after his rainy Saturday morning run and told him that she wanted to foster the little girl Cora had talked about in church, he thought she'd lost her mind. "You *can't* be serious!"

"I *am* serious," Macey replied, crossing her arms. "Grandy would've taken her in."

"Things were different back then," Ben countered, drying his wet hair with a towel.

"How?" Macey asked, even though she'd used the very same logic with her sister.

"People were different. The world was different . . . and your grandmother didn't work."

"My grandmother kept busy. She didn't let anything stop her or get her down. Back then, you did what you had to do. You did what was right and you just kept going."

"We do what is right," Ben said, sounding exasperated. He shook his head in disbelief.

"We could do more," she said, leaning against the counter. "Ben, we've been blessed with this great big house—it's really too big for just the two of us, and we've always dreamed of filling it with little people, but we've only had one idea about who those little people should be. Maybe we've had the wrong idea."

"Mace, weren't we just at your parents' last Saturday when you said there was no way you were adopting?"

"I did, and I still feel that way. But this wouldn't be permanent. I don't know, Ben, it's just . . . well, I keep thinking about my grandmother—she had such an indomitable spirit. She was always the first to volunteer, the first to say, 'Send me,' and I know, even if she had ten kids, she wouldn't hesitate to take in one more. Besides, I find it really odd—almost serendipitous—that Harper's path and mine keep crossing—she was my patient at the office, she got her hair cut at the same salon I use, and now, she shows up at our church. Not to mention *Harper* is a name we both liked for a little girl if we ever had one. Don't you see how this all seems to be happening for a reason?"

Ben took a deep breath and let it out slowly. "Mace, honestly, we don't know anything about her. Not to mention her medical issues."

"I know about her medical issues. I just told you that she's one of our patients. Cora brought her into the office for a follow-up after she was in the hospital."

"Well, if your paths have crossed so often, how come she hardly acknowledged you at coffee hour?"

"I don't know. I bet you'd have a hard time opening up to people, too, if you'd gone through what she has."

"Oh, that sounds like a fun person to bring into our home," Ben said, his voice edged with sarcasm. "You know, Mace, adopting a child is a little more involved than adopting a dog."

"We're not adopting. I'm just saying we should foster."

"Yeah, for now . . . and then you'll fall in love with her and want to adopt."

"Ben, Harper has *no one*, and she will eventually be facing major surgery. How can you be so hard-hearted?"

"Macey, this is crazy, okay? I admit that Keeper has been a wonderful addition, but a kid is a totally different ball game!"

Macey stared out the window at the rain, her eyes glistening. "What happens if no one is her advocate? What if no one steps up to take her in . . . and she dies? How will you feel then?"

"She is *not* going to die," Ben said. "I'm sure someone will take care of her." He pulled off his shirt, picked up his towel, and went into the laundry room to throw both in the washer.

Macey looked out the window at the willow trees, unable to shake the feeling that they were supposed to get involved.

Just then, Keeper peered through the screen door, and she went out on the porch to dry him off. "How're you doin', ole pie?" she whispered as he wiggled all around her.

He stood right in front of her and she wrapped the towel around his noble head, cradled it in her hands, and looked into his sweet brown eyes.

"I was right about you," she said softly, "and I know I'm right about Harper, too . . . we just have to convince your stubborn father."

As she stood, Macey realized the sun was breaking through the clouds, and when she looked across the yard, she saw a glorious rainbow spanning the Savannah sky. "Oh, Ben, come see!"

Ben came out on the porch, and Macey pointed to the sky.

He nodded, seemingly unimpressed, but Macey was undeterred.

"Maybe it's a sign," she said.

"Yeah, it's a sign that the rain's over and the sun's coming out."

He turned to go inside, but Macey wasn't ready to give up. "I think it's more than that. I think it's a sign that we are on the right track."

"Unfortunately, Mace, I don't think I'm on the same track as you." He went inside, and Macey followed, holding the door for Keeper. She had more she wanted to say, but Ben had already disappeared up the stairs, and when he came down, he'd changed into his jeans.

"Where're you going?" she asked with a frown as she opened a new package of bacon.

"Gage needs help with something."

"But I'm making BLTs."

"I'm not hungry." He gave her a peck on the cheek. "I'll see you later."

Macey closed the package, put it back in the fridge, looked out the window, and realized the rainbow had faded. "Oh, Grandy," she whispered, "am I doing the right thing?" She'd felt so certain that her grandmother—and her can-do spirit—were nudging her to step up . . . but Ben's reaction was filling her heart with doubt.

37

"'Hi-ho, hi-ho, it's off to work we go,'" Harper teased as they drove to DFCS late Monday morning, mimicking the words she'd often heard Cora say.

"That's proof right there you been spendin' too much time with me," Cora said as she pulled into the McDonald's drive-through.

"It is not," Harper countered. "Besides, I don't know why you won't let me help you. I could do all kinds of jobs. File papers or make phone calls or . . ."

"Because you need to go to school. *That* is your job right now."

"I don't need to go to school. I already know how to do secretary stuff."

"You *do* need to go—" Cora was interrupted by the static of the speaker.

"Welcome to McDonald's. What can I get for you?"

Cora leaned out her window. "May I please have a coffee and . . ." She glanced over at Harper. "What'd you say you wanted?"

"Are we getting breakfast or lunch?"

Cora looked at the clock and suddenly realized how late it was. "Whichever you want," she said with a sigh.

"A six-piece with barbecue sauce."

"A six-piece McNugget with barbecue sauce," Cora added.

"And fries," Harper piped, "and a Coke."

"And a value fry and a value Coke."

The attendant read back her order. "What size coffee?"

But, before Cora could answer, Harper leaned across and shouted, "Big-ass!"

"What was that?" the voice asked.

"Large," Cora said, giving Harper a look fierce enough to shrivel a tongue.

"How would you like it?"

"Light and sweet!" Harper shouted, ignoring the look.

"Shush, child," Cora admonished.

"That'll be seven-sixty-four. Please drive around."

Cora pulled up to the window and handed the attendant—who was obviously unamused—the neatly folded twenty she kept in the side pocket of her bag for emergencies. The attendant handed her the coffee and a paper bag, which Cora promptly dropped onto Harper's lap, and her change—which Cora dropped into the center console so she could pull away.

"Thanks, Cora!" Harper said, reaching into the bag. "Want some?" she asked, holding out a french fry.

"Oh, I shouldn't," Cora said with a sigh, "but I will."

As they turned onto the busy street, Harper opened the box of McNuggets and pulled the foil off the sauce. "Oh no! He gave me sweet-and-sour!"

Cora glanced over. "I love sweet-and-sour."

"I *hate* sweet-and-sour," Harper said, frowning. "Can we go back?"

"No—I have to get to the office."

"What an a-hole," she muttered.

Cora frowned. "What did I tell you about using that language?"

"I don't care! He's a full-fledged asshole!" she said, sinking into her seat.

"Harper! Honestly! No one is ever going to adopt a little girl who talks like that!"

"I don't give a shit," Harper shouted, tears springing to her eyes. "I asked for freakin' barbecue sauce. Is he some kind of idiot?" And then she flung the sweet-and-sour sauce out the window.

Cora looked in her rearview mirror and then glared at her. "We do not litter!" she admonished in a voice that was growing increasingly frustrated. "You are lucky you didn't hit another car!"

"I don't give a crap!" Harper shouted, tossing the whole box of McNuggets out the window.

"What in heaven's name is wrong with you, child?" Cora demanded, her voice tight with anger. "I paid good money for that."

"I don't care," Harper said bitterly, staring out the window.

"We don't litter," she said, pulling to the side of the road, "and I want you to help pick it up."

"No," Harper said, hot tears trickling down her cheeks. She regretted everything that was happening, everything she was saying, but she didn't know how to stop.

"I don't know what has gotten into you!" Cora said, reaching for the empty paper bag and climbing out.

"Nothing has gotten into me," Harper muttered, rubbing her chest. She watched Cora walking along the road, picking up her food, but when she reached the container of sauce—which had landed in the middle of the road—a car came whipping around the corner and almost hit her.

"That a-hole almost hit you!" Harper said when Cora got back in the car.

"And it would've been all your fault," Cora puffed, trying to catch her breath.

"It would *not* . . ." Harper retorted, and then clenched her jaw, realizing it was true. Why couldn't she say or feel anything right?

After they pulled into the DFCS parking lot, Cora reached into the back seat for her canvas bag full of papers and the McDonald's bag full of discarded McNuggets. She got out, crumpled up the paper bag, tossed it in the dumpster, and marched toward the front door.

Harper watched her disappear and then stared up at the milky sky. She wasn't surprised no one wanted her. Even Cora had had enough. She rolled down her window and listened to the seagulls bickering. One gull—who had a morsel of food in its beak—was playing duck and weave while the other seagulls tried to get it to drop the food, and when it did, they all dove in breathtaking speed. Harper watched the fray until one seagull rose, victorious, into the sky and the game began again. If she were a gull, she would always be the one to get the food, and she would *never* drop it—she would gulp it down before anyone else could take it. In fact, she wished she *were* a seagull—then she could live wherever she wanted and she could soar through the sky and scavenge food. She would never have to depend on anyone, and she would never have to worry about anything—not her heart or school or a home!

She was so tired of not having control over the things that were happening to her. No one on earth seemed to want her; she hated every school they put her in, because all the kids made fun of her; and she was terrified by the idea of having her heart taken out of her chest and a total stranger's put in—how did that even work? How come the other person didn't need their heart any-more? Were they dead? And if they were, well, that was creepy. The question she really wanted to ask was whether *she* would be dead when there was no heart in her chest? And what if the new heart didn't beat? Would she never wake up? That was all way too scary to think about. The doctor had told her not to worry be-cause the operation wouldn't happen until she felt much worse, but she was already feeling worse. She had zero energy and sometimes she couldn't catch her breath. She knew she was supposed to tell Cora, but she didn't want to because she was afraid Cora would tell the doctor . . . and they would take her heart!

She fingered the ring Rudy had given her the day before. It was made from a silver wire that had been tied into a delicate knot. "It's a friendship ring," Rudy had said, smiling, "because we'll al-ways be friends."

Harper had nodded as she'd slipped it on her finger, but now she felt as if she didn't deserve Rudy's friendship—not after she'd almost gotten her mom run over. She touched the chipped pink polish Rudy had painted on her nails.

"Nothing stays nice," she muttered. "Nothing lasts forever." She spun the ring around her finger and then slipped it off and put it in the console. Then she picked up the half-eaten bag of fries, and the change from McDonald's. "Sorry, Cora," she said softly. "I'm sorry to take your money, but I won't be any trouble anymore."

She gripped the handle of the door, considering, and then pulled it open. She ate a fry—now cold—and threw the rest into the sky, causing a cacophony from the flock of gulls, who swooped down in a flurry of flapping and raucous squawking.

"Mine! Mine! Mine!" she teased as they fought for the long greasy strips of potato. Finally, they flew off, still squabbling, and she looked over her shoulder at the door to the building. Then she stuffed Cora's change in her pocket, hitched her backpack onto her shoulder, and hurried toward the park.

∽

38

"I DON'T KNOW WHERE SHE IS!" CORA EXCLAIMED IN A PANICKED VOICE. "I walked into the building; ten minutes later I went out to see what was taking her so darn long and she wasn't in the car. She just wasn't *there!*"

The policeman nodded as he jotted down Cora's explanation and a description. "Do you have a photo?"

"Yes," Cora answered, "although it's not recent—she's probably only five in it."

"How old is she now?"

"Ten," Cora answered, and then corrected herself. "I mean nine."

"Nine?" The officer looked up questioningly. "You don't have something more recent?"

Cora shook her head again. "I don't think so. I'd have to look."

"So, she's nine years old . . . and why did you leave her alone in the car?"

"I did not leave her alone in the car!" Cora cried, wringing her hands because she suddenly realized how bad that sounded. "I thought she was following me inside."

"And how long was she alone in the car?" the officer pressed.

"Oh, Lordy," Cora whispered, closing her eyes in dismay and trying to calculate how long Harper might've sat outside, but her brain was not cooperating—not only was Harper missing, but now, on top of that, she was probably going to lose her job because she'd left her alone. "Five—ten minutes, at most," she answered fretfully. "That child really got my goat today an' I . . . ."

The officer looked up. "She 'got your goat'? How do you mean?"

Cora swallowed, wishing she had kept her mouth shut. "Does it matter? We are wasting precious time! The longer we stand here talking about nothin', the harder it's goin' to be to find her."

"I'm sorry, ma'am, but the details of what happened—how she 'got your goat,' as you say, might actually help us find her."

"I doubt that," Cora mumbled.

"Nevertheless, please explain how she upset you."

"We stopped at McDonald's because she was hungry, and I spent my last twenty dollars to buy her lunch and she threw it out the window!"

The officer looked up. "Why did she do that?"

"Because the attendant gave her sweet-and-sour sauce instead of barbecue."

The officer jotted this detail down in his notebook. "Is she always so short-tempered?"

"She can be."

"And then what happened?"

"I told her we don't litter and I pulled over to pick it up."

The officer looked up. "And . . . ?"

"*And* that's it. I picked up the food and we drove here."

"Did you say anything else to her?"

"Not that I recall. Now, can you please help me look for her?!"

"Ma'am, we are going to look for her," the officer replied in a calm voice.

"You don't seem to be nearly as worried as I am!"

"What time did you discover she was missing?"

"Just after one o'clock."

The officer looked at his watch. It was now one thirty. "Well, she can't have gotten far . . . unless someone picked her up." He looked up. "Is that a camera?" he asked, pointing.

Cora followed his gaze to a small white camera mounted on the top of the low brick building. "It is, but it hasn't worked in years."

The officer shook his head and sighed. "Well, let's assume Harper . . . what's her last name?"

"Wheaton."

"Let's assume Harper left on foot of her own accord. Do you have any idea where she might go? Does she have any friends or relatives in the area?"

Cora swallowed, suddenly praying very hard that Harper had left of her own accord and had not been abducted. God help her, why had she left her alone?

"No," she said. "I have no idea where she might go."

"Do you have any idea why she might run away?"

Cora pressed her lips together pensively, trying to remember. "Well," she began slowly, "when I was picking up the sweet-and-sour container off the road, a car came zipping by, and when I got back to my car she made a comment about it almost hitting me, an' I told her it would've been her fault."

The officer looked up, his brow furrowed. "Is that what you said?"

Cora nodded, suddenly realizing how hurtful that might've sounded to a child who counted on her, to a child who, although she acted tough, was really quite sensitive. "I'm sorry, baby," she murmured to herself. "I shouldn't a' said such a horrible thing. I didn't mean it."

"What was that?" the officer asked, looking up again.

"Nothin'," she said softly, tears welling up in her eyes. She brushed them away. "Can we start looking now? She has a weak heart and she's on the transplant list."

The officer looked up in alarm. "And she's allowed to just be out . . ."

"She is allowed to be out," Cora said, nodding. "Her doctor wanted her name on the list because, and I quote"—she paused to make air quotes—"'although it's not immediately urgent, it is inevitable, and already being on the list would be helpful if her condition deteriorated unexpectedly.'"

Just then, two more police cars pulled in, and the officer glanced over his shoulder. As he turned back to Cora, he noticed several people standing inside the front doors, watching the commotion. "Please wait here, Mrs. Grant," he said. "I'll be right back."

He walked over to talk to the officers, motioned to a nearby park, and then returned to Cora. "Can you get that picture of Harper for me?"

Cora nodded, and the officer followed her toward the building—where the crowd of curious onlookers was now spilling outside. One lady, who was standing near the door, pulled it open for them. "What's happened, Cora? Is everything okay?"

"No, Lorraine, everything's *not* okay. . . . Harper has gone missing!"

A collective murmur swept through the crowd and another woman whispered, "Oh, Lawdy, what next?! These damn kids!"

"*Oh, Lawdy* is right," Cora murmured, brushing back anxious tears.

39

Macey took a sip of her coffee—cold again, per usual—and reviewed the information she'd entered on her laptop. Their newest patient, one-week-old Emmett James Ellison, weighing in at eight pounds, five ounces and measuring twenty-two inches, had just left with his parents. Little Emmett had arrived promptly on his due date, October twenty-third, and everything about him was perfect—from his wispy blond hair, dark blue eyes, and rosy cheeks to his chubby legs and ten tiny toes. The stub of his umbilical cord had already fallen off. His stool had normalized after passing the meconium, and was now breast-milk-fed yellow. His mom, Cassie, had wearily, but happily, reported that he woke up every two hours, like clockwork, with a feisty cry and nursed hungrily. And his dad, Edward, had cradled his new little son in his arms with the confident ease of someone who had a lot of experience holding babies and reported that all was well in the Ellison household: Emmett, their fourth son, had been joyfully received by his brothers, two-year-old Evan, three-year-old Ethan, and five-year-old Ed junior. "We're truly blessed!" he'd gushed, smiling proudly.

"You are indeed," Macey had agreed, mustering a smile. "I've always loved the name Emmett," she'd added. "It was my grand-father's name."

"It's a great name," Edward had said, nodding. "Old names are making a comeback. When we were trying to decide, Cassie liked Emmett, and I liked Elijah, and even though Emmett won out this time . . . next time," he said, smiling at his wife, "it's going to be Elijah."

Macey had reached for the doorknob. "Well, he looks great," she'd said, maintaining her smile. "Congratulations, again. Dr. Hack will be right in." She'd closed the door behind her and leaned against it.

"Why?" she'd muttered, clenching her jaw. "Why are some couples blessed with whole tribes and I can't have even *one*?"

She took another sip of her coffee, closed Emmett's computer file, and watched the screensaver playing on her laptop—it was the same one all the computers in the office had: a slideshow of their cute, young patients. Most of the photos had come from Christmas cards, so whenever Macey looked at them, it made her heart ache—would she ever get to create a card with her own child on it? As if on cue, a photo of the three Ellison brothers, sitting on a beach blanket with their yellow Lab, appeared, and Macey pressed her lips together in a sad smile—Cassie was probably already planning this year's card, an image of little Emmett surrounded by his beautiful, beaming, towheaded brothers.

"Life's not fair," she muttered. The Ellisons had talked so casually about the name they'd picked for their next son, as if it was a given—which it probably was. Cassie got pregnant at the drop of a hat, had easy pregnancies, and popped out healthy, bouncing baby boys, one after another, with no complications whatsoever, while Macey tiptoed through her first month, barely breathing lest she jeopardize the fragile pregnancy . . . and even that didn't work!

She tried to picture Ben holding a baby with the same confident ease Edward Ellison had, but she could only see him looking awkward and unsure, as if he was worried he might drop it, and then she chided herself for not being able to conjure up a more positive image. She'd been telling herself for months she needed to think more positively. She'd read several books on the topic, and they all said that the thoughts a person sends out into the universe—negative or positive—played a role in how things turned out.

"Oh, Grandy," she whispered, looking up at the ceiling. "What am I doing wrong? Why can't I get out of this rut?" She pictured her grandmother's gentle smile.

Oh, honey, she could almost hear her grandmother say, *you are thinking too much! You just need to get out there and* do*! Do what your heart is telling you! Your head certainly has some say in the matter, but when you feel your heart being nudged, you can be sure you need to perk up and pay attention.*

"Hey, Mace," Heather said, interrupting her thoughts as she looked around the doorway. "I'm making a coffee run . . . want anything?"

"I'd love a fresh cup," Macey said, looking up. "I've nuked this one at least ten times."

Heather smiled. "Black, right?"

Macey nodded, and Heather turned to go but then stopped. "I keep meaning to ask you if you're still planning to dress up tomorrow?"

"Oh my gosh! Is tomorrow Halloween?" Macey asked as she glanced at the calendar next to her desk.

"It is, and remember, we're all dressing like Peanuts characters."

"That's right. Do you happen to remember who I said I'd be?"

"You picked Charlie Brown because, and I quote, *I know just how he feels.*"

"Yep, that's me! I'll figure something out by tomorrow. Who are you going to be?"

Heather held her palm to the bottom of her hair and pushed it up stylishly. "I'm going to be Lucy," she said with an air of drama.

"Perfect," Macey teased. "Don't forget your football!"

Just then, Marilyn came into the room to get a file. "Hey, did you guys hear there's an amber alert out for that little girl with the heart condition—the one Cora brought in for a follow-up?"

Macey looked up in alarm. "Harper?"

"Yes," Marilyn confirmed, nodding.

"Oh no!"

"Yeah, and they're not only worried because she's missing, but they also don't know if she ran away or if someone took her."

"Do we have Cora's number?" said Macey, flipping open her laptop.

"Yes," Heather said. "Just look under Harper's name." Macey typed in *Wheaton*, and immediately, Harper's file popped up. She reached for the phone.

"Find it?"

"Yes, thanks."

"Okay, I'll be right back."

Macey nodded as she listened to the phone on the other end go right to Cora's voice mail.

40

HARPER STOOD IN FRONT OF THE SINGLE-LEVEL RANCH WITH HER HEART pounding. The little white house looked a lot smaller than she remembered, and it wasn't nearly as well-kept. The grass was long and weeds were everywhere. In fact, she almost didn't recognize it. She stood on the front step and paused to catch her breath before knocking. She had walked the whole way from DFCS, and even though she'd tried to take her time, the walk had left her exhausted and her chest aching. Still, she'd *had* to come—she just had to talk to Tom. She had no other choice. She just hoped the pain would ease after she'd had a chance to sit down, and maybe have something to eat or drink. She wished she hadn't thrown all those McNuggets out the car window—she was so hungry right now, she'd have eaten them right off the ground!

She took a breath, raised her hand, and knocked tentatively, praying she'd hear Sundance's familiar friendly bark, but the only sound she heard was the breeze whispering through the trees. She stood still, wishing her heart would stop racing, and knocked again, harder this time. She had her speech all set, but if Tom didn't answer, she'd forget everything: how she wouldn't be any trouble; how she'd cook and clean, and walk Sundance *every* day . . . Oh! And how sorry she was about Mary. She tried to see through the window, but the curtain was drawn tight, and there wasn't even a sliver of light to give her hope. She frowned, wondering where they were.

She walked around to the backyard and was surprised to see the swing she'd swung on when she was little. Next to it was the wooden sandbox on which she'd hit her head after tripping on her wagon. She reached up and lightly touched the scar above her eyebrow, remembering the big fuss Mary had made, assuring her that foreheads always bleed a lot. Tom had scooped her up, carried her into the bathroom, and set her on the counter while Mary handed him a cold wash cloth to hold on it while she rummaged through the medicine cabinet.

"Hold still, now," she'd said softly. "I'm just going to put a couple butterflies on it." She'd gently cleaned the cut, but when Harper looked in the mirror, all she saw were funny looking Band-Aids.

"Where are the butterflies?" she'd asked, and Mary had chuckled and pulled her into a hug.

Harper looked around the yard at the long grass covered with leaves. Something wasn't right. Tom always kept the lawn neat and free of leaves. Even the vegetable garden—from which they'd eaten sweet cherry tomatoes right off the vine—was full of weeds. She heard a soft tinkling and turned to see the silver chimes she and Tom had made from flattened silver teaspoons hanging on the back porch.

She climbed the steps, tried the doorknob, and when it wouldn't turn, she slid to the porch with a groan. Her heart had filled with so much hope when she was walking. She was sure that when Tom saw her, he would remember her instantly and exclaim about how much she'd grown. She was also sure Sundance would be so happy he'd wiggle all around her and give her wet, slobbery kisses.

Of course, you can live with us, she imagined Tom saying as he gave her a long hug. *Sundance and I would love your company!* And then she'd pictured herself falling asleep in her old room with Sundance curled up on the end of her bed.

But now, she found herself fighting back tears. *Where were they?* She couldn't even let herself think they might not live here anymore. After walking all this way, she couldn't give up. What if they were on their way home right now? What if they turned onto this street this very minute? If she left, she might miss them—and then she'd miss everything she'd planned, everything that would make her life okay. She pulled her sweatshirt around her. She was cold, tired, hungry, and her chest felt tight. She fumbled around in her backpack, felt a Ziploc bag in the bottom, and remembered she hadn't eaten all the cookies in her lunch from Friday. She pulled open the bag, took out a broken Oreo, and chewed hungrily. Then she pulled Bear out of her backpack, lightly touched the tattered heart on his chest, zipped up her sweatshirt, and wondered what to do. Finally, she determined she just had to give Tom a chance to get home; she didn't walk all this way for nothing! She looked around the porch for a blanket or chair, but there was nothing. The furniture they'd always sat on to eat lunch was gone, so she sat on the frayed welcome mat and stared into the darkness until her eyelids grew heavy, and then pulled Bear against her chest and fell asleep to the sound of the spoon chimes tinkling in the wind.

41

BEN GATHERED HIS TOOLS, TRYING TO SEE IN THE DARKNESS, AND WALKED around to the back of his truck. He dropped everything into the big tool chest in the bed, metal clanking against metal, and turned to survey the house. They were making progress: the new wiring and plumbing had been completed; the cabinets and countertops had been installed; the ancient wide-board oak floors had been sanded, vacuumed, and covered with long sheets of red contractor's paper that would stay down while the walls were painted—hopefully this week. And then, finally, the floors would be refinished. It was the last big job, and once it was done, they would have to stay off the floors for several days, *and* they'd have to keep Gus out— the thought of his nails digging into the fresh wood as he raced through the house made him cringe. Nonetheless, it was starting to look like they might finish in time for the Jacksons to move in before Thanksgiving.

He reached into the back pocket of his jeans for his phone, but it wasn't there, and then he remembered he'd put it in his cooler so nothing would happen to it. He opened the passenger door, heard it ringing, looked at the screen, and realized Macey had been trying to reach him.

"Hey," he said. "I know . . . I'm sorry—I didn't have it on me."
He stood in the darkness, the only light coming from the cab as
he listened to Macey tell him about the amber alert that had been
issued for Harper. He nodded, imagining the little girl Macey now
seemed so determined to rescue trying to navigate the world, and
the darkness, by herself. As she continued to talk, her voice began
to tremble and he felt a knot forming in his stomach. "Okay," he
said finally. "I hope they find her. I'll be right along."

He slid his phone into his pocket and listened to the wind in
the trees. Reluctant though he still was to foster, the thought of
any child being out in the cold was disconcerting, let alone one
with a heart condition. Somewhere under all these stars a child
was in crisis.

He closed the passenger door, and slowly walked around to the
driver's side, but after he'd climbed in, he just sat there, staring
into the darkness, wondering—like everyone else—where a nine-
year-old girl would go.

His thoughts drifted to a long-ago summer night when he
and Henry had run away. The situation had, of course, been different, but they must've been around the same age, and he vividly
remembered the circumstances: Their moms wouldn't let them
camp in Henry's backyard, and in an uncharacteristic moment of
defiance, they'd planned an elaborate scheme to camp near the
lighthouse.

Ben shook his head regretfully, remembering how determined and sneaky they'd been. They'd spent all afternoon gathering food and supplies—enough for a week in case they decided to
never come back—and then they discreetly stashed everything in
the woods behind Henry's house. Like spies, they'd synchronized

their watches and then returned to their respective homes for dinner, a bath, and a little TV.

Afterward, Ben had lain in bed, wearing shorts and a T-shirt, waiting and checking his watch every few minutes. Finally, he'd heard his parents wash up and turn off the lights. He'd continued to wait, watching the second hand circle the face of his watch twenty more times before peeking out his door.

Ten minutes later, he'd pulled into the woods on his bike, his brakes squealing.

"You need to get those fixed," Henry had scolded.

"I know. I'm sorry."

"What took you so long?"

"My parents were watching *The Tonight Show.*"

"I was about to give up."

"Sorry."

"Did you bring a flashlight?"

Ben smacked his forehead. "No, I forgot."

"Great," Henry had said as he tried to strap the tent on his bike.

"Sorry."

"That's all right. We'll manage."

"My mom said it's going to storm."

"Mine did, too, but I don't think so. I mean look at the stars."

Ben had looked up and nodded, but by the time they'd reached their destination, they'd heard thunder. "Maybe we should do this another time. . . ."

"It's fine," Henry had assured him, unpacking the tent.

They'd spent the next half hour setting up, but by the time they'd finished, the wind had picked up and lightning was flashing everywhere. Within minutes, it had begun to pour, and they'd huddled in the leaky tent, hoping the storm would pass, when suddenly it had filled with light. Henry had peeked out and seen the headlights of a park ranger's truck were shining right on them. "Crap," he'd muttered, which was never a good sign.

In hindsight, Ben was certain the idea had been all Henry's, but the punishment had been all encompassing. They'd both been grounded for two weeks—two weeks of their precious summer vacation, wasted!

Ben's thoughts came back to the present. It wasn't a steamy, stormy summer night. It was the chilly end of October, and the missing girl wasn't planning an adventure with a friend. She was all by herself, trying to make her way in life. Ben shook his head. Why was he being so selfish? Why was he only thinking of himself? Macey's words echoed in his head and he realized she was right. He hadn't once put himself in the shoes of the little girl who couldn't find a home. A little girl who had no one to count on, who had no one to love or be loved by. He swallowed, remembering how his mom had come into his room that night, and even though she'd been mad, she'd hugged him and told him she was glad he was home safe. *Home safe.* That was probably all Harper wanted, too—to be home safe.

42

HARPER WOKE WITH A START AND SHIVERED. WILLING HER BODY TO MOVE, she stood and stared into the darkness, realizing that nothing had changed. Tom hadn't come home while she slept. There was no car in the driveway. No light on inside the house. The outdoor furniture was still gone. The yard was still a mess. Tom and Sundance didn't live here anymore, and she had no idea where they were. . . . She'd been so full of hope, but now, she realized, there would be no warm welcome, no *Oh my, how big you've gotten!* or *Of course you can stay with us!* or *We've missed you!* Her eyes welled up with disappointed tears. There was no place for her here. There was no place for her *anywhere.* She stuffed Bear back into the top of her backpack, walked down the steps, took one last look at the swing hanging in the darkness and walked down the gravel driveway, kicking loose stones into the tall grass.

As she hurried through the shadows of Savannah, darkness engulfed her. She heard a woman laugh, tires screech, a horn honk, a man swear, and a dog bark. She heard the haunting sound of a saxophone drifting from a bar, and as she walked by, an angry voice shouting, "F-you, man!" During the day, she would barely notice these sounds, but at night, they pressed around her.

She continued to hurry along the brick sidewalk, hoping no one would notice her, but as she walked by a group of men sitting on a stoop across the street, passing around a brown paper bag, one of them called, "Hey, girlie, where ya headin' in such a hurry?"

"Tha's not a girl," another one slurred, laughing. "You're as blind as a bat!"

"It is so a girl—you're blind! Hey, honey, come on over here and show this damn fool you're a girl!"

Harper's eyes grew wide as she ducked into the shadows of a side street, rubbing her chest.

"Hey! Come back!" the voices called. "We ain't gonna hurt ya!"

"No!" she shouted when she felt a safe distance away. Then she turned a corner and finally began to recognize her surroundings— a couple more blocks and she'd be in Cora's neighborhood.

She slowed down, rubbing her chest again, willing the pain to go away, and finally turned into the familiar driveway. The predawn sky had grown a little brighter so she could make out Rudy's bike lying in the walkway. She picked it up, and as she leaned it against the building, the bell on the handlebar jingled. She approached the door and raised her hand to knock, but then realized they were probably sound asleep. They didn't have to be up for at least another hour—and then they'd be rushing around, having breakfast, getting their books and homework together, arguing, and catching their busses for school. She longed to be part of that chaos, but no, she'd gotten herself in trouble again, made Cora mad . . . and almost got her run over. It was time she faced reality. This wasn't her home and it never would be. She was just making life harder for Cora, and since she didn't want to live with any other foster families, it was time she took care of herself. She bit her lip, stepped away from the apartment, glanced over at Janelle's, and realized she'd planted the dark red mum she'd given her right next to her front door. She smiled wistfully and then headed back down the sidewalk, but as she passed the last unit, she slowed down, remembering the conversation she'd had with Rudy . . .

Mr. Peterson used to live there. He was really nice. His cat was Mc-Muffin's brother. We got them from Janelle when her cat had kittens, and after he learned we named ours McMuffin, he named his Big Mac.

So, what happened to Mr. Peterson?

He died, and now his place just sits empty.

How come no one buys it?

I don't know. His family owns it, I guess.

Harper stopped in her tracks. If no one lived in Mr. Peterson's apartment, maybe she could live there while she figured things out. It would be safe and she wouldn't be a burden to anyone. She looked around to see if anyone was looking, and then she pushed open the rusty gate. It squeaked and she swore as she passed through. She walked up to the front door and knocked lightly—just to be sure. When no one answered, she tried the knob, but it was locked. She looked around, and in the half-light, realized the apartment—because it was an end unit—had a side yard. She walked around the corner of the low brick building, looked up, and saw two windows. Standing on tiptoe, she tried to push open the first window, but it wouldn't budge, so she moved to the second. She pushed with all her might—making her chest ache—and to her surprise, it moved. She quickly threw her backpack in and then pulled herself up, scraping both knees and banging her elbow before finally falling to the floor.

She stood up, pressed her hand to her chest, and closed the

window. Looking around the apartment, she was happily surprised to find it was still furnished. The room she had fallen into was the living room, and there was a threadbare couch with a neatly folded afghan over it, a recliner with a TV table next to it, a small old-style television, a coffee table, two end tables, and a dog bed. *Rudy had mentioned a dog but she'd never finished telling her about it!* She wandered into the kitchen and saw a small round table with two chairs, and on it, two plastic placemats and a napkin holder, still full of napkins. She pulled open the refrigerator but it was dark inside, and except for two cans of Coke, empty. She looked in the cabinets, but they were all empty, too. Finally, she walked down the hall to the bedroom and found a neatly made bed, covered with a faded quilt, two bureaus, and a bedside table with an alarm clock. She stood in front of the shorter bureau, and in the early-morning light, studied several framed photos that were propped there. The first was of an older African-American gentleman with his arms around two young kids. "Mr. Peterson's grandkids," she guessed. There was also a photo of a cat that looked a lot like McMuffin curled up next to a dog. "Big Mac," she whispered, smiling. The third frame was a folding double frame that held two photos—one was of the same man, smiling and kneeling in front of the same dog, and the dog—who was wearing a red-white-and-blue bandanna—had his bowed head pressed against the man's chest. In the second picture, they were facing forward and the man had his arm draped around the dog's shoulders. It looked like the dog had a bandage around his leg.

"I wonder what your name is?" she whispered softly.

She heard a door slam, hurried back to climb on the couch, and peeked out the window. It was Janelle, getting in her car, and

Harper suddenly realized that Cora and the kids would come out soon, too. She watched Janelle pull away, closed the curtain, and sank down on the couch, listening. After a few minutes, she pulled the afghan around her shoulders. Then she unzipped her backpack and pulled out Bear and the drawing pad Rudy had given her. She tucked Bear under the afghan and opened the pad. "Why'd you have to go and die, Mom?" she whispered, lightly touching the picture, and as a wave of sadness washed over her, she pulled Bear against her, and through the blur of tears, traced her finger around his heart.

Five minutes later, Cora hurried her children down the sidewalk to the school bus, but inside Mr. Peterson's apartment, Harper was sound asleep.

43

Cora hadn't knelt beside her bed in years. It was hard on her knees, but she believed God forgave her. After all, he was the one who gave her these old, achy knees. Harper was missing, though, and that was an emergency, so she'd been getting up early, every morning to kneel gingerly beside her bed and storm the gates of heaven.

"I am so sorry I told that poor child it woulda been her fault if I got run over. That was thoughtless and cruel. I didn't mean it . . . so if you could please direct her path back toward this house, I promise I will never, ever—"

Cora stopped, midsentence, and listened to a noise outside—*What was that?* It sounded like the bell on Rudy's bike . . . *but how could that be?* She frowned. If it wasn't so damn hard to get up, she'd go look, but then it'd be hard to get back down again. She sighed. She was down now and that's where she was staying. She continued to listen, though, hoping no one was stealing the bike—even if it would teach that girl a lesson! Rudy was constantly leaving her bicycle in the middle of the walk or on the curb where someone (most likely her poor mother) would trip on it! And she was always riding it without her helmet, too . . . "That child is gonna be the death a me!" she murmured. "It would be just as well if her bike was stolen!" She shook her head in dismay and then bowed it again.

Twenty minutes later she murmured *Amen*, slowly pulled herself up, and made her way down the hall, feeling ten years older than she actually was. She woke the boys and then peered into Rudy's room, too. "Time to get up," she said softly.

"Any news, Mama?" Rudy asked, rubbing her eyes sleepily.

"No news, baby," Cora answered. "You need to get up, though, because we have to get your Halloween costume together."

Rudy sat up. "I don't feel like it. I don't feel like trick-or-treating," she said glumly.

Cora sat down and put her arm around her. "I know you're worried, Rudy. I'm worried, too, but we'll find Harper. The police are lookin' and it's been on the news and they're havin' a search party today."

"I want to help search!" Rudy exclaimed excitedly.

"No," Cora said firmly. "The best thing you can do is go to school."

"Why? Why is that the best thing? That's not gonna help find Harper."

"It *is* the best thing because then I don't need to worry about losing you, too."

"You won't lose me," Rudy protested.

Cora stood. "You need to get up and have breakfast."

Rudy frowned. "You won't lose me," she muttered as she threw off the covers and shuffled down the hall. "Hurry up, Joe!" she shouted, banging on the bathroom door. "I hafta go, too!"

When Rudy finally appeared in the kitchen, Cora eyed her. "What would you like for breakfast? Joe says there's only one waffle left."

"He can have it," Rudy said as he pulled the last waffle out of the box. "I'm not hungry."

"You have to eat something," Cora commanded.

"I'm not hungry," Rudy said defiantly, "so don't cook me anything."

Cora sighed. "You're gonna be hungry."

Rudy shook her head, picked up her backpack, went into the living room. As soon as she sank into a chair, McMuffin hopped up onto her lap and lay down. She stroked her soft fur and thought about Harper. "This is why Harper and me should have cell phones," she called out. "If she had a cell phone, we could just call her and ask her where she is."

Cora came into the room, drying her hands. "That is true, Rudy, but I can barely afford phones for me and Frank."

Just then, Frank came into the room, distractedly looking at his phone. "Besides," he said, without looking up. "If Mom got you a phone, you'd just lose it."

"You're one to talk, Mr. Left Mine in My Locker. A lot of good it'll do you there."

"I didn't lose it."

"I wouldn't lose it, either!"

"You would, too—you can't even take care of your bike."

"I can too."

"Then why was it lying in the middle of the walk when I got home last night?"

"It was not."

"Was too," he said, opening the door to prove he was right, but when he looked out, the bike wasn't there. "You must'a moved it."

"I did not!" Rudy said, gently pushing McMuffin off her lap to look.

Frank stepped outside and saw it leaning against the house.

Cora frowned. "Did you move it, Frank?"

"No, ma'am," he answered. He looked back at his phone for the time. "I gotta go."

"You haven't had breakfast."

"I'm not hungry."

"Ain't nobody's hungry 'round here," Cora said in an exasperated voice. "I don't know why I bother buyin' food!"

"Bye, Mama," Frank said, kissing her cheek. "Love you."

"Love you, too," Cora said with a sigh.

"Oh," he said, looking back. "You tol' me to remind you to find out about the after-school program."

"I have just a little bit going on right now, Frank."

"I know, but the captains are starting unofficial practices next week and it'd be good if I showed up."

"I'll try to remember."

"Thanks." He looked back again. "Let me know if they find Harper."

Cora nodded and waved, but when she went back in the kitchen, she realized he'd forgotten his lunch. She grabbed it and hurried outside to catch him, but he was gone, and she shook her head. "No breakfast, no lunch . . . I don't know how you're goin' to have the strength to play basketball!"

She looked at the clock. "We need to go, too." She saw Joe's empty plate on the table. "Rudy, where's your brother?"

"I don't know," Rudy said. She was back in the chair with Mc-Muffin on her lap.

Cora bustled down the hall and found Joe playing a game on Frank's computer. "Let's go, young man. It's time for school."

"Just a minute, Mama. I want to finish this level."

"One . . . ," Cora began slowly. "Two . . . three . . . four . . ." She was trying very hard not to lose her patience.

Joe groaned and clicked off the game. "You ruin everything."

"I know," Cora said. "That's how life is."

Five minutes later, she hustled them out the door with their costumes in their backpacks.

"You coming to the Halloween parade, Mama?" Rudy asked as they walked to the bus stop at the end of the driveway.

"We'll see," Cora said. "I'd like to, but it depends on what happens today."

As they walked past Mr. Peterson's old apartment, Joe reached in and pulled the old metal gate closed. It squeaked and clattered as it slammed into place.

Cora frowned. "Why was that gate open?"

"So the ghosts could get out," Joe said in an eerie voice. "Ooo—oooo," he teased, hovering around Rudy, flapping his arms.

"Cut it out, Joe!" Rudy admonished sharply. "There're no such things as ghosts!" But as she said this, she noticed that the curtain in Mr. Peterson's apartment was open a little, and she stopped and stared. "That's weird," she muttered.

"What's weird?" Joe asked, following her gaze.

"Nothing," she answered, sounding annoyed and picking up the pace. "Hurry up! The bus is coming!"

✑

44

MACEY SCROLLED TO HER SISTER'S NAME IN HER PHONE AND TAPPED IT. Then she glanced at the time—it was seven fifteen. "If you're not up by now, Maeve, you should be," she murmured, tapping her sister's number. She listed to the phone ring and then to her sister's groggy voice. "There you are! I'm sorry to call you so early, but do you happen to have an old yellow polo shirt?"

Ten minutes later, with a brown marker in her bag, Macey knocked on her sister's door.

"It's open," Maeve called sleepily.

Macey let herself in and found Maeve sitting at the kitchen table with her hands wrapped around a mug of steaming coffee. "Since when do you work nights?" she asked.

"I'm filling in for one of our per diem nurses . . . or in this case, *per noctem.*"

"Wow, good use of your high school Latin."

Maeve yawned sleepily. "Thanks."

"I thought if you were per diem, you had the option to decline work."

"You do, usually, but we're so shorthanded. Because no one

wants to work in a nursing home, our per diems try to find someone to fill in if they can't take the hours."

"How many nights do you have to work?" Macey asked, helping
herself to a cup of coffee.

"Last night was the last. I wanted to be home for trick-or-
treaters."

"Do you have any Halloween candy?" Maeve asked, looking
around hopefully.

"Not yet. I have to get some, so I'm glad you woke me." She motioned to the yellow polo. "What do you need that for?"

"My Charlie Brown costume."

Maeve smiled. "Is that why you have that squiggly line on your
head?"

Macey reached up and touched the line she'd drawn on her
forehead before she left home. "Yes. Why?"

Maeve laughed. "Because I thought it was a Harry Potter scar."

Macey frowned. "It's Charlie Brown's hair."

"Well, don't be surprised if kids think you're Harry Potter."

Macey rolled her eyes. "They won't think I'm Harry Potter.
Harry wears glasses, and besides, the Peanuts gang is our theme,
so they'll be looking for good ole Charlie Brown." She spread the
shirt out on the table and pulled the marker out of her bag. "Plus,
I'm putting a zigzag on this."

"A zigzag?" Maeve asked in surprise. "You're drawing on my
shirt with a Sharpie?"

"I am," Macey said. "You don't wear it anymore, do you?"

Maeve sighed and waved her hand. "Go ahead."

Macey eyed the shirt. "Do you have a ruler?"

Maeve got up, retrieved a ruler from her desk, and handed it to her sister. "Have you heard any more about that little girl? The whole town seems to be looking for her."

"I haven't," Macey said, shaking her head. "I wish they'd find her. I'm trying to convince Ben to foster her. . . ."

"Wait a minute! *You* are willing to foster? After telling me there was no way . . ."

"*Foster*," Macey reemphasized, "not adopt." She sat down across from her sister and took a sip of coffee. "I know I was adamant when you told me about Mr. Olivetti and his brother, but I can't stop thinking about Grandy and what she would do—it's almost as if she's prodding me. Besides, this little girl really needs someone."

Maeve smiled. "I wouldn't be surprised if Grandy *is* prodding you. It would be just like her." She took a sip of her coffee. "I thought you said Harper was a tough cookie."

"I did, and she is, but, you know, *we* were kind of tough when we were little, too. I mean we were competitive and headstrong, so maybe determined is a better word? She's determined because she's trying to survive."

"What about her heart?"

Maeve shook her head. "That just makes me want to help her more."

"Is Ben on board?" Maeve asked, sounding incredulous.

"Not really. But you know how he is—cautious beyond reason."

Maeve laughed. "That's the understatement of the century. Look how long it took him to tell you he loved you! When he finally found the courage to propose, I thought I'd fall off my chair!"

"That's my Ben," Macey said, smiling. "Anyway, the other day, I told him Grandy would take her in in a heartbeat."

Maeve smiled, knowing it was true, and Macey continued.

"He wasn't moved, though. He said—like I did—that times were different back then, but last night, when he came home, he seemed to have had a change of heart. Maybe it's because she's missing." As she said this, a shadow fell across her face. "I hope she's okay."

"I hope they find her," Maeve said softly. "Maybe she *is* the answer to your prayers, Mace. I mean, think about it, wasn't Harper one of the names you picked if you had a little girl?"

"It is." She paused, considering this possibility. "Did I tell you she has red hair?"

"Nooo," Maeve said, laughing. "No wonder she's a tough cookie—she can't help it!"

"Yeah," Macey mused thoughtfully. She stood up, laid the ruler on an angle on the shirt, and started to draw a wide zigzag design along the bottom.

An hour later, she was wearing the shirt when she opened the waiting room door and looked around for seven-year-old Logan Wilson, who was home from school with an earache. "Logan?" she called, and the little boy stood up. Macey smiled as he and his mom approached. "Must be crummy to not feel well on Halloween, huh, Logan?"

Logan nodded sadly and then looked up and saw the mark on her forehead, and his eyes grew wide. "Wait! Are you Harry Potter?"

45

HARPER PULLED BEAR AGAINST HER CHEST AND LAY STILL, LETTING HER eyes adjust to the darkness as she recalled the events of the last twenty-four hours: After climbing through the window and falling asleep on the couch (the first time), she'd awoken to the realization that she'd missed watching her friends get on their bus, and then she'd slumped on the couch, overwhelmed with loneliness, and tried to watch TV, only to remember there was no electricity. She'd searched the kitchen again, found nothing, and opened one of the warm Cokes from the fridge. She took a long sip and licked her lips, savoring the sweetness as the bubbles fizzed down her dry throat. Finally, driven by hunger, she'd slipped out the back door, snuck through the yards, and used the key Cora kept under her mat to let herself in. In the fridge, she'd found a sandwich all made, and even though it was tuna—her least favorite—she'd devoured it; then she'd filled a plastic bag with snacks she hoped Cora wouldn't miss—a roll of Ritz crackers, a bag of potato chips, two apples, and three juice boxes. She'd hurried back to Mr. Peterson's, praying no one saw her, and locked the door behind her.

Now, she realized she must've slept all afternoon because the apartment was dark and she was hungry again. She heard voices outside and knelt on the couch to look. There was a large group of kids walking along the sidewalk dressed in costumes, and she suddenly realized it was Halloween!

She slumped back down on the couch, feeling worse than before—she was missing out on all the fun . . . *and* all the candy! She wondered what Rudy was wearing, and if she'd recognize her. She peeked out the window again, hoping to see her friend, but there were only younger kids walking by. She was trying to decide what to do, when she heard the gate squeak open. Her heart pounded as she listened to voices getting closer. Suddenly, the doorbell rang and she almost jumped out of her skin. She sank into the couch, her heart pounding harder as she listened to a commotion outside the door. The doorbell rang again, followed by loud banging on the metal storm door. "Trick or treat!" a voice shouted. "Yeah, smell my feet!" shouted another. "How the heck can you not be home on Halloween?"

Harper swallowed, praying they'd leave. Instead, someone kicked the door, and called out, "Anyone got any eggs left?" Several voices shouted they did, and then the ensuing silence was filled with the sounds of laughter and eggs smashing against the window.

"Hey! Cut it out!" a man's voice shouted.

Harper held her breath and closed her eyes as the kids ran off, and even though she could hear their voices fading, she didn't dare look. She just rubbed her chest, held on to Bear, and listened to her stomach growl.

She lay back, thinking about what she could eat. She knew she had the crackers and chips she'd borrowed from Cora, but the thought of free candy was making her mouth water. She picked up the flashlight she'd found when she was looking for the TV remote, turned it on, and pointed it at the floor as she walked into Mr. Peterson's bedroom. She opened his closet door and shone the light on the shelves, looking for something—anything—she could use for a Halloween costume. The weak beam of light landed on an Atlanta Braves baseball hat—maybe she could be a baseball player! She continued to look and found a wooden bat in the front corner of the closet—which, she surmised, could double as protection, too, if she needed it. She put the hat and bat on the bed and opened a bureau drawer. It felt creepy to be looking through the belongings of someone who had died, but she really wanted to go trick-or-treating. She rummaged through the drawers with one hand while holding the flashlight with the other. Finally, she found something—an old Atlanta Braves jersey. She pulled it out, spilling several other shirts onto the floor at the same time, and shook it open. It was big, but it would do. She turned it over, spread it out on the bed, and shone the light across the number, 44, and then looked more closely—someone had written something with a magic marker above the name, but because it was script, she couldn't make it out. "I bet he was mad about *that*," she whispered as she pulled the shirt over her head.

Ten minutes later, with the bat in one hand, a plastic bag in the other, and the baseball hat—adjusted to its smallest size—on her head, Harper peeked out the front window. All was quiet, so she let herself out the back door, walked around the end of the unit to the sidewalk, glanced up and down anxiously, and quickly crossed the parking lot to the units on the other side. Another group of trick-or-treaters was just leaving so Harper hurried to get to the door before the woman closed it.

"Oh," the woman said in surprise. "I almost didn't see you," she added, dropping a handful of candy into Harper's bag.

"Thank you," Harper said, peering into the bag.

She hurried off to the next door and knocked, and when the woman opened it, she held out her bag. "Trick or treat," she said hopefully.

"Look at you!" the woman exclaimed. "Bill! Come on out here! You've gotta see this one!"

Harper shifted her feet nervously as an elderly man made his way slowly to the door.

"Wow!" he said, smiling. "If it isn't Hammerin' Hank!"

Harper frowned—who the hell was Hammerin' Hank? Her shirt said *Aaron*.

"Well, young man, that's the best costume we've seen!" the woman sputtered happily. "You get two Snickers!"

Harper shook her head. "I can't have Snickers—I'm allergic to nuts. Do you have anything else?"

"Oh, hon, I'm sorry. That's all I have. . . . I thought everyone loved Snickers."

Harper nodded solemnly. "Okay. Thanks anyway." She turned to go and the man called after her. "Great costume, kid!"

Harper hurried to the next apartment, but just as she was about to knock, she heard voices and turned to see another group coming along the sidewalk, and among them were Rudy and Joe! Harper also recognized the girl next to Rudy—it was Lana the hairstylist's daughter, Kari, who looked so much like Rudy, she could be her twin. Kari Thomas and her mom and brother had moved there from Mississippi. She'd been in the same class as Harper before Latisha had pushed her. She and Kari had even sat next to each other, and when Harper couldn't find her pencil, Kari had given her one and told her to keep it.

"But then you won't have one," Harper said, astounded by her kindness.

"That's okay. I have a pen," Kari said, producing a pen from her pocket.

Harper started to wave to them, but then remembered she shouldn't be seen . . . and they were heading right for her! She ducked behind some bushes and watched them walk to the door. She could make out all the costumes now—the boys were both dressed as pirates, Joe wearing the same costume he'd worn to the Pirate Festival on Tybee Island (Harper had seen the picture on Cora's phone), and Rudy was a purple Crayola crayon (her favorite color), while Kari was an angel with shimmering white wings.

"So they haven't found her yet?" Kari asked, sounding worried.

"No," Rudy answered. "They even had a search party today."

"They think someone might'a kidnapped her," Joe added authoritatively, and Harper suddenly realized they were talking about *her*!

"That's awful," Kari said in a voice that sounded genuinely dismayed. In fact, she sounded so sincere, Harper almost stepped out to assure them she was okay.

"My mom's really upset," Rudy said, pointing over her shoulder. "She won't even let us go trick-or-treatin' in the neighborhood by ourselves."

Harper looked over and saw Cora pulling her coat around her as she talked to Lana. She looked very tired, and Harper suddenly felt sad—she hadn't realized people would miss her enough to search for her. She hadn't meant to hurt anyone or make them worry . . . especially Cora.

46

MACEY OPENED THE FRONT DOOR AND LOOKED AROUND. SHE HAD TURNED on every light with the hope of attracting kids up their long drive-way, but so far, they hadn't had a single trick-or-treater.

"Where is everyone?" she whispered softly, putting her arm around Keeper's shoulders. He wagged his tail and looked around hopefully, too. She sat down on the top step and he plopped down next to her. "No one's even come to see *you*," she said softly, straightening his new Halloween bandanna, which she'd ironed for the occasion, "even though you look so handsome." She gazed down at the jack-o'-lanterns lining the steps and driveway—she and Ben had carved pumpkins every night that week, getting ready. Ben had even put orange lightbulbs in the front porch lights, and she'd made a life-size stuffed witch and sat her in the front rocking chair with a bowl of candy in her lap.

She pulled her sweater around her and stroked Keeper's soft ears. "Never mind not having our own kids to *take* trick-or-treating," she mused, "we can't even get other people's kids to come to our house."

"Maybe that's because they know it's haunted," Ben teased from the other side of the screen.

"Or maybe it's because they know about the curse. You know, because it's built on an old burial ground."

"Maybe," Ben said, coming out, grabbing a candy bar from the witch's bowl, and sitting on the other side of Keeper. The big dog swished his tail happily as he sniffed the wrapper.

"Do you really think that's possible?" Macey asked. "Could this house be cursed? Could *we* be cursed for living here?"

"No," Ben said firmly, ripping the wrapper off and popping the candy in his mouth. He looked into Keeper's mournful eyes. "Sorry, buddy, no chocolate for pups."

"It seems like we're cursed," Macey mused. "Just think about it, the first time I got pregnant was in this house, and every pregnancy since . . ."

"Mace, that's crazy. We are *not* cursed for living here," Ben said.

"Well, what about the widow who walks the halls?"

"What about her?"

"Maybe, because she never got to have kids, she doesn't want anyone else to have kids either."

"That's ridiculous," Ben said. "I think the ghoulish spirits have gone to your head."

Just then, the door behind them slammed shut and they both jumped. "See?" Macey said.

"That was the wind," Ben said matter-of-factly. He watched the swaying trees. "There's a storm brewing out in the Atlantic, and it's supposed to rain all day tomorrow."

"Great. Just what we need."

"It's definitely not what *I* need. The floors in the Jackson house are supposed to be refinished, and a hurricane will put us behind schedule. I don't need the painters tracking mud on the floors before they're finished, either."

"I'm more worried about Harper. What if she hasn't found some kind of shelter?"

Ben nodded. "Hopefully, she has . . . or they find her soon."

"Have you thought any more about fostering?"

"From the way you're talking," Ben said, avoiding the question, "it's not safe for her to live here. I mean, what if you're right and this house is cursed, or the widow doesn't want kids here? Some awful accident might befall her."

"Very funny," Macey said, rolling her eyes, but then she thought about Harper's heart. "I hope nothing bad happens."

"Nothing bad is going to happen," he said, stroking Keeper's soft fur.

"Well, I can't stop thinking about her."

"I can tell. . . ."

"You haven't thought about her, though. . . ."

"I haven't stopped thinking about her," he admitted quietly. "I've been thinking how she must be going through a really hard time right now . . . and she's just a little kid—she shouldn't have to go through something like this alone."

"Does that mean"—she eyed him hopefully—"you'd be willing to give fostering a try?"

Ben shook his head, unable to believe he was giving in . . . again! "Mace, if you think this is something we're supposed to do, I'm willing to give it a try." He stopped and smiled at her. "After all, I know you'll get your way eventually, so I may as well give in now and save myself a lot of trouble."

"True," Macey said, smiling and squeezing his hand. "You're smarter than you look."

"Thanks," he said, rubbing Keeper's ears. "Well, there was

some paperwork to adopt this guy . . . so there's probably a mountain of paperwork involved in fostering a child."

"Probably," Macey agreed. "I'll have to give Cora a call . . . maybe she'll have some news."

"Maybe we won't be approved," he ventured. "Then I'll be off the hook."

"We'll be approved," Macey assured him. "They just have to find her."

Ben nodded thoughtfully, trying to wrap his mind around all the responsibilities being foster parents would entail. "Do you think she'll fit in at the new elementary school?"

"I hope so. I think Mrs. Lyons works there now, instead of at the middle school."

"Our old lunch lady?"

Macey nodded. "Yup, the very same one who let you get a new tray when you spilled your clam roll and fruit everywhere."

Ben laughed. "Wow! Hold old is she now?"

"Well, she wasn't *that* old when we were there—probably in her forties . . . and that was twentysomething years ago, so she's probably in her sixties."

"Maybe she'll look out for Harper."

"If she finds out she's yours, she will."

Ben nodded. He couldn't believe they were having this conversation—a conversation that included possessive pronouns, verbs about caring, and an actual child, all in the same sentence. The prospect of having a child in their care who would attend his old elementary school made him feel more excited than he expected.

"I wish they'd find her," Macey said. "I don't get how a little girl can just disappear into thin air."

"It's a crazy world, Mace. Kids disappear without a trace all the time."

"She doesn't deserve to disappear without a trace. She deserves a chance."

"And we're gonna give her that chance," Ben said. "Right, Keep?" he said, tousling the dog's ears. "We'll find her and then it's *your* job to straighten her out."

Keeper thumped his tail, and they both laughed.

"Well, it doesn't look like we're going to get any trick-or-treaters."

"After all this work," Macey said, shaking her head. "I can't believe no one came."

"Look on the bright side," Ben teased. "We get to keep all the candy."

"*That* is not a bright side—it won't be good for my waistline."

Ben wrapped his arm around her. "There's nothing wrong with your waistline," he said softly, kissing the top of her head and then softly kissing her lips. "And since you didn't get to give out any treats tonight, I'll let you give *me* a treat if you want."

"Ha!" she said. "What kind of chocolate would you like? I have Nestlé Crunch, Kit Kat, Milky Way . . ."

"Hmm . . . that isn't the kind of sugar I had in mind."

"And *what*, exactly, did you have in mind?"

"Oh, you know . . ." he said, pulling her toward him.

"Hmm . . . I think you're gonna have to show me, mister," she teased in her best Southern drawl.

47

Harper flopped wearily onto the couch, unwrapped a snack-size Crunch bar, popped it in her mouth, and washed it down with a swallow of warm Coke. She shone the flashlight on the candy—which she'd divided into two piles—picked up a licorice stick from the nut-free pile, pulled off the wrapper, leaned back on the couch, and took a bite. Chewing slowly, she shone the flashlight around the living room, but when the beam passed over the dog bed, something caught her eye. She stopped, retraced the light's path, and got up to lift the edge of the bed so she could read the letters that were embroidered there. "Keeper," she said softly. "So that was your name."

She walked to the bedroom and shone the light on the pictures on the bureau, picked up the double frame, and held the flashlight so there wasn't a glare on the glass. Then she stared. Was she seeing things? She'd noticed the bandage on the dog's leg before, but now she realized he was actually missing a leg! How the heck did a dog get around on three legs?

She set the picture down, turned away, and felt her foot catch on something soft. Startled, she shone the flashlight on the floor and saw the pile of shirts that had fallen out of Mr. Peterson's drawer. She stuffed them back in, pulled the baseball shirt over her head, squeezed it in on top, and shoved the drawer closed. Then she retrieved the bat and hat from the living room and put them back in the closet, too.

She took another sip of Coke and rubbed her chest. "Stop hurting," she whispered. She heard a sound outside and knelt on the cushions to peek out. By the light of the streetlamp, she saw a woman walking across the parking lot and realized it was Cora. She frowned—why had she parked her car all the way over there and not in her usual spot? She continued to watch and then saw Cora lean over to pick something up.

"Rudy's bike," Harper muttered, shaking her head. She watched Cora push the bike up onto the sidewalk, lean it against the building, and go inside, and when her porch light blinked out, Harper felt a crushing wave of sadness sweep over her. She dropped the curtain and slumped on the couch, her eyes filling with tears. Was her life always going to be this way? If so, maybe she'd be better off dead. The thought made her tears spill over and stream down her cheeks, and she didn't even try to stop them. In fact, if she did die, Cora's life would be a whole lot easier. She wouldn't have to put up with her fresh mouth anymore, *or* try to find her a home. She could just take care of her own kids. She wrapped her arms around her legs and bowed her head. If only her mom hadn't died. If only she could find her dad. If only something good would happen! She huddled like that for a long time, her heart aching not only with physical pain but also with loneliness.

Finally, she wiped her eyes, looked up, and saw the moonlight shining on the dog bed, illuminating the embroidered name.

"Were you a keeper?" she asked softly. She gazed up at the moon above the curtain and remembered something Mary had said when she stayed with them. "'I see the moon, and the moon sees me,'" she murmured. "'God bless the moon, and God bless me.'" The memory filled her eyes with fresh tears.

Resolutely, she bit her lip and wiped her eyes. She was done crying. She didn't want to stay in this empty apartment. She missed Cora and Rudy, and she wanted to sleep on the squeaky cot in Rudy's room. Hiding wasn't making her feel better. It was making her feel worse! She hadn't figured out one thing about living on her own, *and* she was hungry. She popped the last piece of licorice in her mouth, swept the rest of the candy into her backpack, folded the afghan, laid it over the back of the couch, and stuffed the bag she'd filled with snacks from Cora's—which were almost gone— into her backpack next to Bear. She slung it over her shoulder, picked up her Coke, and shone the flashlight around the room one last time. Everything was just the way she'd found it, less two cans of Coke, which she doubted anyone would miss. She switched off the flashlight, put it in the drawer next to the TV remote, walked to the door, pushed in the locking device, and turned it. Then she stepped outside, and without a second thought, pulled the door closed. If she ever changed her mind, she knew how to get back in.

She pulled her sweatshirt around her and walked around to the front, and as she closed the squeaky gate, a gust of wind swept around the building and practically pushed her to Cora's.

PART 3

48

"I NEED TO STOP AT THE OFFICE," CORA SAID, TURNING INTO THE DFCS parking lot.

"Okay. I'll wait in the car."

"No, ma'am. Absolutely not. You're coming in with me."

"Cora, I'm *not* gonna run away," Harper protested. "Besides, it's raining."

"You're still coming in. I have seen enough of the inside of the police station for ten lifetimes! *And* you won't melt," Cora added firmly as she turned off her car and reached for her umbrella.

"Fine," Harper grumbled. She climbed out and was hurrying around to get under Cora's umbrella when a gust of wind suddenly flipped it inside out.

"Nice!" Harper shouted, turning to race for the front door. She pulled it open, stepped inside, and stopped in her tracks. Sitting in a chair outside the front office was Connor Taylor—the boy who'd gotten her kicked out of her last foster home—Mrs. Lewis's. "Well, well, look who it is! How ya doin', shit for brains?"

Connor stared at her as if he was seeing a ghost. "Shut up."

"*You* shut up."

"Oh, go jump in a lake."

"What's the matter? Mrs. Lewis finally realize what a jerk you are?"

"No, smarty-pants. It just so happens I'm going to live with my dad," he replied huffily.

Harper's eyes grew wide—she'd never heard of a foster kid getting placed with a real parent. "Yeah, right," she sneered. "Good luck with that!"

"Shut up. You're such a bi . . ."

Just then, Cora came through the door, looking a little damp, and Connor's mouth clamped shut. "Hello, Connor. How are you?"

"Hello, Mrs. Grant. I'm fine, thank you. How are you?"

"I'm fine, thank you. I hear you're going home with your father today."

Connor nodded. "I am."

"I hope it goes well," Cora said, looking in her bag for her office keys. And as she did, Connor gave Harper a snide look.

"Thank you, Mrs. Grant. Me, too."

"C'mon, Harper," Cora said, and as Harper turned to follow her, Connor gave her the finger—a gesture she promptly returned.

"Why can't you be as polite as Connor?" Cora asked as she unlocked her door.

"Are you kidding me?" Harper asked incredulously. "He's like Eddie Haskell on *Leave It to Beaver*: real polite when adults are around and a dipshit when they're not. He just gave me the finger when you weren't looking!"

"How do you know who Eddie Haskell is?"

"Rudy and I watch the Beav on TV Land all the time."

"Mm-hmm. Well, I really wish you wouldn't talk that way, and you probably gave him the finger first."

"I did not! And I'm sick of everyone thinking I'm the one who starts stuff. I'm the victim here . . . *and* I have a heart condition!"

"Ha!" Cora said, shaking her head. "Victim, my . . ."

"Is Connor's dad nice?"

"Nice enough, I guess."

"Why was he in foster care?"

"I can't really talk about it, baby."

"Why? I'm not gonna say anything."

"Still, I can't—privacy laws," Cora said, riffling through the papers on her desk. She picked up some forms just as Harper plopped into her chair. "No time for sitting. Let's go."

As they walked back through the vestibule, Harper saw Connor in the front office, standing next to a man with a scruffy beard. "Is that *him*?" she whispered.

"Yes."

"He looks kind of sketchy to me."

"Well then be thankful you're not goin' to live with him," she mused. "I don't know what the court was thinking."

"Why? What's wrong with him?" Harper pressed.

"I already tol' you, baby, I can't talk about it," Cora said, holding the door.

Harper rolled her eyes and then hurried to the car. "I'm so glad to go home to your house, Cora," she said after she'd climbed in and slammed the door.

"Easy there, baby—you'll make my door fall off." She looked over. "So you didn't like staying by yourself at Mr. Peterson's?"

Harper looked out at the rain. "No, I missed you . . . and Rudy."

"How could you miss us when we were practically next door?" Cora asked. She was still in shock to learn that Harper had been hiding just two doors down from her, that she had gone trick-or-treating, and that she had snuck into her apartment to "borrow" food!

Harper shrugged. "Have you thought any more about letting me stay?" she asked hopefully. "I promise I won't run away again."

Cora pulled the car over and looked in Harper's eyes. "Baby, you know I love you and I love having you stay with us, but we talked about this: my home is not the right home for you. Besides, remember, I told you this morning that there's a young couple, the Samuelsons, who I know are interested in being your foster parents."

"How do they know about me? Is it because of what you said in church that day?"

"Maybe," Cora said, not sure if this was a good thing.

Harper shook her head. "I don't think it's a good idea."

"Why not?" Cora asked, starting to worry that her new plan might not work out as well as she'd been hoping.

"Because I'm sick and tired of being put in all these stupid foster homes with stupid people who don't give a crap. Don't you see, Cora? It's not working. I just want to stay with you. I promise I won't be any trouble."

Cora sighed. "You aren't any trouble, child. Why can't I get that through to you? I just want to find the right home—a loving home—where you will be happy and thrive."

"A place like that doesn't exist!" Harper said, crossing her arms and slumping into her seat.

"Well, regardless we're taking a ride over to the Samuelsons' house so you can meet them."

"Wait a minute. That's *today*?" Harper asked, raising her eyebrows in alarm. "I thought you meant next week."

"No, baby, we're going today," Cora said with a sigh. She put her car in gear and started to pull onto the road again.

"I'm not staying there," Harper said defiantly. "I don't have my stuff."

"No, you're not staying there," Cora assured her. "We're just going so you can meet them properly."

Harper watched Cora's wipers slap back and forth. "Do they have other kids? Have they even fostered before? Do they know what they're getting into? Are they doing it for the money? Because if they are, I'm *not* interested."

"I already told you, Harper, the Samuelsons are very nice, they don't have other kids, and they're not in it for the money. You already met Macey . . ."

"Yeah, you said that, but I don't remember her."

"You met her at the doctor's office."

"Macey? What kind of name is that? Does she own a department store?"

"It's a nice name, and I truly hope you will try to be polite and not your old sassy self."

Harper frowned. "Is she that woman who wanted to know if I was good at basketball? The one who came up to me after church?"

Cora sighed, praying this day was going to get better. "Lordy, child, could you just give them a chance?"

"She is, isn't she?"

"If she is, what's wrong with that?"

"It's just dumb—that stuff she said about not letting on how good you are so you surprise the other team. What does she know about it?"

"I don't know. She might know a lot, and that seems like a pretty good strategy to me."

"Ha! I think it's better if the other team *does* know how good you are—then you psych them out. She doesn't know squat!"

"Harper, I wish you wouldn't talk like that."

"What? I didn't say anything bad. I was going to say, 'She doesn't know *shit*,' but I didn't."

Cora sighed and looked over. "You need to work on not swearing and not using any unladylike language, and you need to *not* have such an attitude. Where did you get such a badass attitude?"

Harper feigned shock. "Wow! Nice language, Miss Cora!"

"Ha!" Cora said, laughing. "I get it from bein' 'round you!"

"Well, maybe *I* get it from bein' 'round *you*," Harper said, laughing.

Cora shook her head. "Anyway, Macey and Ben live in a big house with lots of room and a nice yard." She looked over. "I know you're nervous because this is how you get—all full o' questions and bein' fresh, but you need to calm down and give this a chance. I think it might just be the answer to our prayers."

"It might be the answer to *your* prayers—you want to get rid of me, but it's not the answer to *my* prayers. If my prayers were being answered I'd find my dad . . . or live with you."

"I do not want to get rid of you!" She looked over. "And I want you to promise me you will not run away again."

"Oh, no," Harper said, folding her arms across her chest. "I'm not promisin' nothing. If I'm not happy, I'm not stayin'."

Cora pulled over to the side of the road again. "Look at me, child," she commanded, and Harper looked at her with eyes full of defiance. "This is going to be your best shot at having a home. A place where people will truly love you *and* take care of you. If you run away, you might ruin that chance. They've already had enough heartache in their lives."

Harper looked at her suspiciously. "Why?"

"Just because. The reason is something they will share if they want to."

"I think you should tell me so I know what I'm getting into."

"Well, I'm not telling you, but if you can't be trusted to not run away, you are only goin' to make life miserable for yourself . . . and for everyone else, including me!"

"I can take care of myself—I already proved it."

"Yeah, you proved it by breaking into someone's apartment and living on soda and Halloween candy for close to forty-eight hours."

"I still did it."

"Harper, for heaven's sake, could you just promise me so I don't hafta worry."

Harper clenched her jaw and looked straight into Cora's eyes. "Fine."

"'Fine' what?"

"Fine, I promise."

"Thank you."

"But you have to promise you'll come get me if I'm not happy."

"If you are truly unhappy, I will come get you. But you have to give it an honest chance. I am not running to the rescue the first time things don't go your way."

"Okay." She paused. "And if they're so nice, you gonna let Rudy sleep over?"

"Yes, I would do that."

"And I can sleep over at your place, too?"

"If you keep your promise."

Harper nodded, seeming satisfied with the arrangement. She looked out the window and saw the golden arches looming ahead. "Do you think we can stop at McDonald's so you can get a big-ass coffee and I can have my last meal?"

"I'm sure it won't be your last meal."

"It might be."

"You promise not to throw it out the window?"

"Yes," Harper said, rolling her eyes.

"Okay, then," Cora said, turning into McDonald's.

"If we eat inside I *can't* throw it out the window."

"Is that what you want?"

Harper nodded, and Cora sighed as she pulled into a parking spot. "You're gonna make me get wet again."

"You won't melt," Harper said with a grin.

"Ha! I might," Cora said, climbing out and reaching out for Harper's hand, but Harper was already jumping over puddles and halfway to the entrance. "Did you look both ways?" she called.

"Yes!" Harper called back, pulling open the door and waiting for her.

49

BEN LOOKED OUT AT THE WIND-DRIVEN RAIN. AS PROMISED, THE TROPI-
cal storm had become a hurricane, but because it was following in
the wake of an autumn northeaster, the track had become much
more challenging to predict. "It just figures we'd get a hurricane
this late in the season," Ben mused. "It's really messing up my
schedule."

"You'll be fine," Macey said, pulling open the junk drawer.

Ben sighed and watched the raindrops trickling down the
window. "Hopefully, we'll dodge a bullet."

"Hopefully we will, but I'd rather be prepared," Macey said,
rummaging through the drawer, looking for candles.

"Maybe it'll stay out to sea . . . or maybe it'll hit New England?
Those hardy Northerners are due for a good thumpin'."

"Still harboring a grudge?" she asked, eyeing him as she set
the candles she'd found on the counter.

"Me? Noo . . . I'm married to one, remember?" he teased, pulling her into his arms.

"I remember," she said, kissing him. She looked over his
shoulder at the willow trees swaying back and forth. "I can't believe

Cora is coming out in this weather. I told her we'd meet them, but she said it's procedure to come to the home where they're placing a child."

Ben nodded and searched her eyes. "You're still sure about this?"

Macey looked up. "I am," she said with conviction. "Are you?"

"I signed the papers, didn't I?"

Macey eyed him suspiciously. "You're getting cold feet, aren't you?"

"No," he said, unable to meet her gaze. "Okay, maybe a little. I just hope we're not making a mistake. I mean this is one hell of a commitment. It's not like taking in a three-legged dog."

"I know, Ben. You've already said that at least ten times."

"Well, it's true. What if she doesn't adjust? What if she doesn't like us?"

"There are a lot of *what-ifs* in life, and I know this is hard for you, but sometimes, you just have to take a leap of faith."

"I'm not a very good leaper."

"That's the truth," she said, laughing. "You have to be pushed, prodded, and pulled."

Ben smiled, knowing it was true.

"Honestly, though, what's the worst that can happen?"

"Um . . . we could be murdered in our sleep."

"Ben! That's not going to happen. She's a little girl."

"I know. I was just kidding. . . ."

"Well, don't," Macey scolded as she pulled away. "Did you bring in firewood before it started to rain?"

"Yes, ma'am."

Macey glanced at her watch. "Cora said they'd be here after lunch."

"Speaking of which . . . what is for lunch?"

"I'm not very hungry, but I'll make something for you."

"Why aren't you hungry? You're not nervous, are you?" he teased.

"Nooo . . ."

"You are," Ben said, laughing. "I'm glad I'm not the only one."

"I just hope she likes it here. I hope she likes her room. I wish we'd had time to do more than just move out the crib and move in a bed and desk."

"I think it's better this way. Now, she can decorate it the way she wants."

"I guess."

"Did you tell your parents?"

"Yes, they're very excited. They want to come over and meet her as soon as she's settled. Did you tell yours?"

"I did. They said they want us to bring her down, too, so they can take her to Disney, but I told them we would have to see how it goes—it's going to be a big adjustment for everyone."

"Listen to us," Macey said, shaking her head. "We don't even know if it's going to work and we're already making plans."

"I hope it does," Ben said, pulling her into his arms again.

"Me, too," Macey whispered. Just then, Keeper, who'd been lying on his bed, pulled himself up and hopped over to nuzzle between them.

"Hey, you," Macey said, laughing. "You don't want to be left out, do you?" She knelt down, and he pressed his copper head against her chest.

"You're so silly," she whispered, hugging him. A moment later, he pulled away, cocked his head, and barked excitedly as he hurried down the hall, wiggling his whole hind end.

Macey looked at Ben and raised her eyebrows. "Ready?"

He mustered a smile. "Ready as I'll ever be."

50

HARPER FELT HER HEART POUND AND REACHED FOR CORA'S HAND. "THIS house is huge," she said as they hurried up the porch steps, trying to escape the rain. "I don't think this is a good idea, Cora. I don't feel so good."

"What do you mean you don't feel so good?" Cora asked, looking down and squeezing her hand. "Does your chest hurt?"

"No, my stomach—it's all queasy inside."

"You're just nervous. You'll be okay."

"I think I might get sick. Are you sure I can't just live with you? Please? I promise I'll be good. I won't cause any more trouble at school . . . and I won't run away ever, ever. I promise! Cross my heart!" Tears welled up in her eyes. "I don't want to live *here*."

Cora knelt down and looked in Harper's eyes. "Baby, it's going to be okay. I promise. I know change is scary. But I really think you're going to like these people."

Harper shook her head as her tears spilled down her cheeks. "No, I don't want to, Cora. Please don't make me. Please take me home. I want to live with you and Rudy and Frank and Joe. I promise I'll be good."

"Oh, child, you *are* already good. It's got nothing to do with that. Now, you have to give this a chance. You have to be brave."

"I don't want to be brave. I want to live with you," Harper cried, flinging her arms around Cora's neck. "Please don't make me!" Just as she said this, there was a loud bark, followed by scampering paws, and she pulled back, eyes brightening. "They have a *dog*?"

"They do," Cora replied, hoping this was a good thing, and then remembering there was another surprise in store for Harper. When she had stopped by for a visit to finalize everything—as was standard procedure when they established a new foster home— she'd been astonished to find her former neighbor's three-legged dog at the door. "You know," she'd told Macey at the time, "my neighbor also had a cat, and the two were inseparable." Macey had remembered the cat she'd seen at the shelter, and later that day, she'd called Cora to tell her she'd gone back to get Big Mac and Cora had laughed. "What about Ben?"

"Oh, he'll get over it," Macey had said, laughing, too. "After all, what's one more?"

"You didn't tell me they had a dog," Harper said, frowning.

"With everything goin' on, child, I forgot."

Harper bit her lip and wiped her eyes, and in the next moment, the door opened and the big golden retriever bounded out. "Whoa!" she exclaimed in surprise as he almost knocked her over.

"Keeper, take it easy!" Macey said. "I'm sorry, Harper. He's usually much calmer than this."

Harper looked up and realized Macey *was* the lady from church and Dr. Hack's office. Now she eyed her suspiciously, wondering what real motive was at play in her wanting to suddenly be a foster parent.

Macey pulled Ben forward into the doorway. "Harper, I know we've met before, but I don't think you've ever met my husband, Ben."

Ben smiled warmly and extended his hand. "Hi, Harper. It's nice to meet you."

Harper nodded, eyeing him warily, but kept her hands stuffed in her pockets. There was no way she was going to be friends the first time she met someone. She turned her attention back to Keeper and the big dog acknowledged her with kisses. She put her hands on his head, looked down at his three legs, and then frowned at Cora. "Is this . . . ?" But a gust of wind sent the rain sideways onto the porch and she never got to finish her question.

Ben held the door open. "C'mon in, before we all get soaked!"

They traipsed past the formal living room, shaking off the rain, and headed to the cozy kitchen. "Cora, would you like a cup of ginger tea?" Macey asked.

"That sounds wonderful," Cora replied.

"I'd love a cup, too," Harper said, her hand still on Keeper's head as she sat at the table.

"Do you like ginger tea, Harper?" Macey asked in surprise.

"Mm-hmm. It's real good with lemon in it—Mary used to make it for me when I didn't feel good."

"Who is Mary?" Macey asked, putting the kettle on the stove.

"Tom and Mary used to foster kids, but Mary caught cancer and died, and Tom couldn't take kids anymore—he was too sad. They had a dog, too. His name was Sundance."

"That's a great name for a dog."

Harper nodded as Keeper rested his head on her lap. "How'd you get Keeper?"

"My sister and I saw him at a pet-adoption event, and they said he'd been in the shelter for two years. No one wanted him because he has three legs."

Harper nodded. "That's like me. No one wants me because I have a weak heart—they're worried somethin's gonna happen . . . and even before that, no one wanted me because I got in trouble . . . a *lot*. Anybody who takes me in, is taking a big risk, right, Cora?" She looked to Cora for confirmation. "I could have a heart attack or somethin' . . . and then there'd probably be an investigation or a lawsuit . . . or, at the very least, an expensive funeral."

Cora—who'd sat down in the chair across from her—listened in amazement as Harper spouted off. "Oh my, baby, you are certainly painting a solemn picture. None of that is going to happen."

"You never know, Cora. You always say, 'Anything can happen' and 'With God all things are possible.'"

"I *do* say that," Cora agreed, suddenly realizing what Harper was doing—she was brazenly and unabashedly trying to sabotage this wonderful opportunity. "But I certainly don't think that is how things will play out in this instance."

Harper sighed heavily as if it were a foregone conclusion and they were foolish to ignore the peril of taking her in.

Macey and Ben exchanged worried glances, wondering what they were getting into, and Cora quickly tried to allay their fears. "Harper has such a wonderful, vivid imagination—you never know what will pop out of her mouth!"

Harper raised her eyebrows at this counterclaim and Macey nodded.

"I never use this teapot," Macey mused, changing the subject as she poured hot water into a beautiful china teapot with blue hydrangeas painted on the side. "It belonged to my grand-mother."

"How come?" Harper asked.

"I never make more than one cup because I never have anyone over, so I usually just steep a tea bag in a cup with a saucer on top."

"You *could* have people over," Ben said softly, watching her.

"I guess I could. I just never feel like it."

"How come?" Harper asked. "You have a great big house."

Macey blinked, trying to decide if this was a compliment. "Thank you," she said finally, giving Harper the benefit of the doubt. "That's a good question. I guess it's because all my friends have kids and they're always off on playdates and doing sports and stuff."

Harper nodded thoughtfully. "Their kids could come."

"You're right, they could," Macey said, dunking the tea bags a few times. The idea of sitting at her kitchen table over mugs of coffee or tea with the other moms she knew, chatting about the school year or complaining about homework while their kids played outside, gave her an oddly warm feeling. She put the lid on the pot. "How about we let this steep for a few minutes and go see your room?"

"Okay," Harper said. "Cora, you comin'?" Harper gently lifted Keeper's head off her lap and stood.

"What about you, Keeper?" Harper asked, tousling his ears as they walked back down the hall to the wide center staircase.

"I'm afraid Keep can't come," Ben explained as he led the way. "He has trouble with stairs." He eyed him. "You stay here, pal."

A shadow of disappointment fell across Harper's face as Keeper stood at the bottom step. "I'll be right back," she whispered, turning to followed Macey and Cora. When she got to the top, she leaned on the railing to catch her breath, and when she did, she realized Keeper had rested his head on the bottom step, his eyes following her.

Macey passed the first door and gestured to it. "This is our room," she said, and Harper peeked in and saw a large, beautiful room with a huge bed covered with a pretty patchwork quilt. "And this would be your room," she said, gesturing to the room across the hall. "I know it's decorated for someone much younger than you right now, but we're planning to redecorate and we thought— since it's going to be your room—maybe you'd like to pick things out."

Harper nodded as she walked into the spacious, bright room with three big windows that looked over the backyard and the river. The walls were painted a pretty ocean green and had creamy white wainscoting along the bottom.

"It's nice," she said softly. "You don't have to change anything." She turned slowly. "Are you sure you wouldn't want me to live in the cupboard under the stairs?"

Macey frowned uncertainly and then realized what she meant. "You mean like Harry Potter?" she asked. "No, we don't want you to live under the stairs!"

Harper pulled out a bureau drawer. Although it was lined with pretty paper, it was empty.

"I thought we could go shopping for some new clothes," Macey offered quickly.

Harper looked down at her too-short jeans and tattered Keds. Other kids always called her pants *high waters* and asked her if she was waiting for a flood. "I guess I could use some new pants."

She sat on the bed and sank into the soft mattress, and then she jiggled it to see if it squeaked. It didn't. She stood up and walked over to the new computer desk under one of the windows and clicked on the lamp. "I don't have a computer," she said, "so I probably won't need a desk."

"We weren't sure if you had one," Ben said. "Macey and I have laptops—which you can use, if you need to. I'm sure, down the road, you'll need one, too, though . . . for school."

Harper stared out the window and bit her lip, fighting back tears—she couldn't believe this was happening. Why were they being so nice? She never expected to be placed with people who were actually friendly and kind—it made her feel funny inside. *It's all too good to be true*, she suddenly decided, *I'm definitely not going to be fooled by all this—they may seem nice, saying they're going to let me help decorate and offering to buy me stuff—but they might just be trying to impress Cora. As soon as she leaves, they might change their tune completely.*

She suddenly reached for Cora's hand. "Let's go," she whispered, trying to avoid Macey's eyes.

Cora frowned. "What's the matter, child? Don't you like your room?"

"It's fine," Harper said in a hushed voice, pulling her toward the door.

Cora gave Macey a puzzled look and allowed herself to be led from the room, and when they reached the bottom step, she let go and sat down near Keeper, who immediately stood up and pushed his head into her chest. Harper leaned over him and buried her tear-streaked face into his soft fur.

"Would you still like some tea, Harper?" Macey asked gently.

Harper wrapped her arms around Keeper's neck and shook her head, and Macey turned to Cora. "How about you, Cora?"

Cora pressed her lips together and nodded. "Yes, please, but if you could just give us a minute."

"Of course," Macey said, nodding. "I also have some chocolate chip blondies that I made last night. Ben, can you help me in the kitchen?" She bit her lip, and when she caught Ben's eye, he raised his eyebrows and shook his head—maybe this wasn't going to go as well as they'd hoped.

"It's not easy for me to get down here you know," Cora said, struggling to settle next to Harper. "You're probably going to have to help me get up."

Harper nodded but kept her eyes focused on Keeper.

"So what's going on?" Cora asked gently. "Before we went upstairs, everything seemed okay. What changed?"

Harper shrugged and stroked Keeper's soft ears. "I don't know. They're too nice—she's saying they're going to let me help decorate, and buy me clothes and a computer . . ." She looked up at Cora, her eyes glassy with tears. "I don't believe it."

Cora sighed and watched her pet the big golden. "Do you honestly think they could be mean and have such a sweet dog?"

Harper shrugged again, considering this, and then a moment later, a big gray tiger cat scooted by. "They have a cat, too?!"

Cora nodded. "They do."

"He looks just like McMuffin."

"He certainly does," Cora said with a smile. "So do you really want to give up the chance to live with this beautiful dog who is obviously in love with you . . . and a cat who looks just like McMuffin?"

Harper shrugged. "I guess I'll give it a chance."

"Good. Now help me up so I can have my tea."

Harper stood up and held out her hands, and as she helped her up, she said, "You still have to come get me if I'm not happy."

"Of course!" she said, pulling her into a hug. "I would go to the ends of the earth for you!"

"Ha!" Harper said, smiling into her old friend's soft bosom. "You'd go to the ends of the earth to get *rid* of me."

Cora pulled back, chuckling. "That's not true, but at least you're smiling."

Just then, Keeper nuzzled between them and Harper stroked his head. "The only reason I'm giving this a try is because of Mr. Peterson's dog . . . and cat," she added softly.

Cora stepped back in surprise. "How do you know about Mr. Peterson's pets?"

"Cora, you know what you always say," Harper said with a grin. "Ain't no flies on me!"

"That's for sure," Cora said, shaking her head. "God help Macey and Ben."

51

"Have a good day, Keep," Harper whispered, wrapping her arms around the big dog's neck. "I wish I could stay home, but the storm's over and school's open again, so I guess I gotta go." After her initial visit to Macey and Ben's house, Harper had reluctantly accepted their invitation to spend the night. *But,* she had told Cora on their way back to the apartment to get her things, *it's only because they have a dog and cat.* Keeper thumped his tail and she held his head in her hands and kissed his brow. "I'll be back. Promise."

"Ready, Harper?" Macey called from the front hall.

"Coming!" she called as she picked up her new backpack and stopped to look in the mirror. She was wearing a new outfit, her favorite of the several she'd picked when she and Macey had ventured out after the storm. They'd met Macey's sister for lunch, and then Harper—who'd decided Maeve was absolutely awesome and funny—had invited her to go shopping with them. This outfit—slim navy capris with a pink flower design and a long-sleeve pink shirt—was one of several Maeve had helped her choose, advising her that pink *always* goes with red hair and freckles. She was also wearing pink canvas Converse high-tops and a pink fleece that was as soft as a cloud.

"Nervous?" Macey asked as they walked to the car, smiling at the outfit.

"A little," Harper replied, trying to sound casual, even though her heart was pounding again. The last two days had gone better than she expected. The hurricane had brushed the coast before heading north, and although it was predicted to gain strength, Georgia had seen the worst it would see. The seventy-mile-an-hour winds and pelting rain had made it hazardous enough for authorities to close schools and businesses, which gave families some unexpected quality time, and Harper's new foster family had made the most of it.

When the power went out, Keeper and Big Mac curled up in the warm glow of the fireplace and dozed as Macey and Ben taught Harper how to play Parcheesi. Keeper had edged closer when they roasted hot dogs and made s'mores, and later, as the storm raged, rattling windows and swaying trees, they'd all tucked safely into sleeping bags with Keeper and Big Mac curled up between them. Harper had gazed into the fire for a long time, pulled Bear close, and fallen asleep with her arm over Keeper's neck. Macey and Ben had lain awake a little longer, talking softly, neither quite able to believe there was a little person in their care, and even though Macey worked in a pediatrician's office, she had definite qualms about the fragile heart beating in Harper's chest, and she prayed nothing would happen.

"Something new for you to worry about," Ben had teased, kissing her good night.

After he'd fallen asleep, too, Macey had continued to watch the glowing embers and felt amazed by everything that had happened. In the short time Harper had been there, she'd already seen the little girl's self-preserving outer shell start to crack, revealing a kindhearted soul who adored animals and had a truly silly sense of humor. She also realized, when Harper drew a portrait of Keeper, that she was a wonderful artist. More than once, she'd had the strange feeling that she was seeing her younger self—a feisty little redhead with a penchant for teasing Ben. "Oh no," he'd laughed goodheartedly, taking it all in stride when she was winning at a game. "I think I'm outnumbered! Keep, you've gotta help me out here!" And the big dog had swished his tail in happy agreement.

"So we're going to the main office first to find out which classroom you're in, and then we're going to stop at the nurse's office and give her your medicine," Macey said. "If you have any problems or don't feel well, you need to go straight to her, okay?"

Harper nodded. "I hope I don't have any problems."

"I hope not, too," Macey said, looking over. "I think you'll like this school. Ben went here when he was your age. It had a different name back then, and it wasn't a charter school like it is now. The way they teach is a little bit different, and they do a lot of fun things."

"How come you didn't go here?"

"I didn't live here till I was in eighth grade."

"Where'd you live before that?"

"Maine."

"That's far away," Harper said matter-of-factly, not sure exactly where Maine was. "How come you moved here?"

"My dad got a new job."

Harper nodded. "I don't know where my dad is."

Macey nodded but didn't say anything—she didn't want to say the *wrong* thing. "Here we are," she said, turning into the school parking lot.

Harper looked at the long, low building and pressed her lips together pensively. "Do they have your number at work?"

"They do. And you have it in your backpack, too."

Harper fumbled around in the pockets of her new backpack, trying to remember where she'd tucked the index card on which Macey had neatly printed their phone numbers. She finally found it, pulled it out, and studied it, trying to commit the numbers to memory. "Are you picking me up?"

"I am," Macey confirmed. When the whirlwind of events had been coming together, making them foster parents, she'd called Marilyn at work to tell her the big news, and Marilyn had told Macey not to worry about a thing—they would manage . . . *and* they were all very happy for them.

"*And* we're having spaghetti for supper," Macey added.

"I *love* spaghetti!" Harper said in surprise.

"I know," Macey said, laughing.

"How do you know that?" Harper asked.

"A little bird told me."

"A little bird named Miss Cora?"

"Maybe."

Harper shook her head and smiled as she climbed out of the car, but when she slung her backpack over her shoulder, she felt a sharp pain shoot through her chest and her smile faded. She clenched her jaw, willing it to go away. She didn't want anything to go wrong today.

52

WITHIN TEN MINUTES OF WALKING THROUGH THE FRONT DOOR, HARPER decided she loved her new school. It wasn't like any other school she'd attended. She followed Macey into the office, where everyone went out of their way to welcome her. The school nurse, Ms. Fisher—who happened to be getting her mail—told her to come by and see her anytime, not just when she *didn't* feel well—which, hopefully wouldn't happen.

Macey finished Harper's paperwork and turned to give her a hug, but the little girl had already turned away. Macey swallowed, taking it in stride, but then Harper surprised her by turning around to give Macey a brave smile and a thumbs-up before following Ms. Fisher—who said Harper's classroom was on the way to her office—down the hall.

"You're going to really like Mrs. Holland," Ms. Fisher said as they walked past several classrooms. "Her two favorite things are animals and art."

"Those are *my* favorite things!" Harper said in surprise.

Ms. Fisher knocked on the last door at the end of the hall and peeked in. "I have a new student for you, Mrs. Holland," she called.

Harper listened to the commotion inside the classroom and felt her heart pounding.

"Come on in, new student!" Mrs. Holland called back cheerfully.

Harper stepped into the bright, airy room and Ms. Fisher introduced her. "Hey, everyone, this is Harper."

Fifteen faces looked up. "Hi, Harper!" they said in unison as Mrs. Holland walked over to shake her hand.

Ms. Fisher handed Harper's paperwork to Mrs. Holland and they spoke briefly outside. Then Mrs. Holland came back in and smiled, her kind eyes seeming to smile, too. "Well, Harper, *you* are just in time. We have a field trip to the Tybee Island Marine Science Center in a couple of weeks and we were just getting ready to watch a documentary about rescuing sea turtles, which is one of the things they do there."

Harper nodded shyly and looked around the room.

"Sam, why don't you show Harper where she can hang her jacket, and then, Harper, you can sit at the desk next to Sam."

Sam showed Harper the cloakroom and then smiled as she slipped behind her new desk.

"Can someone get the lights?" Mrs. Holland asked as she opened the DVD and inserted it into the player.

Harper watched a girl get up from her desk and hurry over to the light switch.

"Thanks, Cara," Mrs. Holland said, aiming the remote at the player and tapping the arrow.

As soon as the first baby turtle swam onto the screen, Harper and the rest of the class were captivated by the plight of the Kemp's ridley sea turtle and the Herculean effort New England beachcombers make each fall to rescue them. When the water temperature drops below fifty-two degrees, the turtles start to seek warmer water, but some have trouble finding their way out of Cape Cod Bay. Volunteers walk the shoreline after every high tide and, if they find a turtle, they move it a safe distance from the water, surround it with seaweed, and notify the Wellfleet Bay Wildlife Sanctuary. A staff member from the sanctuary then heads out— even if it's in the middle of the night—locates the turtle, gently places it in a banana box lined with a soft towel, and brings it back to the sanctuary for evaluation. If it survives, it's transported to the New England Aquarium for rehab, and is eventually transported to marine science centers like the one on Tybee Island, so that it can be released into warmer water.

The class oohed and aahed over every new discovery the volunteers made, especially when it was revealed that more than twelve hundred turtles were rescued in 2014. "Wow!" Sam said in awe. "That's a lot of turtles!"

"It *is* a lot of turtles," Mrs. Holland agreed, turning on the lights. "Now, who can tell me the kind of turtle they rescue the most?"

At the question, sixteen hands shot up in the air.

"Yes, Cara?"

"Kemp's ridley."

"Correct. And what other kinds do they find?"

Fewer hands went up this time.

"Yes, Sam?"

"Green turtles," he answered.

"Good. And does anyone remember the names of the bigger turtles?"

This time, only Harper's hand shot up.

"Harper," she called.

"Loggerheads and leatherbacks."

"Very good!" She paused as she fiddled with the TV remote and then looked back at her class. "Now, everyone, if you would please open your journals, so we can write all this down." She smiled. "Can anyone tell me why we're writing it down?"

Everyone's hand except Harper's shot up this time.

Mrs. Holland picked a boy in the front row. "Jon?"

"Because writing stuff down helps you remember it."

"Right," Mrs. Holland said. "Boy, do I have smart kids!"

As her classmates reached into their desks for their journals, Harper tentatively raised her hand, and Mrs. Holland eyed her. "I bet you're going to tell me you don't have a journal."

Harper nodded and Mrs. Holland smiled. "Well, it just so happens I have an extra one." She opened a closet and pulled out a brand-new navy-blue journal. "Now, don't forget," Mrs. Holland continued, addressing the class. "We can also draw in our journals, so if anyone wants to draw a sea turtle, I have photos up here you can use for reference."

Harper looked through the photos, picked one, walked back to her desk, and spent the next half hour absorbed in shading the delicate wrinkles around the turtle's eyes and on its neck and then tried to meticulously replicate the intricate design on its shell. When she finished, she leaned back in her chair, feeling oddly content, and took the moment to look around her new classroom.

Sunshine streamed through the windows, illuminating all the different study areas—a cozy reading corner with shelves of books and a rug with bean bag chairs; there was a science area with an aquarium filled with goldfish . . . and there was a large cage with two pet guinea pigs! There were also pictures on every inch of wall space: from a huge map of the world to a map of all the constellations in the night sky. There were posters everywhere of every subject from lighthouses to the Iditarod—it was unlike any classroom she'd ever been in! Finally, her eyes landed on a framed print next to the blackboard, and under the title *Class Rules* was an acrostic poem with the word *THINK* written vertically; across from each letter was a matching question: *Is it True? Is it Helpful? Is it Inspiring? Is it Necessary? Is it Kind?* Harper studied the poem, carefully considering the behavior Mrs. Holland expected. She looked back at her drawing, and then realized Sam was looking over her shoulder, too. "Wow, Harper! You're a good artist!" he exclaimed, and immediately, the rest of the class clamored around her desk. Mrs. Holland walked over, too, and nodded approvingly. "Harper, that is beautiful! You'll have to bring it when we go on our field trip to show everyone at the science center."

Harper nodded shyly, her heart swelling with pride.

53

"HOW'RE THINGS GOING?" MAEVE ASKED, TAKING A SIP OF HER COFFEE. The two sisters had met for a quick breakfast before they each had to be at work.

"Okay," Macey said.

Maeve raised her eyebrows. "Just okay? Why? What's going on?"

Macey wrapped her hands around her mug, warming her hands on the chilly autumn morning. "I don't know . . . Harper's been with us for more than a week and it still feels like she's keeping us—or at least me—at arm's length. She adores Keeper and Big Mac—she's constantly wrapping her arms around them, and she even seems to be warming up to Ben, but with me . . . it's different. I mean, it's getting better—the other day when I picked her up from school, she seemed to open up a little . . . I even got her to laugh, but it doesn't last and there're moments when she still seems so wary."

Maeve nodded, swallowing a bite of her Sunny Day Biscuit—a special at another of their favorite breakfast spots, Back in the Day Bakery.

"It's going to take time," Maeve said, brushing the crumbs off her lips with her napkin. "It's a big adjustment and she hasn't really had anyone in her life she can trust. Well, besides Cora."

"I know," Macey said, cutting the cranberry-orange scone on her plate in half. "But she became best friends with you in just one afternoon!"

Maeve laughed. "Oh, well, I can't help it if I have a wonderful, warm personality that draws people in."

"I have a wonderful, warm personality . . . *and* I work with little kids. You work with old people!"

Maeve laughed again. "Hey! My sundowners would take exception to that—they'd say they are young at heart . . . and I think, in some ways, old folks are like little kids. Besides, Harper is sort of an old soul. She's been through—and seen—so much in her short nine years I think she's wise beyond her years."

Macey nodded thoughtfully. "I just thought it would be easier."

"How's she doing in school?"

"She loves it. She's making friends—there's a little boy who sits at the desk next to her—Sam—who she talks about all the time, and her teacher, Mrs. Holland, says she's very smart and adores the two guinea pigs they have in the classroom—their names are Harold and Maude, and she wondered if Harper might like to bring them home over winter break." Macey laughed. "I haven't told Ben yet—just what we need—more animals! But how could I say no? She's like an animal whisperer . . . oh, and did I tell you she's an amazing artist?"

Maeve smiled. "No, you didn't. She and Gage will have to get together—he loves to draw, too. . . . Did you know he went to SCAD?"

Macey took a sip of her coffee and nodded. "Ben told me. He can't figure out why Gage wants to work construction."

"To pay the bills," Maeve said, smiling. "His drawings are incredible, but it's hard to make ends meet. Speaking of construction, though, I heard they finished the house."

Macey nodded. "Just about—Ben said there's a couple little things left—they have to oversee the installation of a granite lamppost and some landscaping, but the Jacksons are moving in next weekend—just in time for Thanksgiving." She broke off a piece of her scone. "Then it's on to the next job. No rest for the weary . . . just like on a farm. By the way, did you ever find out why Gage has no interest in his parents' dairy farm?"

"No," Maeve answered, shaking her head. "He always says it would take a book."

Macey gestured to her plate. "Want the other half of my scone? I didn't touch it."

"You don't want it?"

"No. It's very good, but you can have it." She pushed the plate toward her sister.

"You twisted my arm," Maeve said with a grin. She wrapped it in an extra napkin and tucked it into her bag. Then she checked the time on her phone, and took another sip of her coffee. "We should get going, but I think you need to relax about Harper. It sounds like she's doing great in school, and that is huge," she added, smiling. "It's just going to take time to adjust to all these changes."

"I know," Macey said resignedly.

"How has she been feeling?"

"That's another thing—she never complains, but she gets tired easily and sometimes I catch her rubbing her chest. When I ask her about it, she says it's fine, but I don't know whether to believe her. . . ."

Maeve nodded. "I'm sure she'd let you know if she really didn't feel good."

"I hope so." She smiled. "And as Grandy would say, 'It's always something!'"

"True, but she'd also say to put it in God's hands."

Macey smiled. "Truer words were never spoken!" She drained the last of her coffee. "Ready?"

Maeve nodded. "Is Mom really letting you have Thanksgiving?"

"She is," Macey said, standing. "She said it's time she passed on the torch."

"Wow! I can't believe it!" Maeve said as they walked outside.

"I know, right? That's exactly what Ben said."

"Well, I'm sure you can pull it off—you're amazing, and don't let anyone tell you different." Maeve gave her sister a hug. "No worries about Harper. She'll come around," she added with a smile.

"Thanks," Macey said, "and thanks for breakfast."

"You're welcome." She turned to go, but then looked back. "Let me know what I can bring."

"I will . . . extra wine, for sure!"

Maeve laughed. "You got it!"

54

"How was the field trip?" Macey asked as Harper climbed into her car.

"Pretty good."

Macey waited for her to continue, but Harper just looked out the window. "That's it? Just *pretty good*? Did they like your drawing of the loggerhead turtle?"

"Mm-hmm," Harper said with a nod.

Macey looked over at the little girl sitting next to her. "Everything okay?"

"Mm-hmm," Harper answered, mustering a smile.

"Any chest pains?"

Harper looked back out the window and shook her head.

Macey frowned. "You sure?"

"Mm-hmm. What's for supper?" she asked, trying to change the subject.

"Pizza."

Harper's eyes lit up. "Pepperoni?"

"Is that what you like on your pizza?"

Harper nodded.

"Pepperoni it is!"

"Yes!" Harper said, gesturing with a fist pump.

When they got back to the house, Ben was just coming outside with Keeper, and the big dog bounded over to the car. "Hey, Keep!" Harper said happily, forgetting her backpack and slamming the car door. "Where's your ball?"

The golden trotted happily across the yard, scooped up two tennis balls, hurried back, and dropped them at Harper's feet. She picked them up and threw them, and he bounded away.

Macey watched for a few minutes and then reached into the back seat for the forgotten backpack, slung it over her shoulder with her own bag, and walked toward the house.

"How was your day?" he asked.

"Good . . . busy. I swear there are more kids out sick than in school these days."

"Well, don't bring those germs home," he teased, stepping away from her.

"Very funny," she said, rolling her eyes. "How was your day?"

"Good. Just a couple more details to tie up."

"Great," she said, smiling. "I bet you'll be glad to put this job behind you."

"I will, especially because there's another one waiting . . ."

Macey's eyes lit up. "They took your bid?"

"They did."

"That's so great!"

"It is," Ben said, smiling—he always felt better when he knew for certain they had another job lined up. "How was the field trip?" he asked, watching Harper play with Keeper.

She shook her head. "I asked, but all I got was *pretty good*."

Ben nodded, knowing Macey wished Harper would open up a little more.

"We seemed to be doing so well those first couple days," she said, "when we were all huddled in front of the fireplace during the storm. I don't know what changed."

"Maybe we'll have to do that again—make a fire and watch a movie or play games—we don't have to lose power to do that. Besides, Cora said it might take time."

"I know, but I didn't think it would take *this* long."

"It's only been a couple of weeks."

"It's almost three!" Macey countered.

"You gotta have faith," Ben teased. "Isn't that what your grandmother would say?"

Macey smiled. "It *is* what she would say." She started to walk around to the back porch, and then called over her shoulder. "Pepperoni pizza tonight."

"All right! That's my favorite."

"Harper's, too!"

Ben smiled and then turned to Harper. "You guys coming in?" Ben called.

The little girl looked over. "One more throw."

Ben nodded and followed Macey inside while Harper threw the two balls as far as she could. Keeper bounded off, and when Harper was sure Ben and Macey weren't looking, she rubbed her chest. "C'mon, Keep. Let's go in." She walked slowly toward the back porch and up the steps with the big dog beside her. When she got to the top step, she sat down to catch her breath and Keeper pushed his bowed head into her chest. "That's exactly where it hurts," she whispered, fighting back tears. She pushed her cheek into his long, wispy fur and then heard a familiar tinkling sound above her head. She looked up and, for the first time, noticed the silver spoon chimes, just like the ones she'd made with Tom when she was little. She rubbed her chest again and finally felt the pain ease.

55

"HEY, SLEEPYHEADS," MACEY SAID SOFTLY. "YOU GETTING UP TODAY?"

Harper opened her eyes, blinked at the bright sunlight streaming into her bedroom, and felt Keeper's long body pressed against her blanket. After Harper had come to live with them—and Keeper realized she would be sleeping upstairs—he'd quickly overcome his fear of going up and down steps. "Yes, we're getting up," she said, stroking his velvety ears, "aren't we, Keep?" The big dog yawned contentedly, stretched, and closed his eyes, and Harper laughed. "Well, *I'm* getting up," she said, pushing off her blanket and covering him with it. He peeked out, shook it off, and hopped down the steps Ben had made for him to get on and off her bed.

"How'd you sleep?" Macey asked.

"Pretty good."

"Ben made cinnamon buns before he left, and I just took them out of the oven."

"Yum!" Harper said, smiling a genuine smile that surprised Macey. "Where did he go?"

"He went to meet the man whose house he just finished."

"On Thanksgiving?"

"That's what I said," Macey said, laughing, "but he promised he'd be right back."

"Okay," Harper said, shuffling across the hall to the bathroom. When she came back, Macey had gone downstairs, but she'd left behind a pile of folded, clean laundry. Harper pulled a long-sleeve T-shirt from the pile—another one she'd picked out when they'd gone shopping with Maeve. Maeve had even gotten the same shirt in her size, too. Harper shook it open and read: "I HAVE RED HAIR BECAUSE GOD KNEW I SHOULD COME WITH A WARNING LABEL!" She smiled—she'd have to wear it the next time she saw Cora.

"Harp, you comin'?" Macey called up the stairs.

"Be right down," she called back, pulling the shirt over her head.

She hopped down the stairs and found Keeper already at Macey's feet, watching her every move. She followed his gaze and her own eyes grew wide. "Wow! That's one big-ass turkey!" she said, admiring the twenty-two-pound bird Macey was stuffing, but when Macey looked up with a frown, Harper covered her mouth. "Oops! Sorry!"

Macey nodded and then saw her shirt and smiled.

"Like it?" Harper said, grinning.

"I do," she replied, laughing. "It's perfect."

"Maybe Maeve will wear hers."

"Maybe," Macey said, making a mental note to text her sister. Then she gestured with a stuffing-filled spoon toward the cinnamon buns. "Want to spread the frosting on those?"

"Sure," Harper said, reaching for a spatula. She spread the creamy white substance onto the sweet rolls and then watched, her mouth watering, as it melted and dripped down the sides.

"Yumm," she murmured, licking the spatula.

"You should have one while they're warm."

Harper eagerly scooped one onto a plate. "Want one?"

"You bet," Macey said. "I just want to finish this goopy job first."

Harper eyed the turkey. "Cora says you have to wash your hands with hot, sudsy water anytime you touch eggs or raw meat so you don't get sam-on-ella."

Macey laughed. "And she would be right."

Harper pulled up a stool to watch Macey work, took a bite of her cinnamon bun, and came away with a sugary grin. "How come you have such a big turkey?"

"Because there are a lot of people comin' over."

"There are?"

"Mm-hmm. My mom and dad, and Maeve and her boyfriend, Gage . . ."

"Do they have kids?"

"No, but Gage has a puppy . . . actually, I guess he's more of a dog now, but he still acts like a puppy."

"What's his name?"

"Gus."

Harper nodded thoughtfully. "How come you and Ben don't have kids?"

Macey stopped what she was doing and looked up. Maybe it was because she was caught off guard by Harper's directness, but she found herself being completely honest as she answered, "Ben and I have always wanted to have kids—we love kids, but I've had a lot of trouble carrying a baby, and I've had several miscarriages." She paused. "Do you know what that is?"

"Is that when you lose a baby before it grows?"

Macey nodded, surprised by the awareness of such a young girl.

"I'm sorry," Harper said softly.

"Thanks, Harper."

"Is that why you're getting into fostering?"

"Partly," Macey said, still stuffing the turkey. "I also feel like it's something that's meant to happen." Macey looked over, realized Harper was looking at her intently, and laughed. "Do you know what I mean?"

"I guess so," Harper said. "Sometimes, you just sort of get this feeling that you're s'posed to do something—or *not* do something—and you don't know exactly where it's coming from."

"Exactly . . . but sometimes when I feel that way I wonder if it's coming from my grandmother. She was such a special person—always willing to help people, always being the first to volunteer and even though she passed away a long time ago, I feel like, sometimes, she's nudging me to do things."

Harper nodded. "I know what you mean. Even though I was little when my mom died, I sometimes feel like she's nudging me, too."

Just then, there was a sound on the back porch, and Keeper scrambled to his feet and started barking. "It's just me, silly," Ben said, coming through the door. He looked at Harper. "Well, look who decided to grace us with her presence!"

Harper smiled.

"How come you don't have the parade on?" he asked, turning on the TV on the counter.

"I forgot!" Macey said.

Harper frowned. "What parade?"

"The one-and-only Macy's Thanksgiving Day Parade," he said as the screen flickered on, revealing a tremendous Snoopy balloon floating down Sixth Avenue in New York City.

"Macey has a parade?" Harper teased, giggling.

"Yep! I have my very own parade," Macey said as she washed her hands. As she dried them, she looked at Ben. "Soo . . . how'd it go?"

"Great!" Ben teased with a grin.

Macey frowned. "Great, he loved the house, or great, he paid you?"

"Both," he said, patting his chest pocket.

"Nice," she said. She always loved when Ben got final payment for a big job. "We have a lot to be thankful for," she murmured as he pulled them both into a hug.

"Don't forget Keeper and Big Mac," Harper said, pulling them both down to include the happy-go-lucky retriever hopping around them and the cat who had just wandered into the warm kitchen.

"Yeah," Ben said. "All Keeper's thinking about is turkey!" And they laughed, knowing it was true. Finally, they stood, but Harper moved to Keeper's bed, and pulled Big Mac onto her lap, and then Keeper moseyed over and tried to get on the bed, too.

"You're so silly, Keep," Macey said, laughing and pulling her phone out to take a picture. "Ben, get him to look up."

Ben held a dog treat above Macey's head, and Harper held on to him so he wouldn't get up. "Stay here," she whispered, and just as he turned and licked her cheek, Macey tapped her phone.

"Perfect," she said, looking at the image.

56

"WE'RE HERE!" MAEVE CALLED CHEERILY, LETTING IN A GUST OF CHILLY November air, but before she could even get the door open, the lanky yellow Lab tethered to her wrist pushed his way in and galloped down the hall, towing her along. Laughing and trying to keep the still-warm pumpkin pie in her hands upright, Maeve tumbled into the kitchen. "Happy Thanksgiving!" she said, laughing breathlessly.

"Hi, Maeve!" Harper said, hopping off her stool to give her a warm hug.

Macey watched Harper's exuberant greeting and then held out her hands, palms up, feigning dismay. "I must be a potted plant."

Maeve laughed, set her pie on the counter, and gave her sister a hug. "Happy Thanksgiving, Mace!"

"Happy Thanksgiving," Macey replied.

"Is this Gus?" Harper asked, her arms around the big puppy slobbering her with wet kisses.

"It most definitely is," Maeve confirmed as he and Keeper wiggled around each other. She produced two bottles of wine from her bag, held them up, and smiled at her sister. "Want these in the fridge?"

"*One* can go in the fridge," Macey said, rummaging through her kitchen drawer. "But one can be opened right now." With a triumphant smile she pulled out a corkscrew. "Would you do the honors?"

"Of course," Maeve said, taking off her coat and draping it over a chair.

"You wore your shirt!" Harper exclaimed.

"Of course I wore my shirt!" Maeve said, holding it out by the hem. "We gingers have to stick together!"

"We do," Harper agreed. She looked at Macey. "Macey, you should get one, too."

"Maybe I will," Macey said, surprised but pleased to be invited to join their ginger club and thankful she'd remembered to text her sister. She opened the cabinet and took out two wineglasses. "Where's Gage?"

"Outside, talking to Ben," she said, pouring a glass of chardonnay and handing it to her. "Where are Mom and Dad? They're never late."

"They are today. Mom insisted on making just about everything," she said. "She lets me host, but she still wants to bring half the side dishes . . . and the apple pie, of course! Ben is thankful for that, though—he loves her apple pie."

"Hello! Hello!" A voice boomed from the front porch which triggered the self-appointed welcoming committee to hurry down the hall. "Well, hello to you, too!" they heard the voice say.

"Hi, Dad!" Macey called, hurrying after the dogs to see if he needed help. She unburdened him of the box full of warm dishes he was carrying, and gave him a hug.

"Does Mom need help?" Maeve asked, coming up behind them.

Hal gave his younger daughter a hug. "I think Gage and Ben

are bringing everything else in." He knelt down between the two wiggling dogs to give them a proper greeting and looked up at Macey.

"It's nice of you to host, sweetie, but, honestly, I think it would be easier if we just had it at our house—your mother brought half the kitchen over!" He shook his head and then spied Harper standing in the doorway. "Hey, there's my pal."

Harper smiled shyly. She had met Macey's parents on a couple of occasions already, and although she liked them, she found Mr. Lindstrom's gregarious personality a little intimidating, and Macey had had to ask her dad to be a little less vivacious until Harper got used to him. So with Macey and Maeve looking on, Hal pulled the two dogs close and made them sit.

"What do you think of these two rascals, Harper?" he asked, and Harper nodded approvingly. "Macey tells me you're a dog lover, too. . . . Is that true?" Harper nodded again, and he smiled. Then, out of the blue and without prodding or invitation, she ran into his arms and gave him a hug.

"Happy Thanksgiving," he said softly, looking up at Macey and winking, but she just shook her head and laughed—Harper was full of surprises!

They heard Gage and Ben coming through the kitchen door, and then Ben calling out, "Mace, where do you want all this food?"

"It's piping hot," Ruth called from behind them. "If the turkey's ready, we can just eat."

"Happy Thanksgiving, Mom," Macey said, coming into the kitchen and giving her a hug. "The turkey *is* ready, but I still have to make gravy, so we'll just keep everything warm in the oven for a few minutes, is that okay?"

The petite silver-haired woman looked dismayed. "Okay," she said reluctantly.

"Relax, Mom, it'll still be hot," her daughter assured her.

Ruth nodded, and then realized Harper was watching and tried to make light of it. "Don't mind me, Harper!" she said, giving her a hug, "I just like my food hot!" She laughed at her own eccentricity. "Happy Thanksgiving! How are you?"

"I'm fine," Harper answered softly.

Maeve brought Gage over. "Harper, this is my boyfriend, Gage."

Harper nodded, studying Gage's boyish face and blue eyes as she politely shook his hand.

"It's nice to meet you, too," Gage said. "Maeve tells me you're quite the artist."

She nodded.

"I'd love to see your artwork sometime."

"Okay," she said, a smile lighting her face.

"Gage likes to draw, too," Maeve explained.

Harper nodded, her hand resting on Keeper's head. "I can go get some right now, if you want," she offered hopefully.

"That would be awesome," Gage said.

"Okay! I'll be right back," she said. "Keep, you stay here," she added, gesturing with her hand, and then hurrying excitedly up the stairs. When she got to her room, though, she could barely catch her breath.

"Go away," she pleaded, leaning against the door and rubbing her chest with her fist as tears filled her eyes.

"Please, go away," she begged. "I don't want to have surgery . . . I don't want some stranger's heart."

A few minutes later, Maeve called up the stairs. "We're having snacks, Harp. You coming back down?"

Harper wiped her eyes. "Yes," she called back. "I'll be right there."

THAT EVENING, AFTER THE LEFTOVERS HAD BEEN DIVIDED UP AND SENT home with Hal and Ruth, and Gage and Maeve, Harper curled up on the couch between Ben and Macey to watch an old movie—a favorite of Macey's, but one Harper had never seen.

"Hey, they're just like us when Gus is here," Harper said after the movie started, nodding in the direction of Big Mac and Keeper, who were curled up together in front of the fireplace.

"It *is* just like us," Macey agreed.

"Except, I don't know if Keep could make such a long journey on three legs," Ben mused, standing up to add another log to the fire.

"I think he could," Macey said.

"Maybe," Ben said, still sounding skeptical. He sat down and lay his arm along the back of the couch.

Macey had always loved the movie, *Homeward Bound*, about two dogs and a cat making a long journey home, and she'd often dreamed about sharing it with her own kids someday, but as she watched it now, with Harper, she found it hard to focus on the screen. She found herself listening to the little girl's laughter during the funny scenes and feeling surprise when her small hand gripped hers during the scary ones. As the movie reached its climactic end, Macey was pulled back to the present, though, by the sound of the hapless dog, Chance, shouting, "Turkey! Turkey! Turkey!" and she couldn't help but laugh.

"What do you think, Harp?" Ben asked. "Could Keep make a journey like that?"

"Definitely," she said. "He loves us too much to give up!"

Macey smiled. "Having love like that is probably what got him through having surgery and learning to get around on three legs."

Harper nodded thoughtfully and then wrapped her arms around his neck. "Is that true, Keep?" she asked, and the big dog swished his tail and then gently pushed his noble head into her chest, making her laugh.

57

"Good morning, class!" Mrs. Holland called cheerily, sweeping into the classroom. "Since it's such a nice day out . . . *and* the last day before our winter break, you can leave your jackets on because we're going outside to explore the beach. Let's see what treasures the tide washed up this week, and maybe we'll even see a sea turtle. Then we're going to come back in and write about the things we've discovered."

Harper could hardly believe her ears! She hung up her backpack and then traipsed out into the sunshine with Sam. "I can't believe we're having class on the beach!"

"Yeah, we do this sometimes," Sam said, grinning.

"Remember not to get too close to the water," Mrs. Holland reminded as they walked along the sand, looking for anything that might be of interest. Suddenly, Harper spied a large sun-bleached shell with a long tail. "I found something!" she shouted, and everyone hurried over.

"Nice!" Mrs. Holland said, nodding. "Does anyone know what it is?"

"It's a horseshoe crab," Sam said.

"It is indeed," agreed Mrs. Holland. "Horseshoe crabs have

been around for a very long time. Anyone care to guess how long?"

"A thousand years?" Sam offered.

"More than that! Someone recently discovered a fossil in Manitoba, Canada, that proved the ancestors of horseshoe crabs, like this one, have been around for four hundred forty-five *million* years!"

"No way!" Jon said.

"Way!" Mrs. Holland said. "Unbelievable, right? And not only that, but they aren't really crabs . . . they're chelicerates. Can you say that?"

"Che-lic-er-ates," the class repeated dutifully.

"Very good," Mrs. Holland said with a smile. "Crabs and other crustaceans have antennae, but this critter, as you can see, does not, but he *does* have all these cool eyes," she added, pointing to the different spots on the shell. "Horseshoe crabs are arthropods, so they don't have white blood cells—like we do—to fight infection. They have blue blood—"

"*Blue* blood?!" Sam interrupted.

"Yes, blue blood that's filled with amebocytes, which fight bacteria in their own way—they release a gooey substance that surrounds and blocks germs from spreading."

"Wow! That's so cool!" Cara said.

"It *is* really cool, Cara, because way back when scientists discovered this, they started using the amebocytes from horseshoe crabs' blood to make sure vaccines and other injectable medicines were safe for humans. If the amebocytes started to release the goo, scientists knew the injectable medicine wasn't safe and they had to go back to the drawing board. Today, the test is mandatory for any medicine that is injected with a needle."

"So anytime we get a shot, it's been tested with horseshoe crab blood?" Sam asked.

"It has," Mrs. Holland said, nodding.

"Is that a stinger?" Harper asked, pointing to its tail.

"Good question, Harper," Mrs. Holland said, "That tail looks like it would really hurt, doesn't it? But it's not a stinger. Its purpose is to help the horseshoe crab steer—like a rudder—or turn itself over if it gets turned upside down."

Sam touched the shell with the toe of his sneaker. "Is it dead?"

"Another great question!" Mrs. Holland said, gently turning the shell over. "It is *not* dead. It's just empty . . . which might make you wonder if there's a horseshoe crab now running around the ocean floor, naked."

At this, they all giggled.

"But, no worries!" she continued. "This empty shell is called a molt. As a horseshoe crab grows and matures, it also grows a new bigger shell, and when it's ready and solid, it sheds—or molts—its old shell. That shell is also called an exoskeleton, and because they just get left behind, light and empty, on the ocean floor, they often wash up on the beach. So it's not just kiddos like you who outgrow their clothes . . . horseshoe crabs get new outfits, too!"

"Cool!" Sam said.

"Very cool," Mrs. Holland agreed. "When we get back to the classroom, I'll show you a video of an actual horseshoe crab molting." She picked up the shell and put it in her basket. "We'll take this back in case anyone wants to draw it in their journal."

"Let's keep looking!" Sam shouted, and everyone hurried off, looking for more treasures.

Harper lingered, though. "I'd *love* to draw it," she said softly.

Mrs. Holland put her arm around her. "And I'm sure you will do a wonderful job! But first, are you going to go find us another great treasure?"

Harper nodded and hurried after the other kids.

An hour later—after sitting in a circle and discussing their discoveries: another horseshoe crab molt, a spider crab that was very much alive and skittering down the beach, several sand dollars, three whelk shells, ten hermit crabs, and a striped burrfish puffer—they tromped back toward the school.

"Mr. Fielding is going to love us for bringing half the beach back!" Mrs. Holland said, stomping the sand off her feet and looking at her small troupe of kids. She started counting heads— "Fourteen, fifteen"—frowned, and counted again. "Where's Harper?"

Sam turned around in surprise. "She was right next to me. . . ."

Mrs. Holland's eyes grew wide as she tried to decide whether to have the kids help her look for Harper or send them inside. "Okay," she said, trying to calm her voice. "I'd like you guys to *walk* back to the classroom." She turned to Sam. "Sam, would you please run to the office and tell them I need some help on the beach?"

"Mrs. Holland, do you want *us* to help?" a chorus of voices asked.

"No," she said firmly. "I want you to head directly inside."

"Ohh," they moaned.

"Go along! And Sam, please hurry!"

"Harper!" Mrs. Holland called as she ran back to the beach, scanning the waves. Her biggest fear, anytime she brought her class to the beach, was the water, but all she saw were snow-white seagulls bobbing up and down. "Harper!" she called again and again, running back along the way they'd come. Over the sound of the surf, she heard a faint cry and turned to see the little girl curled up on the sand. "Oh no!" she cried, kneeling next to her. "Harper, what's wrong?"

Harper moaned. "I thought if I sat down, I'd feel better, but it only got worse."

"What got worse?"

"My chest—it hurts so much."

Mrs. Holland pulled her phone out of her pocket and dialed 911.

"I didn't want anything to go wrong," Harper whispered, trying to catch her breath as tears streamed down her cheeks. "Please don't let me die . . ."

While Mrs. Holland spoke to a dispatcher, she saw two of her colleagues running down the beach. She waved and they hurried over, but when they tried to help Harper sit up, she cried out, so Mr. Matheson, the gym teacher, raced back to show the ambulance where they were while Ms. Fisher held Harper's hand.

Within minutes, the ambulance screamed into the parking lot and the kids in Mrs. Holland's class all rushed to the window to watch the commotion. After several minutes, a stretcher was loaded into the back.

"Do you think she's okay?" Sam asked as the ambulance sped away with its lights and siren blaring.

"I don't know," Cara said. "The ambulance is hurrying, so she must be alive."

"I hope you're right," Sam whispered.

58

"MACEY, CALL FOR YOU ON TWO," MARILYN SAID, PEEKING AROUND THE staff room door. "It's the school."

"Uh-oh, Mace, now the fun begins," Melissa teased. "When you're a mom, you're always on call!"

"I'm ready," Macey said, smiling as she picked up the phone.

"Hi, this is Macey . . . ," she said, and then the color drained from her face. "I'll be right there." She hung up the phone, her hands shaking. "Harper had a problem at school and they've rushed her to the hospital! I . . . I have to go!"

"Of course!" Melissa said, suddenly feeling terrible for teasing her.

Dr. Hack—who'd heard the news from the hall—looked in. "Did they say anything else?"

"They said she was having chest pains, and the ambulance was taking her to the Heart Hospital at St. Joe's."

"Okay . . . well, let us know as soon as you can."

Macey nodded as she grabbed her things. "Okay, thank you!"

She ran to her car, her heart pounding, and called Ben. He heard the panic in her voice and told her he'd meet her there.

Macey looked up at the bright blue December sky. "Why, God? Why is this happening?!" she railed. "Is this poor child doomed, just like all my other babies? Why are you doing this to us? Do you think you could cut her . . . *and* us a break? If anything happens to her, it'll be the last time you'll ever hear from me. We stuck our necks out to bring her into our hearts and our home, and if anything happens, we are through!" Tears filled her eyes. "Please don't let anything happen to her. Please let her be okay . . ." She wiped her eyes and tried to focus on the road.

Ten minutes later, she ran through the emergency room doors and found Cora already waiting.

Cora stood up as soon as she saw Macey and hurried over to give her a hug. "The hospital called me because I'm still the only one on her paperwork. Oh, Macey, I'm so sorry I let you get into this! All you need is more worries and heartache."

Macey shook her head. "Don't be sorry, Cora. We are in this because we want to be, but I have more than a few choice words for God."

"I know, baby. I have a few choice words for him, too . . . and trust me, he hears us."

"Do you know anything? Have you seen her?"

Cora shook her head. "No, I just got here, and when I spoke to the lady in admitting, she said they are still trying to stabilize her, and a doctor will come out as soon as we can see her."

Just then, Ben came through the doors and Macey waved. "Any news?" he asked, hurrying over. Macey told him the little they knew and he looked around, half expecting to see a doctor appear. "What did the school say?"

"Just that she was having chest pains, but she was able to tell them what was wrong."

Ben nodded and started to pace—something he always did when he was stressed or didn't feel well. "Why don't you sit down," Macey suggested, and he nodded distractedly and sat next to her, but a moment later, he was up again, and Macey knew it was no use. She looked over at Cora and realized her eyes were closed, but her lips were moving—she was praying. Macey looked around the waiting room—it was decorated for Christmas. She'd been looking forward to celebrating the holidays with Harper—she and Ben had already bought several gifts, including a basic laptop for her to use in school, but now, she just wanted her to be okay.

Finally, after what felt like an eternity, the doors to the hallway swung open and a young doctor came out. He stopped briefly at admissions and then looked in their direction. "Cora Grant?"

Cora opened her eyes and stood. "I'm here," she called. He walked over and Cora quickly introduced Macey and Ben as Harper's foster parents.

"How is she?" Macey asked anxiously.

He took a deep breath and let it out slowly. "Harper is in critical condition. While she was in the ambulance, she went into cardiac arrest, but the paramedics administered CPR, and as soon as we got her in, we used the defibrillator. Thankfully, her heart responded. She's a real trouper."

"She is that," Cora said, nodding and smiling.

"We know she has a weak heart, but we're not sure what brought this on. She was supposed to be avoiding stressful situations." He looked from Macey to Cora. "Has anything happened that might have added to her stress?"

Cora sighed. "What hasn't happened to that poor child? She ran away, was missing for a couple of days. She found a new home with these good people," she said, motioning to Ben and Macey, "and recently started a new school—it seemed to be going well, but that's a lot of change all at once."

The doctor nodded. "That could do it," he said. "With her condition, she needs to be in a stable environment, and she needs to take it easy."

Macey spoke up. "Our home is a stable environment, but every time I ask her how she feels, she says she feels fine."

The doctor nodded thoughtfully. "It's possible she hasn't been completely forthcoming. Do you think she's frightened by the idea of having surgery?"

Macey and Ben looked at each other. "I guess it's possible," he said. "We really haven't talked about it with her."

The doctor nodded. "It's hard to know what's going on in a little kid's head—she might be trying to avoid surgery, especially if she doesn't really understand. Anyway, we're going to do more tests, but I'm also going to recommend she be moved up on the transplant list. That way, when a heart does become available, we will be able to move forward. If we wait, and she gets weaker, we might lose the opportunity. We will also have to do a better job of making sure she understands what is happening so she feels safe—stress on a fragile heart is one of the worst things."

Macey and Ben could barely believe what they were hearing. Ben looked over, saw tears welling up in Macey's eyes, and reached for her hand. The doctor saw her tears, too. "How long have you been Harper's foster parents?"

"Almost two months," Ben said.

The doctor nodded. "You're very brave to take in a child with such a serious health problem, and I promise you, we will do everything we can to help her get better. The risk of rejection is always a possibility, but if we get a good heart and she takes her antirejection medicine—which is essential—it's possible she will recover without any issues. Lots of children even go on to play sports. The important thing is, she will feel better . . . better than she's felt in a very long time."

"Can we see her?" Macey asked.

He nodded. "She's sleeping, but you can see her for a few minutes. And then, if you'd like to come back tonight, after she's been moved to a room in intensive care, that might be best."

He led them to Harper's room, and when Macey saw her, the tears she'd been fighting spilled down her cheeks. Harper looked so small and still and pale. She had tubes and wires crisscrossing her body and an oxygen tube in her nose. The monitor beside her bed was humming and beeping quietly. Through the blur of tears, Macey gazed at her. Where was the little girl who'd laughed while teasing Ben, and who'd fallen head over heels in love with Keeper and Big Mac, wrapping her arms around them every chance she got? And what about poor Keep? What would he think when they came home without her? Would his heart break, too? Macey had always thought the ache she'd felt when she lost a baby was too much to bear, but now, the thought of losing Harper was beyond unbearable—she was a living, breathing child with a sweet, funny personality that had just needed a little encouragement to come out. She wiped her eyes and squeezed Ben's hand.

59

As soon as Cora walked out of the emergency room—where there was no service—her phone started to ring. She looked at the screen and realized she'd missed several calls from Frank, and her worried thoughts raced to her own children.

She picked up, paused to listen, and then answered, "I know I give you a hard time when you don't answer, but I was in the ER with Harper, and there's no cell service in there. Is everything okay?" She paused again. "Yes, she's critical, but stable . . . mm-hmm . . . yes, milk . . . I have to stop at the store anyway, and then I'll be right along. Oh, right . . . I forgot I had to pick them up! I will go there first. I'm sorry you couldn't reach me . . . Love you, too."

She closed the screen and sighed. "There's too much goin' on," she murmured as she unlocked her car.

"I need a new head! And a new body, too, Lord, if you're taking orders," she said, looking up at the now slate-gray sky. "How could I forget to pick up my own children?!" She pulled out of the parking lot and headed to the YMCA to pick up Rudy and Joe, who were finally enrolled in an after-school program so Frank could try out for the basketball team. The program wasn't free, though, and it was going to make it hard for them to make ends meet, but if it helped Frank get a scholarship, it would be worth it, especially after the conversation he'd had with their neighbor. The way Frank told it, Mr. Jefferson had been watching him play basketball at the park and he'd approached him afterward.

"That's some jump shot you've got, Frank."

"Thanks, Mr. Jefferson. Do you play?"

"Four years at point with the Jaguars."

"At Augusta?!"

"Yes, and I still keep in touch with the coach."

"Yeah?"

Mr. Jefferson had nodded. "Yeah. And I reckon you could, too, if you keep playing the way I've seen you play these last few weeks. I'll put in a good word when the time comes . . . as long as you stay on the straight and narrow *and* keep your grades up."

"Thanks," Frank had said, smiling, and when he'd gotten home he'd just about burst with the news.

Yes, indeed, a scholarship would be nice! Cora thought, *not to mention the incentive Jamal Jefferson had given Frank to keep his grades up and stay out of trouble. It would be nice to have one less thing to worry about!*

She pulled up in front of the building and saw Rudy and Joe sitting on the front stoop with one of the staff members. Cora rolled down her window. "I'm so sorry I'm late," she called. "I had an emergency. Thank you for waiting."

The woman nodded and got up to go to her car while Rudy and Joe climbed in. "Mama, all the other kids got picked up a half hour ago," Rudy scolded. "What emergency did you have?"

"I'm sorry, Rudy. Harper had to go to the hospital."

"Oh no! Is she okay?!" Rudy asked, her voice suddenly full of concern.

"Yes, she's okay. But the doctor is moving her up on the transplant list, so it *is* serious."

"Oh no," Rudy whispered again in disbelief. "Can we go see her?"

"No, baby. She's in intensive care."

"Is she gonna die?" Joe asked.

Cora looked at her son's face in the rearview mirror and didn't know what to say. She didn't want to mislead her children, but the situation was grave and she didn't want them to worry, either. "The doctors are taking good care of her, but we need to keep her in our prayers," she said softly.

"We will," Joe said.

"Yes, Mama," Rudy said solemnly, looking out the window.

"How was your day?" she asked, changing the subject.

"Okay," Rudy said. "Kari goes to the after-school program."

"Lana's daughter?"

"Mm-hmm."

"Hmm . . . I wonder if Lana would want to share picking you up."

"Kayden goes, too."

"Yeah," Joe piped, "and he just got a PlayStation Four!"

"Lucky him," Cora said.

"Can *we* get one?"

"Joe, you know if we got one, you'd have to get all new games," Cora said. "What do we do with your old games?"

He shrugged. "I don't know, but it would be worth it because I could get the new *Grand Theft Auto*!"

"Even if we did get a PlayStation Four, you are not getting *Grand Theft Auto*."

"Why not?" he asked in dismay.

"It's too violent."

"Kayden has it."

"I don't care what Kayden has. You're not Kayden."

Joe huffed and crossed his arms.

"Kari has a new bike, too," Rudy said.

Cora looked over. "I'm sorry, baby, but we cannot get a new bike, either. We cannot afford anything new right now, especially since we just signed up for this after-school program."

Rudy looked up at the ceiling in dismay. "I don't even want to go to the stupid after-school program. The only reason we have to go is so Frank can play stupid basketball," she said. "If you ask me, it's a waste of money. *I* could watch Joe."

"Child, we have been through this before. You are nine years old and you are not coming home to an empty house!"

"Waste your money, then!" she huffed.

"Lordy, give me patience," Cora sighed as she pulled into a convenience store to get bread and milk. "Let's go," she commanded. "You cannot stay in the car, either."

"If you won't leave me in the car, why don't you let *me* go in and buy the milk and bread? You can watch me the whole time and you'll find out how responsible I am."

"Rudy, let's just go in together so we can get home. I am making French toast for supper."

"I *love* French toast," Joe said happily, reaching for his door handle.

"I'm not going in," Rudy said firmly, crossing her arms.

Cora looked over. "I know you're growing up—much too fast, and you're becoming more responsible, but I am very tired, and tonight is not a good night."

Rudy stared straight ahead, her arms firmly in place.

"Fine," Cora said, reaching into her bag for a ten-dollar bill. "You may go inside and buy the bread and milk. Make sure you check the freshness date on both and be sure the cashier gives you the correct change."

"Can I go?" Joe pleaded.

"No, you stay right here."

"Oooh," Joe groaned, slumping in his seat.

Rudy's face beamed as she climbed out, carefully looked both ways, and walked proudly across the parking lot and into the store. Cora watched her daughter as she continued down the first aisle to the coolers to pick out a gallon of milk, and then as she reached into the back of the bread shelf to get the freshest loaf. Lugging the milk and bread to the counter, Rudy glanced out at the car as she waited to pay. Cora smiled and Rudy gave her mom a determined nod. Cora continued to watch as Rudy carefully counted her change and then came back outside, even holding the door for an elderly man who was coming in. Before she stepped off the curb, she looked both ways, and then hurried to the car, barely able to suppress the grin on her face.

"Good job!" Cora said as Rudy climbed in, set the milk on the floor, and put the bread on her lap. "You even remembered to look both ways."

"Yes, and I even held the door for that old man."

"You did indeed. You are turning into a very responsible young lady."

Rudy nodded proudly.

"Next time, I wanna go in," Joe piped from the back seat.

"You're too young," Rudy said. "You have to wait till you're at least nine."

"I could do it. I know how."

Rudy looked over at her mother, and Cora glanced in her rearview mirror. "You can help me make French toast, Joe."

"Yes!" he shouted, pumping his fist.

Cora looked back at Rudy and smiled conspiratorially, and Rudy grinned. She couldn't believe how grown up her little girl was getting to be—where did the time go? Before she knew it, Frank would be heading off to college and Rudy would be in middle school. Thank God they were healthy—life was hard enough without having serious health problems!

60

Ben leaned back in the chair next to Harper's hospital bed. He had stopped by on his way home not only to see Harper but also—because Macey had been staying over at night after working all day—to see Macey.

"How's the new job going?" she asked.

"Pretty well. It's going to keep us plenty busy." He paused. "Henry called last night. I told him about everything that's been going on and he said to tell you they're thinking of us."

Macey smiled, picturing their old friend. "Good old Henry. Did he ever send you that cross-country singlet?"

"No," Ben said. "It's no big deal—I don't need it. Anyway, they're going to be at his mom's for Christmas, and he wanted to get together, but I said I didn't know."

Macey nodded. "I can't even think about Christmas."

"I know," Ben said.

"Maeve came by this morning."

"Yeah, Gage told me she was going to."

"Harper was even awake for most of her visit."

He nodded and looked over at the little girl whose fragile body was still crisscrossed with wires and tubes. "What did she have to say?"

"She feels bad for everything we're going through, and she can't believe how quickly Harper's condition deteriorated."

Ben nodded. "I really think the doctor was probably right about Harper trying to hide her symptoms," he said softly. "I'll bet anything she is scared about having surgery. I know I would be if I was told my heart was going to be replaced with someone else's. Can you imagine how that makes her feel?"

"Terrified," Macey replied. She watched Harper breathing softly and knew she was sound asleep. "My parents are coming tomorrow."

"Is she allowed to have so many visitors?"

"The nurses haven't said anything." She smiled wistfully. "I wish we could bring Keeper—that would really cheer her up."

"It would cheer *him* up, too. He is Mr. Gloom and Doom without you guys."

"Speaking of which," Macey said, glancing at the clock. "You better go let him out and feed him."

"Yeah, I'm going. Are you coming home tonight?"

"I am—I need to sleep in my own bed."

"You also need to let your poor pup know you're still alive."

"I know. Maybe I'll sleep on *his* bed."

"No need for that. He's been sleeping on your side of *our* bed!"

"He has? How's he getting up there?"

"I moved the steps I made from Harper's room."

"You're too funny."

"I know," he grinned. "Have you eaten?"

"No. Are there still some leftovers in the fridge?"

"There are. Want me to heat some up for you?"

"Sure, I'm just going to stay a little longer in case she wakes up. I'll text you when I'm leaving."

Ben nodded, stood up, and leaned over to kiss Harper's silky hair. "G'night, little girl," he said softly. She stirred but didn't wake, and then he turned to Macey and kissed her, too. "Safe drive home, big girl."

"Yep. You too, kiddo!" she teased.

Ben smiled. "You haven't called me that in a while."

She laughed. "I know." She waved as he walked out, and then looked back at Harper. She was reluctant to leave—she knew she'd just worry more at home and probably not sleep well, but she really wanted to take a shower and get a change of scenery, and the nurses had assured her Harper would be fine.

Macey's phone buzzed, and she looked at the screen. It was Maeve wanting to know if she was still there. She wrote back that she was but leaving soon, and Maeve responded with a smiley face and said to let her know if she needed anything. Macey sent back a heart, and then tapped the photo icon on her phone and looked at the last picture she'd taken—it was of Harper with Keeper and Big Mac sitting on her lap. It really was perfect—Big Mac was looking up as Keeper licked Harper's cheek and she was laughing. It was the first time she'd seen Harper look so happy, and as she gazed at it, tears filled her eyes.

61

"WEAR YOUR HELMETS!" CORA CALLED FROM THE KITCHEN AS RUDY AND Joe hurriedly tied their sneakers. It was Saturday morning and Kari and Kayden were outside, waiting on the front step.

"Oh, Mama, Kari doesn't wear a helmet!" Rudy complained.

"Well, she should, and you most certainly are!" Cora commanded as she appeared, drying her hands on a dish towel.

Joe finished tying his shoes, and before his mom could make any more demands, he was out the door. A moment later, Rudy heard him swearing as he tried to pull his bike out of the pile of folding chairs, rakes, and outside toys in the makeshift storage area next to their apartment. "Hang on, Joe," she called. "I'll help you!" She pushed open the door and found Kayden and Joe tugging on Joe's bike. "You have to move stuff first," she said in an exasperated voice.

Joe stepped back and folded his arms over his chest. "Fine! You do it!"

Rudy shook her head and surveyed the array of obstacles. "That is why I leave mine out," she said, gesturing to her bicycle lying on the grass. She moved some chairs and then motioned for her brother to help. "Here, pull the rake out of the spokes when I'm moving the bike."

Joe knelt down and freed the rake tines while his sister pulled out his bike. "Thanks," he said, hopping on the seat.

"Don't forget your helmet!" Rudy reminded, holding it out.

Joe groaned, took it from her, and plopped it on his head. "There . . . happy?"

"Clip the strap," she commanded. "It won't do you any good if it falls off."

He rolled his eyes, but did as she said, and then turned to Kayden. "Let's go before I have to put on knee and elbow pads, too."

Kayden nodded and bumped off the curb after him.

Rudy looked over at Kari. "Is Kayden as much a pain in the butt as Joe?"

Kari laughed. "Worse!"

Rudy laughed, too. "Where should we go?"

"Want to go to the big playground?"

Rudy hesitated. "Sure . . . do you have to ask your mom first?"

"No, she doesn't care where we go, as long as we're outta her hair."

"Okay," Rudy said, glancing back at her front door to see if her mom was watching. Then she looked around for Joe and saw the boys jumping their bikes over a small pile of dirt with a piece of plywood on it. "C'mon, J . . . ," she started to call, but Kari stopped her.

"Let them stay here," she said. "Then we don't hafta watch 'em."

Rudy nodded, clicked the strap of her helmet, and followed Kari down the sidewalk toward the street. The playground was only a few blocks away, and they wouldn't be long—they'd probably be back before anyone even missed them.

They rode slowly, each lost in her own thoughts, simply enjoying the clear, crisp morning. When they got to the playground, they discovered—to their delight—they had the whole place to themselves. "I wonder where everybody is," Kari mused as she leaned her bike against the jungle gym.

"Probably soccer or something," Rudy surmised.

"How come you don't play soccer?" Kari asked, sitting on a swing.

"I don't know," Rudy said, sitting on the one next to her. "I guess it's because my mom's always working and I can't get to practice."

"Yeah, me, too. But when I get to junior high, I'm going to try out for the school team."

"Even though you never played?"

"Mm-hmm. I think it looks fun. Besides, how hard can it be?"

Rudy laughed. "You're right. Maybe I'll try out, too. My brother's trying out for the high school basketball team—that's why Joe and I started the after-school program."

"I saw your brother walking to the bus the other morning. He is cute!"

Rudy looked over and frowned. "Frank?! Are you kidding me?"

"I am *not* kidding you, but don't you dare tell him."

"Don't worry—I won't. I don't need anything else goin' to his big ole head! He's already full a himself, bossin' us around like he's the man in charge." As she said this, she backed up, swung forward, and started to pump, and Kari joined her, pumping, too, until they were both swinging high up in the air.

"Touch the sky with your toes!" Kari called.

Rudy laughed as they swung back and forth, higher and higher until they were even with the top crossbar and the legs of the swing set were bumping off the ground.

"I wonder if anyone's ever gone all the way around?" Kari called.

Rudy smiled wistfully, remembering how Harper had always wanted to do that . . . *C'mon, Rudy,* she'd shout. *Let's go all the way around!*

"I'm gonna do it, Kari!" Rudy suddenly called. "Watch me!" Again, and again, she pumped her legs as hard as she could and leaned back as far as she dared as the swing swept forward, and then suddenly, as if she was a toy with a worn-out battery, she stopped pumping and the swing slowed. She dragged the toes of her pink sneakers in the sand, making them dusty.

Kari slowed down, too. "What's the matter?"

Rudy shook her head. "The swings always remind me of Harper, and my mom found out that she's back in the hospital."

"She is? I'm sorry." She put her hand on Rudy's arm. "Is she going to be okay?"

Rudy shrugged. "I don't know—she needs a new heart."

"Oh, man . . ."

Rudy nodded. "I'm sorry to take the fun outta everythin'."

"That's okay. You want to head back home?"

Rudy nodded and they picked up their bikes, but as they rode home, they were each so lost in their own thoughts, they didn't notice Mr. Glover backing his car out of his spot.

62

⌘

"How'd you sleep?" Ben asked, pouring two mugs of coffee and handing one to Macey, who was lounging next to Keeper on his bed.

"Okay," she said, taking a sip, "you know me—too busy worrying to get any decent rest to speak of. How 'bout you?"

"Oh, I've slept better, but Keep had a good night, and that's all that matters." They both listened to him snoring contentedly, just as he'd done all night.

She looked down and stroked his silky ears. "Those are some awfully nice steps Dad made for you to get up on the bed."

Keeper opened one eye and thumped his tail, and Ben smiled. "We'll have to move them back to Harper's room when she gets home." Macey pressed her lips together and Ben searched her eyes. "You can't lose faith now . . . she's *going* to come home. Isn't that what your grandmother would say?"

"It *is* what Grandy would say, but she had a much stronger faith than me."

"Well, your faith has taken some serious hits in the last few years, Mace. It's understandable if it's a little shaky."

"Says Mr. Worrywart himself."

"You're right. I *do* worry, and I *am* worried, but I'm trying to keep the faith. Besides, you heard the doctor—he said she might even be able to play sports if the transplant comes through. That little spitfire could be your basketball protégé someday."

Macey chuckled and started to roll her eyes, but stopped and smiled instead. "I hope you're right, Ben. That would be something." She sighed and gently lifted Keeper's head off her lap. "I better get going. Are you going to stop by?"

Ben looked out the window. "I am . . . a little later, though. I'm going to take advantage of this nice day and get some work done around here. It's starting to look a little neglected."

"Maybe you could fix the drippy showerhead?" she suggested hopefully.

"Maybe," he said, smiling and putting his arm around her, "but I'll probably spend some time outside first, doing a little yard work. All the rain we've been having brought down a million willow branches."

"A million?"

"Mm-hmm."

"Grandy always said if you leave a willow branch on the ground, it'll become a new tree."

"All the more reason I need to get out there. Last thing we need is more willow trees. So, between the branches and the other sticks and leaves, I have my work cut out for me."

"So, nice day equals yard work. I'm sorry, my brain wasn't operating at full throttle yet."

"That's okay. That's why I made Fog Buster this morning," he said, gesturing to her mug.

She took another sip. "And that's why I'm taking it upstairs to my drippy shower."

"Better drippy than no shower at all!"

Macey rolled her eyes.

"Thank you," he teased. "That's what I've been waiting for."

She laughed. "Now, your morning's complete."

"Not quite," he said softly, leaning down to kiss her. "*Now*, it's complete."

"Good," Macey said, smiling. "Can I take my shower now?"

"You can indeed, missy. Get going . . . someone's waiting for you."

Macey nodded and headed up the stairs. She put her mug down on the bathroom counter, turned on the shower, and went into their room to find some clothes. She pulled out every drawer, hunting for her favorite pair of jeans, then turned and groaned when she spied them peeking out of the mountain of clothes overflowing from the laundry basket. She pulled them out, along with a long-sleeve T-shirt she decided could be worn again, grabbed some clean underwear from her drawer, hurried into the bathroom, and closed the door. As she undressed, she stopped to look at her reflection and ran her hand slowly over her flat abdomen. She bit her lip. "Maybe being a mom isn't going to happen in the usual way . . . and maybe that's been the plan all along. If so, I'm fine with it, but please don't take this little girl from us. Please find her a really strong heart that will beat in her chest till she's a hundred!"

63

CORA DID NOT HEAR THE BONE-CRUSHING THUD. NEITHER DID SHE HEAR the squeal of tires as Isaiah Glover pulled forward. All she heard was her next-door neighbor screaming, "Call nine-one-one! Oh, Lord Almighty, somebody call nine-one-one!"

She ran outside and saw Janelle kneeling on the ground next to a bicycle that looked like a mangled metal pretzel. And then she saw Mr. Glover struggling to get out of his car. "What the hell was that?!"

"Janelle! What happened?" Cora shouted. "Is that one of my babies?"

Janelle looked up and saw her friend coming toward her. "Cora! Thank God! Call nine-one-one!"

Cora stumbled forward as if on a blind trajectory. "Is that my baby girl?" she cried as she fumbled with her phone.

"No, Cora, it is not! Stay right where you are and make that call!"

Cora stopped in her tracks and did as she was told. In her panicked rush, she accidently pushed the speaker button.

"Nine-one-one operator," said a calm female voice on the other end of the line. "What is your emergency?"

"I need an ambulance for a child who's been hit by a car," Cora shouted.

"What is your location?"

Cora blurted out the address.

"Is the victim conscious or appear to be breathing?"

"Janelle, is he breathin'?" Cora asked, sounding increasingly flustered as tears welled up in her eyes.

"Yes, *she's* breathing," Janelle called over her shoulder. "Tell them to hurry!"

"Yes, she's breathing," Cora repeated, noting Janelle's use of a female pronoun and feeling it reverberate through her body like a shock wave. "Oh, Lordy! Please hurry!" Cora looked around for her children, but saw only Isaiah Glover leaning against his car with his head in his hands.

"We have an ambulance en route," the dispatcher said, "but stay on the line with me until they arrive."

"Okay," Cora cried, trying to see the child Janelle was shielding from her view. She looked around the parking lot again and saw Joe and Kayden trotting toward them. "Thank God," she murmured, and then commanded, "Boys, stay right there!"

The boys stopped as if they'd walked into an invisible wall and Cora turned back to her neighbor and stepped closer. She didn't want to know the answer to the question forming on her lips but she absolutely *had* to know. "Janelle, who is it?"

"Cora, I need you to keep an eye out for the ambulance," Janelle said, cradling the injured child in her arms.

"Oh my God! Whose child is that?" Cora pleaded when she saw the familiar pink sneakers.

"Where is that damn ambulance?!" Janelle demanded.

But before Cora could repeat the question, the dispatcher

answered, "It should be there any minute. In the meantime, can you please tell me more about the victim? You said *she*. Do you know her approximate age?

"Janelle . . ." Cora began, but then saw the boys edging closer. "Stay right where you are!" she commanded again. "Kayden, where is your mama?"

"Home," he said, looking as if he might cry.

"Joe, have you seen Rudy?"

Joe shook his head. "No, Mama. Kayden and me was riding bikes over the jump." He gestured over his shoulder at the piece of plywood propped on the dirt pile.

"Okay, maybe you boys should run over and get . . ." As she said this, the sound of a wailing siren filled the air and Cora's sentence hung in the air as she hurried toward the road. "The ambulance is here!" she shouted at her phone, and before the dispatcher could even reply she ended the call and began frantically waving her arms. "This way! This way! Over here!"

64

"THEY THINK THEY MIGHT HAVE A HEART FOR HARPER!" MACEY CRIED into her phone.

"They do? Already?" Ben could hardly believe his ears, but then he stopped in his tracks and leaned on his rake, realizing what this also meant.

"I know," Macey said, reading his mind. "It means another child is slipping away."

"Yeah," he said softly. He looked across the river at the pink Savannah sky. "It makes me sad and happy at the same time."

"It *is* bittersweet," Macey whispered, "but it's the only way."

"I know," Ben said, biting his lip.

Macey waited for him to say more. "You there?"

Ben nodded and cleared his throat. "Yeah . . . yep, I'm here."

"Can you come?"

"Yes. Just let me clean up and give Keep his supper. I'll be there as soon as I can."

"Okay." She tapped off her phone and looked out at the setting sun, replaying the conversation she'd had with the doctor just moments before. She had come back from the cafeteria with a cup

of coffee, and he'd peeked into the room and motioned for her to
come out. They'd stood in the hall and he'd told her he had a feeling they would have a heart by that night. It was highly unusual,
he'd added, to have an organ become available so quickly.

Tears filled Macey's eyes as she tried to imagine the heart-
breaking decisions that the family losing their child was struggling with, and she couldn't help but wonder what had happened
to turn their world upside down. As badly as she wanted a heart for
Harper, her own heart broke to think of the loss another family
was suffering. She watched the sun slip below the horizon. Some
people found the end of the day to be peaceful, but as beautiful as
it often was, it always made her feel melancholy. What was it about
the setting sun? Was she just tired by the end of the day or was she
overly sensitive? Maeve often talked about how the setting sun
affected the elderly patients who suffered from dementia, making
them even more disoriented and confused.

"Hey," a voice said, interrupting her thoughts.

Macey turned to see her sister. "Hey," she said, mustering a
smile.

"Mom said I'd find you here. How're you holding up?"

Macey bit her lip. "I'm fine. They think they might have a heart
for Harper."

"Already?!" Maeve whispered in disbelief. "Does Ben know?"

Macey nodded. "He's on his way."

"That's great!"

"It *is* great for us . . . but not for some other family."

"Mace, you know what Grandy would say. . . ."

Macey nodded. "That it's all part of God's plan, I know. But
how can I hope so much for something that will cause heartache
for someone else?"

Maeve pressed her lips together. "It doesn't always. . . ."

"It sure seems like it does. Just this morning," Macey continued, "I was storming the gates of heaven for a heart for Harper, and not once did I really realize that I was praying for another child to not need theirs anymore . . ." She paused. "And now that God's answering my prayer, I feel as if I'm responsible for someone else's loss."

"Oh, Mace, you know that's not how it works."

Macey shook her head. "I'm sure the other family is praying for a miracle right now. They're praying their baby will wake up, smile, and be their old self. So why should my prayer be answered, and not theirs?"

"Mace, you've been praying to be a mother for years, and now that it's actually happening, you're questioning it."

Macey shook her head. "I know," she despaired. "But I don't want anyone else to suffer."

Maeve pulled her sister into a hug. "Your prayers are being answered, and it has nothing to do with someone else's *not* being answered. I don't know why it's happening this way—no one does. It's life—it's the way things happen sometimes."

Just then, the doctor appeared in the doorway. "We're a go," he said. "The nurses will be in to prep Harper for surgery soon."

Macey bit her lip and nodded. "Okay." Harper stirred and opened her eyes, and Macey looked back at the doctor. "May I tell her?"

"Of course," he said.

"Tell me what?" Harper asked sleepily.

Macey sat down on the bed. "They've found a heart for you."

Harper's eyes grew wide. "They have?"

Macey nodded.

"When are they going to put it in?"

"Soon."

Harper bit her lip as tears welled up in her eyes. "Is it a strong one? Because there's no point if it's not strong."

"It's a very strong one," Macey said, silently praying this was true. "They wouldn't give it to you if it wasn't."

"Okay," Harper said, mustering a weak smile.

When Ben arrived, he gave her a confident thumbs-up and Harper returned the gesture. Moments after that, a flurry of activity filled the room as two nurses came in and started getting her ready. One of the nurses reached up to adjust the intravenous tube above her bed and as she prepped a new needle, Harper eyed it warily. "Has that been tested with horseshoe crab blood?"

The nurse frowned. "I'm not sure what you mean, hon . . ."

"Horseshoe crabs have blue blood," Harper explained, "and it's filled with stuff that fights infection by releasing goopy stuff that surrounds germs to keep them from spreading."

"Is that so?" The nurse looked up at Macey and Ben and smiled. "I had no idea!"

Macey and Ben looked at each other in surprise. "We didn't know that, either," Ben said.

Harper nodded as if it was common knowledge. "It's true. That's why scientists use horseshoe crab blood to make sure medicine in needles is safe."

"Well, I'm sure the medicine we're giving you is safe, so no worries," the nurse assured her as she adjusted the bag. "Now, Mom and Dad," she said, looking up again, "it's time to give your little girl a hug and a kiss because we're all set here."

Harper frowned. "They're not my . . . ," she started to say, but then stopped midsentence as Macey leaned down to give her a hug.

It felt odd to have the nurse refer to Macey and Ben as her parents, but it also felt oddly comforting. After all, they had been nothing but nice to her since she'd moved in with them, and now, Macey had practically moved in with *her* while she was in the hospital. No one—except Cora and Mary—had ever treated her with so much kindness before.

Ben reached for her hand. "You got this, Harper!" he said. "Just remember how brave Keeper was when he had his surgery. If he can do it, you can, too!"

Harper nodded and pulled Bear against her chest, but when the nurse realized she still had a stuffed animal with her, she said, "I think you better give that to your mom."

Harper's lip quivered as she looked at Macey. "Will you take care of him?"

"You bet," Macey said. "I won't let him out of my sight. Everything's gonna be fine," she added softly. "We love you and we'll be waiting right here."

Harper nodded and as soon as she let go of Bear, the nurse wheeled her out of the room. Macey watched them go and then looked down at the tattered old bear entrusted to her, and lightly traced the pink heart on his chest.

"She's gonna be fine," Ben said, squeezing her hand. "I have a good feeling."

"*You* have a good feeling?"

"I *do*," he said, pulling her closer. "Everything's going to be okay."

Macey bit her lip and nodded, hoping he was right.

65

MACEY LEANED BACK IN THE STIFF GREEN CHAIR AND GAZED, BLEARY-eyed, at the pile of magazines on the table in front of her—she'd looked through every one of them and then neatly lined them up in order of publication date, newest on top. "You should go home and let Keeper out," she said, glancing at her phone. "It's almost five."

Ben stopped pacing. "I asked Gage to let him out and feed him."

"Oh, okay. What time?"

"Soon, I hope."

"Okay. I just hope the poor dog hasn't given up on us. He's never spent the night alone."

"I'm sure he's fine, but if you want me to run home, I will."

"No, no," she said, shaking her head. "You need to be here."

"What time are your parents coming back?"

"I'm supposed to text my mom when we hear something . . ." Just as she said this, a doctor wearing scrubs walked into the waiting area, and Macey stood up and moved closer to Ben.

"Mr. and Mrs. Samuelson," he said, smiling as he drew near. Macey and Ben both felt a wary relief when they saw the look on his face. "You are the foster parents of one spunky little lady." His kind face looked tired as he continued, "When we were putting her under, she was telling us all about your dog, Keeper, and how he only has three legs, but because he has so much love in his heart he learned to get around . . . and she went right on talking about him until she fell asleep."

Ben smiled. "I reminded her about Keeper having surgery right before she went in—I was hoping it would help her feel less worried . . . I said if he could do it, she could, too."

"That was a good idea," the doctor said with a tired smile.

"How did it go?" Macey asked anxiously.

"Very well—we had a good strong heart, and it started beating right away. Even so"—he paused—"I can't impress on you enough how important her antirejection meds are. There are always risks—but in Harper's case, I think she's going to come through with flying colors. She's a fighter and I think we found the perfect heart."

"Can we see her?" Ben asked.

"Soon," the doctor said, running his hand through his hair. "We're wrapping things up, and she's still going to be out of it for a while, but you'll be able to see her after we've moved her back to her room in ICU. She's going to look a little swollen, but that's completely normal."

Macey nodded. "Thank you so much."

He smiled. "You're welcome."

"Do you know anything about the donor?" Ben ventured.

The doctor shook his head. "The mother wants to remain anonymous, at least for now. Down the road, she may want to meet the children her child saved, but she's still grieving."

"Did they donate other organs?"

He nodded. "All they could."

Macey took a deep breath and let it out slowly. "Wow," she whispered.

The doctor nodded. "It can be a difficult decision, but usually families that decide to donate look back and say knowing their loved one's organs—especially a heart—saved someone else's life helps to ease their loss. We try to encourage people to consider organ donation when they renew their driver's licenses. It makes it easier on families if an individual has already made that decision—then the family doesn't have to guess what they would have wanted."

Macey looked up at Ben. "We should do that."

Ben nodded. "Definitely."

"Okay," the doctor said. "I'm going back. I just wanted to give you an update so you can grab some breakfast or a cup of coffee. A nurse will come find you as soon as we get Harper settled in her room."

They both nodded. "We can't thank you enough," Ben said, shaking his hand.

"Yes," Macey agreed, reaching out to take both of his hands. "Thank you."

He smiled. "You're very welcome."

As he walked away, Ben turned to her. "Coffee?"

Macey nodded. "Just let me text my mom and Maeve." She pulled her phone out of her pocket, but when she looked at the screen, she could barely make out the letters.

"Maybe you should wait till you can see," Ben said gently, putting his arm around her.

"Okay," she agreed, sobbing into his shoulder.

❧

66

"Is there a chapel in this hospital?" Cora asked, wiping her eyes.

The nurse at the desk looked up and smiled sadly. "Yes, it's on the first floor, across from the cafeteria."

"Thank you," Cora replied. She turned and walked slowly down the hall to the elevator, pushed the button, and waited. Finally, the doors yawned open, and when she stepped inside, she just stood there, waiting. When nothing happened, she realized she hadn't pushed the button for her floor. She hit *L*, and as the elevator began its descent, she tried to wrap her mind around everything that happened, but she couldn't come close to comprehending the lost life of a sweet, innocent child. "Why?" she whispered. "She had her whole life ahead of her."

The doors opened and Cora moved, as if on autopilot, in the direction of the cafeteria. When she reached it, she glanced in and saw people getting cups of coffee and trays of breakfast food, their silverware and dishes clinking . . . their lives going on. She turned, looked across the hall, and saw a small sign on a heavy oak door that simply said, *Chapel*.

The sanctuary was quiet and cool, a stark contrast to the busy cafeteria across the hall. As her weary red-rimmed eyes adjusted to the dim light, she noticed a small table filled with votive candles. She paused, remembering how her mother—a devout Catholic— had always lit a candle when she entered her church. Cora reached for an unlit match, held it in the flame of another candle until it sparked, and then lit the candle next to it. She stared solemnly at the tiny flame. Then she made her way slowly up the aisle to the altar and knelt down, brokenhearted.

She had no idea how long she had been kneeling there, praying for comfort and understanding, when the doors swung open.

Cora turned to see who had come into the sanctuary.

"Cora?" Macey said in surprise. "What are you doing here?"

∽

67

One week later, Macey peeked around the door into Harper's hospital room. "Hey, Harp, there's someone here to see you," she said cheerfully.

Harper opened her eyes, and her face—which had taken on a healthy rosy hue—lit up with a hopeful grin. "Did you sneak Keeper in?"

Macey laughed. "No, it's not Keeper . . . but it's almost as good. Maybe better."

"Who?"

Macey stepped back and a familiar face peered around the door.

"Miss Cora!" Harper cried happily.

Cora smiled and reached through the tubes and wires to give her a gentle hug. "We wanted to come see you right after your surgery, but we thought we'd better give you a week or so to recover. How're you doin'?"

"I'm doin' great," Harper replied, beaming. "I had PT this morning and Laurie—she's my physical therapist—said I'm her star patient! She said if I keep it up, they're gonna *hafta* send me home!"

"That is such wonderful news," Cora said, smiling at Macey.

Harper looked around her. "Did Rudy come, too?"

Cora raised her eyebrows. "See for yourself," she said, looking back at the door.

Harper followed her gaze and saw Rudy peek around the door, grinning.

"Rudy!" Harper exclaimed.

"Hi, Harper," Rudy said, keeping her hands behind her back.

Harper eyed her suspiciously. "What's behind your back?"

"A present," Rudy teased, but then, she couldn't wait any longer, and she held out a large blue gift bag with a picture of Dory and Nemo on it. "We know how much you love Dory!"

"What is it?"

"You have to open it and see, silly!"

Harper reached through the tissue paper and pulled out a large stuffed dog. "Oh, wow! He's so cute," she said, pulling him close. "Thank you!"

Harper slowly turned the dog around to see the front of him and then her eyes grew wide. Not only did the dog have a pink heart sewn on his chest, but he was also missing a front leg. "Oh, wow!" she cried. "Where did you find him?"

Rudy grinned and Cora laughed. "We'll never tell," they said in unison.

"That is so cool!" Harper said, showing Macey.

"That is *very* cool," Macey agreed.

"Sooo . . . how are you feeling?" Rudy asked.

"A lot better. I'm so glad you came. I've been so bored."

"You look a *lot* better—your cheeks are so rosy," Cora said, smiling, even though her eyes glistened.

"What's wrong?" Harper asked, seeing her tears. "Why are you crying?"

Cora quickly brushed them away. "I'm not." As she said this, she inadvertently looked at Rudy and caught her eye. Harper watched the silent exchange and frowned—it seemed as if they were keeping a secret.

"Yes, you are."

"Well, if my eyes are a little damp it's because I'm happy you finally got your new heart."

Just then, a nurse came into the room to check on Harper, but when she saw she had company, she offered to come back.

"No, no," Cora said, smiling. "We can't stay," she explained. "We have to get home so Frank can go to basketball practice."

"Did he make the team?" Macey asked.

"Sure did!" Rudy said proudly. "He made varsity, and he's only a freshman!"

"Wow, that's so great," Macey said. "Please tell him congratulations for us . . . and if you let me know when he has a game, maybe we can come."

Harper's face lit up. "That would be fun . . . and then Rudy and I can have a sleepover."

"Ooh, yeah!" Rudy agreed, bumping fists with Harper.

"We can do that," Cora said, nodding as she sat on the edge of Harper's bed and reached for her hands. "I'm so happy for you, baby. You got yourself a good strong heart."

"Thanks, Cora," Harper said, beaming.

"God has blessed you, child."

"Just like you said."

She nodded. "Mm-hmm . . . just like I said. May he continue

to bless you," she whispered, brushing the wisps of red hair out of Harper's eyes. "Almost time for another haircut," she added with a smile.

"Mm-hmm, I'm gonna wait till it's really long . . . so I can donate it again." She looked at Macey. "We're both going to!"

"You are?" Cora said, eyeing Macey.

Macey nodded. "We are, indeed," she said, winking at Harper.

Just then, there was another quiet knock on the door, and they all looked up. "Mrs. Holland!" Harper said, a smile lighting her face. "How did *you* know I was here?"

"Oh, I've been keeping tabs on you," she said, winking at Macey. "Do you really think I could forget after the scare you gave us on the beach?"

Harper's teacher smiled at Cora and Rudy, and Macey quickly introduced them.

"It's nice to meet you," Mrs. Holland said.

"It's nice to meet you, too," Cora replied. Then she looked at Macey. "I'm sorry we can't stay."

"That's okay," Macey said, giving them both a hug. "Just don't forget to let us know when Frank has a game . . . and then Rudy can come home with us and sleep over."

Rudy grinned. "Okay!"

"Bye, Rudy! Bye, Cora! Thanks for my present!" Harper called, smiling and sinking back onto her pillow.

"You're a popular young lady," Mrs. Holland said.

"I know," Harper said, laughing.

"How're you feeling?"

"Really good," Harper said, nodding. She wasn't used to so many people caring about her.

"The kids and I have been worried about you."

Harper smiled. "You don't hafta worry anymore—I have a new heart!"

"We know! That's such wonderful news!"

"*And* I made sure all of the medicine they gave me with needles was tested with horseshoe crab blood, just like you said."

Mrs. Holland laughed, tears filling her eyes. "Oh my goodness, Harper, you are truly a gift to this old teacher."

"Why?" Harper asked, frowning.

"Because you just showed you were listening in class . . . and that warms my heart."

Harper nodded. "I just thought it was really cool, that's all."

"Maybe you will be a research scientist or a doctor someday," Mrs. Holland offered.

"Maybe," Harper agreed thoughtfully. "Although I think I might like to help sea turtles."

"That would be wonderful, too," Mrs. Holland said. "I think you'll be great at whatever you decide to do."

"Thanks," Harper said, nodding shyly.

Mrs. Holland picked up the canvas bag she'd brought with her. "Anyway, I have some presents for you, too. The kids and I were going to wait till you came back to school, but then we decided you might like to have them while you're recuperating."

Harper nodded again.

"First, since you're such a talented artist, Harper, we put our heads together and decided that, instead of a boring old journal, you should have a real artist's sketchbook." As she said this, she pulled a black leather-bound sketchbook out of her bag and handed it to her.

Harper's eyes grew wide in surprise. "Wow!" she said softly, looking at Macey.

"And," Mrs. Holland continued, "we also thought you'd enjoy a book about drawing from nature." She handed the second book to Harper, and Harper began to glance through it. "I hope you don't mind, but the kids drew pictures in the beginning of your sketchbook—they didn't want you to forget all the things we saw on the beach. Sam even drew a wonderful picture of the horseshoe crab molt . . . although he said it's probably not as good as what you would draw."

Harper continued to leaf through the nature book, pausing on a page of birds, and then opened the leather sketchbook to look at her classmates' drawings and notes. "Thank you," she said. "This is one of the nicest presents I've ever gotten."

"You're welcome," Mrs. Holland said. "We also made some get-well cards, and I know Sam worked especially hard on his." She handed Harper a stack of cards tied together with a red ribbon. "You don't have to open them now," she added. "You can open them when you're bored and don't have any company." Harper nodded, lightly running her finger over the ribbon. "We are looking forward to having you back in class, though."

Harper nodded. "I am, too."

"Do you know when you might be back?"

Harper looked questioningly at Macey, and Macey—who was still misty-eyed by the class's kind gesture—regained her composure and nodded. "We're not sure yet. It all depends on how Harper feels. Hopefully, soon."

Mrs. Holland nodded. "Take all the time you need to heal, Harper, and don't come back too soon. You've just had major sur-

gery and there is no rush." She paused. "Well, I know you need
to rest, but the kids have been after me to come by and bring you
their cards and gifts, and they are very anxious to know how you're
doing."

"Please tell them thank you for me," Harper said, smiling,
"and I'm doing fine."

"I certainly will . . . and we will see you soon!"

Harper nodded, and then Macey walked out with Mrs. Holland
to talk for a few minutes.

Harper looked at the stack of cards on her lap, untied the ribbon, and pulled out the card on top. It was a drawing of a heart with
the words "I miss you!" written in the middle of it. She opened it
up and read the neatly written words inside: *Dear Harper, Get well
SOON! Love, Sam.*

68

"I can't wait to see Keep," Harper said as Ben pulled into their driveway. "I haven't seen him in a month!"

Macey nodded—it had actually been more than a month. Fortunately, her parents and Maeve had all taken shifts staying with Harper so she and Ben hadn't completely missed work. "He can't wait to see you, either," she said. "He's been so gloomy, and every time we've come home without you, he's looked all over and then laid down on his bed with his head between his paws."

Harper smiled. "I know how he feels." She looked eagerly out the window as they pulled up to the house, but when she saw Maeve and Gage and Macey's parents all standing on the porch with Keeper and Gus, and a huge banner above them that read, WELCOME HOME, HARPER!, her mouth dropped open. "Holy cow!" she whispered.

Macey turned and smiled. "*Everyone* is looking forward to welcoming you home, not just Keeper."

Before they'd even parked, Keeper was hopping down the steps—it was as if he knew! He stood outside the car, his whole hind end wagging, and as soon as Harper opened the door, he tried to climb in, but Harper laughed and knelt in front of him, and the big dog, making a sweet moaning sound, gently pushed his head into her chest. "Oh, Keep, I missed you so much," Harper whispered into his soft fur. Finally, she looked up, tears in her eyes, and saw everyone watching them.

"That's okay," Maeve teased. "We can wait for *our* hugs."

Harper laughed, stood up, wiping her eyes, and gave them each a hug, including Gus—who Gage had been holding back. "Welcome home, Harper," they each said in turn, smiling warmly, but Harper felt so overwhelmed, she didn't know what to say.

"Okay, everyone," Ruth directed, "inside, or the pizza will be stone-cold!"

Harper's eyes lit up. "We're having pizza?"

"We are . . . *and* it's homemade," Maeve confirmed, putting her arm around her. "Are you hungry?"

"Starving," Harper answered.

The women all headed inside while the men paused to inspect the porch steps. "I can't believe that bottom step is rotting already," Ben complained, pointing to the exposed wood.

"That's what happens when you live near the ocean," Gage said, slapping him on the shoulder. "Salty air and hurricanes."

"Did you prime before you painted?" Hal asked, frowning.

"I did," Ben confirmed, "and it's only been nine years."

Macey came out onto the porch. "It'll be ten years next month."

"Nine . . . ten, it should've lasted," he countered.

"Well, c'mon in before Mom puts the pizza *back* in the oven." They all laughed, knowing how true her warning was.

"Whoa!" Ben exclaimed, walking into the dining room. "You'd think someone special had just come home," he teased, eyeing

Harper. The table was set with a pink linen tablecloth edged with white hearts and a bouquet of beautiful pink roses and baby's breath. There was also a huge bouquet of red heart-shaped balloons tied to Harper's chair.

Gage frowned. "Is it Valentine's Day?"

"It will be pretty soon," Maeve said. "That's why it was so easy to find all these great decorations."

"Duly noted," Gage said with a nod as Ben handed him a beer.

"What kind of pizza are we having?" Harper asked.

"Pepperoni," Maeve replied as she made her way around the table pouring sweet tea.

"Is there any other kind?" Ben teased, elbowing her.

"No other *good* kind," Harper said, grinning and elbowing him back.

"Here we go!" Hal said, carrying in a large pizza and setting it on a pizza stand.

Ben frowned. "When and where did we get a pizza stand?"

"Last week at the party store," Macey said, handing him a heart-shaped paper plate.

"I hope we didn't go overboard with all these hearts," he said, eyeing her.

"Ooh, look!" Harper exclaimed as Ruth put a slice on her plate. "Even the pepperoni is in the shape of a heart!"

"Yes, and that took some time so you better appreciate it!" Maeve said with a smile.

"Sit down and eat," Ruth commanded, putting a slice on everyone's plate. "It's getting . . ." She looked around and chuckled. "You know what it's getting!"

"We're waiting for *you* to sit down," Hal said, standing behind his chair. "And I wish you'd hurry up because I'm starving."

Ruth sat down, and then everyone else did, too.

"Dad," Macey said, "will you say grace?"

Hal nodded, reached for their hands, and asked a blessing for their family and for the wonderful homemade pizza with heart-shaped pepperoni—of all things! And then he added an extra special thank-you for Harper and her new heart. When he looked up, he saw her peeking at him, and he winked.

Harper smiled and reached for her pizza, but then Macey started to speak. "You all go right ahead and eat," she began, "but Ben and I have something we would like to ask Harper."

Everyone looked up and Ben took a deep breath. "Are you sure you don't want to wait, Mace?" he asked hopefully, feeling his stomach fill with the same kaleidoscope of butterflies he'd felt all those years ago when he'd asked her to marry him. "I'm sure your mom doesn't want this pizza to get cold."

"Go ahead and eat," Macey said, eyeing him before plowing ahead. Ben sighed, knowing only too well that once his girl had a plan in her head, there was no turning back.

"So," Macey began again, "even though Cora called us last week with some very good news, Ben and I decided we wanted to wait until Harper came home." She felt her heart race as she turned to the little girl. "And now, we can't wait another minute because, Harper," she said, looking intently into her eyes, "Cora told us that we have been approved to adopt you . . . so . . . if you will have us, Ben and I would love it if you would be our daughter. . . . We would love to officially be your mom and dad."

"Oh, wow!" Harper exclaimed softly. She felt her new heart beating like a drum in a parade, and she wondered how it knew— even though it wasn't really hers—how to respond in a moment like this. She swallowed and looked around the table. Everyone seemed to be holding their collective breath, waiting for her answer, and she blinked back tears and swallowed.

"Do you really mean that?" she whispered, unable to believe someone actually wanted her to be a permanent member of their family.

Macey and Ben both nodded, and Harper pressed her lips together as the tears she was fighting slid down her cheeks. "I . . . I would love that," she stammered. She threw her arms around them and held them for a long time—almost afraid to let go—while everyone else cheered and clapped and the dogs wagged their tails because, obviously, something good was happening. Finally, Harper pulled away and wiped her eyes. Then she looked around the table at each of them. "This means you will *all* be my family . . . my grandma and grandpa . . . *and* my aunt and uncle."

Macey caught her sister's eye and Maeve felt her cheeks flame.

"Oh, hon, Gage wouldn't be your uncle . . . ," Maeve said.

"Hey," Gage interrupted, elbowing her. "I can be Harper's uncle!"

Maeve laughed and shook her head. "Okay, well, if you want to be. . . ."

"Thank you," he said, feigning indignation.

"Uncle Gage!" Harper teasingly rolled his new moniker on her tongue and then eyed him mischievously. "You ready to lose at checkers again?"

"Ha! I think you need to let me finish my pizza before I let you rout me in checkers again."

"Okay," Harper said with a sigh, "but before dessert."

"Is there dessert?" he asked hopefully.

"There is," Maeve confirmed. "We have a heart-shaped chocolate cake."

Ben groaned and shook his head, and Harper looked up at him. "How about you, Be—I mean, *Dad*?" she asked, grinning. "Ready to lose at checkers?"

"Sure," he said, laughing. "Right after I finally get to eat my pizza."

Harper laughed. "Hear that, Keep?" she said. "This is going to be my forever home, too." And both dogs wiggled all around her, wagging their tails happily.

An hour later, as they were getting ready to leave, Ruth pulled her daughter into a hug. "We are so happy for you, Macey, dear. You and Ben are going to be wonderful parents!"

"Thanks, Mom," Macey said. "I hope so! And thank you for the yummy pizza, too."

"You're more than welcome," Ruth replied as she and Hal knelt to give Harper a hug.

"We're so happy to have a dog lover like you for a granddaughter," Hal said. "You take good care of that new heart!"

"I will," Harper said, nodding.

"We're going, too," Maeve said, coming up behind them.

"And we're taking our crazy dog with us," Gage said, smiling. "I think he wore Keeper out," he added, gesturing to the golden retriever snoring in front of the fireplace.

"And *poor* Big Mac can come out of hiding now, too," Maeve said, laughing. She gave Harper a squeeze. "Lunch and shopping again soon, girlfriend?"

"Yes!" Harper said, smiling.

Macey nodded and put her hand on Harper's shoulder. "Harp has a birthday coming up . . . *and* it's a big one, so we'll have to do something special."

"All right!" Maeve said. "When is it?"

"March first," Harper replied. "I'm going to be ten!"

"Wow! Double digits!" Maeve said. "I'm in!"

"Me, too," Ruth chimed. "We can have lunch at the Olde Pink House, my treat!"

"That would be fun," Macey agreed. "What do you think, Harp?"

And even though Harper couldn't understand why an old house—especially one that was painted pink—was such a special destination, she nodded enthusiastically.

69

A̲f̲t̲e̲r̲ H̲a̲r̲p̲e̲r̲ ̲w̲a̲s̲ ̲t̲u̲c̲k̲e̲d̲ ̲i̲n̲t̲o̲ ̲b̲e̲d̲ ̲w̲i̲t̲h̲ K̲e̲e̲p̲e̲r̲ ̲c̲u̲r̲l̲e̲d̲ ̲c̲o̲n̲t̲e̲n̲t̲-edly next to her, Macey collapsed on the couch with her laptop and pulled up the custom greeting card she'd been designing. "What do you think of this?" she said, nudging Ben.

He opened his eyes and looked at the pink card with tiny red hearts sprinkled around the edges. In the center, Macey had downloaded the picture she'd taken of Harper with Keeper and Big Mac on Thanksgiving, and under the photo, the greeting read:

MAY YOUR HEARTS BE FILLED WITH LOVE!
HAPPY VALENTINE'S DAY!
THE SAMUELSONS
BEN, MACEY, HARPER, KEEPER & BIG MAC

"Cute!" he said and then eyed her curiously. "You think we need to send Valentines?"

"Well, with everything going on we didn't send Christmas cards this year, and it's kind of an announcement, too—you know . . . of the new addition to our family."

Ben nodded. "She's such a funny kid—and so different from the tough little kid we met back in the fall. And the way Keeper and Gus and Big Mac are so drawn to her? And she to them? It's amazing. I really think they made a huge difference in helping her adjust to being here."

Macey nodded. "If we had been able to have a daughter of our own, I think she'd be like Harper."

"That's because she's just as stubborn and feisty as you," Ben teased, kissing her softly.

"Maybe," Macey said, sinking into the couch next to him. "Maeve thinks she's an old soul . . . ," she added, recalling her sister's comment, but when Ben didn't respond, she looked over and realized he'd dozed off.

"Must be nice," she whispered.

She turned her attention back to her card, clicked ORDER, closed her laptop, and gazed at the embers glowing in the fireplace. In her mind, she replayed the events of the day: from bringing Harper home to the look of surprise on the little girl's face when they asked her to be their daughter. Just then, one of the embers flickered brightly, and as it caught on a piece of wood and flamed higher, her thoughts turned to Harper's birthday and the plans they'd made. Suddenly, a thought struck her and she nudged Ben. "Do you realize Harper was born around the same time we bought this house?

"So?" Ben said, his eyes still closed.

"Sooo, when we were a young couple signing our lives away on our dream house . . ."

"Umm . . . may I clarify that it was *your* dream house?"

Macey sighed. "The house we *both* dreamed we'd raise our family in. And around that very same time, Harper was born . . . and in all the years since, while we were working on the house and trying to have kids, Harper was going through some tough stuff of her own. Ben, don't you see? It's more than just a coincidence. It's—as Grandy would say—serendipity. It's as if it's all part of a plan that's been unfolding for ten years—a plan we couldn't see until now."

Macey sat up, her voice growing more earnest. "Now I can clearly see the beauty and grace of everything that's been happening: how the events in our lives played out until we were each given—actually, until we were each *ready to receive*—the deepest desires of our hearts. It's so amazing and unbelievable, but that little girl asleep upstairs with a new strong heart beating in her chest is absolute proof that everything Grandy taught me to believe about the tapestry of life is true."

Ben smiled. "I love the way you see life, Mace. I think it's one of the things I love most about you. No matter how many times life knocks you down, your wonderful, buoyant, resilient spirit gets right back up and you find some new amazing way to see things. I think you're more like your grandmother than you realize, and you inspire me to try to see all the little nuances in life . . . and that's what makes me such a blessed man."

Macey swallowed and looked away. She always had something to say . . . she always spoke her mind, but now, with his kind words—telling her she was like her grandmother—her husband had just rendered her speechless. She looked back at him, her eyes glistening. "And the way *you* see me is one of the things that makes *me* such a blessed woman."

Ben reached for her hand and nodded to the front window. She followed his gaze to the candle he'd given her so long ago—the candle that would guide their family home. It was flickering more brightly than it ever had before.

EPILOGUE

"MAY I LISTEN?" LANA ASKED AS MACEY, BEN, AND CORA WATCHED, their eyes glistening.

"Yes," Harper said, lifting her shirt.

Lana gently traced the long scar on Harper's chest and then leaned forward and lightly placed the stethoscope Macey had brought on Harper's chest.

"Oh my," she whispered, her eyes filling with tears. "Oh my, oh my, oh my! That is the loveliest sound I've ever heard." She listened for a long time, and then sat back and searched Harper's eyes. "Thank you, child. I'm so glad you're the one who ended up with Kari's heart. She would be pleased, too, because you're such a good, fine person." She paused and gently touched Harper's cheek. "You know how I know that?"

Harper shook her head.

"Because way back when I suggested you donate your beautiful hair to kids who'd lost theirs, you didn't even hesitate. You didn't blink an eye. That's how I know what kind of person you are, and I also know you're going to do wonderful things with your life. Kari wanted to help people, and she has done that—she has helped four kids! It wasn't the way she or I expected, but I know you will bless lots of people with your life, too, Harper. You and Kari are a team now."

Harper nodded. "I'll take good care of Kari's heart, Lana."

"I know you will, baby, and I would just love it if you would carry her spirit with you, too."

"I will, Lana," Harper said, nodding solemnly.

"Yes, you will," Lana said, smiling. "Will you also come visit me sometimes, so I know how you're doing . . . and so I can listen to that good strong heart again?"

"I will, Lana. I promise," Harper said, hugging her. "Cross my . . . and Kari's heart!"

ACKNOWLEDGMENTS

WITH HEARTFELT THANKS . . .

To my amazing agent, Elizabeth Copps, who encouraged me to "write something new," and then patiently replied to every worried email I sent with calm encouragement—an antidote that always lifted my spirits!

To my wonderful editor, Hannah Robinson, who read *Promises* in a weekend and said YES! And who went on to work beside me, guiding my words until the story was perfect!

To the entire Harper Paperbacks team who have worked so hard to make this book the best it can be!

To Dr. Diane D'Isidori, who took the time to share her knowledge and make Harper's condition, symptoms, and treatment authentic.

To the men in my life—my husband, Bruce, our sons, Cole and Noah—and my daughter-in-law, Leah, who fill my life with joy and inspiration!

To my family, friends, and fans who faithfully read and share my books. I couldn't do it without you!

And to the good Lord above, who has blessed my life so richly!

ABOUT THE AUTHOR

NAN ROSSITER IS THE AWARD-WINNING AND BESTSELLING AUTHOR OF seven novels, including *The Gin & Chowder Club*. She lives in Connecticut with her husband, Bruce, and a noble black Lab named Finn. They are the parents of two handsome sons who have decided to grow up and strike out on life journeys of their own. When she's not working, Nan enjoys hiking or curling up with a good book.

About the author

About the book

Read on

Insights,
Interviews
& More . . .

Meet Nan Rossiter

NEW YORK TIMES and *USA Today* bestselling author Nan Rossiter grew up in Pelham, New York. Some of her earliest memories include riding a green Sting-Ray bike—complete with a banana seat and sissy bar—to the Pelham Library, which, at the time, was a tiny cavelike space tucked beneath Hutchinson Elementary School. It was from the shelves of this library that Nan first discovered the magic of books. Some of her favorite characters included Mrs. Piggle-Wiggle, Pippi Longstocking, and Harriet the Spy. Nan later moved with her parents to a quiet country road in Barkhamsted, Connecticut, and went on to graduate from the Rhode Island School of Design. After freelancing for several years, she began writing and illustrating books for children, including *Rugby & Rosie* (Dutton Children's Books), winner of Nebraska's Golden Sower Award, and *The Fo'c'sle: Henry Beston's "Outermost House"* (David R. Godine). In recent years, Nan has turned her attention to writing contemporary fiction. Her books have been highly acclaimed by reviewers from *Publisher's Weekly* to *Booklist*, and her seventh novel, *Summer Dance,* was the 2018 winner of the Nancy Pearl Book Award.

Nan continues to live on a quiet country road in Connecticut with her amazingly supportive husband, Bruce, and a noble black Lab named Finnegan, who diligently watches her every move and can be roused from a nap in a distant room by the sound of a banana being peeled or a cookie crumb hitting the floor. Finn finds writing to be a humdrum pastime and makes sure Nan doesn't spend too much time doing it, insisting on two long walks a day, no matter the weather. Nan and Bruce are the parents of two handsome sons, Cole and Noah, who have struck out on life journeys of their own, and are both pursuing careers in aviation. Their family has also grown to include their wonderful daughter-in-law, Leah, who adds joy to their lives, and some much-needed female support! Nan is a member of PEO (Philanthropic Educational Organization) International and she hopes that her PEO sisters—and other new readers—will find that her books always include the threads of faith and family.

For more information, please visit www.nanrossiter.com, where you can sign up for her newsletter, or follow her on Goodreads, Facebook, Twitter, and Instagram @NanRossiter. ᗕ

The Story Behind
Promises of the Heart

IT HAS BEEN a long-standing tradition for my family to vacation on Cape Cod. It's part of the reason I set several of my books there. It's also a tradition for us to try to take in at least one Cape Cod League baseball game. That's how it came to pass, one balmy night five years ago, that we were all standing on the hill overlooking the Orleans Firebirds field when a young girl—she must've been between ten and twelve years old—spied our black Lab, Finnegan, and came over to say hello. The girl cheerfully greeted Finn and then told us her parents had gotten her a dog to help her through her recent heart transplant surgery. As she continued to scratch Finn's ears, she shared her love of dogs and told us how much her dog had helped her. Her story was so moving that, when she walked away, my son Noah said, "Mom, you have to write about her!" I had to agree—it was an amazing story, but it was a year before I had the opportunity to draw on that encounter.

I usually know the direction a story will take, but I never know exactly what a character will do or say on any given day. It isn't until I type the characters' names that they perk up and start to lead the way. When I first typed Harper's name, she instantly came to life, and every time I started a chapter with her name, she stepped right up to the plate—as any good character will do—and asked Cora for a big-ass coffee, or started pulling off her bandages, or made an unladylike gesture to Connor, or pulled

Keeper into a fierce hug. Harper's character was inspired by a chance encounter with a young girl who loved dogs and needed a new heart, but she went on to become so much more.

In talking about the process and decisions that went into writing *Promises of the Heart*, I would be remiss if I didn't mention what was happening at the time. I began to write this story soon after I'd left my agent of eight years and the publisher of my first seven novels. I had the support and wise guidance of a wonderful new agent, but still it was a leap of faith. For the first time in years, I was writing without a contract, and the more time passed, the more I worried and second-guessed my decision. My new agent counseled me to depart from familiar characters and favorite settings and write something new. After silencing my internal protests, I set the story in Savannah, Georgia—and then announced to my husband that I'd have to go there for "research"!

When I write, I try to create a story that readers will be able to relate to. I touch on real issues, obstacles, and heartaches that everyone faces at some point, and I always try to weave in a thread of faith. When I started writing *Promises of the Heart*, the first name I typed was Macey, and before I knew it, my strong-willed protagonist was struggling with her fifth miscarriage. While she didn't seem open to adoption, the influence of her late grandmother made anything seem possible. When I typed Ben's name, Macey's overly cautious, hard-working husband came to life and pulled her into a long hug. The stage was set: I had characters with stories to tell, and even though I didn't know where they or their individual plights had come from, as soon as I typed their names, *they* knew.

To make a book—even a work of fiction—truly believable and authentic, there is always some amount of research involved. To verify the details for this book, I researched pediatric heart conditions and their causes. I also met with a pediatrician, a longtime friend who cared for my boys when they were young. Over coffee, we talked about the symptoms Harper would have and what her recovery would be like. While on a road trip with my younger son, Noah, I stopped in Savannah, where we checked out the hot spots mentioned in the book—Goose Feathers Café (where Macey and Maeve have breakfast), Doc's Bar (site of the impromptu class reunion), Tybee Island Light Station (where Ben and Henry go running), and Tybee Pier (where Ben proposed). We also checked out the Crab Shack and Wet Willie's— destinations I'm saving for a future book! ▶

The Story Behind *Promises of the Heart* (continued)

When I'm asked to speak about being an author and about all the trials and triumphs I've experienced, I often mention my faith and the role it plays. I am a believer in prayer, patience, and perseverance. I also believe in God's perfect timing, and even though I frequently questioned how long it was taking to find a new publisher, the stars did finally align!

I may never know if that young girl vacationing on Cape Cod—who is now probably in her late teens—will ever discover that she inspired a book, but I hope that a stroke of serendipity will allow me to thank her one day for the gift she gave me and all of my readers. ～

Macey's Famous Chocolate Chip Blondies

INGREDIENTS

1 cup softened butter (I've used whatever I have on hand, salted or unsalted)

1 cup granulated sugar

1 cup packed brown sugar (I like dark, but light works, too!)

1 teaspoon water

1 teaspoon vanilla

2 eggs

2 ¼ cups all-purpose flour

1 teaspoon salt

1 teaspoon baking soda

12 ounces semisweet chocolate chips

1 cup chopped walnuts (optional)

DIRECTIONS

Preheat oven to 375 degrees F.

With a stand mixer, cream together butter, sugars, water, and vanilla. Blend in eggs. Sift together dry ingredients: flour, salt, and baking soda and add to mix. Blend well. Spread thick dough in a lightly greased 10 ½ x 15 x 1–inch pan. Sprinkle chocolate chips on top and bake for 3 to 4 minutes, until chocolate is melted a little, and marbleize by running a butter knife diagonally through the pan contents several times. Return to oven for 12 to 15 minutes or until golden brown. Cool and cut.

Note: If using walnuts, add them to the dough prior to spreading in pan or sprinkle on top with the chocolate chips. ⌒

Get Involved! Organizations and Charities from *Promises of the Heart*

THERE ARE SO many ways to care for our communities and show love to those who need it most. As we see through the examples of Harper, Macey, Ben, Cora, and even Grandy, the smallest gestures of generosity can have a big impact. Below you'll find information about a few of the organizations and charities in *Promises of the Heart*, but I encourage you to find and support causes you believe in and are inspired by.

LOCKS OF LOVE
Locks of Love returns a sense of self-confidence and normalcy to children suffering from hair loss, using donated ponytails to provide the highest-quality hair prosthetics to financially disadvantaged children, free of charge.
https://locksoflove.org/

ADOPTUSKIDS
AdoptUSKids is a national project that supports child welfare systems and connects children in foster care with families.
https://www.adoptuskids.org/

DONATE LIFE
Donate Life America is a nonprofit organization working with national partners and Donate Life state teams to increase the number of donated organs, eyes, and tissues available to save and heal lives through transplantation.
https://www.donatelife.net/

ADOPT-A-PET.COM
Adopt-a-Pet.com is North America's largest nonprofit pet adoption website, helping more than 17,000 shelters, humane societies, SPCAs, pet rescue groups, and pet adoption agencies advertise their homeless pets.
https://www.adoptapet.com/

Reading Group Guide for *Promises of the Heart*

1. At the beginning of the book, Macey's heart seems set against adoption. What reasons does she give? Do you agree with her thinking? Why or why not?

2. Through Harper's experience, we get a glimpse of the foster care system. Does this justify Macey's wariness about becoming a foster parent?

3. How do Ben and Macey's personalities differ? Do you agree with the adage that opposites attract?

4. Harper has been bounced from one foster home to another, and, as a result, she has an attitude that makes her difficult to place. Around Cora, though, she acts differently. What changes do you notice in her personality when she's with Cora? Why do you think she's willing to open up?

5. Harper and Macey both struggle with not being able to control the things happening in their lives. What are some of these events and how do they cope?

6. Why does Harper run away? What does she learn from this experience, and why does she decide to return to Cora's?

7. Macey and Maeve are as close as two sisters can be, but, like any sisters, they have their differences. In what way(s) do the two girls differ? ▶

8. Although Grandy passed away when Macey was a young girl, she plays a significant role in Macey's life and in the book. In what way(s) does she influence Macey and affect Macey's decisions? What does Grandy's voice represent for Macey? Reflecting on your own life, do you have a loved one—living or dead—whose voice you carry with you? Why do you think that is? What role does this voice play in your life?

9. Ben's unwillingness to take chances is often a bone of contention. What are some examples of this, and in what ways does he change? What thoughts or events trigger these changes?

10. Much like Ben, Harper is very cautious, but she slowly opens up to the Samuelsons. What key moments lead up to her ultimately taking a chance on being adopted? How do the changes she goes through complement Ben's?

11. Harper is like Macey in many ways. In fact, Ben says that if he and Macey had had a biological daughter, she'd be just like Harper. What does he mean?

12. What role does Keeper play in the story? Do you think Harper would have adjusted to her new home without him? Why do you think Harper loves animals so much?

13. Faith and giving are two central themes in the book. In what ways do characters give, and how are they blessed in return?

14. The book begins and ends with the image of a candle in the window. What does the candle symbolize? How is the tradition of keeping a single candle in a window realized in this story?

15. Have you ever felt nudged to step out of your comfort zone to do something positive? Did you take the step? Why or why not? Do you regret your decision? ❧

Have You Read? More by Nan Rossiter

THE GIN & CHOWDER CLUB

SET AGAINST THE beautiful backdrop of Cape Cod, *The Gin & Chowder Club* is an eloquent, tender story of friendship, longing, and the enduring power of love.

The friendship between the Coleman and Shepherd families is as old and comfortable as the neighboring houses they occupy each summer on Cape Cod. Samuel and Sarah Coleman love those warm months by the water, the evenings spent on their porch enjoying gin and tonics, good conversation, and homemade clam chowder. Here they've watched their sons, Isaac and Asa, grow into fine young men, and watched, too, as Nate Shepherd, aching with grief at the loss of his first wife, finally finds love again with the much younger Noelle.

But beyond the surface of these idyllic gatherings, the growing attraction between Noelle and handsome, college-bound Asa threatens to upend everything. In spite of her guilt and misgivings, Noelle is drawn into a reckless secret affair with far-reaching consequences. And over the course of one bittersweet, unforgettable summer, Asa will learn more than he ever expected about love—the joys and heartache it awakens in us, the lengths to which we'll go to keep it, and the countless ways it can change our lives forever.

Have You Read? More by Nan Rossiter
(*continued*)

"Eloquent and surprising . . . I loved this
story of faith, love, and the lasting bonds of
family."
　　—Ann Leary, author of *The Good House*

"Nostalgic and tender . . . summons the
passion of first love, the pain of first loss,
and the unbreakable bonds of family that
help us survive both."
　　　　　—Marie Bostwick, *New York Times*
　　　　　　　　　　　　　　bestselling author

WORDS GET IN THE WAY

FROM THE AUTHOR of *The Gin & Chowder
Club* comes an exquisitely heartfelt and
uplifting novel that explores the infinite
reach of a mother's love—and the gift of
second chances.

　　The modest ranch house where Callie
Wyeth grew up looks just as she remembers
it—right down to the well-worn sheets in the
linen closet. But in the years since Callie
lived here, almost everything else has
changed. Her father, once indomitable, is in
poor health. And Callie is a single mother
with a beautiful little boy, Henry, who has
just been diagnosed with autism.

　　Returning to her family's quiet New
Hampshire community seems the best thing
to do, for the sake of both her father and her
son. Even if it means facing Linden Finch,
the one she loved and left, for reasons she's
sure he'll never forgive. Linden is stunned
that Callie is back—and that she has a son.
Yet in the warm, funny relationship that
develops around Henry and Linden's

menagerie of rescued farm animals, Callie begins to find hope. Not just that her son might break through the wall of silence separating him from the world, but that she too can make a new start amid the places and people that have never left her heart . . .

"Rossiter's second novel is an intimate portrayal of a family in crisis, with good character development and a bucolic setting."   —*Publishers Weekly*

MORE THAN YOU KNOW

BESTSELLING AUTHOR NAN Rossiter weaves a poignant, empowering novel in which three sisters gather to celebrate their mother's life—and find new inspiration for living their own.

Losing their father on the night Beryl Graham was born could have torn her family apart. Instead, it knitted them together. Under their mother's steady guidance, Beryl and her older sisters, Isak and Rumer, shared a childhood filled with happiness. But now Mia Graham has passed away after battling Alzheimer's, and her three daughters return to their New Hampshire home to say good-bye.

Swept up in memories and funeral preparations, the sisters catch up on each others' lives. Rumer and Isak have both known recent heartache, while Beryl has given up hope of marriage. But surprising revelations abound, especially when they uncover Mia's handwritten memoir. In it are secrets they never guessed at: clandestine romance, passionate dreams, joy, and guilt. And, as Beryl, Rumer, and Isak face a future without her, they realize it's never too late ▶

to heed a mother's lessons—about taking chances, keeping faith, and loving in spite of the risks.

"A gripping story of three sisters, of love lost and found, and of a family's journey from grief to triumph. A sure winner."
—Debbie Macomber, #1 *New York Times* bestselling author

"Rossiter's patient, deliberate pacing makes this one a perfect bedtime read."
—*Publishers Weekly*

"Rossiter's writing style is compelling. The setup of the novel provides a number of passages that tug at the reader's heartstrings, and the situations evoke realistic compassion."
—*Houston Chronicle*

UNDER A SUMMER SKY

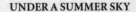

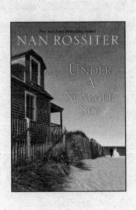

BESTSELLING AUTHOR NAN Rossiter transports readers to Cape Cod with a warm, compelling story of family, new beginnings, and finding the courage to love honestly and well.

The old Cape Cod house that Laney Coleman shares with her minister husband, Noah, and their five boys is usually brimming with cheerful chaos. There's nothing fancy about the ancient kitchen or the wooden floors scuffed by the constant parade of activity and the clicking claws of their two Labrador retrievers. It's a place to savor the sea breeze wafting through the windows, or sip coffee on the porch before another hectic day begins. This summer, life promises to be even busier than usual, because Noah's younger brother, Micah, wants to hold his upcoming wedding on their property.

Although thrilled that Micah has found happiness after past heartache, Laney is apprehensive about having her home turned upside down. She has other concerns, too—her youngest son is being bullied at school, and Noah's father is not the robust patriarch he once was, in mind or body. As the bride and groom's large, close-knit families gather, there will be joyful celebration but also unexpected sorrows and revelations, and a chance to store up a lifetime of memories during the fleeting, precious days of summer.

"The setting, with its sea breeze and quaint charm, is immediately inviting, adding to the overall sense of familiarity that the author so beautifully evokes. . . . [T]o read this book is to feel like you've come home."
—John Valeri, *Hartford Books Examiner*

NANTUCKET

FROM BESTSELLING AUTHOR Nan Rossiter comes a tender, moving story of rekindled passion, set amidst the timeless beauty of Nantucket.

More than twenty-five years ago, Liam Tate and Acadia McCormick Knox fell in love. It was summer on Nantucket, and seventeen-year-old Liam knew that wealthy, college-bound Cadie was way out of league for a local boy who restored boats with his uncle. Yet the two became inseparable, seizing every chance to slip away in Liam's ▶

runabout to secluded spots, far from the world that was trying to keep them apart.

After Cadie returned home to New York and discovered she was pregnant, her parents crushed any hope of communicating with the boy she'd left behind. The silence that greeted Liam's calls and letters couldn't change his heart, but over the years he's settled into a simple, solitary life in his rambling beachfront house. Now he's learned that Cadie is returning to Nantucket for the opening of her son's art show. Over a weekend of revelations and poignant memories, Cadie and Liam have an opportunity to confront the difference time can make, the truths that never alter, and the bittersweet second chances that arrive just in time to steer a heart back home.

"There are moments of pure gold in the story that will undoubtedly touch readers' hearts. With wonderful characters and a charming idyllic setting, *Nantucket* does pack an emotional wallop along the lines of a good Kristan Higgins book."

—RT Book Reviews

FIREFLY SUMMER

BESTSELLING AUTHOR NAN Rossiter's touching new novel reunites four sisters at their childhood vacation spot on Cape Cod—where they uncover the truth about a past tragedy to find their future as a family.

The close-knit Quinn siblings enjoyed the kind of idyllic childhood that seems made for greeting cards, spending each summer at

Whit's End, the family's home on Cape Cod. Then comes the summer of 1964, warm and lush after a rainy spring—perfect firefly weather. Sisters Birdie, Remy, Sailor, Piper, and their brother, Easton, delight in catching the insects in mason jars to make blinking lanterns. Until, one terrible night, tragedy strikes.

Decades later, the sisters have carved out separate lives on the Cape. Through love and heartbreak, health issues, raising children, and caring for their aging parents, they have supported each other, rarely mentioning their deep childhood loss. But one evening, as they congregate at Whit's End to watch the sun set, the gathering fireflies elicit memories of that long-ago night, and a tumult of regrets, guilt, and secrets tumble out.

Poignant yet hopeful, *Firefly Summer* is an uplifting story of the resilience of sisterhood and the bright glimpses of joy and solace that, like fireflies after rain, can follow even the deepest heartaches.

SUMMER DANCE

WINNER OF THE 2018 NANCY PEARL BOOK AWARD

BESTSELLING AUTHOR NAN Rossiter brings together characters from her acclaimed novel *Nantucket* in a powerful, heartwarming love story that bridges past and present.

When Liam Tate was seven years old, his Uncle Cooper opened his heart and his Nantucket home to the boy. In the intervening decades, Liam has found both ▶

Have You Read? More by Nan Rossiter
(continued)

love and loss on the island and, since learning that he has a son, Levi, a new kind of happiness. Yet one piece of his family history remains elusive—the long-ago romance between his uncle and Sally Adams. Now Sally makes a revelation that sets the whole town abuzz: she's publishing a book about what happened during the summer when she and Cooper first met, painting a picture so vivid it feels like yesterday.

In 1969, recently discharged veteran Winston Ellis Cooper III landed on Nantucket with only a duffel bag and a bottle of Jack Daniels. He found a sparsely furnished beach cottage, about as far from Vietnam as he could get. But even here, Cooper couldn't withdraw from the world entirely. Especially once his eyes met Sally's in the flickering lights of a summer dance. The effects of that fiery affair can still be felt decades later. As the story unfolds, there are new lessons for all to learn about life's triumphs and heartaches, and about loving enough to let go. ❧

Discover great authors, exclusive offers, and more at hc.com.